THE BLACK WOLVES OF BOSTON

BAEN BOOKS by WEN SPENCER

THE BLACK WOLVES OF BOSTON

WEN SPENCER

THE BLACK WOLVES OF BOSTON

A Baen Books Original

Baen Publishing Enterprises
P.O. Box 1403
Riverdale, NY 10471
www.baen.com

ISBN: 978-1-4814-8246-2

Cover art by Kurt Miller
Illustrations by Heather Bruton

First printing, February 2017

Distributed by Simon & Schuster
1230 Avenue of the Americas
New York, NY 10020

10 9 8 7 6 5 4 3 2 1

Pages by Joy Freeman (www.pagesbyjoy.com)
Printed in the United States of America

Acknowledgements

Writing a novel is a long and difficult journey.
Thankfully I don't do it alone. Thank you to all
the people who have listened to me laugh and cry and
bang my head against the wall and offered up sage advice.

Heather Bruton
Franklin Bryan
Brian Chee
Ruth L. Heller, DVM.
Laurel Jamieson Lohrey
Nancy Janda
Ellen M. McMicking, D.I.
Nan Nuessle
Hope Erica Ring
Larisa Van Winkle
Nathan L. Yocum
N. A. Young

To my beloved Sunshine Swirl,
from your loving Ink Well.

THE BLACK WOLVES OF BOSTON

1: JOSHUA

Joshua really thought it would be easier to catch a rabbit; he was a werewolf, after all. The stupid things, though, could turn on a dime and kept zigging while his body zagged.

And then there were the trees.

He hit yet another oak tree, this one only about four inches wide, but enough to knock him down and nearly knock him out when he hit it. Acorns rained down on him. It felt like the oak tree was laughing at him.

"Stupid tree." He kicked it while still lying flat on his back.

There was a loud crack and it toppled slowly away from him.

Joshua groaned and slapped his hands over his eyes. He was doing this at night so no one would see him or know what he'd done. People might not notice if half the trees in the Back Bay Fens Park had face impressions but they weren't going to miss a downed tree.

If he were a real wolf, or at least as real a wolf as he got, then catching a rabbit would be easier. Maybe. At least he probably could zig and zag faster on all fours. He had no idea, though, if he was a traditional werewolf who needed the full moon or the newfangled sparkly kind that could pop the wolf out at any moment, like a very violent and hairy sneeze.

Of course, he wasn't sure if he could kill a rabbit if he managed to catch it. And eating it? The more he chased the stupid things, the less they seemed like tiny fried chickens. His stomach growled loudly at the thought of crispy breaded meat.

"Oh shut..." He froze as he realized that he wasn't alone. Someone was standing behind him, just out of reach. Oddly, he hadn't heard them walk up.

"What exactly," the person drawled out slowly in the tone you use on a misbehaving toddler, "are you *trying* to do?" Emphasis on trying, because even the trees knew he was failing.

Joshua lifted his hands and tilted his head back. A tall, lean young man stood looking down at him with his head tilted slightly in confusion. His long hair was pulled back into a hipster's ponytail. He was wearing a long black coat and a white scarf that fluttered in the chilly wind.

"Landscaping," Joshua said. "I'm the new tree guy for the city of Boston."

"Oh." The man eyed the toppled oak. "I see. I've been watching; you've run into a dozen trees now."

"I'm testing them for rot," Joshua stated firmly. "It's very hard to tell from the outside. You got to thump them good. Like a pumpkin..." He was babbling like a complete idiot now.

The man tilted his head in the other direction. "Aren't you a little short for a tree trimmer?"

Joshua growled in annoyance and climbed to his feet. Not that it helped. Life had always been unfair to him, starting with his last name and ending with turning him into a very inept werewolf. Along the way, for complete shits and giggles, it had made him embarrassingly short too. Joshua only came to the man's shoulder.

Smells had been driving Joshua nuts since he'd woken up a werewolf. It had been the scent of the rabbits that started the entire *trying* to catch them fiasco. This man smelled of expensive cologne and something faintly sweet that triggered a strange urge to rub against him. Joshua stepped back a couple of steps to lessen the effect; he didn't want a repeat of the fire hydrant incident. Stupid dogs. At least, he assumed it was dogs. He couldn't imagine there were other werewolves out there, walking around on autopilot like he seemed to be half the time, pissing on fire hydrants without realizing what they were doing.

And to top everything off, his stomach growled again. Loudly.

"You're hungry." The man stated it as a fact.

A growl of anger slipped out without him even knowing it was coming. His temper had become something separate from

him; it roamed around him like a high school bully looking for victims. Joshua closed his eyes and took a deep breath and found his center. He normally was a much calmer person than this, but normally he was a much less hairy person than this. He actually had five o'clock shadow for the first time in his life.

"Are you some kind of tree police?" Joshua asked without opening his eyes. "Do you feel as if you have some kind of civic duty to come out here and—and—annoy the hell out of me?"

"Well—yes—I do have a civic duty to stop you—that is—if you needed stopping. If you'd kept to simple tree assault, I would have just kept watching. It was fairly entertaining, in a train wreck kind of way. You've moved up to tree homicide."

"Homicide?" Joshua opened his eyes to give the man an annoyed glare. "That implies intent. At most, this is tree slaughter. Maybe even just reckless endangerment—it might not be dead."

They eyed the tree in silence. His kick had sheered the tree trunk off five inches from the roots, leaving behind a jagged white stump, flowing with sap.

"No, that's dead," the man said.

"Yeah." Joshua had to agree. It occurred to Joshua that this person might be undercover cop or some off-duty park ranger or a very lost Canadian Mountie or something. He'd seen Joshua destroy a piece of public property worth hundreds of dollars. The man might try to arrest him. That wouldn't end well for either one of them.

Joshua bolted.

He was out of the park and halfway down the street before he was fully aware that he was running. Another two blocks before he realized that he had no clue where he was going. Another block before he realized that, wherever he was heading, he was getting there amazingly fast. He was running faster than the cars on the street beside him. Not that they were going all that fast, but he was running at least forty miles per hour and he didn't feel...

He missed the fact that the street ended. He missed the turn. He didn't miss the wall.

He hit it and kept going, smashing through wood and drywall in a cartwheeling blur of destruction. There were shelves of pots and pans and dishes and Halloween decorations. Somewhere along the way there was a glass display full of knives.

He came to a stop on the far wall beside a display of jack-o-lantern cookie jars, surrounded by broken china and drifting clouds of plaster. He'd tripped some kind of burglar alarm, probably by flagging half a dozen motion detectors, and a bell was ringing loudly. There was a butcher knife stuck in his thigh. He stared at it, hyperventilating with fear.

He had a knife in his right leg. A big, big knife. In his leg. The two together just looked so wrong it seemed like it had been photoshopped.

People died from things like this! This could kill him. Maybe. He was a werewolf. Knowing what kind of werewolf he was would be very useful right now.

He couldn't catch his breath. He was getting lightheaded. He didn't know if it was from hyperventilating or blood loss or both. He closed his eyes and tried to center himself. He was sure that his judo sensei never had this in mind when he taught Joshua how to meditate.

He heard the crunch of footsteps through the rubble. Oh good! The cops must have shown up. They could get him an ambulance—after they arrested him for something. Breaking and entering. Or just plain breaking. Lots and lots of breaking. His breathing sped up and he opened his eyes.

The tall dude from the park was walking cautiously toward him.

Joshua was beyond caring if he was the police. He pointed at the knife in his leg with both hands and whimpered. "Can't. Breathe."

The dude gave him a long, slightly confused, stare. Pulling a paper bag from the nearby service desk, he crouched beside Joshua. "Here. Breathe into this."

The name of the store was "Kitchen Kitsch" and the paper bag was red with white spots all over it. The bag inflated and deflated like one of the Mario Brothers' mushrooms. He couldn't stop whimpering. He sounded like a kicked puppy and it was freaking him out nearly as much as the knife.

Joshua took the bag away from his mouth long enough to pant out. "Call 911." Which got him another long stare. "Call 911!"

The dude pointed to the left. "Look over there!"

"Huh?" Joshua couldn't see anything beyond scattered pots and pans and a wall of Halloween decorations.

The man jerked the knife out of Joshua's leg.

Joshua yelped and lashed out in sheer reflex. It wasn't a solid hit but the man tumbled away from him, taking the knife with him. "You're not supposed to take it out! Only doctors are supposed to take it out! Don't you know basic first aid?"

"You're a werewolf." The man called from behind a display of vampire kitchen timers. "You can only be killed by cutting your head off."

It was comforting for only a moment. Then Joshua realized that the dude still had a seriously huge knife in his hand.

The part of him that was crying like a kicked puppy took off running. Unfortunately it took the rest of him with it.

"No! Nononono!" He cried even as he bolted. This was what scared him about being a werewolf. He wasn't in control of his body anymore. Because of his last name and small size, he'd always been a target of bullies. He'd learned early that they could hurt him but they couldn't control him if he didn't let them. And then he learned martial arts and they couldn't even hurt him anymore. In the last twenty-four hours, it had been as if he was strapped into a rollercoaster: all he could do was go for the ride and scream a lot. His fear was that the ride would be through other people. He'd become like the monster that made him, tearing his way through humans like they were so many blood-filled water balloons.

He was away from everyone he loved, but he wasn't away from people. There was a city full of strangers he could kill.

He knew nothing about werewolves but what was in the movies. He hadn't even believed they existed until he was attacked. The tall dude, though, knew.

Joshua managed to force his body to make a left-hand turn at the corner, and again once he was across the street, and then a third time. He came looping past the Kitchen Kitsch where the tall dude was standing in the hole in the wall.

"You're really conflicted about this running away part, aren't you?" the dude said as Joshua dashed past him.

"Yes!" He tried to put on the brakes but his body kept running. He could smell his own blood on the man and his body wanted nothing to do with that.

The dude wasn't standing in the hole as Joshua came looping back toward the Kitchen Kitsch a second time. Joshua was afraid he'd lost the man. He was so focused on the opposite side of the street that he nearly ran into the glass door that opened out in front of him. A hand caught him, jerking him into the building.

He tumbled through a roll and came up in front of a steaming tray of crab rangoons. They were fried golden brown, still
so hot that they burned his throat a little going down. Next to
them were giant-sized pot stickers, the outside fried crispy and
the inside a big ball of heavenly-tasting ground pork.

"Don't use your fingers." The dude shoved a plate into his hands.

"I can't pay for this. I don't have any money." Joshua thumped
a heaping spoonful of sesame chicken onto the plate and ate like
a dog. He was sure that's not what the man meant by "don't use
your fingers" but at the moment, it was all Joshua could manage.

"I'm treating you." The man filled another plate with beef and
broccoli and handed it to Joshua. "Sit down and use chopsticks.
I'll bring you more food."

The man brought four plates filled with meat dishes. He
watched Joshua stab the beef chunks with his chopsticks and went
off to find forks. He carefully slid two across the table and then
sat on the other side of the booth to watch Joshua wolf down
the food as fast as humanly possible.

"Mank mou," Joshua mumbled around garlic shrimp.

"You're welcome."

Joshua realized the man wasn't eating, so he pushed one of
the plates toward him.

The man waved off the offering. "I'm allergic."

A weird silence fell at the table as Joshua ate. It felt too comfortable to be eating with someone he didn't know. His father
liked to say that just because someone was being nice to you at the
moment, it didn't mean they were good people. The dude looked
as if he could be a college student but there was something about
him that made him feel much older to Joshua. Maybe it was the
way he sat; patient stillness, like an old man who had been alive
so long he wasn't impatient for the moment to be over. His eyes
were dark, dark brown. Crow's feet were beginning to form at the
corners, but they seemed more like laugh lines. At some point in
his life, the man had smiled a lot, but he wasn't smiling now.

Joshua blushed as he realized he was sitting, staring into a guy's
eyes. And the guy—all clean and elegantly dressed—was staring
back as if sizing him up. And he'd just bought Joshua dinner.

He swallowed down the mouthful of food he was currently
chewing and asked, "Is this some kind of a date? It better not
be. I'm not gay. Not there's anything wrong with being gay. I'm

not . . ." At least he was fairly sure he wasn't. He was seriously lacking in terms of interaction with girls, with the exception of sparring partners, since he was the only boy in class of similar size. It probably was better not to bring that up. "I'm not."

The man laughed. "No, not a date. You'll have more control if you feed the beast. Hungry and scared, there will be no talking to you."

"Who the hell are you? How do you know about werewolves? No one believes in werewolves. And how do you know that I am one? It's not like I'm wolfing out on you. And how is it your 'civic duty' to scare the shit out of me?"

The man laughed again. "I'm Decker, Silas Decker. I have a gift and need for tracking down magical creatures. I was out looking for—" He paused as if he had forgotten what he had been really looking for. "—something when I spotted you."

"And?"

"And?" Decker echoed, confused by Joshua's question.

"How do you know I'm a werewolf?"

"Really? Chasing rabbits in the dark?"

"Okay, that's suspect but why did 'werewolf' leap to mind instead of just—I don't know—desperate for a pet? Crazy?"

"Kicking down a tree?" Decker gave him a look that said "just accept it." And then, sighing, he glanced away. "There are two types of werewolves. Feral werewolves are deadly uncontrollable monsters that kill everything in their path. Anyone that survives their attack—which are fortunately few in number—becomes a feral werewolf too. The other type is a pack wolf. And they're very dangerous, but law abiding. They could be your next-door neighbors and you'd never know. The thing is, pack wolves are the world's best parents. They live for their kids. Any little baby pack werewolves come with a set of big, ugly parents that will rip the throat out of anyone that says 'boo' to their kid. So I see you and you're acting like a feral werewolf, but if you're a pack wolf, and I kill you, I'd be calling down a world of hurt on my head."

"Wait! What? There are good werewolves and bad werewolves? Which am I?"

"That is the question I've been trying to figure out for nearly an hour now. The thing is, if you were feral, there wouldn't be anyone still alive in this restaurant. But if you were a pack wolf, you'd know it."

Joshua opened his mouth but all the dots finally connected and the light went on. Decker wanted to know if he'd get in trouble if he killed Joshua. Telling Decker that he didn't have protective monster parents would be a bad idea. "I—I might. You said that pack wolves could be my next-door neighbors and I wouldn't know. Who knows, maybe my parents are—wolves. Or—or I could be adopted. I always suspected that. Family reunions are like living in the land of the giants."

"You're starving. You're broke. And you've got a backpack stashed under the nearest bridge. Maybe. If that homeless guy didn't take it yet."

Joshua leapt to his feet. "What homeless guy?"

"The one I made up." Decker tapped the table. "Sit."

Joshua wavered. It really didn't feel safe to stay with the man but he'd come to Boston looking for answers. He wasn't going to find anything if he bolted from the only person so far that knew about werewolves. He sat down. "Is there a cure?"

"Pardon?"

"A cure! You get bit by a werewolf and you become one. It's some kind of disease. There has to be a cure."

Decker slapped a hand over his eyes. He sat that way for several minutes. He kept taking a breath as if he was going to say something but then would sigh it out without speaking. "That's—" he finally said. "That's not how it works."

"Are you sure? How do you know it's not?" It occurred to Joshua what he should have asked Decker first. He leaned over the table and whispered. "Are you a werewolf?"

Decker's body started to quake. It took Joshua a minute to realize that the man was silently laughing at him.

"This is not funny!" Joshua felt the other inside him stir with his anger and focused back on shoving food into his mouth. Feed the beast. Feed the beast. "I want to be able to go back home. I got kicked out of the hospital for breaking things. I tore the door off my dad's pickup, flooded the bathroom, and nearly electrocuted my neighbor to death. Our cat is scared of me. He won't come near me and he peed in my bed! I just want to go back to how I was."

Decker continued to laugh silently without taking his hand from his eyes. He finally canted up his hand to look at Joshua in confusion. "How did you electrocute your neighbor?"

Joshua blushed with embarrassment. "Does it matter?"

"I'm just curious."

"I snapped the faucet off the sink in the upstairs bathroom." The entire disaster had been a lesson in plumbing. "Our house is old. There aren't any shutoff valves for those pipes. You need to turn off the water main for the whole house. I didn't know how to do that and my parents weren't home. I ran to my neighbor's to get help and put my hand through their door when I went to knock. By the time we found the main and got the water turned off, it was raining in the kitchen. It turns out that the two-twenty line for our old electric stove isn't properly grounded. Mr. Buckley went into the kitchen to mop up the water and it nearly killed him." Up to that moment, Joshua believed that nothing could be more frightening that being attacked by a werewolf. The universe seemed determined to prove him wrong. "I had this weird vision—or something—while I was having an MRI that I should go to Boston. After the ambulance took Mr. Buckley to the hospital, I packed some clothes and left home."

"Your poor parents," Decker murmured. "To leave, thinking their child was snug in their safe nest, and to return—bough broke, nest in ruin, and the chick is lost."

"I don't think 'chick' is the correct metaphor here."

"It is a little forced."

They fell silent as a tiny Asian woman came to clear the table of plates. She left a little tray with the bill upside down, pinned by two fortune cookies. Decker flicked the plastic-wrapped cookies toward Joshua and took the bill. His eyebrows rose in surprise as he read the total.

"Did they charge you for two?" Joshua asked.

"It's just I have not bought food at a restaurant for a very long time. I'd forgotten how expensive it is."

"Do you have enough?"

"Yes. Don't worry about it." He took out a wallet and pulled out a fifty-dollar bill. "Eat your cookies."

The first fortune read, "Accept something that you cannot change and you will feel better." He dropped the slip of paper on the table and opened the second cookie. The fortune said, "Depart not from the path which fate has you assigned."

Decker cocked an eyebrow at Joshua's face and picked up the discarded fortunes. "See. No going back."

"I don't take advice from baked goods," Joshua growled. "They're just random nonsense."

"They used to be random nonsense for you, but not anymore. Men live by logic; a flipped coin always has equal chance of landing heads or tails. Monsters live by magic; the universe is no longer random for you. You are now ruled by fate."

"What the hell does that mean?"

Decker held up the slip of paper as if it was proof. "It means that you becoming a werewolf is part of something much bigger than your own personal tragedy."

Joshua considered the possibility that he should amend his father's advice of "just because they're nice doesn't mean they're necessarily good." Maybe he should add, "just because they recognize that you are a werewolf doesn't mean they aren't crazy." Who knows, maybe Decker thought everyone was a werewolf. The man just happened to finally run into someone that was.

Decker's phone played "Für Elise" in dubstep. He took it out of his coat's breast pocket and eyed it. "It keeps doing that."

Shades of Joshua's mother.

"Someone texting you," Joshua said.

"Texting?" Decker looked dubious. "It's a phone."

So like his mother.

Joshua took the phone from Decker. At least he could be fairly sure it would be just a text and not someone sexting Decker since the man seemed clueless. There had been a missed call at 6:43, 6:47 and 6:51, all from someone named Elise. At 6:52, the first text was received.

"Are you awake yet? I didn't think you could sleep in. Call me." And then. *"Freaking hell, I need help."* And then. *"Damn you, you better not let the battery die on that thing after I bought it for you."* And then, *"I need backhoe. Backhoe. Backhoe. Damn autocorrect! BACKUP!"* This was followed by a string of symbols and numbers that looked like someone had pounded randomly on the screen. *"Help! Now!"*

"I need to go." Decker stood up and then froze in place, looking confused.

"You don't know where you're going?" Joshua guessed.

"Not quickly; I'd have to slowly divine her location. Does she not say?"

They peered together at the screen.

"She gave you the phone?" Joshua said. "Okay, hold on, let's see if she has loaded any kind of friend finder app. Bingo. There she is."

Judging by the pins on the map, they were not far from Elise.

Decker strode purposely for the door, his long black coat tails flowing behind him. Joshua realized that he was letting the one person who might be able to help him get away. He dashed after Decker.

"Elise is Grigori Virtue," Decker said as they ran down the street. "Which you know nothing about. How to put this? Long, long story which we do not have time for, yadayadayada."

"That is so not useful."

"I'm trying to figure out how to condense several thousand years of history into a few short sentences as we're running toward certain mayhem. The Grigori are religious lunatics. Heavily armed religious lunatics—with magical powers—who will kill you if they think you're feral. Okay, that covers it."

"Wait—these lunatics—are these the good guys or the bad guys?"

"That's a fluid condition, changeable by day, if not minute by minute. I worked with her grandfather Saul and her mother Lauretta, which is the only reason Elise trusts me as far as she does. I will warn you that if you anger her, she knows that she can shoot you with no fear of actually killing you. It will hurt really, really bad, but it will not kill you. Make no mistake, though, she can also shoot you to kill you. That's the heavily armed part of religious lunatics; she's loaded for werewolf."

"And this is your friend?"

"Elise would shoot me if I called her my friend. Stick to ally. Better yet, how about 'associate.' Yes, I think associate would be safest thing to call her."

"Well, you must like her if we're running to save her."

Decker glanced at him sharply and then laughed. "*We*, hm? Yes, I'm very fond of Elise. More importantly, she trusts me—somewhat—which means we can work together. Most would not give me the benefit of doubt. If Elise were killed, some other Virtue would take over this area. That person would have good reason not to trust me—Elise had been killed in my territory—and would hunt me down. For my own safety, I have to keep Elise alive."

"So who are the bad guys?"

"Huh?"

"Who is trying to kill Elise?" Joshua assumed that the label of "Virtue" made her the good guy in this scenario.

"Elise? Who knows? Knowing Elise, the question is probably 'what' not 'who.' Especially if she's asking for help."

Joshua hadn't realized from the map that they were going back to the park until they crossed the street and plunged into the wooded darkness. The winding paths, arched stone bridges, tranquil ponds, and lush green had not been what he'd expected of Boston when he left home. He had expectations of big city and skyscrapers fringed by nothing but pavement and row houses.

Once into the wooded darkness, though, they stopped, unsure which way to head. The map indicated that they were nearly on top of Elise. A storm wind tossed the trees, promising incoming violence. Dried leaves skittered across the cement path like hordes of dark mice.

"She's close by." Joshua tried to hear if anyone was calling for help. It was impossible to hear over the thrashing leaves that all whispered like a thousand voices. "Here, give me your phone again."

Joshua switched to the phone app. Elise was the only contact entered into Decker's list. Oh, that was so sad—even Joshua had two-dozen contacts on his list. It explained, however, why the man didn't understand his phone. Joshua tapped Elise's cell phone number. A dozen feet away, the Toadies "Possum Kingdom" started to play.

"I can promise you," the lyrics sang out of the darkness. "You'll stay as beautiful, with dark hair and soft skin . . . forever. Forever."

"That isn't good," Decker walked in a circle as Joshua retrieved the phone from the bushes. "Not good at all. We need to find her. Quickly. My way is too slow. Can you track her?"

"Me?"

"You can do that now." Decker tapped his nose. "Just follow her scent."

"Me?" Joshua repeated, feeling something that could have been horror. Did Decker fully expect him to embrace his werewolf-ness and do something he'd never tried before with a woman's life on the line? Joshua struggled to keep in control with cold logic. "I have no idea what she smells like."

Decker pointed at the phone in Joshua's hand. "Her scent should be on that."

Joshua sniffed cautiously at the phone, not expecting to be able to smell anything. There was, however, a rich "other" on the slick surface. Baby powder. Rose-scented soap. Sweat. A murky oily smell he couldn't identify. Okay, assuming that was Elise, could he actually track her? He shoved the phone into his back pocket so it wouldn't distract him and then walked in a circle, sniffing.

Decker stayed quiet and impossibly still while Joshua hunted for the scent.

The night smelled rich and complex. The cinnamonlike death of the autumn leaves tossed by the storm wind. Green of bruised grass. He could smell the damn rabbits. And then, unexpectedly, Elise and blood. He started forward, afraid of what he'd find.

Down the path, over an arched bridge, they came to a small playground with swings. A woman sprawled in a pool of blood.

Decker caught his shoulder and pulled him back. "That's not her."

"But she's hurt." Joshua pointed at the woman on the ground.

"She's dead." Decker tightened his hold. "Something's wrong here."

The wind started to pick up, tugging at them with a thousand little hands. It caught up sticks and dead leaves and swirled them about the shadowed playground. The swings gave rusty cries, swinging as if used by ghosts. The hair on Joshua's neck rose and he sank down without thinking, until he crouched nearly on all fours, growling lowly.

Someone came running up the dark path. Joshua only caught the impression of a slim figure wielding two long knives before Decker pulled him back.

"No!" Decker shouted. "He's with me."

"God Almighty, Decker, you finally checked your phone? And where in Heaven's name did you find a wolf in Boston?" A stunningly beautiful girl walked out of the shadows. Her black hair spilled down over her shoulders in loose curls. She wore tight black clothes and held two long daggers that gleamed in the darkness. A pair of pistols hung low on her hips, tied down like a Western gunfighter. Heavily armed religious nutcase: check. This was Elise.

"What are you hunting?" Decker ignored her questions, still pulling Joshua backwards.

"A huntsman," Elise stuck her daggers into sheaths strapped across her kidneys.

Decker breathed out a curse. "What idiot made one of those? Who is it hunting?"

"Don't know." Elise skirted the body in a wide circle to join them at the edge of the playground. "And don't know. It's got five hounds already."

"Six!" Decker shouted as the wind howled louder. Dead leaves by the thousands whirled and danced, circling the body.

"Stop it, Decker!" Elise cried. "My blades don't work on them."

"I can't!" Decker shouted. "It's too late. The ground is tilled and wet with blood. The seed is planted. We could only stop it at this point by killing the huntsman!"

"Stop what?" Joshua growled.

Suddenly the wind roared and all the dead leaves rushed toward the body.

"That!" Decker pointed.

Sticks joined in the whirlwind of leaves, sucked from the nearby trees and undergrowth. The maelstrom collapsed inward, growing denser. The roar deepened to an animal-like growl and the bracken became a dark beast.

"Oh," Joshua whispered in shock. "Oh, shit."

His voice attracted the beast's attention. Its eyes were hollow pits with something glistening deep within the darkness. A snarl of fear bloomed out of Joshua's chest. He dropped down to all fours, his fingernails scratching deep lines in the cement.

"Don't lose control." Decker gripped Joshua's shoulder hard.

"I can't kill the hounds," Elise whispered. "They regenerate too fast."

"Just slow it down," Decker said.

Elise unsheathed her daggers and leapt forward. Her gleaming blades left contrails on Joshua's vision as she met the beast halfway. The blades slashed through the hound's dark side. Bits of leaves and sticks sprayed from the wound that vanished instantly.

The hound dodged Elise and leapt snarling at Joshua. He reacted without thinking. He caught hold of the beast by its throat and shoulder. His fingers crunched through brittle leaves and found solid skeleton within. Turning with the creature's momentum, he flung it at the nearest tree. It shattered on impact.

"Yes!" Joshua cried.

The wind caught the leaves and sticks and whirled them up. Roaring, the hound amassed together again.

"Oh, you've got to be kidding me," Joshua whispered.

"Get back," Decker shouted.

From someplace Decker had gotten a massive dark red sword. For some reason, it was scarier than the hound. Joshua didn't know if something could gleam with evil, but it made his hair crawl just looking at it. He scuttled backwards away from it, snarling.

"What the hell is that?" Joshua cried.

"You don't want to know," Decker stated calmly.

It was Joshua's experience that when people said that, he definitely did want to know. Not knowing led to bad, bad things.

Decker charged the hound and rammed the sword tip into the center of the beast. The leaves collapsed into a tight ball around the sword and then fell to the ground. Decker stood panting, the sword level, his face twisted hard as if he was in pain.

"You good?" Elise backed away from Decker, daggers ready.

Decker gave a deep, husky laugh. "Oh, I'm good."

"Don't lose it on me."

Decker took several deep breaths and then nodded. He lowered the sword. "I'm fine."

"The huntsman?" Elise asked.

Decker pointed. "It's that way, but it knows I'm here."

There was a shitload of questions Joshua wanted to ask, but he stuck to the thing that was scaring the other two.

"What exactly is a huntsman?" Joshua said.

"It's a magical construct." Elise watched Decker closely. "It finds, captures and teleports a target to its maker. It is used to collect powerful creatures like Decker."

"Teleports? Powerful creatures like *Decker*? What does that mean?"

"It means we need to stop it fast." Decker started down the path. "Every person the huntsman kills becomes a seedbed for a hound."

Elise sheathed her daggers and gave Joshua a hard look. "Did you just judo throw that hound?"

Joshua spread his hands in confusion. She made it sound bad. "Brown belt judo. I would be black belt if I weren't a minor. Legal responsibilities and all that."

"Wolves don't learn judo." Elise's voice was full of suspicion.

"Stranger things happen!" Decker called back as he disap-peared into the darkness. "All the time! Especially around us!"

Elise trotted down the path, calling, "There aren't any wolves in Boston, Decker. If there were, we wouldn't have the mess we have! Where did you find a wolf?"

Joshua trailed after the two. Obviously everything he thought he knew about the world was wrong.

It was Saturday night.

Friday had been Halloween.

As part of trying to nail a scholarship for college, Joshua had joined the prom committee. Their first fundraiser was going to be a haunted house at the Dwyer barn. They'd gotten permission to leave school early to set up. Joshua spent the afternoon knowing that he didn't fit in. Prom was for popular kids and Halloween was for little kids. He used to love the holiday, running around with his friends in the autumn night, doors opening up to warm brightly-lit houses, people happy to see little monsters at their door, praising them for the work they'd put into their costumes. All happy. All nice. All fake.

He was too old to trick or threat. He was too dorky to fit in with the popular kids.

At dusk, a real monster showed up at the barn.

Joshua wanted the world to go back to making sense. He needed it for his own sanity's sake. He'd lost everything else in the last twenty-four hours; it was all he had left. His classmates were dead. He'd fled his family to keep them safe. He had no money, no place to live, no idea where to go except to follow the two deadly people who knew what the world was really like.

Elise was explaining her day. "I picked up a police report out of Framingham this afternoon."

Joshua was surprised to hear the town name. He'd taken the Lake Shore Limited to Framingham, using up most of the fifty dollars he had to his name. From there, he'd connected with the Boston commuter lines. He'd only had enough money by then to buy a ticket to Yawkey Station. Feeling lost and alone, he'd retreated into the park a few blocks from his stop.

"The Framingham PD had found a seedbed," Elise contin-ued. "They had no idea what it was. From what I could tell, the huntsman made his first hound there, which meant its target was close by. I've been calling you since sunset."

"Framingham," Decker murmured and then, after a long pause. "Yawkey."

With a roar, another hound came rushing out of the darkness. It tried to slip past Decker to lunge at Joshua. The man skewered it with his scary long sword. After the monster collapsed into leaves, he turned to look at Joshua. His eyes were totally black and his breathing was ragged.

"The huntsman knows I'm here," Decker said. "But it's closing on us."

"Maybe you're the target," Elise said.

"It wouldn't have started in Framingham. Any enemy of mine knows that I never venture that far out."

Elise followed Decker gaze. "Where did you find a wolf in Boston?"

"Here," Decker murmured. "In this park. Chasing rabbits. Killing trees."

"Killing what?" Elise said.

"A newly made wolf, connected to their magic, not protected by the pack," Decker whispered. "Someone is playing a deep game."

"He's the target?" Elise asked.

"Yes, someone wants him very, very badly." Decker tilted his head, thinking through the problem. "When he bolted from his parents' house, he was only hours old. I'm thinking that the Wickers had a hand in making him. He'd slipped through their fingers when they went to collect him. They need to catch him fast, before he draws the Wolf King's notice. Any place else, he'd be one of many, but in Boston, he stands out because he's the only one."

Go to Boston's Prince, the black wolf had whispered in his dream, *Run!*

He'd come to Boston looking for a prince. Was the Wolf King the same as a prince?

"We could just kill him." Elise pulled one of her pistols.

"Hey!" Joshua backed away from her.

"No, you can't." Decker drifted sideways, blocking Elise. "The boy isn't feral. Killing him would violate the Grigoris' treaty with the Wolf King. You'd be starting a war that the wolves would win."

Elise huffed but holstered her gun. "You could kill him. You don't have a treaty."

"Nah." Decker reached out to pat Joshua on the head. "He amuses me."

This would be a whole lot more comforting if Decker didn't have solid black eyes and smelled wild and dark as the night.

Decker ruffled Joshua's hair and turned away. "The huntsman is coming with the other four hounds."

"Are you going to be able to take four without losing it?" Elise said.

Decker laughed. "I doubt it. Kill the huntsman fast and I won't have to."

Elise frowned at Joshua. "Keep your head down and don't let them get ahold of you. If they snare you, they'll drag you through a tear in realty and we won't be able to save you."

The wind rose. Over the thrashing of leaves, Joshua could hear the growling roar of the hounds closing in. He thought of just fleeing. The huntsman was killing people in his wake, though, to make hounds. So no, they had to stop it. And by "they," he meant Decker and Elise because he didn't know what the huntsman was, let alone how to kill it. He hadn't been able to hurt the hound.

The hounds came in a solid wave. Decker stabbed one but the other three kept coming. One of the hounds tackled Elise, and she went down cursing. Joshua caught the third hound as it leapt at him and flung it toward a tree. The fourth slammed into him and they went tumbling into the darkness. The beast filled his nose with the scent of blood and dead leaves and tree sap. All his sparring never prepared him for an opponent that could grow vines around his arms and legs. He locked down on the fear coursing through him and focused on leverage. *Fight the opponent, not yourself.*

The hounds could be broken by hard impact. He got his legs under him, did a quick roll, followed by a hard body slam pin. The hound howled as it shattered with the sound of a thousand little twigs snapping. It sounded like someone was beating a Rottweiler with a dead Christmas tree. Joshua rolled again and flung it away from him. As it reformed, Decker stabbed it.

"Thanks—" Joshua yelped as Decker caught him by the collar and slammed him into a tree.

The man felt like static electricity against Joshua's skin. Decker snarled, showing sharp teeth.

Vampire! Vampirevampirevampirevampire!

Decker lunged for Joshua's throat.

"Decker!" Joshua punched him. It felt like hitting a stonewall. He caught the man—vampire—by his dark hair. "No! Not me! I amuse you! Remember?"

Decker breathed hard against Joshua's throat. And again. And again. After the fourth time, Joshua realized that the vampire was laughing. "Yes," Decker finally whispered. "You amuse me."

"No biting?" Joshua said hopefully.

"No biting," Decker whispered.

"Goddamn you stupid shrubbery!" Elise cried, rolling around on the ground, slashing at the last hound. "Stay dead!"

Decker took a deep breath and whispered, "Don't let me kill her. She is dear to me, despite all appearances."

Joshua nodded, ready to agree to anything at this point. He had no idea how he would actually stop Decker if the vampire attacked Elise, nor was he sure that Elise wouldn't simply kill them both. And somewhere out there was a monster that scared them all.

Correction, the monster was standing over Elise.

It was a mishmash of horrors. The bottom part was a more solid version of the hounds with wicker and grapevines forming a pony-sized dog body. The upper part grew upwards through a scarecrow straw-stuffed body, creating a centaur from hell.

Joshua whimpered as he recognized the bloody ripped shirt. It was Frank Cahall's number seventeen football jersey. It was layered over Kevin's black hoodie. D.J.'s ever-present expensive headphones hung around its neck. The neon glow stick necklace that Chris had been wearing before being beheaded looped under it. The jack-o-lantern that Joshua had carved and left sitting on his parents' front porch snarled down at him, some brilliant red light source blazing within the cavity.

There was no question as to its target. It was there for him.

As Joshua stared in horror, the huntsman lifted up a bow. The weapon was the huntsman's left hand. The bowstring shimmered like a strand of moonlight. It drew the gleaming string taunt with its thumb. Its fingers grew long and pointed. It took aim at Elise, still pinned to the ground by the hound.

"Decker!" Elise shouted.

Decker leapt between the huntsman and Elise.

Joshua tackled the hound, tearing it from Elise. He flung it at a tree, smashing it to pieces.

Elise drew her guns as she rose from the ground. "Decker, move! Don't block my shot!"

The bowstring twanged as the huntsman released it. The four arrows struck Decker with a loud thud.

"You idiot!" Elise opened fire with both pistols at the huntsman as Decker staggered backwards. The bullets flared as they hit, burning their way through the stuffed clothing, lighting the huntsman on fire.

The monster didn't stagger or scream. It drew back the bowstring again.

Joshua snatched up the scary sword that Decker had dropped and plunged it into the huntsman.

"No!" Elise screamed.

...a forest surrounded him, massive trees stretching up to a canopy far, far overhead. Sun dappled the leaf-strewn ground with shafts of pure gold light. The scent of lush green vegetation filled his senses. He took a deep breath, feeling at peace. This was home...

And then he was flat on his back, looking up at faint stars and a worried Elise gazing down at him. Behind her a pile of leaves, sticks, and scraps of clothing burned. The flames crackled and popped; the firelight dancing off the leaves overhead.

"What a stupid ass move!" Elise cried. "You could have gotten us all killed! Keep your hands off his sword!"

Decker started to snicker. He was lying on his back a few feet away, four arrows sticking out of his chest. His eyes, though, looked normal.

"Do you want to be kicked?" Elise turned her attention back to Decker. "Stop making everything sound like a double entendre!"

"I did not say anything; you did," Decker pointed out. "Ow!" This was because Elise had yanked out one of the arrows. "Ow! Ow! Ow! That wasn't nice."

"I can stick them back in and take them back out in a *nice* way." Elise shook the last arrow at him.

"No!" Decker waved both hands to fend her off. "No, that's fine! Thank you, Elise."

Elise flung the bloodied arrows into the fire. The flames leapt up as if she'd poured gasoline onto it.

Decker got shakily to his feet. Despite Elise's casual treatment, he didn't look very good. Joshua steadied him before he could fall forward onto his face.

Elise ignored them to shine her flashlight on what looked like a hunk of meat.

"What is that?" Joshua really hoped it wasn't what it looked like.

"A heart." Elise confirmed his fear. "The Wickers make huntsmen by sacrificing a human. The victim's life force fuels the spell. Their heart will find the target and forms the huntsman."

"That's a hu-hu-human heart?" Joshua said.

"Yes." Elise cut black threads that crudely stitched shut a hole in the heart.

"What are you doing?" Joshua winced at the awful squishing noise that the wet meat made when she pushed fingers into the opening.

"Getting the heart stone." She pulled out a small bloody item that looked like a pinkie.

"Oh geez, that's so gross," he said. "Why do you need that?"

"If the Wickers recover it, they'll be able to send another huntsman after you."

"Oh! Yeah! We don't want them to get—get—get the what?"

"Heart stone." She wiped the blood from it and held it out to him.

It was a loop of silver about the size of a small donut. One edge was engraved with the face of the man in moon. "Why is that called a heart stone? It looks like it's made out of silver."

"You don't recognize it?" She held it out to him. It made an odd rattling noise.

"No."

"Odd." She pocketed it. "A heart stone needs to be something extremely unique to you for it to work. A baby tooth. A custom-made engagement ring." She took a square of leather out of her other pocket. "A handmade wallet."

Joshua slapped his hand to his back pocket. It was empty.

"Hey! What are you doing with my wallet?"

"Finding out who you are." She pulled out his student ID and squinted at it. "Is this really your name?"

He braced himself for the inevitable teasing. "Yes."

"You poor child." She handed it to Decker.

The vampire gave a surprised laugh before Joshua snatched the card out of his hand. "That has to be an Ellis Island misspelling."

Joshua doubted that spelling it different would have lessened the lifetime of teasing. His dad would insist on the embarrassing pronunciation.

"It's not a werewolf family name." Elise continued to dig through his wallet. His emergency contact and library card followed. "He's seventeen. Freshly bitten."

"He's clearly not feral. If he was, he'd be trying to tear open your throat instead of looking at you like a hurt puppy." Decker patted Joshua on the head. It was surprisingly comforting. "Nor could he have helped me find you quickly. You know how slow my method can be at times."

Elise gave Decker a dark look then studied the empty billfold of Joshua's wallet. "Take him home with you."

Joshua wasn't sure which of them she was talking to or which house she meant. He didn't want to go back to his parents' with monsters chasing after him.

Elise made herself clear when she realized that they were both standing still, staring at her. "The Wickers won't know where the huntsman spawned. Even if they pinpointed Framingham, that's twenty miles out. Where you live is one of the best kept secrets in Boston. Your place is warded against nearly everything. No one will be able to find him if he's with you."

Decker glanced behind himself before pressing a hand to his chest. "Me?"

Elise snorted. "I'm not going to drag a newborn werewolf with me while hunting Wickers. I'd be hip deep in ferals before he learned how to control his wolf."

"You're not going alone..." Decker started.

Elise cut him off with an angry stab of her finger. "I'm not doing that vampire in the trunk thing again. It's entirely too freaky. Besides, I want to take my Jeep, not a rented sedan with no clearance. If he's a pack wolf, then there's a pack. Someplace." Elise had apparently taken her phone out of Joshua's pocket while he was unconscious. She photographed his emergency contact card and then typed in his home address. "It looks like Albany is the closest pack. Was he from Albany?"

It took Joshua a minute to realize that she was talking to him and that "he" meant the werewolf that had bitten him. "I—I don't know. I didn't recognize his car; it was a black BMW i8. It had New York plates; KJV 2341."

She handed back his emergency contact card and empty

wallet. "And he didn't tell you anything before or after he made you a werewolf?"

"I don't think so."

Up close she was breathtakingly beautiful and very scary. "You know his license plate but you don't know if he mentioned werewolves?"

He took a step backwards and looked down so he could think. The bonfire threw uneven light and shadows so it looked like something was reaching for him. He backed up another step. "I don't remember a lot of last night. When I woke up in the hospital, I couldn't even remember my name. The police showed me a picture of his car; they wanted to know who drove it to the barn. I was a little freaked out about the amnesia, so I memorized the license plate."

"How do you know it was the werewolf's car?" Elise turned away to stir the fire, making it burn brighter. Driving back the shadows.

"After they left, I remembered him getting out of it," Joshua said. "It was like a circus act: little car, big, big man. After he got out of the BMW, he changed into a wolf. That's when I realized why I felt so—wrong. I was a werewolf."

"And you know nothing at all about werewolves?" Elise collected the sticks that had been the hounds and added them to the flames. The jack-o-lantern leered at Joshua from the bonfire.

"No," Joshua whispered. "Nor about witches and vampires or any of that stuff."

"This doesn't make any sense," Elise murmured and Decker nodded in agreement. "Pack wolves only change their own children."

"I don't think he was trying to change me," Joshua said. "He killed ten other kids from my school. They say the only reason I'm still alive was someone killed him first."

"Who?" Decker asked.

"*How?*" Elise cried.

"I don't know." Joshua rubbed his shoulder. "I only know that the paramedics had to pull his body off me."

Elise was shaking her head. "You can't kill a werewolf with a normal weapon. I don't think even a chainsaw would work. They heal too fast. A silver blade will work, but short of silverware, no one makes silver knives. The metal is too soft to hold a decent edge. Trust me, you don't want to be stabbing at a werewolf with a butter knife as it tears you to pieces. So it's freaky weird that a lone pack wolf shows up at a barn in the middle of nowhere and someone there has a weapon that can kill him. Did they shoot it with silver bullets?"

He spread his hands helplessly. "I don't remember."

"That's normal," Decker said. "The amnesia that is. The werewolf bite is a magical wound; it opens a gate between you and the source of the werewolf's powers. When you're first opened up to magic, it burns part of you away."

Elise pointed at Decker. "Take him home." She turned and pointed at Joshua. "Make sure you don't hurt Decker or I'll make you sorry."

Joshua was all for bolting from the park. He never wanted to come back. He hated everything about it: the gymnastic rabbits, the badly placed trees, and the rampaging monsters.

It had been a weird, weird night. Joshua's brain had shut down somewhere around the time that the huntsman showed up. He'd collected his backpack from its hiding place and followed Decker the whole way to the Yawkey subway station before his brain finally engaged again.

"What the hell just happened?" he asked while Decker fed money into the ticket machine. "How did we win?"

"We got lucky." Decker handed him the ticket the machine spat out. "I don't fully understand the pack's magical power, but it's not like most monsters'. The pack is like a tightly woven net; all the members sharing one central power. Most other supernatural beings are a solitary pinprick through which massive power can flow. There's no on or off switch, it's just a flood that wipes out the individual and they become the power. I'm a freak of nature as a vampire; I have an off switch. It gets stuck on when I stress it out, and I become a true vampire if I can't turn it off."

"Like when you almost bit me?"

Decker herded him through the turnstile. "Not my finest moment, but yes. Part of my nature is that I don't need blood to survive; I can tap power from other monsters. If I get too much, though, I overload and can't break free. I could become something that lives to drain all life essence from everything around me. The huntsman should have destroyed any hold I have on myself."

"Which was why you wanted Elise to kill it while you dealt with the hounds."

"Yes. Because you struck the killing blow, the huntsman's power was defused by your connection to the pack's magic." Decker glanced away. "Thank you for protecting Elise."

The train rumbled up to the platform. The doors slid open and Decker stepped on. Joshua realized he hadn't actually thought everything through. His parents always told him not to go anywhere with strangers. They could be dangerous. A vampire definitely qualified as strange and dangerous.

Decker turned and saw that he was still standing outside the subway car. He waved Joshua forward. "Come on. Come on." He said in the sort of voice that one used with a puppy.

Joshua blushed. If he didn't get on, he wouldn't be able to actually finish the conversation. He still didn't know anything useful about being a werewolf and there were monsters chasing after him. He stepped onto the train seconds before the door slid shut.

"Look," Joshua said. "Usually when I'm going to go stay over at someone's place, they have to call their folks and make sure it's alright. This is kind of freaking me out."

"My parents died a long time ago."

Awkward.

"You don't have any place to go, right?" Decker asked. "Or do you have family in town?"

"No. I-I just had the weird dream in the hospital that I should come to Boston." It sounded stupid aloud. At least he assumed the Prince of Boston would be in Boston. Someplace.

Decker nodded but didn't comment on the dream. "And you don't have any money? Nothing to buy food with?"

His running away from home would seem stupid if it wasn't for the whole "monsters chasing you." And to be honest, he hadn't known about that part. It wasn't like he was some little kid that should be under constant watch. "I was going to go to college next fall. I had it all planned. Harvard was my top choice but I needed a scholarship. That was a real long shot. I'd figured that I'd end up at Syracuse like my sister Bethy. She's a senior there. I wanted to have an apartment instead of living in the dorms. I figured I'd just get bullied in the dorms—like usual—only worse."

Decker raised an eyebrow, apparently confused by the change in subject. He thought for a moment, tilted his head, and asked, "Do you know the story of Bluebeard?"

It was Joshua's turn to be confused. "The pirate?"

"That's Blackbeard. Bluebeard is about this woman who gets married to a man who'd been married multiple times but all his wives had mysteriously disappeared. He gives his bride the keys to his castle and tells her that she has full run of the place, as long as she never uses the key to a small room in the basement. Eventually she goes to see what's in it and finds the bodies of his previous wives hung up like butchered pigs."

Joshua squinted at Decker, trying to figure out the point of this story. "You've got dead bodies in your basement?"

Decker covered his eyes and shook his head, laughing silently. "I *am* the dead body in the basement! And people are like that. You try to tell them to stay out of one room and no matter how many times they promise not to, sooner or later, they just have to find out what you're hiding. It never ends well. As recently as fifty years ago, it got villagers with torches showing up, trying to kill you, blaming you for everything from a recent murder to low sex appeal."

"Okay." Joshua still didn't see the point.

"I've been trying to live alone and it's not working. I need someone. A housekeeper."

"Like Alice?"

"Alice?" Decker echoed, mystified.

"On *The Brady Bunch*. Alice was the housekeeper. Always in a maid's dress."

"I was thinking more like Mr. French."

"Who?"

Decker sighed. "Obviously before your time."

Joshua doubted that the vampire actually needed a housekeeper. He wasn't sure why Decker was even making the suggestion. "Look, I wouldn't look good in a maid's outfit."

"I don't know. A little black corset dress with a white apron?" Decker drew indecent lines where the outfit would start and end. "Stockings and garter belts? A white ruffled headband and a black ribbon choker?"

"In. Your. Dreams."

Decker snickered. "Okay, what I really need is a guard dog. Someone that can move around in the daylight. Chase off intruders. Bring in the daily paper."

"I'm not a dog."

"You're better than a dog, because you talk and clean up after yourself and drive a car."

Joshua burned with embarrassment. "I don't have a driver's license. I don't even have a learner's permit because my parents have never been able to figure out what they did with my birth certificate." He needed it to get a social security number too. He didn't remember his folks being so weird about the paperwork with his older sister. As always, it sounded so lame that he added on their other excuses. "They couldn't afford the additional insurance while my sister is in college. And my folks have an old Dodge half-ton pickup with a manual transmission and I—I'm having trouble with the clutch." Because he couldn't reach the freaking pedals, but he didn't want to mention that.

"Ah, the all-important clutch." Decker somehow made that sound dirty. "You can learn to drive, something that's beyond the average Rottweiler." He took a deep breath and confessed. "I need someone I can trust. Someone that knows I'm a vampire and won't be trying to kill me or sell my story to newspapers. Someone who has a hope of surviving if I lose hold of the monster inside me. Someone who amuses me."

Joshua studied the vampire. In the flickering lights of the subway, he looked like a normal college student. If Elise was his closest friend, then the man was very much alone. And wasn't everything Decker said true for Joshua? He needed someone that knew he was a werewolf. Someone that had a hope of dealing with the wolf when it finally manifested. Someone who found him amusing, not frightening?

"Okay, but no maid outfit."

Decker grinned but made no promises.

The subway slowed and pulled into a station.

Decker stood up. "Come, this is us."

2: ELISE

Elise stopped at the first service plaza on the Mass Pike. She had a quarter tank of gas, but it was two hundred and sixty miles to Joshua's home in Sauquoit, New York. Ignoring the signs on the gas pump, she called in her report.

Clarice answered with a sleepy, "Central. Ow!"

"Are you okay?" Elise asked.

Clarice had bright copper hair and the porcelain skin that went with it, which meant she bruised spectacularly. She was also a klutz. "No biggie. I just kicked my desk." She yawned deeply. "Report?"

"It's Elise. The huntsman is dead and I've secured its target."

"Oh good." There was a clicking of keys as Clarice entered the information into the logs. "And the Wickers that made it?"

"I'm looking for them now. I think they're in the Utica area of Central New York. Is anyone else there? There was a wolf attack at a barn on Friday night. It was related to this."

"The Wolf King is on the warpath in Belgrade." Clarice must have put Elise on the speakerphone. Her voice floated away from the pickup, and was joined by the sounds of coffee making. "He popped up on our radar when he and half his Thane went through customs. All hell let loose there. We're not sure what's going on."

"I said Central New York."

"Yes, I know." Another faint "ow" as she burned herself on the coffee she'd just made. "Whatever is happening in Belgrade has all the wolves rattled. After I heard about the attack in Sauquoit,

29

I called Albany and Syracuse to see if it was one of their wolves or a true feral. The Baron of Syracuse said we should mind our own business. I took it to mean that the wolf wasn't a feral, otherwise it would be our business."

"What did the Marquis of Albany say?"

"That the Thane are looking into it. I got the impression that he'd talked with the Castle, been told *something* that was obviously incomplete, put clues together, but didn't totally trust the answer he'd come up with. He chose to be rude instead of giving us false information. Why?"

Clarice manned the phones at Central because she had a rare magical gift of insight. She could sense patterns from the barest of clues. Also, no one really wanted her playing with knives.

"A wolf tangled with a Wicker's puppets and ended up dead." Elise ticked off what she'd pieced together from the clues. "The sole survivor had been bitten but didn't go feral."

"Bitten? Fudge, I missed that." There was a long pause. "Oh geez, yeah, this has Wicker fingerprints all over it. The news media suddenly detoured off all the weird stuff on the case. You need to go down the whole way to the social media of the victims' family members to get the nitty-gritty. The reporters are churning out buckets of crap, but it's all been whitewashed. You're looking at a big coven. There's no way only one or two witches are running this show. And you're right, the wolf must have been a Thane; I've talked to the two nearest Alphas. Good call."

A big coven. Elise whispered a curse.

"Oh geez. Nonononono!" Clarice cried.

"What?"

"I spilled my coffee! Grandmother is going to kill me."

"You spilled it in your laptop?"

"I'm not allowed laptops anymore. Grandmother said I was going to personally bankrupt the family, which is totally mean of her. I make a ton of money day trading in my spare time. She got me a wireless keyboard and wall mounted my monitor. I'm not allowed to touch the desktop tower. This is the third keyboard this week. Maybe if I can—" Clarice gave a startled squeak and the phone went dead.

Elise tried calling back three times before giving up. Clarice must have killed the phone too. It meant Elise was on her own.

3: SETH

Seth Tatterskein never knew that werewolves were so good at hiding.

In the three years that Seth had lived at the Wolf King's Castle, there was always at least one burly Thane guarding the front door. They were in Manhattan, facing Central Park and tucked between museums. It meant that anyone might innocently walk through the impressive bronze doors, from Japanese tourists mistaking the Castle for a museum to the desperate homeless. Then there was a weird off chance that someone who actually knew that it was the Wolf King's Castle was crazy enough to want to try to take on the king and his Thane. For all those reasons, the entrance was normally kept locked and guarded.

The door had been unlocked and there wasn't anyone standing guard.

Seth stopped in the marbled foyer, dropping his luggage around him. "Hello? Hello?"

Had something happened while he was in the air? He had assumed that his phone calls, as he hopped from one airport to another, had gone unanswered because no one wanted to tell him that his cousin Jack Cabot was dead.

Thirty hours earlier, thousands of miles away, he'd felt something thrust through Jack with a searing blow that would kill a human. More blows followed as someone or something stabbed Jack again and again. And there was nothing Seth could do other than howl in fear and rage.

It was like all the times Seth had felt strangers die in Boston while he was stuck in New York City. Only worse: this was Jack. His big brother, best friend, fierce protector, loyal follower and only living relative all rolled into one. And now Jack was possibly dead.

Seth closed his eyes and focused on the tenuous connection he had with Jack. Somewhere far away, Jack clung to life. Seth growled in frustration. If Jack had been attacked in Boston, Seth would be able to pinpoint his location, know if anyone was with him and figure out if Jack was safe or not. Jack was somewhere west of New York City, not east. Seth needed someone else to fill in the holes as to what was being done to save his cousin.

Seth opened his eyes and scanned the empty entrance hall. If Jack was still alive, why was everyone avoiding Seth? He sniffed, testing the air for blood and gun smoke. He picked up Eric Hoffman's scent. Lowest dominance of the Thane, Hoffman often pulled door duty. Hoffman had been standing at the doorway until a few minutes ago. He probably watched through the spyhole as Seth paid the taxi driver. Hoffman unlocked the door and vanished.

"Hello?" Seth slammed shut the front door. It boomed loudly and echoed. "Hoffman?"

Where was everyone? Why hadn't anyone answered his phone calls? Seth had spent nearly fourteen hours trying to reach someone at the Castle before leaving his grandfather's funeral early. (His Uncle Efrain, the new Earl of Guadalajara, hadn't wanted Seth to fly internationally as an unattended minor, but one of the few benefits of being the Prince of Boston was that only the Wolf King could stop Seth from doing what he wanted.) It took another fourteen hours to work his way to Mexico City and then Atlanta and finally Newark. One of the Thanes should have met Seth at the airport with one of the Wolf King's limousines.

Hoffman had been at the door. Where was he now? Where were all the other Thanes? The Wolf King had thirty-one of them living at the Castle.

The lounge was empty; normally at this time of night two or three of the Thanes would be relaxing in the leather armchairs. The billiards room was dark and silent, as was the music room and the theater. Seth checked the library, the ballroom, the formal dining room and the throne room. No one. Nor was there any sign or scent of bloodshed or invaders.

"Where is everyone?" Seth shouted. His voice echoed through the empty castle.

Seth realized then that Hoffman had to be hiding from him and that the Thane was doing a damn good job. Seth looped back through the entrance hall, opening doors and staring intently into the dark rooms. Listening. Sniffing.

Who knew that werewolves were so good at hiding?

Seth hadn't played hide and seek since his little brothers were killed along with the rest of his family. Searching for Hoffman made him remember how helpless he'd felt the day they died. The Thane had pinned Seth to the throne room's floor as his family was torn to shreds in Boston. He could do nothing but scream and beg. When his father died, his power roared into Seth like a supernova. Becoming the Prince of Boston burned out everything that made him Seth; for a few confusing weeks, he was spared the memory of ever having little brothers.

When he started to remember, Jack had been there, keeping him from breaking into a thousand pieces.

"What happened to my cousin?" Seth roared. The coat closet, tucked in a dark corner of the entrance hall, was the only possible hiding place left. He ripped the door off and flung it away from him. The force embedded it into the far wall.

The walk-in closet was cedar-lined and filled with rarely used winter coats. Werewolves only needed outerwear to stay dry, not warm. A light brown tail was sticking out between two camel-hair wool coats. It'd been wagging when he ripped open the door. At the boom of the door hitting the far wall, the tail slung down to tuck between the back legs of a large werewolf.

"Hoffman!" Seth shouted.

"I don't know!" Hoffman wailed, slinking deeper into the coats. "I don't know, Seth! Your highness! Please don't hurt me!"

"I'm not going to hurt you!" Seth growled. "Get the hell out here and tell me what you do know."

Hoffman had twelve years, three inches and fifty pounds on Seth, but was lowest dominance of the Thanes. The man overcompensated with muscle T-shirts to show off his tribal tattoos. The ink showed through his camel-colored fur as bold black markings, making him look like some kind of weird zebra.

"Cabot forgot his phone in the kitchen again," Hoffman whined. "You know how he's always setting it down and forgetting it. When you called, Isaiah picked it up, guessed Cabot's password, and listened to the message you left."

Seth cursed. Jack always used the same two passwords: December twenty-eighth and March seventh. They were Seth's and his half-brother's birthday. "Why didn't Isaiah call me? Why didn't anyone answer the Castle's landline?"

"Isaiah said, until we found out what happened to Cabot, we shouldn't talk to you. It would upset you more if you knew that we didn't know where Cabot was, let alone what happened to him."

Utter bullshit! Isaiah was the Wolf King's son, a twenty-nine-year-old going on five. Isaiah didn't care how upset Seth got. In fact, Isaiah routinely chose the path that annoyed Seth the most.

"It's been a full day!" Seth shouted. "Haven't you found anything out?"

"We thought Cabot was in Mexico with you!"

Jack had been an angry ten-year-old when Seth's parents were joined in an arranged marriage. Apparently he had choice things to say about the ancestry of the Guadalajara pack. When Efrain called the Castle to let the king know that Seth's grandfather was dying, his uncle made it clear that Jack wasn't welcome in Mexico. The Wolf King's lawyer, Bishop, had flown with Seth in a private jet down to Guadalajara. Shortly after they arrived, however, Bishop had taken off with said airplane on some other business for the king.

"Did anyone tell Alexander?" The Wolf King usually knew when something had happened to one of his Thanes. Jack was a special case; Alexander had shifted Jack back into the Boston territory after the rest of Seth's family had been killed. The knowledge that Jack wasn't directly under the king's protection had eaten Seth with guilt the entire way back to New York.

"Alexander is in Belgrade; he left Friday morning. We couldn't remember who all went; so we called Bishop to see if your cousin was with them. Bishop told us that the king sent Cabot to someplace in Upstate New York. He went with Samuels. We should call Samuels."

Hoffman made it sound like a collective of Thanes huddled around the phone acting with Borg-like hive intelligence. What most likely happened was that Isaiah made the phone call and told the Thanes loyal to him what he'd learned.

"And?" Seth snapped.

"And what?"

"Did Isaiah call Samuels?"

"He's not answering his phone."

Wolves didn't have pockets. It was possible that Samuels wasn't answering because he left his phone with his clothes. It was comforting to know that at least his cousin wasn't alone. How quickly had Isaiah followed up on Seth's desperate calls? After spending Friday trying to learn something by phone, Seth spent Saturday hopscotching his way back from Mexico on commercial flights. It had been a frustrating twelve hours topped by another hour in the taxi with the awful knowledge that Jack wasn't anywhere near New York City.

Seth felt Jack get stabbed on Friday. It was now nearly midnight on Saturday. "When did Isaiah try to reach Samuels and how many times did he try?"

"Sometime this morning, after he got hold of Bishop, and then again at dinner, after he found out you were heading back from Mexico."

Twice. Twice. Two Thanes missing—one of them seriously hurt—and Isaiah had made only two phone calls.

Seth swore, making Hoffman cringe. Seth resisted the sudden urge to hurt someone because it wasn't Hoffman he wanted to kick hard. It was Isaiah. Hoffman was just one of the many Thanes that expected the Wolf King's son to rise to power and take them with him. Most of them were the weaker Thanes who were sick of being bottom of the dominance order at the castle.

And most likely the reason Isaiah hadn't done anything was because losing Jack would devastate Seth.

Hoffman knew nothing else about what had been done about Jack, which wasn't surprising. He wasn't sure where Isaiah was either. The best he could guess was that Isaiah had taken one of the cars from the Castle's extensive motor pool, thus exiting via the garage.

Hoffman did know that most of the Thanes had left the Castle once they learned that Seth was on his way home. The last fight between Seth and Isaiah that had gone to blows was when Seth was fourteen and Isaiah was twenty-seven. Isaiah started it by ambushing the boy. Seth ended it by breaking five of Isaiah's ribs, his collarbone, his right arm, and the north wall of the library.

The Thanes might be loyal to Isaiah but they weren't stupid.

There was one person that couldn't or wouldn't hide. Whether Seth could trust him was something he was never sure of.

The Castle's massive gleaming kitchen, extensive larder and well-stocked wine cellar were the personal territory of Cook. As a man, he was a tall, blond Dane. He was always in the kitchen, dressed in chef whites. Even now, close to midnight, he was setting out bread and meat onto the long stainless steel island.

He glanced up as Seth came through the swinging doors from the dining room. He looked down immediately since he wasn't dominant enough to meet Seth's angry gaze. No one but the king was. It didn't mean that the male couldn't dig at Seth. Thirty years he'd served the Wolf King but he still spoke with a thick accent. "Was it safe for you to leave your uncle like that—what with him just into his power? Alexander would have normally shepherded him through the amnesia, as he did with you."

"Efrain didn't need me." Seth paced on the other side of the stainless steel island. "My grandfather has been bleeding out his powers for years. My uncle has been the Earl of Guadalajara in every way but name until last week. He had a few hours of amnesia." Which was nothing compared to the weeks that Seth had been lost to himself when his father died, making him Prince of Boston. "Where is Jack?"

Cook cut a round dark loaf of rye bread into thin slices. "I was feeding Bishop. He'd been tied up expediting a new passport for the king to go to Belgrade; it was being complicated by the normal problem of Alexander being born before all this silly paperwork was invented. Anyhow, I was feeding Bishop lunch when the Ithaca police department called him. They talked to him about a stolen car that had been found in a lake. He made me put a second piece of bread on his *smørrebrød* so he could carry it and he headed off to see the car."

Smørrebrød was the Danish open-faced sandwich he was making now. Cook treated it as an insult to his cooking to add more bread to it.

"Ithaca?" Seth seized on the name. The city wasn't a Source point so it was geologically stable enough that it didn't require a wolf pack. It was protected by an overlap of three different territories: Binghamton, Syracuse and Buffalo. It made sense that the Wolf King's lawyer would be called in to handle any large legal mess since it wouldn't be clear which territory should shoulder the responsibility.

Cook spread a thick layer of liver pâté onto the pieces of rye bread. The rich smell reminded Seth that he hadn't eaten anything all day. Cook's food was good but it still struck Seth as strange and exotic. "While Bishop was in Ithaca, the Prince of Belgrade called saying that the situation was worse than he thought. He needed help immediately. The king wanted Bishop in Belgrade, so he had Samuels call him and order him back."

Alexander was born when humans were still struggling with the concept of forging metal. He did not use phones and barely tolerated things like cars and airplanes. Because the Thanes constantly had to act as go-betweens for the king, everyone ended up knowing snippets of information. The problem was not all the random pieces went to the same jigsaw puzzle.

"Does this have anything to do with Jack?" Seth asked.

Cook shrugged and topped the liver pâté with slices of salt beef and meat jelly. "I'm telling you what I know. After Bishop got back, the king called in Samuels and Cabot. They came through the kitchen, arguing over which of them would drive. Samuels said that since it took nearly five hours, they could take turns. They asked me for something to eat on the road. Cabot put down his phone and forgot it." He took it out of his pocket and gave it to Seth. "I did not notice until it started to ring."

Hard evidence that all lines of information had been cut filled Seth with grief. Where was his cousin? What happened to him?

Ithaca matched up to the vague northwest direction he was getting when he focused on Jack. The city, though, was in the middle of nowhere. If he guessed wrong, he could be hours from wherever the two Thanes had actually gone.

Cook added raw onion rings and garden cress to the *smørrebrød* and pushed one of the plates across the island to Seth. "Eat. You're scaring everyone."

A hungry wolf was a dangerous wolf.

Seth picked up the heavily loaded rye bread. After a week of spicy Mexican food like his mother used to make, it was an assault of rich, earthy flavors. He knew the *smørrebrød* tasted good but it made him homesick for a home that no longer existed. His parents were dead and their house had burned to the ground. All he had left was his cousin, hurt and possibly dying. The *smørre-brød* tasted of death and sorrow.

"Who did the king take with him?" He went to the drink refrigerator for something to wash the taste out of his mouth.

Cook named the Thanes that had gone to Belgrade. The list made Seth growl in frustration; Alexander had taken everyone that Seth trusted.

"Where's Isaiah?" Seth asked.

"Out," Cook stated plainly. Either he didn't know or he didn't want Seth to know. Seth wasn't sure which. Isaiah had been the little motherless boy before Seth showed up. Worse, Isaiah's mother had chosen to abandon her son when she committed suicide. It was one of the many reasons why Isaiah didn't like Seth.

"Did anyone call Bishop and tell him that they couldn't get hold of Samuels either?" By "anyone" Seth meant Isaiah but he was being diplomatic. He was never sure which of them Cook favored. Perhaps Cook was truly neutral as he seemed—if he was, he was the only Thane out of thirty-one.

"They tried." Cook kept to the plural. Maybe someone other than Isaiah actually acted on the information. "No one could get through to Bishop."

Seth took out his phone and dialed Bishop. After nearly a minute of silence, a recording cut in, explaining that all circuits were busy. A second and third attempt got the same result.

The king would only send one Thane unless he thought the mission might be dangerous. Alexander would know where they were, even from the other side of the world. He would know, just as Seth knew, that Jack was hurt. He would know, and he would do something.

Unless something on the other side the world had his complete attention.

"What's wrong in Belgrade?" Seth asked.

"There was a massive breach; larger than the one that killed your family. It leveled part of the city and killed the prince before Alexander arrived."

"Did Alexander get the breach closed?" The dark, cold tears in the fabric of reality were what Seth hated most about being the Prince of Boston. He'd never been allowed to see one but he could feel them when they happened. Normally they were tiny rips allowing through only small things like growlings and skitterscratches. Jack would sit on Seth in New York as Alexander took Thanes to Boston to close the breach and hunt down anything that slipped through the opening. The Thanes couldn't feel the breach or sense the monsters at a distance; they hunted by scent alone for creatures that Seth could track from hundreds of miles away. Seth would be stuck in New York as people died in his territory. Seth thought there could be nothing worse before Jack disappeared to some place where Seth couldn't track him.

"Alexander closed the breach," Cook said. "He has half the Thanes with him, killing what came through the tear. The biggest problem is that the prince's nephew inherited his power, not his sons. Those idiot Serbian wolves started to fight over if the boy was the true prince or not. When the heir is lost to alpha amnesia, that's when he's vulnerable."

Seth snorted. "The power goes where it wills." His uncle Efrain had two older brothers. When the power started to leech out of his dying grandfather, though, it slowly became apparent who was the true heir. Any power struggle was dealt with years ago. "Is Alexander bringing the new prince back to New York with him?"

"No. He's several years older than you."

When Alexander arranged Seth's trip to Mexico, Seth thought it meant that the king was finally going to allow him to act like a prince. There were princes scattered across the world that could have guided the new earl through the amnesia. Seth thought that his other responsibilities would quickly follow; that Alexander would allow him to return to Boston, deal with the breaches, and protect his territory. There would be no more three-hour delays as the Wolf King drove the hundreds of miles between the cities. There would be no more people dying needlessly.

Shortly before Seth left for Mexico, though, Alexander announced that Seth would be attending Columbia University just a few blocks away. Seth growled softly. If he had to sit on his hands and feel people die for the next four years, he was going to go slowly mad.

"If he's not bringing the new prince here, then the king is staying in Belgrade until the amnesia wears off?"

Cook went still and silent as he realized the logical end to the conversation.

If the Wolf King wasn't returning, then Isaiah could ignore the situation until Jack was dead.

"You can't go looking for him," Cook said quietly.

"No one can stop me."

In theory he wasn't allowed to drive between nine p.m. and five a.m. He only had a junior driver's license. Nor was he allowed to take the Porsche Boxster, since it was considered Isaiah's car, despite the fact that the registration only had Alexander's name on it. He decided that karma gave him certain privileges. If Isaiah was going to put Jack's life in danger, Seth could take his Porsche.

4: DECKER

If Decker had known what adorable noises werewolf puppies made when distressed, he would have gotten one years ago. Joshua huddled by the front door, trying to look all directions at once, making cute little whimpers.

"When was the last time you actually cleaned?" Joshua finally cried.

"When I moved in. 1959." Maybe grinning wasn't the right approach. Decker smoothed away a smile with his hand. "It will go fast. I'll help you at night. And maybe we can talk Elise into helping..."

"Oh, she'll just burn it all down!"

Decker considered and then nodded. "Yes, she has threatened to do that in the past."

He tried to see his home with fresh eyes. He'd grown used to the clutter. At first it had been a relief to be alone, safe from accidental discovery, no longer afraid that his "trusted" servants would grow too curious for their own good. (To be fair, the last disaster wasn't his servant's fault but the results were the same.) The house, though, had been huge and empty and echoed.

Once he realized how clutter could soften the hollowness of his existence, he abandoned all pretense of cleaning. He left things where they were laid; there was plenty of space. Finding what he needed in the clutter was never a problem; all he needed to do was focus his gift on what he wanted.

Every now and then he'd move a pile that had grown too

large, shifting it to one of the upstairs rooms by the armful. It wasn't until the last year or so that he'd noticed that he was running out of space. It was only in the last month that he realized that the clutter was a symptom of an illness. He was sick of the loneliness.

He'd gone out looking for a cure. His gift had taken him clear across the city to find a wolf puppy running into trees. He could not remember the last time he'd laughed so much. Pure luck had dropped Joshua into his lap. Decker would have to be careful not to scare his puppy. And at all costs, he mustn't let it escape.

To someone young, the job probably looked Herculean in scope. Fifty years of clutter filled the house to bursting.

"We'll get it cleaned up in no time." He tried for reassuring. "One room at a time. We don't even have to do all the rooms. We could just do the rooms you're going to use."

"Me?"

"I only use the library when I'm awake." Decker waved toward the large room. Its floor-to-ceiling built-in cherry bookcases were what made him choose the oversized house. At some point, however, the pleasure he found in reading dimmed. He'd continued buying material out of habit. The room was a static flood of books, fallen piles of novels creating cascades, as the volumes sat waiting to be read.

The clutter had been the first symptom of his illness. The second was that he'd stopped reading altogether. Of late, he didn't even want to stir from his sleeping chamber. He really needed to keep hold of this puppy if Joshua was the cure to what ailed him.

"There are five bedrooms. Maybe six." He hadn't been upstairs to check them for a decade. "We can clear out one for you. Two if you want. Down here on the first floor, there's the front parlor..."

"The what?"

"It's the room you receive visitors in." Not that he ever had visitors beyond Elise.

"A living room. Okay."

"Yes, a living room!" He remembered that was what the real estate agent had called it. (She'd unfortunately been sensitive enough to be scared silly by him; the woman endlessly repeated the house's features like a mantra.) "With a fireplace and original moldings. A large dining room, an updated kitchen with a butler's pantry and first-floor laundry room." No, he shouldn't be listing out the rooms. Joshua was whimpering again. "But we can start with just one room. One of the bedrooms. You'll need someplace to sleep." There was the small matter that the stairs were currently impassable.

"Where's the bathroom?" Joshua asked.

Decker stared at Joshua as he tried to remember if there were bathrooms.

"There are bathrooms, right?" And then blushing bright red, Joshua added. "I've got to pee."

"I think there's one..." Decker scanned the house from the foyer. There were lots of doors he never opened; maybe there was a bathroom behind one of them. Surely there were toilets somewhere in the house. When he was born, the world operated with chamber pots and outdoor privies. He'd noticed the outside accommodations disappearing but he'd never had need for whatever replaced them. He had a shower in his sleeping chamber, along with a dressing room. The house had been newly remodeled when he bought it. Surely the contractor had put in modern plumbing. Or was it before toilets moved indoors?

Joshua opened the coat closet, peeked in and closed it. "Nope." He went to next closed door, blocked shut by a stack of newspapers hip high. He unearthed the door enough so he could crack it open. "Oh, here's one."

"Voila!" Decker waited until Joshua disappeared into the small room before frantically clearing the steps up to the second floor. He hadn't felt this way since he was a human teenager. He'd forgotten it wasn't a totally comfortable feeling.

There was a lot of mysterious swearing and banging and the clatter of china on china coming from the bathroom. The pipes started to rattle and knock from air inside the plumping. Decker didn't think urinating was that large a production—at least it wasn't when he still needed to do it.

"Is everything okay?" He called, flinging newspaper and junk mail over the railing at reckless speed.

This resulted in more whimpers and curses from the bathroom. "I'm fine!" Joshua cried after a moment. "All the water was turned off! I don't think anyone ever used this bathroom before!"

That was entirely possible. Would it scare Joshua if Decker confirmed that? It was probably better to delay confessing to all the oddities that living with a vampire might include for as long as possible. Decker neared the top of the staircase and began to use the smallest bedroom to the left as a deposit for all the clutter. Hopefully Joshua would be the practical sort and want the larger bedroom on the right. It had its own bathroom, if Decker remembered correctly.

Decker found the light switch and flipped on the overhead. *Oh. Oh, dear.* It was much worse than he remembered. *Rally! Rally! The puppy is washing its hands. What a good little puppy!*

Decker shuffled clutter as quickly as he could, grabbing piles from the big bedroom and flinging them madly into the much smaller room directly across the hall. He managed to clear the first three feet into the room before the water shut off and the bathroom door opened.

"Up here!" Decker called as casually as he could manage.

Joshua came up the stairs cautiously. "What was all that noise?"

"Just moving some stuff around. I was thinking you might like this room. We could clear it out tonight. It would only take a little while."

Joshua peered into the room. "Cool! Is that round area part of the tower? The ceilings are so high! You could play basketball in here. This is like ten times bigger than my bedroom back home."

Yes!

Luckily Joshua was wading through the clutter and missed Decker's victory dance. The boy reached the bay windows and peered out them. "I—I haven't transformed into a wolf yet. It will be a full moon on Wednesday. I looked it up. Will I change then?"

"No," Decker said with more authority than he really had. He scrambled to back up his claim. "Other creatures are affected by the moon, which is the basis of the legends, but werewolves aren't. Ferals run unchecked until they're killed. Pack wolves can choose when and where they transform. You don't want to piss a wolf off, but you can sit at a table and talk with them."

"Do you think we should set up a cage, just in case?"

Cage? He didn't think they made cages that could hold werewolves. Not a good answer. What could they use as a reasonable substitute? "There's a room in the basement. It was the coal cellar. The previous owner bricked up the chute and it has a good solid door." Dusty as hell; it made him glad for gas heat. "Don't worry too much about it. Even if you lose control, you won't be able to hurt me."

At least, he didn't think so. The boy was scared and needed the reassurance, even if it wasn't totally true.

Shifting the clutter was like looking back in time—through a fogged-over window. Certain things like the hula-hoop he remembered distinctly. Uncoordinated creatures of the night with supernatural strength should not play with toys that could become projectile weapons. Luckily he'd learned that lesson before beheading anyone. Nor could he ever forget the box full of unfortunate experiments with tie-dye. He had rainbow color hands for a year. He finally soaked his hands in strong lye to remove the stains and let his unnatural healing deal with the damage. The stack of 45s, however, mystified him. When had he bought them? When did he get the lava lamps? Did he ever think the shag area rug actually looked good?

Joshua unearthed the phonograph player. Surprisingly, he had no clue how it worked. Once Decker explained it, Joshua insisted on playing the 45s as they cleaned out the room. Most of the songs the boy had never heard and Decker didn't remember, so it was much as if they were both hearing them for the first time. "Wild Thing" by the Troggs went onto repeat play for half an hour, Joshua bouncing with the music as he carried things out.

The campy "Monster Mash" by Bobby Pickett only got halfway through the song before Joshua took it off. It was too soon for him to make light of his new status.

"Do you?" Joshua asked as he shuffled through the records, looking for something emotionally safer.

"Do I what?" Decker eyed a curtain of beads. What had he been thinking?

"Do you sleep in a coffin?" He'd stopped the song where Dracula was complaining from his coffin.

How much creepy could Joshua take?

"I—I—I've found that coffins are safe. There's nothing like waking up and discovering that rats have gotten into your bedroom." Too much info. "It's like sleeping with blankets over your head." If the blankets were pillowed and then stapled to wood. "I've got the king-sized version, not one of those little narrow things." This was probably not helping. The song had probably called up all the horror movie images of dark crypts full of dead. The boy might be desperate for a place to stay the night, but tomorrow he'd be alone all day, with plenty of time for second thoughts. Time to think where Decker might be sleeping. At any time, he could bolt and Decker would be helpless to stop him. "It's like a bed. The walls of my sleeping chamber are muted blue and the accents are suede, polished gold, and crystal."

Joshua laughed. "Accents are suede, polished gold and crystal? Did you hire an interior designer?"

"Actually I did. A very good one. Once I dissuaded him from using a monochrome color scheme and burnt orange shag rugs, things went smoothly."

Joshua laughed and put on "Stay" by Maurice Williams. A simple song, but it struck Decker to the soul.

"Oh won't you stay, just a little bit longer, please let me hear, that you will."

What a stupid song to be crying over.

They'd cleared the room down to the wood floor. The curtains were in tatters from sun rot. The walls were dirty white. The overhead bulb seemed too harsh. Every little sound echoed loudly. At least the floor was in wonderful shape, due to the fact it had been protected by clutter for decades. They used the ugliest of the tie-dye experiments to dust mop the floor and walls. Decker tried not to panic over how horrible the room looked even empty of the clutter.

"I just realized there's no bed." Joshua laughed and unrolled a shag carpet that once lived in the front pallor.

"I'll buy you one." Decker felt sunrise racing toward them. He would have to shut himself away and pray that when he woke, the boy was still there. "We can go out for dinner and then pick a bed out."

Anything to cement Joshua into his life. The last few hours had been filled with moments of joy, the first time in decades he'd felt the emotion.

Joshua stretched out on the carpet, yawning deeply. "Dinner and bed?" Joshua yawned again. "M'kay." And then how that sounded sunk into the boy's awareness. "I told you no maid's dress."

Decker grinned but refrained from the easy taunt. Once he'd fallen asleep, the day would pass in a blink of an eye, and the moment of truth would be quickly at hand. Would Joshua stay?

Surely if the puppy stayed for a day, all would be good. So he promised solemnly, "No dress. Big steak dinner." Or what was that thing Elise always talked about? "Or a clambake. Lobster, mussels, crabs, steamers, quahog, sausages, potatoes, and corn on the cob." It always sounds like the entire kitchen dumped into a pot, but Elise loved it. "I liked a nice rack of lamb when I was young."

He realized that Joshua's breathing had deepened and the boy was asleep on the carpet. He sat watching him sleep for as long as he could, wondering if he should wake him up and *ask* the boy not to go. In the end, he patted his puppy on the head and went to lock himself away from the unstoppable day.

5: JOSHUA

Joshua had been running in nightmare slow motion through the elementary school playground with the entire high school football team in pursuit. When they were in first grade, Frank Cahall couldn't run without falling down. The high school quarterback had no such limitations as they wove through the monkey bars and swings. Frank wore the torn, bloody jersey that he'd been killed in. In the shadows, Frank shifted into the wooden centaurlike huntsman.

Then the dream changed in time and space.

Joshua had gotten to the barn to find out that he was going to be the star pitcher in the Deep Game. The barren cornfield was standing in as a baseball diamond, complete with massive digital scoreboard. The PA system blasted his theme song: "Wild Thing." A werewolf cartoon flashed on the board, dressed in a baseball uniform. Joshua stood nervously on the threshold of the barn door, Clark Kent glasses on, wondering how everyone knew he was a werewolf. It was supposed to be a big secret, the whole reason he was wearing the glasses and looking even more nerdy than normal. He didn't want to go out onto the playing field, once he was out there, the killing would start.

He couldn't see the stands or bleachers or the crowds that they held. He could, however, hear the audience. They shouted along with the song. "Wild thing! You make my heart sing!"

He wavered on the threshold, not wanting to go out into the bleak cornfield and let the killing start.

49

"There you are." Daphne appeared beside him, slinky black witch's costume on. He really didn't see why all the guys were acting like idiots over her. Yes, she was striking with long red hair and vivid green eyes. When she was posed for the audience, she was lovely, but all the other times she stomped about, all knees and elbows. She was so tall, thin and awkward that at times she seemed like a basketball player in drag. She obviously had never gotten into sports or dance or anything that made her comfortable with her own body. With another personality, the awkwardness would be endearing, but as she was, it puzzled the hell out of him why the entire male population had lost their minds over her.

Daphne had been in the barn with the jocks, forcing them through more and more embarrassing feats. Why was she even paying attention to him? He had his disguise on. No one should even be paying attention to him.

"Have you been dodging me, dogface?" She scowled at him, not bothering to make herself pretty.

He felt to see if he was still wearing his disguise. Was his nose bigger? Were his ears showing? What about his tail? "No, of course not."

He had been dodging her ever-growing entourage. She'd started with the football team, all of whom had hated him since first grade. He wasn't sure what he'd done in kindergarten to inspire such collective hate; one would think he'd remember.

"Bark like a dog," Daphne commanded.

He didn't understand how she was getting away with it, but he'd seen her pull this stunt again and again all week. Anyone that hesitated got more of her attention and like a flock of angry birds, her entourage followed her focus. He could take them one by one, but not all nine at the same time. He barked and kept barking, which was what the people she ignored normally did. It was what Superman would do.

"Hell," Daphne breathed. "Bases are loaded. You need to strike out the next batter, Dogface, or everyone loses."

At least, that was what she'd said in the dream. Part of his mind detached from the action and remembered that they had this conversation in the barn, not out in the privacy of the cornfield. She had said something else, something he hadn't completely caught because the football team been laughing too loudly at Joshua barking like a dog. He lost it now under the howl of the unseen audience, up in the bleachers, viewing the Deep Game from safety.

"Wild thing!" The fans cheered for him.

He'd walked out to the pitcher's mound. A clown car started to circle the playing field as the crowd continued to sing. "You make everything groovy, Wild Thing!"

Daphne was on her phone, swearing softly. "Are you sure he's the one? You've always told me that younglings are resistant. Every time I've pushed him, he rolls." She gave a little growl of annoyance. "Yes, everything is ready. Is Garland going to come back me up for this? What was that?"

Joshua didn't want to walk onto the playing field, but staying close to Daphne had its own dangers. No one else seemed to notice the toy vehicle wheeling closer. If he stayed at the barn door, he'd be trapped with all the others. He walked purposely out toward the pitcher's mound. As he walked, the night darkened, the stadium lights dimming and the stars brightening. The ground roughened to the recently shorn cornfield. The night grew still and biting cold. A hint of snow scented the air.

"Wild Thing!" the crowd shouted somewhere in the darkness, the "wild" nearly a wordless roar.

The clown car looped closer.

"What do I do?" Daphne fearfully asked the person on her phone. She hadn't noticed that he'd walked away. "Should I bring him there? Hey, Dogface, we're . . . Two?"

"We're two?" Joshua's attention was wholly on the car. The monster was in the car.

"Oh, no! What do I do?" Daphne cried from far away.

"Run?" Joshua whispered, fearful to draw attention to himself. Running usually worked well for him. They were a mile from anything, though, and the sun had already set.

The clown car stopped. A huge beast unfolding himself out of the driver's seat. The creature wore a human mask; Joshua thought it might be Samuel Jackson.

Joshua stood frozen on the pitcher's mound, downwind of the beast. The barn door was a golden square in the distance.

"Dogface!" Daphne shouted. "You're up!"

Samuel Jackson started to growl. He took off his mask, revealing the beast. He dropped down onto all fours and stalked toward the barn.

Joshua stood transfixed. He had seen the impossible. He wanted to bolt, run from the Deep Game, but it was his time to take stage center. From the darkness, the now invisible crowd roared for him to show his true self.

"Wild Thing! Wild Thing! Wild Thing!"

"No," Joshua whispered. "I don't want to play."

But the screaming had started in the barn. The game had begun . . .

Joshua jerked awake. Outside seagulls screamed in thin shrieks. He stared at the ceiling wondering where he was. It was a high white ceiling with crown molding and an old bare light fixture. The walls were dirty white. The room was oddly shaped, like someone collided a circle onto a long rectangle. Sunlight streamed in from a half circle of windows, cooking him slowly with UV.

Where was he? Not his bedroom. Not the hospital.

Then he remembered. Decker's incredibly messy house.

I'm living with a hipster vampire who has a serious hoarding problem.

The seagull screams grew closer as the birds flew past the house. Echoes of the dream washed over him.

I'm a werewolf.

He'd woken up in the hospital like this. Disoriented. Echoes of screams. The smell of blood. The feel of fur. The sense of something else inside of him. Not him. Not human. The police arrived before any of his memories returned. His parents hadn't had the courage to tell him what had happened. The police had photos that explained it all too clearly.

"I don't even remember getting to the barn," Joshua told the police. "D.J.—Dennis Kean—was supposed to pick me up for school. I had a bunch of stuff for the haunted house that I couldn't take on the bus. I remember sitting on my front porch waiting." The smell of fresh carved jack-o-lantern beside him, leering as if it knew what was in store. Despite the sunshine, the day had been chilly enough make his ears cold. Of course, he hadn't been able to find any of the winter hats except for one of his dad's. It was a dorky thing like what Sherlock Holmes wore. He kept taking it off and turning it in his hands. Should he leave it behind and freeze his ears off or just buckle down and wear the stupid thing, knowing that the universe liked to make him the butt of all jokes?

Normally he wouldn't worry. After years of fighting, he'd gotten to the point where he could kick the butt of any kid in school and everyone knew that. At football games and such, the bullies of the school were normally in school uniform and had a host of similarly dressed idiots to beat the snot out of, so he was safe there. Tonight, there would be no other team to distract them.

Wear the hat or leave it? Which did he decide? He couldn't remember. "Was I wearing a hat?"

"Is that important?" the policeman asked.

When he was sitting on the porch, waiting, the hat had been important. It certainly wasn't now but it seemed as if the presence or absence of the hat might start him down the right path to remembering what happened. "D.J. was supposed to pick me up." Joshua was the only senior without a driver's license. "He was late. I remember waiting for him. I don't remember anything else."

He realized then that D.J. was the very dead body he'd seen in the photos. For the first time, the wolf filled him and overflowed. It started with soft whimpers of distress. At first he wasn't even aware that he was making them. He glanced around the room, looking for the hurt puppy, before he realized the noise was coming from him. Awareness only made it worse as he tried to control the whimpers and couldn't. He hunched over, not wanting these strangers to see him losing it like a little kid. He pulled the sheets over his head as the whimpers became high-pitched keening.

It was only after the police left and his mother coaxed him out from under the sheets with jelly donuts, that he remembered being at the barn. It was like a gif image, a handful of seconds of standing in the cornfield, his breath misting in the bitter cold, as he stood listening to distant screams.

It was another four hours before he remembered the werewolf. By then he'd left a trail of broken hospital equipment behind him and had a vision of a wolf telling him to go to the Prince of Boston.

In thirty-six hours, his life disintegrated into nothing.

No parents. No money. No future. No idea what in hell he was doing.

He wasn't even sure if his vision had been "real." Certainly there'd been no wolf at the hospital talking to him—he was positive of that. He had a dozen witnesses that verified that he'd been alone when he thought he saw the talking wolf. Unless the wolf could also teleport.

The huntsman had definitely been very real.

Decker was most likely asleep until sunset if he was anything like the vampires in the movies. Elise was going to go looking for the Wickers and didn't want Joshua underfoot. He didn't want to piss her off—not after she threatened to stab Decker with the same arrows she'd just jerked out of the vampire. He didn't want to wander around lost looking for a person that might be a figment of his imagination.

"Hi, I'm looking for a prince. He may or may not be a were-wolf. Yes, a talking, teleporting wolf told me to find him. Would you know where to find the Prince of Boston?"

"No, not doing that," he muttered, and sighed. "What the hell am I supposed to do now?"

The seagulls shrieked outside. He shuddered as it made him remember the screams of his classmates. The forensic photographs of kids he'd known all his life, torn open, torn apart.

He flailed for something sane and logical and doable.

"Clean house. Yeah, that's what I should do."

It was slightly ironic that his mother had a mild obsession with reality TV shows based on hoarding. She seemed to think that without periodic shocks to her system, she'd slide into such behavior. She'd watch an entire season on Friday nights and wake Saturday morning, gird her loins, and launch into frantic deep cleanings. Joshua had learned to maintain his room neat and orderly to keep the cleaning tornado at bay.

Years of exposure to the TV shows had ingrained the process into him. Last night, they'd broken the OHIO rule of Only Handle It Once. All they'd done was simply shift the mess around; they hadn't actually done anything lasting with it. If he were going to tackle the entire house, he'd first need lots and lots of garbage bags.

And a dumpster.

His stomach growled loudly.

And some food.

His parents had a strict rule: always leave a note on the refrigerator saying where you're going. Decker had a great deal of paper—swimming with it actually—but no workable pens, pencils, markers, crayons, or lipstick (Joshua was getting desperate for a writing tool). Joshua resorted to a lump of charcoal from the fireplace. Then he discovered that Decker had no refrigerator.

Joshua stood staring at the large empty hole in the kitchen.

On *Hoarders*, there was always a refrigerator. Scary-ass refrigerators filled with repulsive mystery food.

Where the hell should he put the note if there was no refrigerator?

If he had tape, he'd stick it to the back of the front door. He considered attempting to close it in the door, so Decker would see it sticking out. He abandoned this idea when he realized how many of the interior doors had scraps of paper caught between the door and the frame.

Well, if he weren't back before Decker woke up (but he should be) then the vampire would probably check his room. It was very odd to think of the big empty room as "his" bedroom but Joshua had already slept there once and the vampire definitely gave it to him.

That line of thinking veered Joshua too close to making him wonder about the actual sanity of staying with Decker. Really, he knew nothing about the man—vampire—person. But if Joshua left, where would he go? Where would he be safe from whoever sent the huntsman after him without endangering innocent people? The full moon was just days away...

Right—deep clean the hoarder's house—a simple easy mind-numbing task. He was starting to understand his mother's obsession.

The only clear spot in Decker's house was the foyer table. (It was also one of three pieces of furniture in the entire house. Seriously? Eleven big rooms and the man only had one chair and two tables?) The night before, Decker had carefully put his phone in its charger by the front door. There was a post-it note on it stating: LET IT DIE AGAIN AND I WILL CUT YOU!

"Note to self," Joshua muttered. "Don't piss off Elise."

Luckily Decker's phone wasn't password protected. Elise must have turned that feature off so not to confuse Decker. According to Google Maps, there were several supermarkets within a few blocks of his current location. Wherever that was. He zoomed out on the map. Cambridge. Harvard was just down the street!

He sighed at dreams lost. He'd busted his butt for a year to score amazingly high on his SAT and ACT tests. Combined with his honor roll grades and the fact that he'd competed at state-level in Judo, his guidance counselor had said he'd probably qualify for a scholarship at any university. It was the only way he could have gone to college; his parents couldn't afford to pay for it.

Harvard had been a dream; he could have only attended if he'd gotten a full scholarship. He doubted that he'd get one but he was going to give it his best shot. He also planned to apply to schools where the cost of living was lower. He wanted out of Sauquoit; away from the people that made growing up there hell. He wanted more than the hand-to-mouth existence of a minimum wage job. He wanted to be something that was guaranteed to make money. Accountant. Banker. Lawyer. Anything. Except a werewolf.

Well, those dreams were all toast.

Deep breathing always worked for dealing with the idiots that bullied him in school. It wasn't coping as well with a life going down in flames.

He scrambled to think of the positives.

He had no plans when he left home. He spent the entire train trip sure that he'd be sleeping on the street. He'd worried about wolfing out if someone tried to rob him or molest him, or arrest him. He didn't want to hurt anyone. He thought that he might freeze to death if the weather suddenly turned colder.

Positive: he had a roof over his head. A massive bedroom with a tower. It could not get cooler. Well—a bed would be a plus—but Decker made it sound like he was welcome to stay as long as he wanted. The vampire had talked about painting the room any color Joshua liked.

Vampire.

He was living with a vampire.

That still freaked him out.

Deep breath.

Positive: Decker seemed like a good person. A bit eccentric but that probably was a result of living for a long time. Decker had called the record player "a gramophone" at one point, which apparently had been the forerunner of the one they were using. He explained that gramophones had been hand-cranked since most houses didn't have electricity yet. It was amazing Decker

understood the cell phone at all, considering that he was probably born before telephones were even invented. Before electricity
was invented.

Positive: Decker was fun to be around. He didn't seem ancient
to Joshua. Decker didn't even seem as old as Joshua's parents; maybe
because he looked only a few years older than Joshua. Hanging out
with Decker was how Joshua hoped college life would be like. It
turned out that Decker had actually read *The Hobbit* and *The Lord
of the Rings*. (Most "fans" Joshua's age hadn't.) Decker had also read
Dune and all of Kurt Vonnegut and Ray Bradbury, and books that
Joshua had never heard of but sounded interesting. They'd talked
about the architecture of the house. Decker said it was a shingle-
style which had been common in Cambridge and that it mimicked
many of the details found in Queen Anne style. He knew what a
gable was (the attic had two) and called the garage a carriage house.

Joshua's stomach growled, reminding him that there was a
reason he was looking up supermarkets on Decker's phone.

Decker had dropped his house keys on to the table along with
his wallet. The man had no ID, no credit cards, only a thick wad
of fifties. Last night Decker had broken a fifty to cover Joshua's
dinner. Somehow the vampire had burned through all of the
change because there wasn't anything smaller in the wallet. It
felt wrong to take a large bill without asking first. If there had
been a couple of one-dollar bills, Joshua might have been able
to take them without feeling guilty. He couldn't bring himself
to take a fifty; it felt too much like stealing.

He noticed that there were several ten-gallon milk cans on the
floor, each filled to the brim with coins. One can was only half
full. Decker had unloaded his spare change into a metal flower
vase sitting on the table. It was approximately one-tenth the size
of the big cans on the floor. Apparently when the vase hit full,
Decker poured the coins into one of the milk cans.

Joshua grinned. These were clearly hoarded coins. *Something*
had to be done with them. He might as well start the process.

It rained the whole way to Star Market.

Navigating via phone, Joshua ended up in the back alley
behind the store. The block-long wall had been painted with a
huge mural that depicted all the little shops that must have been
torn down to build the massive grocery store. Very real windows

were surrounded by fake old-fashioned buildings, painted people and flat 2-D animals. The area had once been very rural with cows and horses. Or at least, that's what the painting showed. Joshua stood in the rain and stared at the seemingly unending mural, feeling oddly removed from reality.

Odder yet was the sudden realization that this painting of rural Cambridge depicted a time *after* Decker was born.

Joshua wondered what had happened to his life. How did he fall so far from the sane and normal? What happened to his ordinary world? Becoming a werewolf was one thing—where were all these other weird things coming from? Vampires. Witches. Monsters. Why were they still just myths when they were real? He felt as unreal as the people painted onto the wall. Maybe he was dreaming. Maybe he was really in a coma back in Utica and all this was some kind of drug-induced nightmare.

He stalked around the corner to find the loading dock to Star Market. Down the block, and around the next corner he finally reached the front door, sopping wet.

The coin machine was just beyond the carts. He stood dripping and sniffing as he poured the coins out of the metal vase. The place smelled amazing with hot roasted chicken, fresh baked bread, and donuts. He growled softly as the machine slowly clicked through counting the quarters, dimes, nickels and pennies. He was so hungry, his stomach felt like it was twisting into knots.

The vase was nearly empty when he realized that the security guard was watching him intently.

Did the guard think he'd stolen the money? Technically, he had, but he was fairly sure that Decker wouldn't mind. It wasn't like he'd stolen a large amount of cash.

The coins stopped falling. He glanced at the total.

Two hundred and forty dollars.

Holy crap.

"Is that a funeral urn?" the guard said.

It took Joshua a moment to realize that the guard was talking to him. Only the words didn't make sense. Funeral urn? "W-w-what?"

The guard pointed at the metal vase in Joshua's hands. "That's a funeral urn—isn't it? It looks like the one that my girlfriend's father is in."

Of course Decker had a funeral urn sitting in his foyer. What else would a vampire keep coins in? A coffin would be too big.

The guard was standing there, waiting for an answer.

"I-I-I don't know. I just found it—sitting around—in the garage." Garages were full of weird stuff. They were almost as bad as attics and basements. "I thought it was a metal flower vase."

"It's probably worth a couple hundred dollars," the guard said. "I saw on 'Antiques Roadshow' once a guy brought in a copper urn. There's a surprisingly large market for old funeral urns. Doesn't that beat all? I really don't understand it. I always thought it was a little creepy to have a dead family member sitting on the mantle. Especially when you're making out. I hide my girl's father in the closet; first thing I do when I get there. Last thing I do before I leave is put him back on the mantle."

Joshua stared at the urn in horror. Was it a used urn? Had someone been dead inside it? His skin started to crawl with the need to wash his hands.

The guard pointed at the coin machine. "You need to hit accept and get a receipt. You can either cash it out at the service desk or take it to one of the cashiers."

Joshua stabbed the screen to get the receipt. Luckily there were sanitary wipes next to the cart rack and he could disinfect his hands immediately.

From there he went straight to the Bath & Body aisle and found hand soap. His family always used unscented Dove because his older sister was allergic to everything. She'd moved out but they continued to buy it. He tossed shampoo, a comb, a toothbrush and toothpaste into his cart. What else did he need? Toilet paper was a must before last night's Chinese hit bottom.

Cleaning supplies were next to the toilet paper. He grabbed the giant economy roll of garbage bags. He eyed the prices of brooms and mops with dismay. Those were going to have to wait for another coin run—and next time, no creepy urn.

What else did he need? Stationery was beside the cleaning supplies, so he picked up a notebook and a pack of ballpoint pens.

His stomach growled impatiently. It wanted food! A lot of it!

There was a little cooking stand set up by the refrigerated section run by a young woman with dark purple hair. She was heating chunks of sausage links and setting them out on a plate with toothpicks in them. He'd eaten half before he could stop.

The woman backed away from him, big brown doe eyes going

wide. Her nametag read: *Winnie*. Her lipstick was as purple as her hair.

Joshua blushed as he licked his greasy fingers. "I'm sorry. I didn't get breakfast."

Her doe eyes went wider and she shook her head. "No, no, no, it's okay. You can have all of them. A hungry wolf is a dangerous wolf."

"What?"

Winnie's white cable sweater was too big for her and the sleeves covered half her hands. Her fingernails were the same bright purple as her lips as she caught herself just short of chewing on them. "Everyone knows it! It's like one of those Snickers commercials. You know 'when you're hungry you're not yourself?' Just eat them all. It will be safer for everyone if you do."

He was still trying to process "Everyone knows" when he realized that he'd wolfed down the rest. "Who..." He nearly swallowed one of the toothpicks. He fished about in his mouth and discovered there were three total. He felt like he was doing the magic trick where the magician pulled endless bright colored scarfs out of his mouth—only with toothpicks. "Who is everyone?" He didn't know! How did everyone find out? Was there some secret meeting that he'd missed, like the one in school on puberty? He'd been sick that day and came back to find everyone looking bewildered but unable to explain. (Really, the human species was how old and that's the best that public schools could do?)

"Everyone that knows about werewolves." She edged away from him. "See a wolf, feed a wolf. The safest way to go, to keep your fingers and toes; feed a hungry wolf Ho Hos."

"You're kidding." He wondered which aisle Ho Hos were in. Back home they were with the baked goods in one store but with cookies in another.

The squeak she made might have been "No."

He tried another tack. "How do you know about werewolves?"

"I'm a medium; I channel spirits. It's not as fun as it sounds. But anyone with a gift knows about the Prince of Boston and his family...or to be more exact, his lack thereof."

"Huh?" Channeling spirits didn't sound fun to him. It sounded creepy. Did Decker say anything about the prince? They'd talked about a lot of things last night but very little had to do with werewolves. He'd mentioned his vision but had forgotten to explain exactly what the black wolf had said to him.

"They're all dead," Winnie clarified. "That's why there's no wolves in Boston. Except you. Whoever you are. Who are you?"

"I'm not sure any more." Joshua didn't want to tell Winnie his name; his parents probably had an Amber alert out on him or something.

"Hm?" Winnie tilted her head, squinting slightly, as if listening intently. "Fred says you're one of the black wolves of Boston and that I shouldn't be afraid of you."

"Fred?"

She pointed upward. "Spirit guide."

He glanced up. Something loomed over them. Tall and willowy, bending to fit under the high warehouse ceiling. It was dark yet insubstantial, less like a shadow and more like the absence of light. He leapt backwards, snarling.

"It's just Fred!" Winnie cried. "He's my spirit guide! He won't hurt you. Here. Have more sausage." She chopped off big slices of the sausage, stabbed toothpicks into them and shoved them uncooked toward him. "Sorry. Most people can't see him. Wolves can. I forgot."

Joshua couldn't resist the allure of the meat. Still growling, he darted forward and stuffed the offered slices into his mouth. Fred smelled of fresh dirt and earthworms. The scent reminded Joshua of an open grave and it raised the hair on the back of his neck.

He'd eaten three big slices of uncooked sausage before he thought to ask if they were safe to eat raw.

Winnie held up the package and pointed to the label. "They're organic fully cooked sweet apple chicken sausage. They contain only hand trimmed, fully cooked, uncured premium organic cuts and organic spices. These sweet apple sausages add the subtle flavor of apple and spices to your favorite meal."

"Is that your sales pitch?"

She squeaked, dropped the package. "Yes."

He felt guilty for scaring her and a little mind-boggled too. Him? Scary? All five foot two and a hundred twenty pounds? One of the reasons he always got bullied—despite the fact that he could beat the snot out of most guys—was the fact he couldn't look intimidating even when he tried. It was like he had a giant neon sign over his head that read: HARMLESS DORK PLEASE KICK ME.

Even spirit guides could read the sign. "Fred said I was harmless."

"No, no, he didn't say you were harmless." She waved her hands as if to ward off an attack. "He said I shouldn't be afraid of you. That's not the same. You have to be careful with spirit guides. They mean exactly what they mean and nothing else."

"So he might actually be warning you that I might wolf out on you if you're afraid?"

"Yes!" She smiled brightly. The smile wavered as she parsed the statement more. "Have more sausage!"

He ate the offered slices, growing aware that he'd gobbled down two full packages. He was in the process of cleaning her out of samples. "Won't you get in trouble if you let one person eat them all?"

Winnie opened another package. "I'm not liking this job as much as I thought. It seemed so simple. Cook yummy chicken sausages and get people to try it so they'll want to buy it. It's kind of a captive audience. People are here to buy food! Most of them are hungry. But it's really strange and boring."

"Strange?" *Werewolf strange?*

"Everyone keeps saying the same thing! 'Where's the pancakes?' Seriously. Even the people who are vegans say it. I'm starting to think there's some evil spirits involved. Like all those chickens aren't happy with me. But that's probably the lithium."

If it wasn't for the looming shadow, he'd think she was just a little crazy. Maybe a lot crazy. Considering his life lately, though, she was par for the course.

"I take it to inhibit my powers," Winnie said. "Lithium that is. Fred hates it. I don't like it. Makes me drink like a horse and that means I have to go pee constantly. Wait. It's eat like a horse. Drink like a fish." She wrinkled her nose. "That makes me sound like a drunk. I'm not sure why you only mean 'booze' when you say that. Fish are in water."

"You're taking it so you won't hear Fred?" Joshua wondered if Fred would stay with her if Winnie couldn't hear him. Would Joshua still be a werewolf if he never turned into a wolf?

When would he turn into a wolf? Decker said it wouldn't be during the full moon.

"No. Fred is fine. He's been my best friend since I was three. We had marvelous tea parties. Of course—through high school—he

was just about my only friend. Teenagers are so judgmental. It's
that when you're open—you're *open*—and that's bad. Just about
anything could walk in and set up shop. The lithium is barring
the door against such things. But it screws up my normal gig.
People hire me to talk to their relatives and such. Freshly dead
are really still too freaked out about the whole 'dead' thing to
contact unless you're barn door kind of open even with Fred herd-
ing them in my direction. Marie Antoinette? Easy peasy lemon
squeezy to talk to. A real challenge to my high school French. I
have no idea what she's doing in Boston of all places. But she's
been dead long enough to know all the ins and outs. I'll be trying to get hold of someone's Aunt Gertrude and in pops Marie
wanting to have tea and cake and talk about the latest dress
fashions. One summer I put on twenty pounds because she kept
taking me out to the Royal Pastry Shop on Cambridge Street.
She's addicted to their cannoli and Italian rum cake."

Channeling spirits was starting to sound extremely creepy
to Joshua. "She just takes you over and makes you eat pastry?"

"Yeah. Hard on the hips and hard on the wallet but basically harmless." Her lip quivered slightly. "Seeing a *Marie Claire*
magazine nearly makes me cry thinking how lonely she must
be. Everyone has closed up shop or moved out of Boston for
the duration."

"Duration of what?"

She cut up more sausages. "Until the prince returns, Boston
isn't safe for me to keep the doors wide open. There are dark
things that can take me and hold me tight and I wouldn't be
able to break free."

"Who is the prince?"

She paused and gave him an odd look. "You're a werewolf."

"Yes. At least, I'm pretty sure I am. I haven't actually changed
into a wolf yet. I'm just going on the assumption that since I
was bitten by a werewolf that I'm one. I am—aren't I? At least,
everyone keeps telling me that I am. I have gotten freaky strong
and I keep growling. The first few times I did, I scared myself.
I thought there was a wolf standing behind me."

Winnie stared at him with big doe eyes. "Geez Louise! I
thought I had it rough." She pulled a strand of purple hair to
her mouth and nibbled at it for a minute, clearly thinking hard.
She squinted, tilting her head, listening.

The hair on Joshua's neck rose as he heard—murmuring under the Muzak playing "Witchy Woman"—the whisper of wind through leaves and the scrape of bone against wood. "Is-Is-Is that Fred?"

"What? You can hear him? Jack could never hear him. Which was good since... Oh! Shoot!"

"What's wrong?"

"Oh, it always turns out that when I suddenly think about someone for the first time in ages—especially if I clearly remember exactly what they looked like—it usually means that something horrible happened to them." She sighed deeply. "Jack was always polite to me. Fred freaked him out so he rarely got close enough to be anything else. Oh my god, he was so good looking, even though he never seemed to know it. There was a secret cult among the girls that didn't know he was a werewolf. The rest of us knew it was pointless."

"Because he was a monster?"

"Oh no. Werewolves are kind of like good Jewish boys, only more so."

"What does that mean? I'm from a small town. I don't know any Jewish people."

"Werewolves only marry werewolves. Oh, I really hope he didn't die. That would suck. He really took the guardian shtick seriously. He didn't like Fred but he always made sure no one teased me. A total white knight in shining armor complete with steed; a Harley Iron 883. Oh God, he was so hot on it. I used to go to school early so I'd see him ride in." She closed her eyes and shivered. "The pulse of that big engine against my skin; it really tripped my trigger. I would have put out for him in a heartbeat."

Joshua felt a blush burn its way up his face, all the way to his ears. He didn't have much experience interacting with women. There were the girls in his Judo classes and his sister; both of which were usually trying to hurt him. He really didn't know how to reply to that.

Fred spoke again with a rustle of wind through invisible leaves and scratch of finger bones.

"Oh! Jack told you to go to the prince? What are you doing here?"

"I-I-I have not a clue. Shopping?"

She stared at Joshua, wide eyed. The great shadow-that-was-not-a-shadow folded so it peered over her shoulder at him. There were notably darker points that seemed to be eyes.

He found it very unnerving. "Yes, shopping. Getting toilet paper and such." He fished out the rolls as proof. "I should let you go back to work."

"You really don't have a clue—do you?" she said.

No? Yes? Which would get him into more trouble?

"Maybe?"

"Okay. That's it. I quit." She took out her phone and started to text someone.

"Quit? Quit what? Quit your job? Don't do that!"

She waved one hand to silence him. "This job bores me silly and you *obviously* need help. I'm letting them know I've got a family emergency and need to leave."

"I'm shopping!" He waved the toilet paper roll violently.

"Yes, I see. You can pay for that before we leave."

"You can't just quit. You need money."

"Oh! You're right." Winnie turned to face Fred. "I need money." The shadow darted away.

"What's Fred going to do? Mug someone?"

Winnie laughed. "No, no, he's just going to find—I don't know—whatever he finds. Let's go! It's almost noon already and I want to be home before dark." She lowered her voice. "They mostly come out at night. Mostly."

She stayed with him long enough to dump a dozen packages of Ho Hos into his cart and then disappeared. The smell of chocolate cake and crème made it impossible to take them back out. He picked up bread, peanut butter, packets of tuna fish, and some bananas as food that didn't need to be cooked.

He was amazed at how expensive the few items in his cart were. He handed over the receipt from the coin machine and got six twenties as change back.

Winnie suddenly appeared beside him to snatch one of the twenties from his hand. "I need to borrow this for a minute. Fred found something."

"Hey!" He picked up his bags. "If Fred has money why do you need that? That's all the cash I have and it's not really mine."

"This will just take a minute." She walked to a blue vending machine. The state of Massachusetts was outlined on the side with the words "The Lottery" written inside the lines. In a starburst above it was the word "Instant." As she fed the twenty into the bill acceptor, Joshua realized it dispensed scratch off lottery tickets.

"Wait! No! What are you doing?"

"Getting money. Fred says that one of the tickets is a winner. Go on, hit a button."

"What? Me? I don't know which one is the winner; Fred does!"

"No, that's not how it works. For me, it's a random chance, one in a hundred million to win, or something like that. For you, it's not. You're governed by fate."

"What if it's not my fate to win?"

"There's a dozen places you could have gone to buy food, but you came to this store while I was working here. A mere four-hour window. You were fated to meet me: someone who knows Jack. If you hadn't met me here, you would have met me someplace else. I might have run you over in the street or something. So you're obviously fated to meet me. I can only help you if I can leave work, which requires me to have money. You *need* to win money for me so I can help you."

He stared at her, dismayed and bewildered by her logic. Surely this was not how the universe worked.

She pointed at the machine with both hands. "Push a button!"

He turned to eye the machine. Why was it harder to believe in fate than believing in werewolves, vampires and spirit guides? The tickets were all expensive; some were twenty dollars apiece.

Was it fate that he'd met Winnie or pure coincidence?

Only really one way to find out. He stabbed the button for a Mega Fortune ticket that cost twenty dollars.

"I'll cash this in and I'll give your money back." Winnie fished around in the vending slot and pulled the ticket out. "How do you play this one? Okay you scratch these and these and... Oh my god. Oh my god. Oh my god."

She started to bounce up and down.

That looked like they'd won. He glanced back to the machine to see what the ticket paid. The top prize was ten million dollars.

"No frigging way," Joshua whispered.

Winnie started to squeak as she bounced like a giant squeaky toy. Suddenly she gripped him tightly by both shoulders. "This means fate put us together! With super glue! It's like we're star crossed. It must be super-duper important that I help you!"

6: SETH

"Ithaca" had been a random collection of data to Seth. He knew it was a small college town, home of Cornell University, and stable enough not to need a werewolf alpha to keep the area safe. He wasn't prepared for how remote the town was. After hours of winding his way through darkness on what seemed to be back roads claiming to be major highways, he dropped down a long, steep hill into the tree-lined center of town. The city had been built in the flat valley beside a large lake. Everything seemed clean, neat, moneyed and peaceful.

At the first red light, he closed his eyes and focused on his cousin.

He had guessed horribly wrong. Jack wasn't in Ithaca. Jack was somewhere far away in the northeast. Weaker. Closer to death.

"Shit!" Seth leaned back in his seat, rubbing at his eyes with the heels of his hands. What the hell should he do? He couldn't even guess how far away Jack was. It could be hundreds of miles. He'd already driven nearly five hours in the wrong direction. At this rate, it could take him a day or more to slowly triangulate where Jack was.

A car came up behind him and beeped. The light had turned green.

He drove through the empty dark streets. He needed to find Jack quickly.

At the first empty parking lot, he pulled in and parked. Bishop's number got him an "all connections are busy" message. He ran through the phone numbers of all the Thanes with Alexander. Fifteen identical results. He checked the newsfeeds for Belgrade. The city was in chaos. The humans thought that an unused transit tunnel under the city had collapsed, taking out dozens of buildings. Hundreds were dead and fires were burning unchecked in the bohemian neighborhood of Skadarlija.

Bishop had come to Ithaca to talk to the police. Seth was going to do the same thing.

His phone directed him to a stark white stone building with the words "Hall of Justice" written over the door in giant letters. He sat in the idling Porsche staring at the entrance. The dozen squad cars confirmed that it was the police station.

"Seriously? Hall of Justice?" He snorted as the image of the Justice League's headquarters flashed through his mind. "I am Batman."

He could use a few super friends. And one of his uncle's flaming Mexican coffees or something. He was so tired he was getting silly. And someplace to park. There wasn't any street parking and all the lots within sight had signs reading: police vehicles only. It would be a stupid move to illegally park in front of a police station. He'd be stranded if they towed the Porsche instead of just ticketing it.

He rolled down the window and called out to a police officer walking toward the building. "Officer? Where's a legal place to park?"

He was tired. The police officer was a tall, wide-shouldered woman with a pixie haircut.

She walked cautiously to the side of the Porsche, eyeing him with suspicious. "Does your father know you've got his baby?"

"My father is dead. This is my car." He lied about the second part.

She blushed but didn't apologize. "There's a parking garage across the bridge." She pointed down the street toward a narrow ravine. "I'm sure your fancy car would have found it if you asked it."

"I was looking for the police department," Seth said. "I want to talk to someone about a stolen car."

"Well, you found it. Come back after you park your car." She glanced at her wristwatch. It was a rugged military-grade timepiece. "I come on shift in fifteen minutes."

The parking garage had a vending machine selling Monster energy drinks. Yawning, he debated the flavors. Mean Bean Java Monster? Anti-Gravity Monster Energy Extra Strength Nitrous Technology? What the hell was "Nitrous technology"? He fed in a fistful of coins and two rumpled dollar bills and punched the top button. Nothing happened. He checked the digital display. Yes, he'd put in enough money. He pushed the second button. Third. All the buttons.

"Give me the damn can!" He punched the machine. It rocked to the side. He caught it as it started to fall. "Don't! Stop that!" He shook it hard. With a nervous rattle, it dropped three cans out of the slot. Two of them rolled across the floor in a desperate bid to escape.

Seth righted the machine. His father had warned him there would be days like this. His father had warned him of a lot of things. "When you're Prince of Boston..." It was mostly useless advice now. "You will need to be firm but respectful with your uncle. He was a Thane but you will be the prince." His uncle was dead. "Your little brothers will push your patience, but you must protect them from everything, including your own anger." His brothers were also dead.

His father said nothing about Jack, because Jack left Boston to serve the king once he came of age. The last three years had been hard on the Thane, trying to be at once father and older brother to a boy he couldn't hope to control.

If Seth lost Jack, he'd be utterly alone.

Despair rushed through him so strong he wanted to howl. He accidently crushed the can he'd picked up. Luckily it was a non-carbonated coffee. The cold dark liquid poured through his fingers. "Oh freaking hell." He dumped the leaking can into a nearby trashcan and chased down the cans that rolled to freedom.

"Hold it together for the police," Seth muttered. He cracked open the second can of iced coffee. "Going full out wolf will only make them shit their pants."

Scaring people was a lot less useful than it sounded.

The female officer's desk placard read "Freja Kjeldsen." From the back, her wide shoulders made her look male. From the front, she had the chin of a linebacker and a flat chest. He suspected that she didn't give a shit that people mistook her for a man, otherwise she wouldn't cut her dark hair so short. On the left side of her neck, she had a long-legged spider tattoo. Wasn't there some spider monster boss in a video game with the name Freja?

She ignored him after a glance at her wristwatch. She apparently wasn't on duty yet. He locked down on a growl of impatience. He didn't want to stand there waiting if she couldn't help him. "Officer Kjeldsen, I need to talk to someone about a stolen car."

She glanced at her wristwatch and grunted. Her shift must have started as she pulled her keyboard toward her. "Name?"

"Seth Tatterskein."

"Can you spell that?"

Seth did and then realized that she was entering it into a form. "I'm not reporting a car stolen. You recovered a stolen car? It was found in a lake?"

She frowned. "Wait. Tatterskein? Are you related to Gerald Tatterskein?"

"He was my father. Someone with the Ithaca police department called my lawyer and said . . ." And Seth suddenly realized why the police called Bishop. He'd assumed that the car had been stolen recently and one of the three local wolf packs were involved. There was only one reason, though, why his father's name would be brought up.

"You found a '96 Dodge Viper? Black? Custom gold pin-striping with a wolf head front panel, driver's side?" Seth had charged Jack's phone during the drive. He took it out, entered the password and opened up the photo album. The Viper was the first picture in Jack's album. "This one?"

She frowned at the picture. "Yes, that's the car. Divers found it in the lake mid-September. What do you know about this car?"

He opened his mouth and then remembered his father had killed two people the day that the Viper had been stolen. What had Bishop told the police? "My lawyer was here; Edward Bishop of King's Law. Didn't he explain?"

"He's your lawyer? He talked to our Lieutenant Townsend." She cleared her computer screen. "He's head of the investigative division. He's not in today."

In other words, Seth was going to have to wait until tomorrow.

"Please. My cousin is missing." He flipped through Jack's photo album to find one of Jack's selfies. The first picture Seth found was of both of them in Times Square. "This is him. Jack Cabot. He left New York City after talking to Bishop about the Viper. Something has happened to him." Because he couldn't explain how he knew, Seth added, "No one has heard from him since Friday morning. Did he come here to follow up?"

He thought she would dismiss him as an alarmist. It had been only forty-eight hours since Jack walked out of the Castle, not a huge amount of time for a grown man, considering the driving distances involved. She studied the picture longer than necessary, linebacker jaw flexing. She knew something and was considering tactics.

"I would remember him," Officer Kjeldsen said finally. "He didn't come here. Have you called your lawyer?"

"He's in Belgrade. I haven't been able to reach him. There was some kind of disaster—part of the city is on fire—and it's taken out all communication lines. Why? Did something happen to my cousin?"

"I really can't answer any of your questions..."

"My entire family was killed in a house fire three years ago while I was visiting Jack in New York City." That was the official explanation of his family's massacre. "He's all I have left. I need to find him, make sure he's okay. I'm afraid he might be hurt."

She sat for a minute, staring at him and tapping her pencil on her desk. "I'll do an information trade. You first."

"Trade?" Seth had so many secrets he couldn't tell police.

"All we told your lawyer over the phone was that we found a twenty-year-old Dodge in the lake. He shows up five hours later. You're what? Nineteen?" She missed his age by three years. "You've got a lawyer on retainer and are driving a Porsche. You've got to be stinking rich. Why did your lawyer drop everything and push the speed limit to get here from New York City in that short a time? For a freaking twenty-year-old Dodge?"

Obviously Bishop hadn't told them anything. What should he tell her? There was no guarantee that she would tell him anything useful. She probably was just trying to milk him and had no intention of giving him information.

But Jack wasn't in Ithaca, nor anywhere close. Seth would have to drive blindly, and Jack had grown weaker over the hours. He had to find Jack soon.

"It's not the car that is important," Seth cautiously started. "The people that stole it killed my father's first wife. The car is the only lead we've ever had."

"Oh! Bishop said nothing about a murder."

Seth spread his hands, trying to look innocent. "I don't know why. Maybe he's trying to keep my family's name out of the news."

Seth knew he was setting bridges on fire. He was willing to risk anything to get to Jack. "Her name was Anastasia Tatterskein."

He needed to start with the half-truths. He'd been taught early never to discuss his father's arranged marriages. "She was born in Moscow. She came to the United States as an exchange student when she was thirteen. My aunt was her host mother. Jack was five when Anastasia arrived. He was ten when she was killed. He's never gotten over her death. He loved her like an older sister."

After Anastasia's murder, the king had insisted on Seth's father take a new wife immediately. It was why Jack had been so angry at the joining of Seth's parents that he'd gotten himself banned by the Mexican pack.

"When and where was Anastasia murdered?" Officer Kjeldsen said.

"Tyringham, Massachusetts on March fifteenth." His father always disappeared on the date to grieve privately while his mother raged about the Ides of March. It had etched the date into Seth's brain. "My family has an isolated mountain lodge outside of Tyringham. The land is totally backed by Beartown State Forest. Anastasia was there with my father. They'd gotten snowed in the night before. He'd gotten up early, shoveled out the driveway and gone to town for groceries. While he was gone, she was shot a dozen times."

"And there were no suspects? Your father was cleared of the murder?"

Seth stared at his foot rather than look at her. If he did, he'd frighten her. "We know who killed her. It was a cult that practices black magic; they use human sacrifices in their rituals. They cut up their victims and combine them with silver and myrrh and pieces of wood to create—" he caught himself. Most humans didn't believe in magic any more than they believed in monsters. "— items that they believe hold magical powers. There were three to seven people." Three was the minimum because his father had killed two and one had gotten away in the Dodge. It was one of the many secrets Seth needed to keep. "They came in multiple vehicles. One of their cars got stuck in the snow. They couldn't get it free, so they took the Viper. After they fled the lodge, they disappeared. My family has never been able to find any clue to their whereabouts."

His father killed two of the coven that day. A witch at the lodge. A warlock just a mile from the Lee interchange on Mass Pike. His grandfather was still alive; the power to track people through their territory hadn't passed to his father yet. His father had guessed blindly and gone cross-country to get ahead of the warlock.

Seth got his anger under control. He looked up to meet her eyes. "These are dangerous people. If my cousin followed some kind of lead on them, he could have fallen into a hornet's nest full of trouble."

"You think your lawyer discovered a lead when he was here?" Officer Kjeldsen said.

"Yes. Bishop was my family's lawyer when my father married Anastasia. He dealt with her funeral arrangements. He could have seen a clue in something that seemed insignificant to you. Bishop met with Jack and an hour later my cousin drove out of New York City."

Officer Kjeldsen tapped the desk with her pencil, flipping it on each tap. Tip. Eraser. Tip. Eraser. "Okay. Let's look at what we pulled from the car. It would be useful to know what triggered all this."

She gave him a long lecture on how she would *show* him what was found in the car. He couldn't touch it in any way. Chain of evidence required that items be handled by a minimum number of people, all of them authorized. Standard stuff. Bishop had drilled police procedures into Seth. As the Prince of Boston, Seth might need to make bodies disappear. Shit happened; he would be responsible for cleaning it up.

As she talked, Officer Kjeldsen let slip that the lieutenant in charge had been off sick since Friday morning and she was bucking for a promotion.

She had Seth wait in an interrogation room while she got the case files out of storage. It was a big cardboard box marked: Cayuga Lake Jane Doe 34.

Seth realized he hadn't asked the most important question.

"There was a body in the car—that's why you're so interested in what I know."

"Yes. A woman. Coroner says she was between eighteen to thirty years old. We found ten different driver's licenses in the car. Ten different names. All with the same woman's photo. They appear to be stolen identities. It's possible that none of them are her real name. We've been attempting to track down next of kin for all the IDs."

Each photo license was in a separate plastic bag. The driver had been a waifish Latino woman. The only name that seemed remotely Latino was Wonder Woman Alvarado, which didn't sound real at all. The rest ran the gamut from Orli Cohen to Kyung-sook Kim. In half the photos she sneered confidently at the camera, obviously proud of her long glossy dark hair and good looks. In the other pictures, she looked like a frightened prisoner, stripped of makeup and her hair hacked short. His gut was telling him that this was one of the Wickers' puppets, one that they'd controlled over months instead of a few hours as they normally did.

If the car was in the lake by sheer misfortune, then the driver would have simply vanished for the Wickers as well as for his family. By contacting next of kin, the police most likely reached the coven. They had set up a collision between Jack and the Wickers. The question was where? Why not here?

"Did any of the next of kin come look at this evidence?"

"Yes." Officer Kjeldsen studied a sheet of paper. "A woman came in three weeks ago. The lieutenant accessed the files the day she was here. She was a clotheshorse with a red Bentley. She parked in our lot, ignoring all the signs. Jenkins went out to give her a ticket and came back panty whipped. He followed her around like puppy, holding the doors and fetching her coffee."

Definitely a witch. She could have left one of the policemen on post-hypnotic script to contact her if anyone else looked into the case. It might explain the officer who was out "sick" immediately after Bishop's visit.

Seth clenched his hands tightly. Of all the things in the world, a witch was the most dangerous to werewolves. They knew all the wolves' weaknesses and they had an unlimited supply of human puppets to throw at wolf packs. At one time, wolves killed any witch that crossed their path, but the treaty with the Grigori changed that. Now only witches that worked blood magic were killed, and only after being screened by the Grigori.

Larger plastic bags followed the small ones out of the box. They held a rusted gun, two large meat cleavers, the tattered remains of a purse, a plastic drinking cup from Roy Rogers, and a nylon windbreaker with a rusty zipper. Seventeen years in water had destroyed most of the evidence. Why were the police even bothering to follow the case so closely?

"There was something else in the car," Seth guessed. This was Wickers after all. "Was it a severed limb or something?"

She eyed him. Her silence alone confirmed it. After a long silent debate with herself, she finally admitted, "A human head in the trunk. Wrapped in a black garbage bag. We've got it at the FBI labs for identification."

So they were treating it as a murder case.

Officer Kjeldsen pulled out an evidence bag containing a small lump of leather and fur. Seth gasped and snatched it up.

"Hey! I said don't touch!" Kjeldsen put out her hand for it.

Seth reluctantly gave her the plastic bag. He'd gotten a close enough look to recognize it.

She squinted at the contents. "What is this?"

"It's a hat." His grandmother had made it with yarn, leather and fur. Water had rotted it into a shapeless mass but the wolf ears were still recognizable. In his concern for Jack, he'd forgotten about his half-brother Ilya.

The Wickers had stolen his father's firstborn. They'd taken Ilya out of his crib and driven off with him. His father had gambled that Ilya was in the warlock's car. He'd been devastated when he discovered that he was wrong.

Had Ilya died in the lake?

Seth scanned the items on the table. Purse. Nylon windbreaker. Plastic cup. All the little items belonging to the puppet stayed in the car. Except for the hat, there was nothing else related to an infant. "Did the windows break when the car crashed? Could anything small float out?"

"All the glass is intact. The victim didn't have her seatbelt on when the airbags deployed. Coroner says it looks like she'd been knocked unconscious and then drowned."

Bishop had helped clean up the dead Wickers before the police were notified of Anastasia's murder. He had been a frequent visitor to Boston when Seth was growing up. Bishop would have recognized the baby hat; Seth and all his baby brothers had worn one. Bishop would have realized that Ilya could have been in the Dodge Viper when it was driven away from the lodge.

It was possible that Ilya's body simply hadn't survived being submerged for seventeen years. Something, though, made Bishop send Jack someplace north. Someplace not within Seth's territory but between here and Tyringham.

"She stopped someplace," Seth said with certainty. The answer was on the table in front of him. He just had to look.

"Probably," Kjeldsen said. "It's like two hundred miles to Massachusetts state line. She would have needed to stop for gas someplace." She pointed at the Roy Rogers cup. "There's only a handful of Roy Rogers in the state and all of them are on the Thruway."

Seth scanned the other bags. The smallest evidence bags held scraps of paper inside a gallon-sized Ziploc storage bag. He leaned close to study them. One was receipt from an auto repair place in Utica. The other was a deposit envelope from First Niagara Bank. He typed Utica into his phone GPS system. The town was just off the New York Thruway. "What was in the deposit envelope?"

"A cashier's check made out to one of the IDs. This one. Wonder Woman. It was drawn on the account of a New Hartford law firm that closed doors fifteen years ago. Both partners are dead. We're trying to track down any clerical staff that worked there. The check is for twenty thousand dollars."

New Hartford was a small town bordering Utica.

"What's the date on it?" Seth asked.

She checked. "Oh shit. March fifteenth."

Ides of March.

A puppet flees Massachusetts with a baby, most likely without a script in place to control her actions. She went via the Thruway until the Viper broke down near Utica. Facing possible kidnapping and murder charges, she had to be in a panic. Obviously via the auto repair place, she got the Viper running. In New Hartford, lawyers gave her twenty thousand dollars. In Ithaca she died without the baby in the car. The logical explanation was that she sold the baby in Utica.

"I know where my cousin is." It would take Seth two hours to get there.

7: ELISE

Elise left Boston after midnight. Massachusetts was a sea of darkness after an hour of suburban sprawl. She climbed up and over the Berkshire Mountains, the wind blowing dead leaves and promises of winter storms. She played rock music loud to drown out the fear that the dark wind blew through her.

Hunting Wickers was a dangerous game of cat and mouse. The witches could turn most normal humans into puppets and hide behind them. A very powerful witch could remotely control their puppets by implanting scripts like post-hypnotic suggestions. It meant that Elise could be fighting puppets in Utica while the Wickers searched Boston for Joshua. She was betting heavily that the Wickers didn't know that the boy had taken the train. A huntsman wasn't an urban-friendly tool; it drew too much attention to the Wickers' activities. They probably cast the spell thinking he was hiding in a tree fort near his house. By now they would have realized something had gone very wrong but without the heart stone, they wouldn't be able to recast the spell. Probably. It made her uneasy that Joshua didn't recognize the moon-shaped loop of silver. It had to resonate strongly with his soul; otherwise the spell wouldn't have worked.

Dawn rose on farmland. Rolling pastures lined the highway with solitary barns standing like islands. She spotted distant woods marking where the land lay too rugged for farming. Prime Wicker country.

Utica sprawled in a broad wooded river valley. The wide

streets lay in an orderly grid system. Four- and five-story buildings were scattered randomly through the city, as if someone had gone through and weeded out structures. It seemed that Utica had been a base of power back in the age of the Erie Canal but now was merely a truck stop along the New York State Thruway.

Signs off the highway pointed out the Amtrak train station, Saint Elizabeth Hospital, and the various law enforcement agencies. She stopped at a large gas station with four islands of pumps to stretch, fill up her Jeep, and consider her options.

Joshua was from the town of Sauquoit, six miles south of Utica. The town was so little that she couldn't find any information on it beyond the fact it did have a post office. Satellite pictures of the area showed that the town was little more than a string of houses lining the country roads with backyards giving way to farmland and woods. News stories had ten dead teenagers at a barn Friday afternoon, a late Friday night discovery of the mauled body of a Reed Wakefield at his home, and the murder of Joshua's neighbor, Joseph Buckley, sometime Saturday afternoon.

Wakefield most likely was a Wicker; killed by the same werewolf that showed up at the barn. Buckley may have been the sacrifice made to create the huntsman. It was difficult to tell, as the news stories contained fewer and fewer details instead of more. Clarice was right: the Wickers had recovered from the disasters and taken control of the media. By Saturday evening, the news reports dropped all mentions of Buckley, Wakefield and the wolf. The only stories posted Sunday morning defended the decision to issue an amber alert on the seventeen-year-old Joshua and details of the mass funerals that would take place Monday.

Twelve people dead in three separate murders meant that the local police departments would be overloaded. If the Wickers seriously wanted Joshua captured, they would worm their way into the police search for the missing teenager. The New Hartford department had used volunteers to comb the fields around the barn for additional victims. The Wickers probably inserted themselves into the pool of concerned citizens and took control from there. Only one in a million humans was immune to their powers. The sheer number of law agencies involved was the limiting factor; even the most powerful witch could only control a handful of people at the same time.

Elise could guess who was a witch; she needed to be in the same room with the Wicker to be sure. The problem was that any witch could recognize Elise instantly as a Grigori. Any humans in the room with them would become an instant tool for the Wicker. The trick was to catch the witch alone.

Elise considered her options. All the local law enforcement agencies would be keeping tabs on the case. None, though, would be eager to share information with her. Law enforcers tended to be control freaks. The irony being that her family predated everything in the United States. The FBI. The CIA. The Boston City Police were started in 1838, nearly two hundred years after the werewolves and the Grigori arrived to protect the city. Since her family operated internationally, she had official Interpol credentials. The badge raised a few eyebrows in large United States cities and suspicion in small ones.

She eyed her phone. It looked as if her best bet would be the U.S. Marshals.

The U.S. marshal, Thomas Stewart, was wearing blue jeans and honest-to-God black cowboy boots. His jeans hid all but the unmistakable toe and heel. His navy blue polo shirt had the star within circle symbol of the marshals. Otherwise he looked like any other law enforcement officer with open carry pistol, badge, and handcuffs attached to a thick leather belt.

She had caught him in the parking lot, just getting out of his car. He held a large Dunkin' Donuts coffee and looked like he desperately needed it. He stared at her face, ignoring her badge. There was grey in his mustache and goatee and his hairline was receding. She guessed that he was old enough to be her father. It was always creepy when they were old.

Elise moved her badge to in front of his eyes. "Interpol," she repeated.

Stewart blinked several times before refocusing his attention to the billfold with the gold badge and picture ID. "Huh? Interpol? Wh-wh-what?"

She waited impatiently for blood to return to the big head.

A moment later, Stewart managed to ask, "What brings Interpol to Utica?"

"I'm chasing a cult." As far as modern police were concerned, witches were part of fairy tales. Cultists, though, police believed in. "There's six dead in the Boston area. We think it's linked to your murder of Joseph Buckley."

The "we" was because cops liked dealing with organizations, not individuals. There were only a handful of Virtues on the East Coast and even fewer Powers. To outsiders, her family seemed like nothing but loose cannons. She focused on Buckley's murder because it would be difficult to explain what happened at the barn in terms of "cult activity."

"Why are you here talking to me instead of..." Stewart glanced at her face and lost the thread.

She blocked his view with her phone playing the video of Joshua's parents making a passionate plea for anyone knowing his whereabouts to contact a tip line. "We believe the cultists are still in the area attempting to locate the sole survivor of the animal attack. The speed at which the parents called a press conference suggests that they're being manipulated by the cult without their knowledge. These cultists are very good at moving into an area, working their way quietly into people's trust and then using it against them."

"That still doesn't explain why you're talking to me." He tried to look around the phone.

She shifted it to keep the phone blocking his view. "Can you identify all the people in this video?"

"That's the parents of our missing boy. Sandy and Walter. They're good people. They own a garage here in town." Stewart knew the family personally then.

"Not Joshua's parents," Elise said. "The people in the background, especially anyone who looks as if they're trying to stay out of camera range."

He studied the screen, nodding. Something she was saying was clicking with something he'd already noticed. "You think that these cultists inserted themselves into the investigation?"

"Yes. These cultists are very good at tricking groups of people into thinking they're trustworthy. Basically X will trust the cultist because of Y; Y will trust them because of X. Their belief loops without any external proof that their trust is well founded. Once the cultists are firmly entrenched, they're assumed to be a trusted member, even in a close-knit community."

At that point, it became difficult to determine who was a puppet and who was simply deluded by pretenses.

He cursed. "Everything went batshit crazy on Friday. There haven't been wolves in this area for nearly a hundred years and then we have two attacks in one day. I was thinking it had to be something like Satanists or something after they found Joe Buckley yesterday. Tied up like that with herbs stuffed in his mouth and his lips sewn shut with thick black thread. Coroner says he was still alive while they were cutting out his heart."

He'd seen Buckley's body, either in person or via forensic photographs.

"You're involved in the case?" Elise asked.

Stewart blushed slightly and studied the tips of his boots. "I—I stuck my nose in when Joshua went missing yesterday. I got all my nieces and nephews into judo. He and his older sister are part of our dojo. They're good kids. Well, she's a firecracker. He's dorky as all hell but he's got grit in spades. Buckles down, does the work, pitches in to help without being asked, avoids fights even when he could clean the floor with the other kid, always where he's supposed to be when he's supposed to be there, or he makes sure people know why he isn't. A really good kid. And he's gone. Just gone. New Hartford police are saying he ran away from home; that's not the kid I know. Something's happened to him. I want to find him before he ends up like Joe Buckley. This cult thing worming their way into a group—that makes sense because the New Hartford PD suddenly can't find its ass with both hands. They 'lost' all the clothes from the crime scene yesterday. They're saying that the clothes might have gotten accidently mixed into the trash and ended up in the incinerator. What kind of idiot does that?"

The clothes hadn't been lost; they'd been used in making the huntsman. The lie was merely to cover that they had been taken. The Wickers definitely had someone on the inside of the New Hartford Police Department. Elise was glad that she hadn't gone straight to them.

"Who do you know at this press conference?" Elise asked.

He tapped on the screen to pause the video. "Like I said, Sandy and Walt. That's their daughter, Bethy."

All three were tall, willowy platinum blondes. Between their butchered last name and fair coloring, she guessed that the family had originally been either Scandinavian or Slavic. Elise couldn't see any family resemblance to Joshua. He seemed too short and mousey to be genetically related.

Stewart continued to name people clustered around Joshua's parents.

"Rob Harpur, he's the guidance counselor at the high school. He and Walt went to school together. Joshua has been working his butt off to get a scholarship to college. William Cosby is our representative; he's up for re-election. That's Dahlia Wakefield..."

"Wakefield, as in Reed Wakefield? The man mauled in his house?"

Stewart nodded. "His wife."

Dahlia was the epitome of a Wicker. She wore a red fox jacket, diamond studded fingernails, and Coach handbag. Wickers had a need to be recognized as powerful and important.

Covens liked to work in groups of three to thirteen people. The members weren't necessarily related. A group of unrelated people moving into an area would raise flags. The coven would use one family name to draw less attention.

"What can you tell me about Dahlia Wakefield and her family?"

Stewart shrugged. "The first eight hours or so, everyone ran in circles, screaming and shouting. None of the kids had any ID on them. They'd changed into costumes for the haunted house. All of their wallets and purses were locked in one of the cars. The kids were so torn apart we weren't sure how many there had been. We spent hours scouring the fields around the barn, making sure a kid hadn't run off wounded and was lying unconscious in the undergrowth."

He must have been part of the search teams since he used "we" in the tone that meant he'd been stomping through the fields personally. "Half the kids in the county were out at one haunted house or another. When the news got out about the attack, every parent who couldn't get hold of their kid showed up at the hospital, freaked out of their mind. It was a circus; only this time the lion act had gotten out and eaten part of the audience. It was well past midnight before anyone got out to the Wakefield house to break the news about their daughter, Daphne. The officer found the front door broken down and Reed Wakefield torn apart in the foyer."

"Had they been living there long?"

"No. They'd just moved in a few days before Halloween. Everything about them seems a bit off but there hasn't been time to find anything out. It's been thirty-six hours since the 911 call about the barn was made and twenty hours since Joshua disappeared and his neighbor was found dead. Three different crime scenes and twelve people dead and one boy missing. There was no sign of a struggle and Joshua wouldn't go without a fight. He might have just wandered off. The first few hours at the hospital, he had no idea what his name was or where he lived. But I think he remembered something from the attack and—and—"

He scrubbed at his hair, looking close to exhaustion. "I don't know. I've been racking my brains trying to figure it out. I've even went back to the barn a couple of times, thinking he might have gone there. Some of the older kids are keeping a vigil at the dojo, although that's a real long shot. It's ten miles from his house to downtown Utica and when he was released from the hospital yesterday, he barely remembered where he lived."

The Wickers had to be walking on eggshells. They had a newborn werewolf roaming loose; one trained to fight. They couldn't be sure what the dead werewolf had told Joshua before he was killed. Their only hope was to take Joshua unaware and cage him before he could react. And they had to act before his pack arrived in force.

Which should have been Friday night. Maybe they were already here.

"Did anyone run the license plate of the mystery BMW?" Elise asked.

Stewart snorted with disgust. "I did after those idiots at New Hartford PD ran in circles all day yesterday. It's leased by a company in New York City. King Properties. It sounds like a real estate firm. I managed to get through to someone this morning. They said that it must have been stolen. Their records show it's supposed to be in a garage on . . ." He paused to consult his note. "Central Park West."

Elise pressed her mouth tight on a curse. She was glad that he was still looking down; she couldn't keep the dismay off her face. The company existed solely to manage the Wolf King's extensive motor pool and far-flung properties. It meant that the dead werewolf was definitely a Thane carrying out the king's orders.

What did the Wickers do to piss off the Wolf King? Before they killed his Thane? What pulled both the Wickers and the Thane to a barn in the middle of nowhere? Was the Thane there for the Wicker, or was the Wicker there for something the Thane was after? Joshua? How random was it that he was the only one to survive? The boy seemed to think he simply got lucky but this was a Thane, not some random pack wolf. Thane killed anything they set out to kill, as the Wickers found out.

"We're still trying to find the men that were in the car," Stewart said. "There's been no sign of them."

"Them?" Elise seized on the most important word in his statement.

"Rob Harpur says that there were two men at the high school Friday afternoon. Big guys in business suits. They felt like mafia to Rob. They came in the BMW and walked around the halls, obviously looking for someone. Rob spotted them at Joshua's locker and tried to get them to leave. He went to call the police. The idiot drama teacher chased them out of the costume room and told them where the kids were."

The two "men" both had to be werewolves because wolves rarely associated with anyone outside their pack. They were probably both Thanes as most wolves didn't bother to dress up. Alexander liked formal wear for his heralds/enforcers. It was as close to a military uniform the wolves could get and remain hidden in plain sight.

Two Thanes and only one was accounted for? What happened to the second one? It put a different light on the two separate attacks.

"Are they sure that Reed was killed by the same wolf?" Elise asked.

"Actually, no." Stewart glanced at his watch. "I'm surprised that it didn't make the news. For some reason, New Hartford thinks there's a second wolf. They're passing around special ammo and doing a blanket search, starting at Wakefield's house in about an hour."

"Special ammo?" Hollow points would only mean pissed off werewolves and dead law officers.

Stewart took a pistol magazine out of one of the leather pouches on his belt. "I don't get this 'special ammo.' Looks like crap to me. I'm sure the hell not going to use it. Nothing about this case makes a whole lot of sense."

The magazine was loaded with silver bullets. The police would stand a chance if they actually used the ammunition. But if they were like Stewart, they'd use their own trusted ammo. At that point, it became Russian roulette for the werewolves. There was no way to get this many silver bullets in thirty hours. The Wickers expected a war with the werewolves and came prepared.

"Wait. The Wakefield house?" Dead Wicker. Silver bullets. Wolf hunt. The witches must have had some kind of magical construct that wounded the Thane. There would be no other reason for the wolf to still be in the area. "Was there a lot of foliage inside the house? Branches and leaves and vines?"

"A shitload of it."

A newborn and a wounded Thane running around loose, both immune to the witches' powers. No wonder the Wickers were working slowly and cautiously. One misstep and they'd be missing limbs.

And lucky her had to find the wounded werewolf before the police department—or the town was going to be mourning a lot of dead cops on top of dead teenagers.

8: JOSHUA

Winnie had a purple Vespa that matched her hair. It had little violets painted all over it as if someone had sprinkled it with flowers. Joshua had grown up with dirt bikes; to him two wheels and a motor was the essence of masculinity. (His sister rode dirt bikes but she loathed pink and would kick anyone's ass for calling her a "girl." His mom kept to four-wheeled ATVs. His parents' motto seemed to be "a family that gets muddy together, stays together.") There seemed something intrinsically wrong for a scooter to be so girly-girl. He supposed it could be worse; it could be a pink motorcycle.

"Her name is Violet." Winnie buckled on a black helmet with Hello Kitty eyes and whiskers bracketing the visor. She added in a whisper, "She's very temperamental."

"It's leaking oil," he pointed out. "It needs a new gasket and probably new spark plugs."

Considering how much money they'd just won, she could just get a new Vespa. A fleet of them.

"You have a scooter?" Winnie's black leather motorcycle jacket had a Hello Kitty stitched into its shoulder. Just so wrong.

"Dirt bikes. Mostly Yamahas and Kawasakis. Nothing Italian like your Vespa, but they're single cylinder, four-stroke engines." As she continued to stare at him, he added, "My parents are both mechanics. They have their own shop and tow truck. I grew up helping out when I wasn't at school or at the dojo. I could take a dirt bike apart and put it back together before I could do algebra."

87

His parents would rather show him how to take apart engines and put them back together than help him with his math homework, but that was a different story. Helping out at his parents' garage (better known as "free slave labor") was another reason he wanted to go to college. Customers had this weird idea that his folks shouldn't charge so much for labor, ignoring the fact that his parents needed to pay for the loans on the garage and all their tools, insurance, electricity and an endless list of other incidentals. His parents should have been doing better money-wise but people were constantly bartering with them and bouncing checks. His mom and dad were too nice for their own good. He knew they would love for him to take over the garage but he didn't want to be fighting every day for a decent income.

Could he win a decent living by being a werewolf? What a weird and unexpected benefit. He wasn't sure that what had just happened was repeatable. If it was, it implied an even stranger future than he'd thought.

"So, she just needs a new gasket?" Winnie knelt down to eye the fresh drips of oil under the scooter. "And here I thought she might be possessed. My cousin had a car that was possessed. It constantly tried to kill him but it never needed gasoline."

She swung her leg over the seat and hitched forward to make room for him. "Come on. We've got to scoot!"

"Where are we going?" He wasn't sure that if it was totally wise to run off with a stranger—and Winnie definitely qualified as strange. She did, however, have ten million dollars in her pocket that theoretically belonged to them both. And he didn't even know her last name.

"We're going to my granny's," Winnie said. "We need to do a jam session to find out what's going on with Jack."

Harrowing was not a word that Joshua had ever considered using before.

No other word, however, came close to describing Winnie's driving.

The only warning he got was when she canted her head to look up at Fred and said, "Fastest route to Granny's, avoiding pigs."

He was about to ask "what pigs?" when Fred flitted away and Winnie took off after the spirit guide at full throttle.

They cut between buildings via passageways barely wide

enough for her handlebars. They flashed through intersections against the light. Winnie drove on sidewalks, through parks, and over a pedestrian bridge that crossed the Charles River. Oddly there were no pedestrians in their way, no matter how erratic a path they took. Unfortunately the same couldn't be said of cross traffic. Boston drivers used their horns and curse words that Joshua had never heard shouted before but never their brakes.

After taking several one-way streets in the wrong direction, they cut into a vast parking lot for some kind of warehouse with dozens of tractor-trailer trucks that blared horns at them. Fred led the way through a narrow a hole in a fence, across a pedestrian crosswalk, through a gate that Joshua was sure should have been padlocked shut, and down into an abandoned unlit tunnel.

By then it was fairly obvious that when Winnie said "pigs" she meant the police.

Joshua's grandmother lived in a big Victorian in Saratoga Springs. Her hair was titanium blond via monthly visits to a beauty parlor and always hair sprayed into a perfect hairdo. She favored turtleneck cashmere sweaters and wool skirts and low-heeled dress shoes.

The fact that they parked in front of a tattoo parlor warned him that Winnie's grandmother was not like his. There was a porcupine drawn in tribal style on the window and the name of the shop wrapped around it: Sioux Zee's Quill Pig Tattoo. Heavy metal music thundered somewhere close by. As they neared the shop, the noise grew louder and he realized that it was coming from within the building.

Winnie opened the door and the music hit them like a wall of sound.

Joshua followed, feeling bewildered and lost. Why was he here? Winnie had swept him up and carried him away like a leaf in a storm wind. Decker had said that as a monster, random chance no longer applied to Joshua. That he'd pulled the winning lottery ticket out of thin air seemed to prove it. It did seem to indicate that fate had taken him to the one person in Boston who knew all about werewolves. Destiny also gave him ten million reasons why he should stay.

Fate and destiny were the words his AP English teacher used

to describe the setup in *Macbeth*, and that turned out badly for Macbeth.

The tattoo studio's door opened to a large long room with high ceilings. The floor was polished dark oak. The walls were exposed red brick. There were five black leather adjustable chairs set up as tattoo stations with black enameled tool cabinets. On the walls were animals drawn in the same tribal-style as the shop's logo, obviously tattoos, but framed like paintings. In the very back was a metal spiral staircase that led up to the second floor. A sign warned off customers with: Quill Pigs Only, Others will be Neutered.

The artist nearest the door was a girl slightly older than Joshua. She wore her long black hair swept up into a bun that was pinned into place with hummingbird-tipped hairpins. Her halter-top and low rider jeans showed off her full-body tattoo of green and ruby feathers. She glanced toward the door and then focused back on her client, an extremely muscular, metrosexual man. "Ooooh! I should have known!" Hummingbird girl carefully peeled a stencil paper from the man's upper body, revealing the interlocking jagged black lines of a tribal tattoo that wrapped his left shoulder. "Sioux Zee is on the warpath. She just kicked on the metal a few minutes ago."

"Shoot!" Winnie glanced toward the ceiling speaker as if noticing the music for the first time.

"Shape shift nose to the wind," the voice of the male singer growled over heavy bass through vibrating speakers. "Shape shift feeling I've been. Move swift all senses clean. Earth gift. Back to the meaning of wolf and man."

Coincidence or did Winnie's grandmother know that Joshua was coming?

"Oh man!" Winnie cried. "Metallica?"

"Busted!" A male artist at the next station called out without lifting his head. His female client was lying face down in the chair as he inked a tribal crow with wings spread across the woman's shoulder blades.

"What did you do to piss her off?" The hummingbird girl laughed and held up a large hand mirror to her customer. "Do you like it? Is it a go?"

"She probably quit her job again," the male artist guessed accurately. "It was too boring."

"Mark!" Winnie stomped her foot. "It's not my fault! I'm meant to do one thing and I do it well. I just suck at everything else."

"What do you do?" the male customer asked as he examined the stencil marked on his shoulder.

There was a moment of stunned silence in the room as everyone stared at him. Then Mark started to giggle.

Winnie put her hands on her hips. "I'm a broadband communication specialist."

"What's that?" the client asked.

The hummingbird girl tapped the mirror, calling the client's attention back to the stencil on his arm. "Is it a go on your tattoo?"

"Yes, it's awesome!" the client said.

The hummingbird girl picked up a needle gun. "Great! Let's get started."

Winnie caught Joshua and pulled him through the long room to the spiral metal staircase.

The second floor of the studio was Sioux Zee's private sanctuary. It was the same basic design of polished dark oak floors and exposed brick walls. A lone tattoo station of adjustable chair and black enameled toolboxes sat next to the stairs. That area was stark and clean. The rest of the room was a wonderland of odd and unusual items that fought for Joshua's attention.

Most riveting were the skulls of fierce animals that Joshua couldn't identify. They were the size and shape of small dogs and large cats but with multiple rows of saw-blade teeth like sharks. Two had horns like sheep. One had what looked like a third eye-hole.

The second most riveting thing was the array of a dozen antique rifles and shotguns mounted on the wall. They had beautifully engraved stocks and well-oiled barrels. They put his father's small collection of hunting guns to shame. As he studied them longer, he realized that the engravings were weird and mystical-looking and set his neck hair on end.

The third most riveting thing was a large old fashioned safe standing open. There was no cash inside, but a dozen thick, leather-bound books and a collection of crocks wired shut and covered with odd runes. The jars were even more unsettling than the guns, although he couldn't tell why.

The fourth most riveting thing was Winnie's grandmother.

Sioux Zee was a tall leggy woman with long stark white hair down to her knees, a choker of turquoise, silver and bone, a two-tone leather vest, skinny blue jeans and knee-high buckskin boots. She was leaning over a big, ugly, dangerous-looking man. Her tattoo gun buzzed as she carefully inked in an odd complicated set of runes on his right shoulder.

"Granny! Granny!" Winnie cried. "You're never going to guess—oh—well—you probably could guess—although this might surprise even you. Maybe."

"You quit your job," Sioux Zee stated coldly without looking up.

"T-t-that's the start of my news..." Winnie whined. "It gets better. Well—better then worse and then maybe totally horrible."

Her grandmother glanced hard at Winnie and then looked beyond her granddaughter to see Joshua for the first time. She jerked back with a gasp.

Which alerted the big, ugly, dangerous-looking man that something was wrong. He lurched off the table with a growl. "What's wrong, Sioux Zee?" He caught sight of Joshua. "Can't you read, shrimp? This is off-limits, you little..."

"Brutus!" Sioux Zee smacked the man hard on his bleeding shoulder where she'd just been working. "Look before you swing! Use that thick skull of yours for something other than breaking open walnuts."

Brutus squinted at Joshua and then his eyes widened. "Shit!" He took three giant steps backward. "Where did you find a wolf?"

Was "werewolf" printed on Joshua's forehead? He scrubbed at his brow.

"The supermarket," Winnie said. "Deli aisle, next to the cold cuts. He was lost."

"I'm was not lost! I was shopping!" Joshua held up his plastic shopping bags as proof. The last word came out more of a growl than he intended. Everyone took two steps back from him.

"I'm going now." Brutus edged around Joshua, keeping Winnie between them. "We can finish up my protection runes some other time."

Sioux Zee huffed as Brutus escaped. She followed him, calling, "I need to clean that and bandage you first! Brutus! Don't make me hit you again!"

"Sit! Sit!" Winnie pointed at a poker table in the far end of the room.

"Okay." The table was edged with leather. Eight brass cup holders were embedded into the surface between hardwood grooves to hold poker chips. "This is hard core."

"Granny loves poker. Don't ever play with her. She's a shark."

He'd been "outvoted" (read that as: tricked) into playing a card game with his cousins last Thanksgiving called Craits. (He thought they'd made up the game but later found the rules online.) He'd been hopelessly confused the entire afternoon. Tens reversed the order from clockwise to counterclockwise or back again. Eights were wild. Fives forced everyone else to draw a card. On and on and on. He suspected at the time, and later confirmed, if he'd been shown the rules first, he could have kept up. The gameplay wasn't as complex as chess; it was just that his cousins never explained any of the rules. The sheer number of special cards and speed of play made it impossible to keep the rules straight.

There was a thick leather-bound book open on the table. It smelt old. The pages were handmade linen paper. The handwritten words were in an elegant lettering that was either Arabic or Cyrillic or some other alphabet that Joshua didn't know. The large, carefully drawn, and footnoted rune matched the one that Sioux Zee had been inking onto Brutus' shoulder.

Joshua realized that light shimmered over the table, like a heat mirage off a hot parking lot. He couldn't tell what was causing the illusion; the area was cooler than the rest of the room. Gazing at the book while the empty eyes of the strange skulls watched him, Joshua felt like he was deep in the middle of a card game whose rules everyone else knew.

"What's this?" Joshua pointed at the book.

"That's Dorothy." Winnie carefully closed it and patted its gilded cover. "Everyone thinks that the universe is one big dollhouse; that we're nothing but Barbie dolls. Some of us get put in fancy outfits and set on the shelf and admired by all. Some end up naked with their hair hacked to pieces, covered with mud, but well-loved. Others are accidently tossed on the fire Christmas morning and end up one unhappy lump of wax. People act like we're taken out of a box, moved around only by forces we can't control, and end up back in the box. But that's not how the world works. That's not what we are. The universe is more like a box of tissues."

"Crank!" Ian slapped down a Two card. Wayne threw down an ace. "Two crank!" Julian quickly slapped down another Two. "Three cranks!" Joshua frowned at the cards on the table, trying to figure out what he was supposed to do. Throw down a Three? His cousins started to laugh—again—at the fact that he had no clue what was going on.

Joshua took a deep breath. "What do you mean by box of tissues?"

"It's layer upon layer upon layer of realities. And we exist as some weirdness that we can't explain yet. We don't have the words. We're atoms, or electrons or quarks or something. We're part of the tissues but we're not. Heaven and hell, they're just one quantum state away, two or three tissues up or down, and we merely have to change particle state to move to that existence—to that tissue. Most people around us are only aware of the tissue, but a handful like Brutus and I can see a layer over. You've been changed to a higher state or something so that you live on two worlds at the same time. Earth and whatever universe your wolf exists in when it's not here. Dorothy and Fred, they're from another world too, but they're also at a higher state than us, and can move around in our world too. And all those dead people that haven't moved on to heaven or hell? They're partially in our world or they're in Dorothy's and Fred's world or they're in some gray space between them."

"Okay," he said slowly, trying to wrap his mind around it. "Dorothy is a spirit guide like Fred?"

"Yup." Winnie carried the book to the safe. "She was my father's spirit guide. He copied these runes from a book that had been damaged when someone tried to steal it back before the Revolutionary War. Even though it was too damaged to read, it had been passed down through my family for safekeeping. My father teamed up with a friend that went to M.I.T. to use some kind of scanner to recover the information. Dorothy guards over it now that he's passed on."

Winnie carefully tucked the book between the other leather-bound tomes inside the safe. "Brutus is open enough to see what most people can't, which makes him valuable as an employee for certain businesses, but it also makes him vulnerable. The runes close him off to anything that could take him over."

"Couldn't you use these runes instead of drugs?"

"I don't want to close down for good. I just need a little time. A few months, then all will be golden again when the prince returns."

"Who's the prince?"

"Seth Tatterskein."

"Where is he and why has he been gone for so long? Doesn't he know that you need him?"

"He knows. It's just that he was only thirteen when his family was massacred and he inherited his father's power."

"Oh, wow." Joshua had been feeling sorry for himself because he had needed to leave his family. At least he had someone to go back to once the dust settled.

Winnie nodded. "Yeah, really, right? Seth needs to grow up before he can take on full responsibility for Boston. He's sixteen now. His birthday is around Christmas. The expectation is that he'll move back when he turns eighteen. Maybe. If the Wolf King lets him. But it's not like Boston has totally gone to hell; Seth is holding back the worst of it just by existing. I can feel him sometimes, late at night, checking to see if I'm still me and not something else. Something dangerous."

"That sounds—creepy."

"It's like when Granny comes in and checks under my bed when I'm sleeping. It was annoying until the night she found a growling hiding under it and shot it." Winnie pointed at one of the skulls with saw-blade teeth. "That one there."

"Holy shit! That was under your bed?"

"Yeah, during a new moon last fall. Most dangerous time in Boston is after the fall solstice as the year dies. I'm like an open door to things like that. So, no, the prince checking on me isn't creepy. I know that if things go horribly bad, it won't be just Granny trying to deal with the mess."

Sioux Zee came back up the steps, her boots ringing on the metal treads of the spiral staircase. "I swear, I boasted out loud, when I was either too young or too drunk to remember, that I couldn't be surprised. Something heard me and took it as a challenge. I suspect it was while I was drunk, because your father was like a rock. He was so predictable I always knew what he was going to do next, even get himself killed. Like a rock, you couldn't stop him once he got moving. You," Sioux Zee wagged her finger at Winnie. "I never know what impossible mess you're going to fall into next."

"Granny!" Winnie whined. "I didn't do anything except go to work!"

Sioux Zee sighed. "And that's the truly frightening part."

"I got paid." Winnie patted her various pockets until she found the lottery ticket and held it up as evidence. "Well, sort of. It's two birds with one stone kind of deal. It's a day's wage—and then some—and proof that I was fated to meet…meet…meet…" Winnie turned to Joshua. "You know, you never told me your name."

"His name is Joshua." Sioux Zee huffed and took the ticket to examine it closely. "If you bothered to watch the news, you'd know that. He disappeared from his home in Central New York yesterday after a wolf tore apart half the boys of his graduating class. There's an Amber Alert out for him. His parents were on the evening news begging for information on him."

"They were?" Joshua cried. "I left a note on the refrigerator." Not that it actually said where he was going. He claimed he was going to see an online friend and they shouldn't worry about him. He figured if he mentioned Jack's instructions to find the Prince of Boston, he'd only convince his parents that he was mentally unstable. (Personally Joshua thought he was a little crazy for picking Boston as a destination but Jack's command was the only thing he could think of while trying to decide where to go.) "I—I—I don't know what the hell is going on. Why is this happening to me? I had a normal boring life until yesterday. There has never been a real monster under my bed or anyone else's bed. No real vampires or ghosts or those things—whatever those are." He pointed at one of the skulls with horns. "Why didn't I ever hear about them before? Why is this happening to me?"

"The odds of encountering real magic or real monsters are the same as winning the top prize in the lottery." Sioux Zee waved the lottery ticket at him.

"Those odds are millions to one!" Joshua protested. "Since yesterday, I can't swing a cat and not hit something supernatural."

"You're no longer human. Normal odds don't apply to you; that's how you ended up with this ticket." Sioux Zee put the ticket in the massive safe. "And you're still a minor." She closed the safe and spun the lock. "You can't collect the winnings until you're eighteen."

"But-but-but-" Winnie started. "I can collect it. Or you can, Granny. And then we can share it."

"It's ten million dollars," Sioux Zee said. "The state officials are going to rake anyone who tries to collect it over the coals. The first thing they'll do is ask you where you bought the ticket. If you turn it in tomorrow, they'll pull the security tapes at the supermarket. And who actually pushed the button? A minor with an Amber Alert out on him; the sole survivor of a massacre who vanished without a trace. There's no way that's going to stay quiet. I'm guessing that he's got a world of trouble chasing after him. Winnie, child, you've fallen into a big pit of trouble, no need to pull a basket of rattlesnakes in with you."

"Oh pooh." Winnie deflated.

"I do have trouble chasing me," Joshua admitted reluctantly. "Or at least, I did. I'm hoping I lost it."

"Certain troubles you need to kill to stop," Sioux Zee said.

"Kind of did." Joshua explained meeting Decker and Elise and the fight with the huntsman.

Sioux Zee huffed at the news. "The heavy hitters are all in the game."

"Joshua came to me!" Winnie cried. "And it was Jack that sent him! I have a connection to Jack."

"In your mind." Sioux Zee moved to clean up her tattoo equipment. "Jack told Joshua to go to Seth, not you."

"This is fated!" Winnie cried. "You're refusing to admit it because you don't want to get me involved but I'm already involved. And I'll stay involved as long as I want. Jack was good to me and if something happened to a Thane, then we should know what's going on before everything blows up in our faces."

Sioux Zee crashed equipment together loudly for a minute before finally growling out, "Fine. We'll do a session. Minimum time, though. You need to keep tightly shuttered if there's heavy hitters stirring things up."

Winnie squealed and clapped her hands. "Fred! Fishing time!"

Fred washed over Joshua, an intense wave of cold and dark and the smell of fresh dirt.

"What the heck?" Joshua leaped back, growling. Fred had vanished. Maybe. Being that the spirit guide had been just a smell and a lack of light, Joshua had to peer about the room to be sure. "What do you mean: fishing? Why did he do that?"

"It's all just a crap shoot." Winnie motioned for him to help her lift the wood cover to the gaming table into place. "Tons of people die but only a few of them stick around to talk. Some because they have unfinished business. Others? No idea why they stay. Marie Antoinette? I have a theory that she thinks God's idea of fashion is scruffy men in loose robes and she wants none of that. She likes men in tight breeches."

Sioux Zee lowered thick blinds and then drew heavy curtains. The fabric completely blocked out the sunshine. "Basically Fred goes out and finds someone whose psyche responds to yours."

"To me?" The photographs that the police had shown Joshua at the hospital flashed through his mind. "Oh, I don't think this is a good idea. Those kids didn't like me in the first place. They're probably are really pissed off at me now that they're dead."

Winnie waved off Joshua's objections. "It's unlikely Fred could get any freshly dead to travel this far."

"I have had a really boring life up to now," Joshua said. "The only other dead people that I would know are my mom's parents, and they died when I was really little. I think the only thing they could tell you about me is my potty training."

Winnie lit a candle in the center of the table. "The dead have secrets that they're longing to tell."

Sioux Zee turned off the overhead lights. With a flare of a match in the dim room, she lit incense that smoldered next to the lone candle. "Given a chance to talk, the dead rarely say anything trivial."

Winnie took out her phone and started a music app playing a recording of ocean waves. The sound of restless water filled the room, waves crashing on some invisible shore and rushing back into the unseen sea. With the darkness closing in and the ocean waves filling the space, Joshua felt more disconnected from the real world than ever.

"Do we have to do this?" Joshua asked. "The lights and candles and everything?"

"Yes," Sioux Zee stated firmly.

"There's power in light," Winnie explained. "Life is drawn to it. Death flees it. A recently deceased spirit won't enter the light."

"And the incense?" Joshua wrinkled his nose against the scent. Normally he liked the smell but there was something different about this. It seemed as if he could smell darkness. Not the black of night but something darker and enclosed, like a cave.

"Certain scents lure spirits closer." Sioux Zee pulled the weight on what looked like miniature grandfather clock. There was a bronze bell at the top engraved with runes. The pendulum started to swing, ticking loudly. With each swing, the miniature hands of the small clock moved toward twelve. "Unfortunately it attracts everything. There's a window of opportunity, and after that, it gets too dangerous. The timer will shut everything down. It's a failsafe, one that human negligence and curiosity can't override."

"And the recording of the ocean?" Joshua whispered as the women settled into silence.

"It's Winnie's focus," Sioux Zee whispered. "She needs to concentrate to open up enough to let a spirit talk through her. Even housed in Winnie, the spirit probably won't be able to hear you. I'll ask it questions. Now, quiet, so Winnie can focus."

Joshua didn't want to believe in ghosts but the séance was about to happen whether he believed in them or not. The spirits were as real as everything else that had happened to him in the last thirty-some hours.

With a rush of wind that sent the candle flickering Fred returned. The room grew colder and somehow more still.

Winnie took a deep breath, bowing her head slightly so her hair fell across her face. Another deep breath, she relaxed more, and then she jerked rigid. Her breath quickened and she peered upward through the screen of purple hair.

She locked gaze with Joshua. "Shit. Gandhi was right. Karma bites you in the ass in the end." It was Winnie's voice but pitched deeper with a faint Southern accent. Her gaze slid to Sioux Zee and her eyes narrowed. "Do you have a cigarette? I would kill for a smoke."

"What's your name?"

The ghost snorted. "Shit by any other name still stinks. It doesn't matter what my name was. I just needed a computer, a printer, and a lamination machine, and voila, I could be anyone."

"The name you were born with if you want a cigarette."

The ghost laughed bitterly. "It was a stupid name. My mom was a new age hippie into peace, love, tie dye, crystal healing, reincarnation and spiritual beings. She named me Wonder Woman Alvarado. Try going through middle school tagged with that. I might have had a chance if my father hadn't been picked up for identity theft the day before I was born. He wanted to call me Jazmin after his mother. He would get out of jail and tell me that my name was Jazmin. He would get picked up again for running some con or other, and my mother would force me to answer to Wonder Woman. I tried to go by Diana Prince once and that pissed them both off. You can call me Jazmin."

Sioux Zee leaned back, opened the black metal toolbox behind her and took out an unopened pack of cigarettes, matches, and an ashtray.

Jazmin snorted at Winnie's purple fingernails. "I always said I wouldn't be caught dead in nail polish. You want the mark's eyes on your face. Not on your hands." She opened the pack and tapped out a cigarette, laughing silently, so it nearly seemed like she was sobbing. She flipped the cigarette that she'd taken out, and started to slide it back into the pack, filter first. When she realized what she was doing, she shook her head. "My mom always did that with her smokes. Her lucky cigarette. I thought she was crazy, always talking about crystals and negative energy and magic. I thought it was all bullshit until I met Linden."

She lit the match with practiced ease and leaned back to take a deep drag on the cigarette. "Linden. Linden. Linden. He was the real deal. He had powers that made my mother look like a girl scout with a Ouija board."

Another deep drag and she settled back to tell her story. "I was in Fort Lauderdale when I met him, running a fortune-telling scam on the snowbirds. With my parents, it was only natural that I ended up running cons like that. My mom gave me this bottomless pit of new age craziness to bullshit with and a touch of power to back it. 'Persuasion' was what Linden called it. My dad taught me how to read marks and steal credit information and get out before the law came crashing down on you. I had a pretty sweet setup running. Linden came sweeping into my place like a king. Gorgeous man. He reeked of money and power. I thought I'd hit the jackpot. I was shit out of luck and didn't know it. Do you have anything to drink in this shithole?"

Sioux Zee took out a bottle of Jack Daniels whiskey and a shot glass.

"Oh, my boy Jack! How I have missed you!" The ghost moved for the bottle.

Sioux Zee shifted the bottle out of Jazmin's reach. "Tell me about Linden."

The room went frosty cold. "Give me the bottle if you know what is good for you."

"I'm the real deal too," Sioux Zee said. "Just a different flavor. You mess with me, and you'll be in a cold dark place forever. Tell me what I want to know and you can have the shot. Tell me more and you can have another."

The ghost licked Winnie's lips and took a drag of the cigarette. "Linden Wakefield was a scary ass warlock. Not like that chick on *Bewitched.* No twitching the nose or chanting spells or anything. He'd just tell you to do something and you did."

"He was Wicker?" Joshua asked.

The ghost squinted at him and then looked to Sioux Zee. "I can see him but I can't hear him."

Sioux Zee poured a finger of whiskey. "Did Linden make things with wood and herbs and dead things?"

"God, yes." The ghost tossed down the drink and then shuddered at the burn of the whisky and bad memories. "We'd grab some wino off the street and go out into the woods and make these creepy-ass things." Jazmin pushed the glass toward Sioux Zee. "You can't get drunk enough to get it out of your mind. My mother was always going on and on about magic like it was a good thing full of light and happiness. Real magic is the stuff of nightmares."

She tapped the empty glass impatiently on the table. "More."

Sioux Zee lifted the bottle but didn't pour. "Tell me how you know this wolf."

The ghost frowned at the woman in a silence measured out by the ticking timing device. "Give me the bottle and I'll tell you the plan."

"A glass. Your information is years out of date."

"Oh no, it's not or he wouldn't be sitting here." The ghost pointed at Joshua. The hairs on the back of his neck rose. "It was a long-range plan. They planned big changes using him."

Sioux Zee poured a shot glass and pushed it toward Winnie. "I'll be the judge. Egomaniacs are always thinking that they're going to change the world. It's the ones that know their weaknesses who do."

Jazmin tossed down the shot and pushed the glass back. "Oh, Linden knew his weaknesses. That was what it was all about. Why he came to my place in Fort Lauderdale. See, Linden was like a god. A vengeful god. Someone flips him off? He'd have them walk in front of a bus. Someone cut him off in traffic? He would follow them to the next red light, get them to roll down the window, and calmly tell them to drive off a bridge. Only he was a god on a very short leash."

"What did Linden plan to do with the wolf?" Sioux Zee tapped the whiskey bottle on the table as if reminding the ghost of the possible reward. "Get to the point. Quickly."

Jazmin laughed bitterly. "What is time for me? I'm the one that got the short end of the stick in all this. See, it was just dumb luck that Linden even showed up at my place. I'd gotten in a fight with some meth head and he scratched my left cornea, so I needed to wear an eye patch for a while. Customers liked the flair that it gave me. *'A pirate fortune-teller! Oh! Ah!'* After my cornea healed, I wore the eye patch as a prop. I even got a freaking parrot. I figured that if I had to skip town, the eye patch would make it harder for the police to find me. The problem was that Linden was looking for a one-eyed fortune-teller."

"He walked into my place, sat down at my table, and put a gun in front of me. Told me to shoot myself. It was like he put a pack of cigarettes in front of me. I picked it up, put it in my mouth and pulled the trigger as naturally as lighting up. Click. Click. Click. I sat, crying my eyes out, but I couldn't stop pulling the trigger. Click. Click. I thought it was like Russian roulette, that there was only one bullet and sooner or later I'd hit it. There wasn't—it was empty. Linden laughed at me, took the pistol, loaded it up and handed it back. I couldn't even see because of the tears burning in my eyes but I could feel that the gun was heavier. I knew I was going to die."

"I started to blubber out promises. Money. Sex. Kill someone. Find anyone. At 'find anyone' Linden had me put the gun down and talk."

"Whom did he want you to find?" Sioux Zee growled.

Jazmin banged the shot glass on the table. "If you want to know, pay up."

Sioux Zee glanced at the timer. It had just two minutes left. She gritted her teeth and poured another finger of whiskey into the glass. "What was his plan? What does it have to do with this wolf here? Where is Linden now? Here in Boston?"

"Linden beat me to the afterlife by a day; torn to pieces by a pissed off papa werewolf. It freed me of his control, though, and I ran, for all the good it did me. His coven is still alive and kicking. They're an incestuous group of people just like him. His daughter wife Belladonna and their little hell spawn Garland and all the rest. Little petty gods. Able to make most people kill themselves with a word. They wanted to rule the world. They thought it was their birthright to be kings and queens. Instead they lived like cockroaches; scuttling for darkness every time the lights were turned on. See, the angels and the wolves—they're immune to witches. They'll kill a witch if they find it. At one time, the angels and wolves fought one another and witches could take advantage of the chaos. But for the last thousand years, there has been a treaty…"

"This is all ancient history!" Sioux Zee snapped.

"I'm getting to it." Jazmin tapped the shot glass again.

Sioux Zee ignored the demand. "Get to it now!"

"Linden heard about a real-deal fortune-teller, a woman with an eyepatch. That's what he was doing at my place. His coven was combing the country to find her. They needed her to pinpoint the right wolf. My little pirate shtick brought them down on me. What kept me alive was I knew all the tricks of hiding, so I also knew all the tricks of finding."

"You found her?" Sioux Zee snapped. "What did she tell him?"

Jazmin tapped the shot glass on the table, indicating that she wasn't going to talk any more without whiskey. "Come on, it's good. You want it. You know you want it."

Sioux Zee poured the whisky. "What did she tell him?"

"Very little that made him happy. He thought they were all set to go. They had a little wolf all picked out to grab; finding the fortune-teller was supposed to be a last-minute safety check while they were waiting for the right moment. If the shit hit the fan, it would take out everything within miles, so Linden decided to take the time to be careful. The bad news was that the puppy's bitch mother had been messing with the milkman. If the coven used the puppy, most of East Coast would go under in a major shitstorm. The good news was him." The ghost pointed at Joshua. "The stars aligned and all that shit with him. The problem being, they might also align for all his little brothers, if they were born. The apple never falls far from the tree. Linden was out of patience. He decided to do it the messy way."

Sioux Zee shot Joshua a sharp look. "Still ancient news."

The ghost laughed. "Do you know what the one-eyed fortune-teller said that was all so true? Half of knowing the future is knowing the 'why,' not the 'what' in past events. Sure you're sitting there, so confident you know what happened, but do you know why?"

The hands of the clock were nearly at twelve.

"What do they plan?" Sioux Zee cried. "How are they going to 'use' the wolf? What will they do next?"

"Next? They drown Boston in darkness and..."

The timer hit zero and it rang the bronze bell. Joshua felt the tone, like it had struck him in the chest and resonated all the way down to his toes.

Winnie collapsed backwards in her chair, breathing fast as if she'd just run a race. "Oh geez, why do I always get the foul-mouthed smokers?" She dug through her messenger bag to find a pack of gum.

Sioux Zee flicked on the overhead lights and blew out the candle. "Foul-mouthed smokers are the people that usually have unfinished business when they die."

"I don't understand," Joshua said. "What does this have to do with Jack Cabot? I thought we were trying to find out about him."

"Where were you when you talked to Jack?" Winnie asked.

"Inside an MRI machine at Saint Elizabeth's." Joshua blushed as he fumbled to explain. "I really wouldn't call it 'talk' so much as had a very odd—very odd but intense 'vision.' They were afraid I might have some brain damage so they were running all these tests. They put me in the MRI machine. It's very loud and surprisingly scary. I was trying to do deep mediation to stay calm. And then suddenly, he was there. Well, not *really* there. It was like one of those dreams where you think you're awake until really weird shit happens. I thought I felt a wolf lying on top of me, his head on my chest, pinning me down. I could feel his fur and he was really heavy. He said 'You are not safe here. Go to the Prince of Boston. Run!' I broke the MRI machine; I punched a hole in it. They were very upset with me."

He had already torn the bathroom door off its hinges, broken his bed and reduced both his IV drip thingy and the automatic blood pressure machine to small pieces in similar panic reactions. He didn't want to stay at the hospital after his vision of Jack. The hospital wasn't hard to convince that breaking protocol and releasing him early would be best for everyone.

"I didn't want to hurt anyone, so I left home. I could have gone to New York or Buffalo or stopped at Albany. Because of what Jack said in the vision, though, I came to Boston."

"Your vision sounds like a projection through the pack magic," Winnie said. "With the Boston pack reduced to two or three individuals, the ties between the wolves might be stronger than normal. Jack is a Thane and most likely Seth's heir."

Downstairs the front door chimed as a new customer came in.

Sioux Zee stood up. "My next appointment is here. It will be dark soon. If you're taking him home, you should go soon."

She started down the steps.

"Granny," Winnie called after her. "Do you think Jack might still be alive?"

Sioux Zee paused to give her a sad look. "I wouldn't get your hopes up. If Joshua's part of the Boston pack, then only Jack or Seth could have changed him. According to the news, the wolf that bit him is dead."

"Oh pooh." Winnie slid down in her chair to disappear under the table.

Joshua froze in place, unsure what to do. Girls were unknown to him except the ones that didn't like him; they always just wanted him to go away. Older women were his mom and sister; neither ever turned to him for comfort. He felt like he should *do* something. He leaned sideways to look under the table.

Winnie huddled underneath, rubbing tears from her eyes. "I always thought that I was so weird because, when push came to shove, I'd be able to do something that no one else could do. That I could help. I could matter. Now something horrible has happened to someone I know—someone who was always nice to me—and this is all I can do?"

Winnie sniffed loudly and guilt stabbed through Joshua.

This was his fault; he just wasn't sure how. There were people dead. Lots of them. He hated that they might have died because of him yet he didn't have a clue why. He'd always been a dorky little nobody at school. The most interesting thing about him was his judo but he hadn't been able to raise the money to compete at the national level. He wished he could remember what happened at the barn.

Witches had sent the huntsman after him. The ghost seemed to recognize him. Fred claimed that Jack had sent him to Boston. What was so special about him that all these weird things were after him? He wanted to know.

"You meditate on the ocean sound to contact the ghosts," Joshua said. "I was trying to meditate when Jack talked to me. Maybe I can meditate and channel his spirit."

He'd tried lots of quick meditations since he'd left the hospital, but nothing deep and focused. If this was a video game, though, the initial vision would have been an indication that certain keystrokes could recreate the ability. Up. Up. Down. Down. Left. Right. Left. Right. B. A. Ho! Ha ha! Guard! Turn! Parry! Dodge! Spin! Ha! Thrust! Channel werewolf ghosts. Achievement unlocked.

"Oh! Oh! That's a marvelous idea." Winnie crawled across the floor to his feet. "I'll ride shotgun since you've never done it before."

"Ooookay." He wasn't sure how she was going to do that.

She leaned up and took his hands. "I listen to the ocean because I imagine I'm a whale. I start out swimming just under the waves. The deep: dark below me. The surface: a shifting gleam above me. Take a deep breath."

Joshua closed his eyes and breathed deep. Usually it wasn't hard to meditate. He'd learned how when he started martial arts in second grade. When he closed his eyes, however, all the weirdness wanted to crowd in. Fred's fresh grave scent. The rustle of wind through invisible leaves as the spirit guide moved around them. How the dead leaves of the hounds had crunched under his fingers when he grabbed hold of them. The cries of seagulls outside the windows. The screams of his classmates at the barn.

He struggled to relax. *Breathe deep. Be calm. Find your center. Be in the now. Anything that happened before this moment, forget.*

Another dozen deep breaths and he settled into the calm that meditation usually brought.

"Now slide down into the darkness," Winnie whispered.

She gave him a slight tug and they seemed to fall downward, through the floor. He jerked and opened his eyes.

"It's okay." Winnie tightened her hold. Her hands were warm and soft.

He realized that he was growling softly. "It wasn't like that at the hospital. I didn't slide into the dark."

"Can you remember what you did at the hospital? You lead; I'll follow."

He closed his eyes again. His mother clung fiercely to his hand as she sat beside his hospital bed. Her hands were surprisingly small, like she'd shrunk sometime during the nightmarish night. Her palms had been dry from the harsh soap that she used to strip engine grease off every night.

She had to be worried sick about him. He knew that she would have fought to the death to protect him. Against werewolves and witches, though, all she could have done was die.

Breathe deeply. Be calm. Exist in the now.

It took longer for him to find his center the second time.

In the dark stillness, Joshua became aware that Winnie was breathing in time with him.

At the hospital they'd wheeled him away from his mother's anchoring presence into the stark cold room with the MRI machine. Once he was on the table, the technicians had moved out of sight, leaving him alone in the hospital gown that barely kept him decent. He suspected that since he was in the pediatrics unit, they'd given him a child-sized gown. It was purple with puppies romping on it. It was so short that he felt like he needed fig leaves to stay decent, especially when the female technician tucked pillows under his legs, canting up his knees.

He pushed that embarrassing memory away.

The MRI bed slid into the chamber. A moment later, a loud jackhammering noise started. He'd closed eyes tight and tried to flee inward. The way had been shadowed, but not completely dark. He felt like he was running through a thick forest. He didn't know yet what he was; the wood seemed safe and welcoming.

Could he find his way back to the forest?

He focused; trying to remember. It had been so simple at the hospital. Just close his eyes and there it was. Of course that was before the black wolf showed up to freak him out.

Once he concentrated on the quality of the darkness, he realized that he'd found his way back to the shadowed forest. Night seemed to press close. He could still feel Winnie's fingers laced with his. He could smell Fred hovering close. The two were with him in the woods.

Was Fred the reason it seemed so dark? Last time it seemed brighter, even though it had been late at night. He tightened his hold on Winnie's hand and cautiously moved forward. What was this place? Where was it? Somehow it felt familiar, but meditating had never taken him to someplace so real. Was it because Winnie was with him? No, he'd been here at the hospital but the sense of *déjà vu* ran deeper than that.

Something gleamed in the distance. For a moment he thought it was a searchlight cutting through the darkness. He realized it was a massive gleaming animal racing toward them.

"Not good!" Joshua cried trying to backup. "Not good at all. Run!"

The beast hit him like a hot wave. There was a flashing impression of fur and muscle and a rumbling growl as loud as thunder. Then heat poured over him, into him, until he was drowning in the warmth.

He flailed wildly, snapping open his eyes. He lay on the wood floor of Sioux Zee's tattoo studio. Winnie huddled in the corner furthest from him, eyes wide in the darkness. They seemed alone in the dim room but he could *feel* a massive foot pressing down on his chest, pinning him in place. The candle on the table flickered, throwing shadows on the far wall. And then the shadows moved independent of the flame. A massive head glanced at Winnie and then turned back to study him.

The ghost wolf standing on his chest—that was there but not there—filled the room, its back brushing the ceiling. Its panting blasted over him, warm and smelling of ancient forests. He could feel it staring angrily down at him.

"This isn't what was at the hospital!" Joshua whispered to Winnie. "Can you make it go away?"

Winnie squeaked.

"I'll take that as a no," he muttered. The great head leaned close and he had the distinct impression that it was smelling him. "What is it?"

She whimpered in fear.

The ghost wolf glanced again at Winnie. A growl rumbled like thunder in the enclosed space. "Keep your hands off what is mine!"

The weight on Joshua's chest vanished. The room brightened. The candle stopped flickering.

"Holy shit!" Joshua breathed. It seemed worth repeating. "Holy shit! What the hell was that? Is it gone? Are you okay? What was that?"

"The Wolf King!"

"The what?" Joshua said before remembering that Decker and Elise had talked about a Wolf King. "You mean the king of werewolves?"

Winnie nodded and kept nodding.

"Are you okay?"

The nodding became a violent "no." "I think I peed myself."

9: ELISE

The Wicker house was easy to find; Elise merely had to follow the caravan of vehicles heading down the narrow country road. It seemed as if the New Hartford Police Department had called in favors with every law enforcement officer in the state. The good news was that no Wicker could control this many people. Unfortunately, they'd only need one or two well-placed puppets who could command the rest of the herd.

The road went past the Sauquoit high school, three stories high with ten-foot-high glass windows. It looked surprisingly large and moneyed for such a small town. At some time in the past, the area had been well-to-do. Three or four hundred feet more and the caravan turned onto an even narrower street and stopped just short of a railroad crossing.

The Wicker house sat on a large parcel of land, set back from the street another hundred feet. A winding driveway led back to the two-story farmhouse with a large river rock chimney and a wrap-around porch. It was a modern house pretending to be something old. It was too small to house a large coven; its size confirmed that the property was a temporary base.

Yellow police tape kept the caravan from turning into the driveway. The police cars that she'd been following pulled onto the grassy shoulder, already cut deep with ruts.

A small media circus had gathered, unpacking satellite dishes and cameras. Elise tucked her Jeep between two production trucks. She had wondered why the Wickers were delaying the hunt. The witches obviously wanted a lot of people between them and the werewolf. A set start time maximized the turnout of monster fodder.

Elise wished that she could simply sit and wait for the Wicker to show up. She couldn't kill the witch in front of so many police officers and expect to be able to walk away. It would get messy. Yes, when push came to shove, her family did lean toward "kill them all and let God sort them out." It made the Grigoris' lives much simpler. Heaven was a nice place; good people went there. Bad people got what they deserved.

It would piss off her grandmother, though, and that was to be avoided at all costs.

A cameraman spotted her as she climbed out of her Jeep. He'd been about to lift the camera to his shoulder. His eyes went wide and his pupils dilated. "Wow. Hello gorgeous! Who you are with?"

"I don't date losers like you." Insults were now her kneejerk reaction to how men acted around her. Depending on the guy, one or two dozen cutting remarks generally got them angry enough to actually see her. She didn't like the type of person it was making her. Not that she was the sweetest person in the world to start with, but she was starting to feel like a weird cross between a swan and a spitting cobra.

"I meant your network." He started to point the camera her way.

"Unless you want to eat that thing, do not point it at me." She pulled her pistol and aimed it at the lens.

Really, she didn't like that pulling a weapon was her first reaction. Or that her second reaction was thinking about pistol-whipping him and stuffing him into the equipment locker on his truck. Other women didn't have to be this hostile—right?

"Okay! Okay! Not filming!" He jerked the camera off his shoulder and back-pedaled, bouncing off vehicles as he went.

She stalked across the road, muttering darkly. "Is it really too much to ask, God, for one person—beyond Decker—who won't go brain dead every time they look me in the face?"

There was yellow tape where the front door had stood. The frame and part of the wall around it lay in the high-ceilinged foyer. The wolf had caught the warlock in the hallway just beyond it. Blood painted the walls and ceiling for eleven feet from a werewolf tearing the body to pieces. Eleven parts, to be exact, according to the coroner's report that the U.S. marshal had shared with her.

Elise ducked under the tape and followed the blood trail. At the end of the hallway, the wolf had barreled into a big farm kitchen.

There had been something made of wood and blood sacrifice waiting for the wolf. The end result must have mystified the police. Sticks and leaves and something long dead littered every surface along with swathes of blood from the wounded wolf.

Something glinted among the dead leaves. Elise toed aside the dead foliage. It was a silver bread knife tied to a branch. The small-town police, overwhelmed by violent and bizarre massacres, had missed the silverware. Even if they'd seen it, they wouldn't realize what it indicated.

The witches had known what was coming for them. They'd prepared.

So the werewolf wasn't just wounded, it was poisoned. It wouldn't heal until its wounds were washed clean with Earthblood. That explained why the Wickers knew that it had to be somewhere close by, nearly dead.

"Hey!" A male voice shouted at the end of the hall. "That's a police line that you just danced under, Missy!"

"Interpol!" she shouted back, following the splattering of blood to the garage entry. Some of the coven had escaped while the construct bought them time. The garage door was smashed open from the inside and there were tire marks on the driveway, racing away from the house.

A man came stomping up the hallway toward her. "I don't care which news agency you're with, get back across the damn road and wait with the other vultures!"

"Interpol." She pronounced it slowly and held up her badge. "As in international police. As in the United States Justice Department. As in federal agent. Interpol."

"What?" He snatched the badge from her. He was a tall beefy man with a bulldoglike face. His nametag stated Chief R. Dietz. His uniform patch identified him as New Hartford Police Department. From what she'd been able to gather, Sauquoit didn't have its own police. "French police don't have jurisdiction here."

Dietz studied her photograph and then glared at her. He could have been gay, but the lack of understanding of complex structures that he should know was a classic symptom of being under a witch's power.

"I'm a United States federal agent who works on the behalf of the Attorney General and Homeland Security." It was a greatly simplified version of the command structure in Washington, D.C. It usually required diagrams to explain who had control over what. The bureaucracy usually worked in the Grigoris' favor since no one was ever sure who to complain to.

He frowned at the badge again. "What the hell does Interpol want with a simple murder case?"

Simple? Elise laughed despite the fact that her heart was racing, making ready for a possible do or die fight. "I'm investigating the trafficking of endangered species."

"Trafficking? Like drugs?"

Oh, this man was ratcheted tight if he wasn't following that.

"Illegal importing of animals on the endangered list. It's possible that this is a critically endangered red wolf, or endangered Ethiopian wolf or a near-threatened maned wolf."

"What the hell does that mean? Are you a tree hugger here to stop this hunt?"

"No, I'm trying to trace how this animal got here in the first place. Wolves are extinct in this area, so clearly someone brought it here."

"We've looked for kennels and animal sanctuaries..."

"You've checked the registered ones. I'm looking for unregistered places with European ties."

All bullshit but he nodded slowly, grasping what she was implying.

"Were you given ammo?" He held up two magazines for her. "Everyone should take one. It's loaded for wolf."

She took the nine-millimeter clip magazine and made a show of loading it into her pistol. He was working off a script. Like post-hypnotic suggestions, he'd keep to the script until the witch showed up to supervise the hunt. Obviously he'd been told to gather up a hunting party and arm them with silver. Short of knocking him unconscious and tying him up, Elise had no way to get him off script. Killing him would also work but that would be bad.

She desperately wanted to search the house for clues on what the Wickers intended to do with Joshua. The Wickers obviously thought he was still in the area. They were standing their ground to find him. As long as they thought he was in the Utica area, he was safe in Boston.

There wasn't time to search the house. The Wicker could arrive at any moment and the werewolf was someplace, poisoned, and obviously too wounded to move. She had to get to it before the police could close in on it. A single bite would instantly make one of the hunters a feral werewolf. From there, chaos would spiral outward.

The house's backyard edged a dense woodlot of sugar maple, shedding brilliant red leaves. Elise stood on the edge of the yard and considered the layer of dead foliage. Strange how leaf-covered ground could seem so threatening.

There were witches, and there witches and then there were *witches*.

Wickers took the word to a scary level. Just about anything could be lurking in among the leaves or hidden in the woods besides one hurt and very pissed off werewolf. Luckily the media circus was in full swing in the front yard. The house shielded her as she pulled her daggers. Nerves jittering with fear, she walked into the woods.

The dead leaves crunched under foot. Occasionally a hidden twig would snap, making her tighten her grip on her daggers.

It was times like this that she wished her faith was stronger. Oh, she knew there was a God. The proof was written on the face of every member of her family and all the monsters she'd killed since she took up her daggers. What she doubted was that God gave a damn about his creations. Look at what he'd done to Decker; given him a divine gift and then twisted him hard by having him attacked by a vampire. As a man, he'd been persecuted for God's touch on him. Because of his faith, he couldn't even kill himself and go on to the afterlife that he believed in, even after he'd become a monster. What kind of creator did that to its creations and could still be called "loving"?

The wind sent the leaves skittering. She pranced sideways, startled.

"Oh God Almighty, maker of heaven and earth!" She blushed and glanced about to see if anyone had witnessed her fear dance. No. Her forefathers, however, were probably snickering at the moment. They had to be a little perverted despite being angels—hence the reason they'd slept around with human women.

The werewolf's blood trail was easy to follow; the wolf bled heavily as it staggered through the woods. The officers sent to tell Daphne's "parents" the bad news had been at the house late Friday night; they'd missed the blood splattered on the dead leaves in the darkness. Saturday the police had been distracted with Joshua disappearing and the murder of his neighbor. The Wickers had been busy regrouping, trying to capture Joshua, and sacrificing Joshua's neighbors for the huntsman. It had been a busy Saturday for everyone involved.

There was no way the hunters would miss the blood trail today.

Elise followed it through the woods, heading downhill. The werewolf needed Earthblood to cleanse his wounds. It was unlikely he'd find any. He'd reached the railroad crossing and realized that it would taint anything that lay beyond. He lay there for some time, bleeding out, before crawling across the gravel and creosote-soaked ties and metal rails to the shallow stream beyond.

Sauquoit Creek ran too polluted for Earthblood, but gave him something to drink, so he was still alive when she found him. She cursed softly at the sight of him. He was a massive black male. Ferals were only slightly bigger than a Rottweiler. Normal pack wolves tended to be slightly larger than Great Danes. This wolf was built more like a black bear. Her family had legends that the Wolf King was like a polar bear crossed with an elephant when he was angry—huge and white—but it was unclear if that was true or not. Most people did not survive witnessing it.

He growled softly without opening his eyes.

"Seth?" Elise kept her distance.

He breathed out a bitter laugh. "Everyone forgets there's more than one black wolf of Boston still alive."

"Cabot." She'd forgotten about him. Jack Cabot was the prince's cousin. He was the youngest of the Wolf King's Thanes. If he hadn't been wounded, she would have been seriously outclassed. Even hurt as badly as he was, he might be able to kill her.

He opened his eyes for a moment, focused on her, and then closed his eyes with a laugh. "I never thought I'd be happy to see a Virtue in person. I knew I'd be in deep shit when it happened, but I thought I'd at least start on my feet."

"The Wickers are using the local police as puppets. They've

armed the cops with silver ammo. A hunt for you starts in a matter of minutes." She scanned the area. There was no way she could carry him any distance. There was no safe hiding place nearby. She would have to get her Jeep. "I need your promise that you'll not hurt me while I'm trying to save your ass."

His laugh ended with a whimper of pain. "I want to live. For Seth's sake, I need to live. I've been lying here realizing how messed up he's going to be if I don't make it. I'll promise almost anything."

"That you won't hurt me?"

"I will not hurt you unless you do something stupid, like trying to shoot those silver bullets you have at another wolf."

Close enough. "I'm going to get my Jeep. I'll be right back."

"I'll be here." He closed his eyes.

A powerful witch could walk into a car dealership, pick out a car, and have it given to them, all the proper paperwork signed and sealed. The more expensive the car, the more powerful the witch.

There was a red Bentley sitting in the Wicker driveway. Elise took a deep breath as she realized that the witch had walked away with a two-hundred-thousand-dollar car. No wonder the Wickers could keep Dietz on script from miles away. It was possible that such a powerful witch could control all the police at the house.

Elise wanted to kill the witch, but now was not the time. Just as she was nearly immune to a Wicker's ability, they were immune to hers. The Wicker would see her coming and throw every puppet in the area at Elise. She needed to catch the witch without its meat shield.

Elise drove her Jeep down the railroad, straddling the right rail. The right of way dropped off steeply on either side; she really hoped that no train came while she was driving down the narrow raised bed. A quarter mile up the tracks, she reached Cabot.

"You need to get up." She opened the passenger door. "I can't lift you."

He heaved himself up, growling lowly. It was impressively loud and scary as hell.

She backed away from him. "Do you have to do that?"

"Being angry helps," he snarled. "We're strongest when we're pissed off."

"As long as you remember that I'm not the one you're pissed at."

"I know exactly who I want to kill. I saw her just before that damn thing in the kitchen laid into me. A tall brunette with red fox jacket and big gold earrings. Late thirties, early forties. She just glanced back toward me and said 'kill it' and walked out. Walked." He nearly roared the word and flung himself into the passenger seat of the Jeep. It rocked under his weight. "Like I was nothing."

In place, he subsided, panting.

"You done?" Elise did not want to get in beside the angry werewolf.

He took deep cleansing breaths before murmuring, "Yes. Done. Get me out of this place. Please."

The nearest Earthblood spring was in Ferris Lake Wild Forest, over an hour away. Cabot lay silent the entire way. Much as she wanted to ask him questions, she didn't want him angry again while she was trapped inside the car with him.

The spring was deep within the park. The Earthblood spilled out a granite outcrop to gather in a grotto. Despite the overcast sky, the "water" shimmered with the telltale gleam of the pooled magical liquid.

She waited until after he'd half fallen out of the Jeep and crawled into the grotto's pool. Red clouds formed and drifted away as the Earthblood cleansed his wounds.

"I was expecting Samuels to come and laugh at me," Cabot whispered. "We did rock-paper-scissors and I picked what sounded easier."

"A Wicker deep in the country? Easy? Amateurs." She pulled out her phone and found the photo of the dead wolf. "Is this Samuels?"

Cabot breathed out and closed his eyes. "Yes." He was silent for a minute before speaking again. "I suppose I did get the easy job then. The witch he was going after?"

"Dead."

"And the others?"

"What others?"

"The seniors were doing some kind of haunted house to fund their prom. Eleven kids had gotten out early for it. Samuels would not have gone down without a fight. What about the other kids? Was there collateral damage?"

She showed him the collateral damage.

"Jesus." He breathed and closed his eyes against it. "We royally screwed this up."

"You were after Wickers. What did you expect?"

"We weren't! Not originally! The first we knew that there were Wickers in the area was when we walked into the school. That damn smell: myrrh and fresh bruised greens and something dead long enough it started to rot. We decided to split up. I'd follow the witch's trail back to her lair. Samuels would go on to the haunted house."

"Why were you at the school?"

"Wolf King's business."

"Don't give me that bullshit."

Cabot snarled, showing teeth.

She slapped him hard on the snout. "There's dead scattered all across the tri-state area and you'll be out of it for days yet. I need to know what I'm dealing with here."

He swore, rubbing his snout with a huge paw. "I don't know! Alexander said merely that a youngling was a senior at the school and that we were to find him and bring him back. Only there's no pack in this area; the closest is Albany. Their younglings go to a private school the pack owns. If a youngling goes past thirteen without being changed, it's usually because they chose not to become a wolf. Those kids go to a boarding school on the West Coast. Alexander didn't give us a name; he just said that we'd know him when we found him. There was a youngling; we tracked his scent through the school. He was in among the bunch of seniors heading to the haunted house."

She hadn't realized that younglings smelled different from normal humans, since they weren't werewolves until they were bitten. She'd always assumed that younglings were humans. If the Thanes could pick the youngling out of a crowd, then the boy wasn't completely "human."

It meant that Samuels had gone to the barn without knowing which of the kids was the missing youngling. Was Joshua actually the child that the Wolf King sent the Thanes to find? Cabot couldn't tell her.

He rose to his feet and shook, spraying her with Earthblood.

"Hey!" Elise backed away from the grotto.

"Sorry." He stretched and changed. He was a flowing dark

gleam as if his entire being became glowing liquid. It started black and shifted to a dappled green and then stabilized to bare skin and honey brown hair.

Cabot made a tall, muscular man. Seriously ripped. His shoulder-length hair was surprisingly honey-colored, a blond nearly dark enough to be brown. His thick eyebrows, beard and chest hair were darker still. His eyes were a golden color. Fringed with the black lashes, they almost seemed to gleam.

The men of her family were just as angelic in their looks as the women. They were elegantly beautiful to the point of being androgynous. (Their gaydar was utterly useless as even straight males hit on them.)

Cabot's face was pure strength, drawn in rugged lines. Every part of it alone suggested brute force. The solid square jaw, the high cheekbones, and prominent brow ridge could have been ugly, but together they created a raw animalistic handsomeness that was impossible to deny.

Elise realized she was staring and turned around, blushing. "You could warn me you were suddenly going to be naked."

"Sorry." He gave a slight laugh, as if he was too weak for anything more. "I'm not thinking clearly. I assumed you had some clothes I could put on. The police are looking for a wolf, not a man."

He wasn't the only one having trouble thinking. Did she have clothes he could wear? He wasn't fitting into her spare clothes. She remembered that she had a fresh pair of coveralls for Decker. (He had a thing about not ruining his fine tailored clothes and monsters tended to spawn in the sewers.)

"Yeah, I think I might." She headed toward her Jeep. "You'll have to go commando."

"I'll live." He was trembling when he reached her side.

"Sit." She shoved a towel at him. "Put this on until you're bandaged."

He wrapped it around his lean hips and perched on the narrow back bumper of her Jeep. He had dozens of wounds on his muscled torso. The shallow ones were already angry scabs but the deeper punctures were seeping blood. "You know my name. What is yours?"

"Elise."

Various types of magic had a smell. The scent of his change clung to him. It was a soft, woody smell like sandalwood, mixed with a rich sun-warmed grass. He leaned against the frame of her Jeep, eyes closed, as she bandaged the deepest of his wounds. His skin was surprisingly soft, like a newborn's, only it covered hard muscle. She tried to remember what Joshua had felt like when she'd checked his pulse.

She realized he'd opened his eyes and was watching her. "What?"

"I know our people aren't always on the friendliest of terms. You could have left me to die. I owe you."

"Yes, you do." Elise snapped her mouth shut after her kneejerk reaction had spoken for her. He hadn't done anything remotely like the mouth breathers. If anything, she was the one quietly lusting...

She blushed hot at the realization. *Oh, you hypocrite*! She ducked her head and tried to focus on bandaging him. Unfortunately it meant focusing on his body. How their legs had to tangle together for her to get close enough to apply the bandages. The heat of his body. His scent.

Questioning him would be safer than working in silence because without anything to think on, she found herself wondering if he tasted as good as he smelled. "So you don't have any idea what the Wickers are planning?"

"I think they're after our youngling. After I tore their construct apart, I noticed that the house was practically empty except for a handful of textbooks and some enrollment papers from the local high school. The house was a staging area."

"Did the Wolf King tell you the name of the youngling?" Were they looking for Joshua or was the boy merely more collateral damage?

He gave her a long measuring stare. "Why are you interested in our youngling?"

"The Wickers are standing their ground after tangling with two Thanes. I want to know why."

He closed his eyes. "I didn't get around to exchanging names with the Wickers. They might not realize who the hell came tearing through their kitchen."

"They know the car at the barn belongs to the Wolf King. Only an idiot couldn't put the two and two together."

He fell silent. He breathed so deeply that she wondered if he'd fallen asleep.

She busied herself with putting away her first aid kit. "You need to put on clothes and get into the passenger side before you can pass out."

His edge of his mouth lifted in a ghost of a smile. "I know what I need to do but I'm not sure that I can."

"Do you need help?"

A tired laugh. "Unfortunately, yes."

The next ten minutes proved to be the most conflicted of her life. Putting pants on a man turned out to be as sexy as taking them off. Nor could she just stop there as Cabot's wounds and the coveralls' design made it necessary for her to put both arms around him and pull the back up so he could get his hands into the sleeves. She wanted it to be an innocent act done without awareness of the heat of his body or how their hips pressed together. That she couldn't keep either out of her mind made her angry with herself; she was reacting just like the mouth breathers.

He slumped against her, head on her shoulder, breath warm against her neck. "I know that I'm weak as a baby. I'll recover after a night's sleep. Hopefully. I need to go back. If the Wickers were after the youngling and are standing their ground, then the kid is still in the wind. I need to find him and get him to safety."

He wanted her to take him back. Until he got back on his feet, he also needed her protection.

At least, she was fairly sure that was what he was saying. Wolves were usually fairly straightforward creatures. Not like some monsters that twisted words around until yes was no and the sun was the moon.

"You're suggesting an alliance?" she asked to be sure.

"Yes. I need your help. You're going after them, aren't you? We can work together."

It was ironic that she'd had an hour to think on the drive to the Earthblood and she hadn't considered the ramifications of saving him. He wasn't a human law officer who could be turned into a weapon against her. Nor he was the clueless puppy ignorant of all things related to Wickers, Grigori and werewolves. This was a Thane. The only danger that he posed was to her libido. There was no good reason not to agree on an alliance.

"Yes, I'm going after them. We can work together."

Oh, God help her.

10: SETH

Driving to Utica from Ithaca was like playing a redneck version of Grand Theft Auto.

Seth had taken back roads out of Ithaca since they led in the direction he could sense Jack. The two-lane "highways" could barely qualify for the name except they showed up on his GPS system as actual Interstate routes. The Porsche's powerful engine and the twisting roads through farmland and state forests tested his driving abilities.

Every light he hit was red.

Children and animals darted out onto the pavement with annoying frequency. The cats and dogs and whitetail deer he expected. The cows and bison and alpaca tipped the experience to surreal. (Since when were there bison in Central New York? And what were they doing standing in the middle of the freaking road?)

Half of the vehicles were slow-moving Subarus, it being the older redneck car of choice. The other half were a dangerous mix of impatient pickup trucks and random giant farm equipment.

The GPS claimed it was a two-hour drive. Between the bison herd and the slow moving tractors, it had taken three hours. Seth pulled the Porsche into the Utica gas station that Wonder Woman Alvarado had used. The gas gauge read empty and he felt blurry at the edges from exhaustion and hunger.

The Wolf King's power washed over Seth as he climbed out of the low-slung sports car. Half a world away, the strength of

Alexander's presence was still stunning. Seth leaned against the Porsche's roof, growling softly. He'd hoped that he could find Jack before the king realized Seth wasn't safe in Mexico anymore.

A phantom brush of fur. A massive ghost nose drawing in his scent. A great shadowy foot prodding at him. Alexander didn't seem angry. He seemed puzzled. Was it because he didn't expect Seth to be in New York?

Seth's phone rang. He didn't even have to look at it to know it was Bishop. How much more trouble would he be in if he didn't answer? He was fairly sure he knew why Alexander had sent Jack to Utica, but he wanted to verify his guess. Of course, Bishop was going to order him back to New York City.

Seth was tempted to punch the top of the Porsche but that would dent the roof. He was in enough trouble already. He answered his phone. "Yes?"

"What are you doing there?" It wasn't Bishop. Alexander was actually growling through the tiny speaker. Somewhere in the world, pigs were flying.

"Looking for Jack," Seth said. "You know he's hurt. Samuels isn't answering his phone."

"Samuels is dead."

It was like getting punched in the stomach. Seth bent in pain. Samuels had been a good friend; one of the few people at the Castle he trusted as much as Jack.

Alexander continued. "There's a coven of Wickers in that area."

"The ones that killed Anastasia?" Seth asked.

"Most likely, which is why it's too dangerous for even you to be there alone. Go back to the Castle."

"I need to find Jack."

"Isaiah is on his way. He'll deal with the Wickers when he gets there. Go home."

Alexander hung up, confident that he would be obeyed.

"Boston is home." Seth growled at the lost connection signal. He closed his eyes and focused on Jack.

Something had changed during his drive to Utica. Jack's connection to the Source was no longer blocked. He must have found a pool of Earthblood. Seth focused harder, pushing through the link between them. Seth wasn't Alexander; he couldn't project strong enough to make Jack aware that Seth was looking for him. Seth could tell, though, that Jack had been stabbed a dozen times in the chest. His cousin lay in the magical spring; so weak he could barely move. He was so vulnerable that it scared Seth.

Jack's emotions, however, had changed; he was no longer afraid. With the Earthblood, Jack had found safety.

"Are you okay?" a man called.

Seth opened his eyes. A news camera truck had pulled into the neighboring gas pump. The passenger with network-worthy good looks was coming toward him, a mix of concern and reporter curiosity on his face.

"I'm just tired," Seth said truthfully enough. He'd slept on the way back from Mexico but that had been scattered across a half dozen flights. "And I can't figure out how to put gas in this stupid car."

The man laughed. "The engine is in the back, so the gas tank is in the front on the passenger side. You just push on the access panel to release it." He crossed to the other side of the Porsche and pushed against the gas cap hatch, which was out of Seth's line of sight. "But you need to have the car unlocked first."

Seth had automatically locked the car when he got out. He used the fob to unlock the doors. The man pressed again on the side and the hatch thumped open. "Thanks."

The man stayed on the other side of the car, watching Seth closely. "You know any of the kids that were mauled?"

Years of living at the Castle made it so Seth could keep the shock off his face. Wickers in the area. A dead werewolf. Collateral damage had to be expected. "No." And because that seemed too short an answer, he expanded with, "I go to a private school. I was in Mexico until last night—family funeral. How many kids were killed?"

"Ten. The one survivor has disappeared." The reporter waved across the street at an auto repair place. "So, you don't know Joshua?"

Seth swore softly. The reporter had assumed that he knew the victims, which meant they were probably Seth's age. Ilya was ten months older than Seth.

"Joshua is seventeen?" Seth asked. "Almost eighteen?"

"Yes, that's him. Do you know where he might be?"

"He's missing?" Seth felt dread start to rise.

"His parents took him home from the hospital, ran out to do some errands, and came home to find him gone."

Hospital implied that the boy was hurt. There was a world of difference between bitten and merely clawed. A werewolf's bite was a magical wound that opened up the person to the Source. The change would have been instantaneous. If the resulting werewolf wasn't anchored, they became feral.

His family had lost a full generation when a newborn wolf bit a youngling. Seth's great-grandfather had been blessed with nine healthy children. He'd taken all of them to the Tyringham lodge to celebrate his oldest son being changed into a wolf. He'd made the mistake of leaving all the children alone afterwards except for his infant son, Seth's grandfather. The newborn wolf lost his temper with a younger sister who hadn't been changed yet. He nipped at her, meaning only to scare her. When his teeth broke skin, he created a magical wound through which power could flow. She instantly went feral. She killed him, and mauled all their baby siblings. The ones that didn't go feral were torn apart. The surviving monsters descended on Tyringham. A bloodbath followed.

Normally only an alpha wolf could safely change a child. The alpha used their connection to the Source to anchor the newborn within the pack. Could Thanes safely change a youngling into a newborn werewolf?

"Was Joshua bitten?" Seth asked.

The reporter dismissed the injury with a wave. "They're worried he has some kind of brain injury. He had amnesia when he woke up. He lives near Woodford State Forest. They're afraid he's wandered off."

Seth cursed. Amnesia was a side effect of being changed. If Joshua was in human form when taken to the hospital, then he wasn't a feral. It didn't mean he was in complete control of his wolf; that took time and training. In the meantime, he could accidently create a feral that would kill him and everyone around him.

"So you know him?" the reporter asked.

"No." Which got him a look of disbelief. "I think I might have met his father."

The dead puppet had gotten the Viper repaired at the garage. Had she sold Ilya to the mechanics? Was Joshua his long-lost brother?

More importantly, where was Joshua now?

If he was bitten, then he was a newborn werewolf. There was no "maybe" about it. Since Joshua was still a minor, he was a puppy and automatically the responsibility of the nearest alpha. And at the moment, that meant Seth.

Joshua's family seemed to have nothing to hide. Their home address was listed with their phone number.

It was small house; it looked like the entire thing would fit in the Wolf King's ballroom. A large metal Quonset hut garage in the back of the property dwarfed the house. Life, for Joshua's family, was apparently all about cars.

A solid wall of trees edged the sprawling yard. According to the map, the woods extended a mile on private land to meet up with a large state forest. Seth could see why people thought that Joshua had simply wandered off and gotten lost.

Seth pulled cautiously into the driveway. Somewhere in the area were Wickers who'd already killed one Thane and badly hurt another. Seth turned off the motor and listened to the quiet ticking of the engine.

He'd grown up with stories of how his infant brother had been picked up helpless from his crib and carried out of the mountain lodge. His kidnappers tracked Anastasia's blood through the snow. His father had howled himself hoarse when he realized he'd chased after the wrong car; that he'd forever lost his first-born son. The only child his father would ever have with his childhood sweetheart, the girl he'd loved nearly half his life.

It would be a miracle if Joshua were his lost brother.

The important thing, though, was he was a newborn werewolf. He wouldn't be able to fully control his transformation into a wolf. One bite would create a feral, and then there would be an uncontrollable monster loose. It was a cascading disaster waiting to happen. It might be smarter to wait for backup now that Seth knew what was going on but if he hesitated, dozens of people could be killed.

The back door was unlocked. It surprised Seth until he remembered that the family thought Joshua might have wandered off in a fit of amnesia. They didn't want to lock Joshua out on a cold autumn day. Seth opened the door and slipped in.

Water from an upstairs bathroom had flooded down through the kitchen's ceiling the day before. The plaster still dripped. The range sat pulled out from its cove and unplugged. The receptacle looked half-melted; char marks followed the path of water down the wall to the floor.

Seth eyed the dripping ceiling. "Oh, yeah, someone is having trouble with their new wolf strength."

There was more than one reason why his family normally took newborns camping for a month. Broken faucets, toilets, doors, lamps, and electronics got to be expensive. Seth had spent an entire summer shifting chicken eggs from one basket to another to learn control.

The living room reflected a modest income. Worn furniture. No paintings or artwork. Ancient TV. The items normally displayed on the fireplace mantle had been shoved aside to make way for a multitude of photos of Joshua. Afraid that he was already dead, Joshua's family had built a shrine to him.

Seth stared at the pictures, trying to see his father in the boy. Joshua didn't belong with this family. His parents and older sister were willowy tall, blue-eyed and blond. In other words, everything Joshua was not. He didn't look like a Tatterskein either; he was far too short and mousey. However he ended up with this family, though, it was obvious he'd been raised with love. A toddler sat awe-struck on Santa's lap. An eight-year-old grinned widely to show off missing baby teeth. A pre-teen had grease up to his elbows and smeared across his face as he did male bonding under the hood of a muscle car. A teenager looked embarrassed by his mother's hug.

Seth was assuming that the boy was Ilya. If Joshua was his lost older brother, then Ilya had had a good childhood. One that was a far cry from the horrific death that Seth's family had always imagined. Furthermore, if Joshua had been found and returned as an infant, he would have died with the rest of their family.

"Good for you," Seth whispered to the pictures.

Seth started to turn away when he noticed that one of the photos had fallen to the floor. Joshua's parents stood outside their business in Utica, infant in arms, snow on the ground. In the background was the Dodge Viper with a wolf head painted on front panel.

The only reason that this picture would be on the mantle would be that Joshua was the infant in the photo. It was proof that Joshua was Seth's long lost brother, Ilya. Seth put the photo into his wallet.

Was Joshua also now a werewolf?

Seth took a deep breath through his nose. The house been closed up for the approaching winter. Trapped in and circulated by a forced air furnace, the room held a heady soup of scents. The family had had Chinese takeout the night before; General Tso's chicken and Mongolian beef masked the fainter scents.

He growled in annoyance and closed his eyes to focus tighter on his sense of smell. Yes, there, the scent of a youngling. Fainter still was newborn werewolf; Joshua had only been in the house an hour or two before disappearing. Under the food and youngling and werewolf was something else. Seth breathed deeper.

There was something dead in the house.

A cat yowled from somewhere in the house. Another howl followed. It was a call that demanded that a stupid human come and find out what was the matter.

Seth gathered his power close to him and followed the sound upstairs.

The smell of carrion came from the bathroom. The sink's cold-water faucet had been snapped cleanly off, creating the downstairs flood. A seal-point Himalayan sat in the battered bathtub. The cat glared at him. It wanted a human, not a werewolf, to obey its summons.

"Good kitty." Seth's experience with cats was limited to those he met at the Dr. Huff's office.

The cat hissed.

"Yeah, yeah, I know." The cats at Dr. Huff's never liked the big bad wolf either.

Something fluttered under the Himalayan's front paws.

"What did you catch?" He leaned closer, making the cat hiss again.

A snitch fluttered its paper wings, trying to escape. Its twig legs scratched against the tub's porcelain as it clawed at the smooth surface.

"Shit!" Seth ducked back into the hallway. He didn't want the Wickers knowing he was in the area. The magical construct worked as a spy, communicating back what it saw and heard. The coven needed to use a freshly harvested human eye to create the snitch. None of the dead teenagers at the barn had been missing their eyes. The town's body count just went up by one.

How to catch the snitch without the Wickers knowing that the Prince of Boston was the one who caught it?

His first impulse was to use his hands. The construct couldn't hurt him and he was trained to fight barehanded. A human, though, wouldn't want to touch it.

He scanned the bathroom from the door. What could he use as a weapon? Yesterday's flood must have triggered a massive cleanout, as the room was bare. The only object in the room was a toilet plunger.

The things his father never warned him about.

He leaned in, picked up the toilet plunger and braced himself for a fight.

As he moved closer to the tub, the cat hissed and fled. The freed snitch darted forward, careened off the tile wall and headed for the open door. He smacked it out of the air with the plunger and then stomped the red rubber end over it. It buzzed angrily under the suction cup.

"Gotcha!" He glanced around the bare bathroom again. "Now, how to kill you?"

A magic wound like a werewolf's bite would work, but there was no way he was putting it in his mouth. A silver knife? He doubted that Joshua's family had real silverware, but he should at least look.

He felt vaguely like a robber going through the kitchen drawers and kitchen cabinets. Nothing silver. Not even candlesticks.

Out the kitchen window he spotted a charcoal grill.

Fire would work.

He found a flat cookie tray and slid it under the plunger. He carried the unwieldy trap downstairs and out the back door. Joshua's parents were orderly people; all the needed utensils for a cookout were carefully organized. All that was needed was a dishcloth to drape over the snitch so it couldn't report who was burning it. He used tongs to hold it over the fire and spray it with lighter fluid. The flames leapt greedily up. Under the thin cloth, the snitch's paper wings thrashed.

If the Wickers had snitches in place, then they didn't have Joshua.

Was Joshua lost in the woods? Had he gone feral?

Once Seth was sure that the snitch was nothing but ashes, he stalked through the yard, sniffing. He found Joshua's scent overlaid by that of multiple people. He followed it to the Quonset hut garage. Unlike the house, this was locked tight. He gave the side entrance a hard push and the dead bolt broke the frame.

Someone had run a gasoline engine in the tight confines in the last two days. Neat and orderly continued in the garage. Along the near wall was a herd of ATVs, motorcycles and dirt bikes. There was an obvious void where one of the bikes had been taken. Four pegs by the door used to hold four helmets. Only three hung there now. Seth sniffed at them. Joshua's was missing.

The newborn hadn't "wandered off," he'd fled at full speed.

"Way to go, big brother."

The snitches were in place in case Joshua contacted his family or came back home. The Wickers had lost track of his brother. Joshua would be safe from the Wickers as long as he stayed hidden.

The question was: where did Joshua go?

Upstairs had once been two bedrooms. The largest had been split into two claustrophobic bedrooms for children of opposite gender. Joshua's room was just big enough to wedge a bunk bed into it. The lower bunk had been removed to make space for a desk. Seth's shower at the Castle was bigger.

The room was surprisingly clean; especially for a teenage boy whose life had been turned upside down. There were no dirty clothes or books or papers on the floor. Even the small closet was neatly organized. To Seth, nothing seemed to be missing. There was even a phone sitting in a charger on the desk.

He picked up the phone. It turned on as he lifted it out of its cradle. A swipe put him at the passcode screen. Seth tried 0000 and 1234 and 4321 without any success.

"Not a simpleminded man, are you, Joshua?" Seth scanned the room for a possible clue. What would Joshua use for his passcode? Above the desk was a bookshelf. On the left side were a half-dozen textbooks. The rest of the shelf was science fiction and fantasy novels. No real clues there, at least nothing obvious.

A corkboard hung to the left of the desk. Pieces of Joshua's life were pinned into place. A straight "A" report card. An SAT score higher than Seth's. Applications to half a dozen colleges. Joshua ranked his applications with sticky notes. He wanted to go to Harvard or Boston College or Northeastern University but would settle for Syracuse or Rochester or Albany. Red-penned

Amtrak schedules explained the latter three; he wanted to get to school and back via the train.

Seth unpinned the applications. All the little boxes were filled out with Joshua's personal information. His birthday was listed as February twenty-ninth instead of Ilya's date of March seventh.

Neither was his passcode.

Joshua had left his social security number blank on all the applications. Seth scanned the corkboard. A note reminded Joshua to get a copy of his birth certificate from his "mom" and apply for a social security number.

"She can't supply what she doesn't have." Seth folded up the Harvard application and tucked it into his pocket. The others he repinned to the corkboard.

Joshua's phone vibrated in Seth's hand with an incoming text.

The screen identified the contact merely as "George." "Your folks are on the news again, asking for information on you. Where are you? No one knows where you are. I called everyone."

If George had actually contacted "everyone" that Joshua knew, then the newborn werewolf wasn't hiding with friends. All things considered, that was probably a good thing.

The phone vibrated again. George asked, "Are you okay, Kickboy?"

Kickboy?

Seth noticed for the first time that there was a shelf above the closet door. It held dozens of martial arts medals, ribbons and trophies. Werewolves didn't compete in most high school sports; their speed and strength would draw unwanted attention. A youngling didn't have any advantages over a normal human. The number of trophies was impressive considering Joshua's small size.

"Wow, you rock, big brother." Seth put the phone back into the charger. The room painted a picture of a boy who was organized and compulsive over the smallest of details. Joshua had left his phone on purpose, most likely so he couldn't be tracked via its GPS. He'd probably deleted any telling information. It was a dead end.

Down the hall, the Himalayan howled, announcing it had caught a second snitch.

Seth swore. He should have guessed that there would be a second one. The Wickers would be economical; they'd use both eyes of their victim to make the snitches.

He leaned into the bathroom to grab the toilet plunger again and followed the howling.

Joshua's older adoptive sister fared better in the room division; she'd wedged a full-size bed on eighteen-inch risers into her bedroom. A dormer gave her space for a low dresser with piece of plywood hinged to the top so it could double as a desk. The room seemed partially stripped of belongings as if his sister had been the one who fled the house. Most likely she'd gone off to college. Otherwise it was much the same: clean, compact, focused on sleep and study, sprinkled with martial arts trophies.

The howling came from under her elevated bed. Seth got down on his hands and knees.

Up against the far wall, the Himalayan pinned a second snitch. The cat hissed at him and then dared to growl at him. Him! The Prince of Boston.

"Damn, you're one stupidly brave cat."

Seth leaned back to eye the bed. It touched three walls. He wasn't even sure how they'd gotten the mattress and box-springs down the hall, through the door and into the space. It wasn't wedged tight, it simply had nowhere to go if he tried to move it. Maybe they'd built the room around the bed.

When his father warned him he'd have rough days as the prince, his father probably wasn't envisioning a fight with a magical construct and a large house cat under a co-ed's bed with a toilet plunger.

He crawled under the bed and chaos erupted.

It hadn't occurred to him that his body would block both the snitch and the cat from escaping. Or that by blocking "flee" for the cat, he'd trigger "fight" instincts. The Himalayan became a howling cyclone of claws as the snitch flitted about madly, looking for a way to escape. Seth stabbed with the plunger, trying to nail the snitch to the wall. Every time he'd thought he had it, the cat would leap in the way. He didn't want to reduce his brother's cat to a pancake.

He swung his leg out, trying to pin the cat. It wrapped itself around his leg and latched all four sets of claws and its needle-sharp teeth into his leg just below his groin. He roared, abandoned trying to trap the snitch with the plunger and merely grabbed it with his free hand.

"What the hell?" a woman shouted.

He'd been so focused on the snitch and the cat that he missed someone coming up the stairs.

He jerked up, taking the bed with him. A tall, willowy blonde stood in the doorway with a bamboo kendo practice sword in hand. "Who the hell are you? What are you doing in my house? Why are you under my bed?"

He stood panting, plunger in one hand, snitch in the other, and the damn cat wrapped around his leg. Seth breathed in her scent. Yes, it was her bed that he'd just upended, the frame still lying across his shoulders like an ox-yoke.

This was going to be fun to explain.

Was he still fully human? Yes. Yay him; years of practice just paid off.

Now what did he tell her? What was a good and rational reason to break into someone's house and molest their cat under a bed?

He had nothing. He was too tired to be that creative.

So he went with the truth.

"Catching this." He held out the snitch as evidence.

She took a step back, raising the sword into strike position, before glancing down at his hand. "What is—Holy shit!" She jerked back. "It moved! What the hell is that?"

The snitch fluttered its paper wings and flailed with twig legs, trying to get free.

He forgot for a moment that he had the toilet plunger in his left hand. He raised it, saying, "I need to—ow! Ow!" She'd whacked him twice with the bamboo sword, both head shots. It stung but she couldn't actually hit him hard enough to hurt him. She would need a silver weapon or a Mack truck for that. "Shit! Just wait!"

He blocked a series of blows with the toilet plunger. She was fast; he only managed to block her because he was a werewolf. He managed to get her to back up by advancing. The Himalayan kept hold of him, growling fiercely and occasionally raking at his leg with its back claws.

They went down the steps and across the living room before she realized that he was just blocking and not attacking. At that point, she grew reckless and started to swing without trying to guard herself.

"Just. Let. Me. Show. You. This!" He smacked the sword hard.

The plunger broke and the sword went flying out of her hand. He thrust his hand with the snitch forward, trying to make her stop and look at it.

She caught his wrist and threw him onto the ground.

He was starting to get seriously pissed off, which was a very bad thing. He struggled not to growl or radiate his power. She was just freaked out right now. If he terrified her, there would be no talking with her. Ever. (Although he was getting to the point where he didn't care.)

At least the cat had let go of his leg.

"What kind of bug or whatever is that?" she asked.

Oh thank God, now that she thought she had him pinned, she was actually looking at what he held in his hand.

"Is that calculus?" she asked..

What? Oh, the snitch's wings. The Wickers would have used items they found in Joshua's house to make it. In this case, a calculus textbook.

"I've been trying to show it to you," Seth said. "It's not a living creature. It's like origami on crack."

"Who the hell are you?"

He didn't want the snitch—and thus the Wickers—to hear. "Look, can I deal with this thing first and then talk?" To keep the conversation on a "normal" level, he added, "It's really creepy."

She let him go and backed away. Her stance reflected the martial arts trophies in her room; she braced for a second round of fighting.

He motioned for her to follow him out to the grill.

She was conditioned not to harm a living creature. The snitch seemed living enough that she flinched as he tore off the wings. He turned them this way and that so she could see that they were pages from a math book. Even detached, the wings continued to move feebly. He tossed them onto the white-hot coals.

"That's so weird. How is it..." She gasped as he ripped open the body to reveal the human eye. "Oh, God, tell me that isn't..."

"It is." He tossed everything on the fire. "Everything you think you know about the world isn't true. There is such a thing as magic. There are monsters and witches and warlocks. They killed someone to make that thing so it could spy on your family. They want to find Joshua. They'll take him if they find him."

She turned without a word and walked back into the kitchen.

Seth wished he had more experience with women. His exposure was limited to a handful of hours at school and those girls were from New York City high society. None of them would have attacked him with a bamboo sword. They'd have either ignored him like a crazy guy on the subway or barricaded themselves into the bathroom and called 911 or asked him out on a date. He could hear Joshua's sister running water in the kitchen, so it wasn't any of the above.

After attacking people, it turned out that Central New York girls offered their victims coffee, tea, water, soda, or whiskey combined with any of the above. Seth accepted a coffee and watched her mix herself an Irish coffee.

"What's your name?" He'd been spoiled by a week in Mexico. This coffee was horrible stale ground stuff out of a can.

"You break into my house and destroy my bedroom without knowing my name?"

"I know your last name." He doctored the coffee with the brown sugar and heavy cream that she'd gotten out to make her Irish coffee.

"Elizabeth." With her voice threatening to break, she added, "Joshua calls me Bethy." Her voice went back to annoyed steel. "Who the hell are you? And don't try to tell me that you're a friend of my brother's. Joshua doesn't know anyone who drives a Porsche, or dresses in hundred-dollar jeans, or talks with a Boston accent so thick you could cut it with a knife."

"My name is Seth. I'm Boston."

"Yeah, I got that." Actually, she hadn't got what he meant but he was glad she didn't understand. It made it more likely that her family were innocent dupes for Anastasia's killers.

She pointed toward the smoking grill. "What—what—what the hell is going on? Why would anyone want to kidnap my brother? He's a dork. I mean he's a good kid. Too good. It's like deep down he thinks if he's really, really good everyone in the family will finally accept him."

"They want to kidnap him because he's adopted."

She snorted into her coffee. "Really? How do they know? Most people don't. We used to live in Whitesboro when Joshua was little, so our neighbors here in Sauquoit don't know. We don't tell people. We haven't even told Joshua. He has no idea why half my family are total shits to him. Why our father's parents are paying for everyone's college education except his. He tries so hard to be perfect. I keep telling my mom that they're only hurting him. He should know that it's not him; it's our family who are a bunch of jerks. They're narrow-minded, racist assholes." She laughed bitterly. "You're not supposed to think that about your grandparents but there's no other words for it. It doesn't matter if was his mother was Latina, or if my parents found her broken down alongside the road too poor for a tow or that she basically sold Joshua to us. He was two weeks old! We're the only family he's ever known."

"And the worst of it?" she whispered. "I was a horrible spoiled brat when I was little. I was four and so happy to be the center of my parents' world. I didn't want him." She wiped at a tear. "I didn't understand. My mother nearly died having me. She couldn't have any more children, but she didn't want me to be an only child. She had a younger brother who had died. She would have given anything to have him back. She wanted that for me. But I didn't want a baby to take my place, so I was awful to Joshua, for a long, long time."

"Your parents didn't know Joshua's 'mother' before the day they gave her a tow?"

Bethy wouldn't be derailed. "My parents called me and told about the massacre and that Joshua was in the hospital hurt and they didn't know how bad. I should come home, just in case he didn't pull through. All I could think of was how many times I'd told him to drop dead."

Seth understood completely. He had hated being the oldest. He'd been forced to be endlessly patient with his baby brothers, to take responsibility for any fight even if he hadn't started it, and to hand over beloved toys without anger. He was going to be prince. More importantly, he was going to be a newborn werewolf while they were still vulnerable younglings. He needed to learn to never strike out in anger.

He'd thought being oldest was the worst.

The worst was actually losing his little brothers.

The pretense of coffee was abandoned. Bethy poured a straight shot of whiskey into her empty coffee cup. "The funerals start tomorrow. Someone came up with the bright idea of staggering them so the kids from Joshua's high school could go to them all. The stupid reporters are turning it into a media circus. If I had another microphone shoved in my face, I was going to lose it. Dad told me to go home before I hurt someone."

"Where do you think Joshua went?" Seth asked.

"I don't know!" Bethy started to cry. "He kept freaking out at the hospital so they'd given him a bunch of strong sedatives. They said he'd probably sleep all day. Mom and Dad brought him home from the hospital and he went straight to bed."

A newborn werewolf would burn through any sedative in minutes.

"Joshua broke the passenger door on Dad's pickup; he snapped it off at the hinge. They had to wire it into place to get home. Dad went to the junkyard to find a replacement. Mom had to take a dish to D.J.'s parents because he—he—he's dead, and I was supposed to stay with Joshua. He was asleep! I thought he would be fine. We didn't have anything to eat in the house. I thought I could run into town to the store. I was only gone for an hour. I came back and the house was a disaster zone and an ambulance had been here to take our neighbor to the hospital..."

Seth stomach knotted. "Your brother attacked your neighbor?"

"No! Mr. Buckley was electrocuted by the flood." She pointed at the blackened 220 outlet. "Joshua called 911 and did CPR until the paramedics showed up. He was here when they were here, but by the time I got home, he'd disappeared."

The truck door. The bathroom faucet. The next-door neighbor. Joshua was clever enough to realize that, as a newborn werewolf, he was dangerous to everyone around him.

"Where would he go to hide?" Seth said.

"Hide? You think he ran away?"

"I'm not saying he's a coward..."

"Oh, he would run if he was being chased! The track coach wanted him to go out for the hundred meters, but that would mean being naked in locker rooms with jocks. The idiots around here made Joshua's life living hell. My parents are so clueless that it always made me want to scream! My dad thinks because he was teased as a kid that he knows what Joshua is going through. My dad was always the tallest kid in his class and completely normal. Joshua has always been dorky. The only time he isn't doing all his weird fidgeting is when he's fighting."

"Weird fidgeting" was typical for their people. Younglings weren't directly connected to the Source but they were close enough to have their behavior influenced by it. It was one of the reasons why that his family maintained a private school where younglings would be sheltered from the public eye. Normally the more wolflike the youngling, the easier time they had controlling the wolf once they were transformed. It was good that Joshua "fidgeted."

"No, someone took him," Bethy stated firmly. "Someone had been here. They took stuff. Stupid stuff."

"Like his calculus book?" It sounded like Wickers had raided the house for material attuned to Joshua.

"Yes! I couldn't convince Mom and Dad that Joshua wouldn't take all that shit with him. Why the hell would anyone take a twenty-pound jack-o-lantern with them? Someone was here and they took him!"

Seth eyed the kitchen. Yes, there'd been a flood, but there was no sign of a struggle. Joshua knew how to fight and now had werewolf strength to back it. "I think he took a motorcycle."

"What? Oh, he wouldn't...! We didn't think to look... That little..." Bethy charged out of the house.

Seth followed her to the garage. There was a digital keypad that he'd ignored earlier beside the big steel doors. She flipped up the cover and typed in the code.

"Oh, that little shit!" she cried once the door had rattled up high enough to reveal the empty space in the line of off-road vehicles. "That stupid little shit!" She turned in circles, hands in her hair, scanning the land around them. "I'm going to kill him! Where the hell would he go?"

That was what everyone wanted to know.

"Someplace he couldn't just walk to," Seth pointed out. "Is the bike street legal?"

"No! It's his Kawasaki. It's a dirt bike. Besides, he doesn't have a driver's license yet. But there's trails all over the county, he could be literally anywhere."

Anywhere covered a lot of ground. During the same time frame, Seth had traveled from Guadalajara, Mexico, to Utica. Since Joshua didn't have a passport or a driver's license, he was limited to dirt trails or public transportation.

Seth remembered the Amtrak schedule pinned up on the corkboard in Joshua's room. "How much money would he have on him?"

"How the hell would I know?" She stalked back to the house. "He normally works at my family's garage in Utica, but not this year. He found out that my folks could only afford to send him to the local community college. If he wants to go anywhere else, he needs a full scholarship. He spent most of the year studying and got a freaking amazing SAT score. At school this year, he's been doing all the club shit that colleges like you to do to prove you're a joiner. That's why he was at that stupid barn in the first place. Prom committee. And oh my god, if I hear one more 'at least he was supposed to be there' from someone, I'm going to slap them. I don't know why half the freaking football team was at the haunted house when it was supposed to be a prom committee event—maybe the football team was being nice for once—but don't you dare imply that any of them deserved to live more than my brother."

"So he had only a few hundred dollars?" Seth asked.

"You've never been broke?" she cried.

"I've never had money that was strictly mine. I'm not allowed to take a part-time job."

She glanced at the Porsche.

"It's my guardian's car," Seth said. "But, yes, I'm clueless. You said he can get anywhere on the dirt bike. Can he get to the train station?"

"Oh, that little shit!" She started for her car, a vintage black Mustang with a custom flame paint job.

Seth took that as a "yes." "How much would he have for a train ticket?"

She paused, door open, one foot in her car. "He wanted a laptop for school. Mom and Dad said they'd match half. They bought it in August, just before classes started. He had less than a hundred dollars left over."

Seth knew from experience that he could get from New York City to Boston for that amount. Joshua could easily reach Albany or Syracuse. How far would he run? Which direction?

Bethy slammed her car door and her Mustang rumbled to life.

"Where are you going?" Seth asked. Joshua had a full day's head start. He wasn't in Utica anymore.

"If he took the train, then he had to ditch his dirt bike some-place. I'm betting he put it in the storage shed at the garage. It's the only place in Utica where it would be safe and yet my folks wouldn't have noticed it by now."

11: ELISE

There were no rooms in Utica. Not at the Super 8. Not at the Days Inn. Not at the Radisson. The female clerk at the Holiday Inn said, "It's the massacre. We've got all the people here for the funerals tomorrow, the out of town news crews and police helping with the manhunt and big game hunters..."

"Big game hunters?" Eloise had left Cabot in the car after the first strikeout. She glanced nervously out the lobby windows at her Jeep.

The clerk misunderstood her fear. "The wolf is dead. No one has seen hide or hair of a second animal. You don't have to worry."

"Look, I've been awake for nearly forty hours." Elise had tried to book online only to be told that Syracuse had the nearest opening. She was not going to drive another hour. She *couldn't* drive another hour, not without risk of falling asleep and going off the road. There was something about Cabot's deep breathing as he slept in the passenger seat that acted like a sedative on her. "I've been to most of the places in town, asking for a room. Please. I'll take anything."

"Hold on." The clerk took out her phone and texted someone. "My cousin just bought a bed and breakfast across town from this little old lady. It's a big mansion in the downtown historic district. The place has a lot of interesting history behind it. My cousin completely remodeled it, so it's all new inside. She hasn't got the online booking set up yet. She might have a room." She gave a slight laugh. "My cousin is asking if you're one of the heavily armed nutcases."

The clerk didn't actually ask Elise if she was. Elise volunteered nothing.

The clerk typed back something while explaining her cousin's fear. "She was in Starbucks when some out of state idiot walked in with an assault rifle. Scared the shit out of everybody. Okay, she says she has one room left. It's two hundred a night with breakfast included."

"I'll take it," Elise said.

She forgot to ask how many beds it had.

"Interesting history" meant that the Italianate mansion had at one time been a brothel. The hip new owners decided to take the ball and run with it. They remodeled to embrace all things hedonistic. They'd painted the walls a deep red. They'd furnished the room with a massive four-poster bed, a tufted fainting couch done in red velvet, dark stained wood floor, oriental rugs, and suggestive paintings.

"Not a word," Elise growled to Cabot, who leaned heavily on her.

"I'm not saying anything."

The only positive thing about the room was it had a private entrance in the back via a small covered porch. She was able to get Cabot inside without anyone seeing them. She guided him to the bed.

"I thought I'd recover faster than this," Cabot whispered.

"It's only been two hours since you washed the silver poison out of your wounds." She checked the time. "I'm starving. I need to get something to eat and then crash for a while."

"Food sounds wonderful." He unzipped the jumpsuit. Several seams had split during the trip. He skinned off the too tight shoulders. The sudden reveal of skin made Elise's breath catch in her chest. She looked down so all she could see was his feet. He slumped back to lie in the bed with an exhausted sigh.

"Clothes would be good too. Maybe some shoes." He wiggled his toes. How could even his feet seem sexy to her? Was it because they had no blemishes? No callouses. No dry skin. Just male strength contained within perfect skin.

She eyed the fainting couch. If she were five feet tall, she might consider sleeping on it. No, she was going to need to share the king-size bed with him.

This was going to put new meaning in the phrase "strange bedfellows."

She hit Utica's Kmart first to pick up clothes for Cabot.

Shoes, socks, underwear, jeans, shirt, jacket. She wasn't sure if he needed the last but it would help him maintain the illusion of being human. Everyone else in town wore multiple layers against the autumn chill. Elise wore hers to hide her weapons.

It surprised her how much stuff it took to clothe a human being despite wearing clothes every day of her life. She never saw it collected together. When she was eleven, she'd flown to Greece to train without any luggage. She returned to the United States with nothing more than her knives and guns. Her studio loft had a stacked washer and dryer; she did her laundry in small loads. Trips like this were never premeditated enough to allow packing.

The store employees were changing out the Halloween items for the Christmas decorations sprinkled lightly with Thanksgiving baking. The candy had been picked over but she found packages of full-sized candy bars. She considered them insurance against having to deal with a hungry wolf.

Not for the first time in her life, she wondered how normal people lived.

A normal woman wouldn't be trolling through Kmart, buying clothes for a man that had been a wolf when they met. A normal woman spending a night with an impossibly sexy man wouldn't be considering candy bars for "protection."

Was it any wonder that she often felt lost?

Yes, her family had neat little blueprints on how to live the life of an angelic warrior, but it rarely dealt with all the quiet alone time between the hunting and the killing. She'd spent her childhood angry with her mother for spending so much time with Decker. Now that it was her turn, she was discovering that there was no one else. In Greece with her cousins, she couldn't imagine wanting the company of normal people. Moving to Boston had isolated her in ways that she hadn't imagined possible in a city full of people.

A flock of college students fluttered past her, intent on scoring cheap candy. They were an uneven number of boys and girls, weaving in and out of the displays. It was impossible to tell if any of them were paired up, what relationships tied them together, who was best friends with whom, and who had just tagged along.

How did they do that? How did they become a group like that? How did you find people?

She'd tried and failed miserably. She didn't even know where to start looking.

Maybe her attraction to Cabot was because deep down she knew she wouldn't have to explain the knives and the guns and odd scars. That he could carry on a full conversation while making eye contact. That her reaching out to touch him wouldn't trigger a near-rapist response. (Her handful of attempts at dating had ended with broken jaws and black eyes.) That he was like Decker, only actually alive and breathing twenty-four-seven instead of dead half the time. (Okay, so Decker wasn't actually "dead" dead during the daytime but it was close enough in her book.)

Did this deep loneliness trigger a need for physical contact? Or was it the need for physical contact that created the deep loneliness?

She turned the corner to find herself in the "sexual wellness" aisle.

"When I said 'God help me' I didn't expect this kind of answer." She supposed that if the flesh was weak, she'd better be prepared. She had never bought condoms before. Her handful of sexual encounters weren't planned and such things as condoms were an afterthought. So far she'd been lucky. She didn't want to press her luck, not with a werewolf. She scanned the boxes.

"Almost as if wearing nothing at all. Forty condoms? Let's not get carried away; I'm not even sure if I'm going to be needing one. Flavors and Colors? What the hell? It's not a lollipop. Pure ecstasy? Ribbed? Extra large?" She'd purposely not gotten that good of a look. "He can't be huge if that wasn't the first thing that I noticed when he changed shape. Could he?"

The college students suddenly came swooping through the section. She blushed hotly and grabbed a random box. It wasn't until she was two aisles over that she saw that she picked up a thirty count variety pack.

"Oh, hell."

God worked in mysterious ways.

Greek was her comfort food and she was in serious need of comfort. There was a Greek restaurant in town that did takeout. She ordered skewers of lamb and pork souvlaki, pita bread with tzatziki dip, dolomathes, tiropita and baklava. It could have fed four people but she didn't want Cabot to have any excuse to be hungry.

When she came out of the restaurant, there was a pack of wolves waiting for her.

With one Thane dead and another badly wounded, she should have expected to be hip deep in wolves. The five males ringing her Jeep were in human form, but there was no mistaking what they were.

Cabot's blood and scent would be all over her car. She had explaining to do.

"Peace be between us for the good of both our people!" she said as she backed away from the restaurant door. She didn't want innocent people to get caught up in this. "Let us stand as allies, not as foes!"

She recognized the Wolf King's son from his file photos. He was a handsome man. He'd gotten his mother's alabaster skin, rich auburn hair, vivid green eyes, and delicate features. He'd cultured a regal appearance with a three-hundred-dollar haircut and an Armani suit. He looked more like a model than a werewolf, but there was no mistaking the magic that he radiated.

"You're soaked in wolf blood!" Isaiah growled. It was a deep menacing sound that set the hair on the back of her neck on end.

Elise would normally kill anything that made her feel this threatened. She didn't dare pull a weapon; she'd never get a second shot off. "Cabot tangled with a Wicker construct. He had silver poisoning; I needed to drag him to an Earthblood spring." She lifted up the bag of food as evidence. "I'm taking him something to eat."

"You closed with a wolf with silver poisoning?" Isaiah said with disbelief.

"He was lucid," Elise said.

"Why are we bothering talking with her?" one of the Thane at Isaiah's back snapped. By his thick Italian accent, he was probably Luis Silva, a grand nephew of the Prince of Rome. "The Grigori are nothing but homicidal leeches. The world doesn't need their kind anymore."

Isaiah shrugged and Silva took it as permission to attack.

The Thane leaped forward, roaring.

Something big, square, dark blue and flying fast hit Silva at chest level. It struck with such force that it smashed Silva sideways into the building. It wasn't until the object stopped moving that Elise realized that it was a big blue USPS mailbox still anchored to a square of concrete.

"Seth!" the other three Thanes cried while backpedaling quickly.

At first glance, the Prince of Boston was not impressive. Yes, he was tall and wide shouldered, but so were the Thanes. He was still puppy-lean, dressed simply in jeans and gray polo shirt. Nothing about his face and stance indicated he was angry, but his rage crawled over her like static electricity. He didn't need a silk suit to be princely.

"What the hell do you think you're doing?" the prince said quietly. He carefully positioned himself out of striking distance from both the Thane and Elise. "What are you even doing here, Isaiah?"

"Bishop called." Isaiah stepped back. "He said we were to make sure you were safe or there would be hell to pay."

"He told you that there were Wickers in the area," Seth stated as a fact, not a question.

"He said that *something* killed Samuels and wounded Cabot," Isaiah said. "He said it *might* be Wickers. It's suspicious that there's a Grigori here, armed to the teeth, reeking of wolf blood."

"Eleven people are dead!" the young prince shouted and then got his voice back to a low growl. "Half the police in New York are here. Of course there's going to be Grigori looking into it. That's what they do."

Isaiah cringed back. The Thanes retreated a dozen feet, whimpering in fear.

"Go find Samuels' body!" The prince pointed toward the heart of town. "He deserves a decent funeral."

The four Thanes fled, obeying him instantly.

Isaiah took a dozen steps after them before managing to stop and turn. "Father wants you back in New York City where you're safe. If you're killed, Cabot won't be able to take Boston. It will turn him feral."

"Jack is not your concern," the prince said. "You made that clear."

"We couldn't get through to Samuels or Bishop," Isaiah stated.

"Is that the royal 'we,' Isaiah?" the prince asked.

"One day," Isaiah stated like a promise. He turned on his heel and stalked away.

Seth's lips curled back into a silent snarl. He made it clear who he thought was more dangerous; he ignored her until Isaiah turned the corner. Only when they were alone did he turn to look at her.

It was faint, but she could see the resemblance between him and Cabot. He was a younger, darker version of the Thane.

"Do you have enough for three?" Seth asked.

It took her a second to realize he meant the food.

"Yes."

He nodded and pointed toward the bed and breakfast. "I'll follow you to where you've got Jack holed up."

Cabot had stripped off the coveralls and climbed under the linens while she was gone. He came thrashing out of the bed when the young prince followed Elise into the hotel room.

"What—what the hell!" Cabot half-fell out of the bed, naked. "Seth?"

"Clothes!" Elise threw the Kmart bag at him.

"Why aren't you still safe in Mexico?" Cabot fought with the plastic shopping bag. "What are you doing here?"

"Looking for you." Seth paused to take in the red walls and nude paintings. "This is not how I thought I'd find you."

"This is not what it looks..." Cabot paused, staring into the bag. He glanced up to give her a confused look.

She'd forgotten to take the condoms out. "I-I-I like to be prepared for anything."

"Ooookay." He took the package of colored briefs and tossed the bag on the bed. "You can't be here, Seth. It's too dangerous. Go home."

Elise tried to find someplace safe to look as he pulled on the briefs. She hadn't noticed *Leda and the Swan* on the wall by the bathroom door. She didn't recognize the artist but the subject was unmistakable. Unlike other more classical versions, Leda was a petite woman lying prone under a massive swan. Her back was arched in ecstasy. Her legs gripped tight her avian lover, urging it on, instead of fighting it off.

Elise blushed hotly.

Still not safe to look in Cabot's direction. Maybe she should have stuck with the extra large.

The Dream of the Fisherman's Wife was on the wall by the

door. *Who the hell furnished this room?* No wonder the owner had asked if she had children with her when she checked in.

"You can't be here," Cabot was saying. "Go home."

She risked looking back at the Thane. The briefs left little to the imagination but there was actual clothing covering him.

"I'm not leaving without you." The young prince hugged his cousin roughly.

Cabot winced in pain. His wounds hadn't completely healed yet. "Seth, please, I'm a Thane first before a Tatterskein. My duty is to my king before my prince. He set me on a mission. An important mission."

"You're all I have left." Seth released him to pace the room restlessly. "Isaiah is here with Silva, Russo, Tawfeek and Hoffman. They can deal with the Wickers."

"I have things yet to do." Cabot fished one of the T-shirts out of the bag. "Please, please, please, just go home."

"Ilya isn't in Utica anymore," Seth said.

"Who?" Elise asked.

"Ilya?" Cabot stood a moment, mouth open, as he worked through some mental problem. When he came to the solution, he swore loudly. "Ilya! Oh, how could I be so stupid? Ilya! He's alive? Where is he?"

Seth spread his hands in ignorance. "He bolted. He could be anywhere on the East Coast."

"Damn it. I can't believe I screwed this up so bad." Cabot attempted to put on the blue jeans. He would have fallen if Seth hadn't caught him. "We need—we need to..."

"We need to eat." Seth steadied Cabot as he finished dressing. "And then sleep. You're not going to be any use to anyone the way you are now."

Cabot sighed. "Fine, but you need to stay with me where it's safe."

Everyone knew that hungry wolves were dangerous wolves. Elise decided to hold her questions until the two had a chance to eat.

It was a surreal meal. The room had no tables or chairs, so they sat on the floor and ate with their fingers. The food was comfortingly familiar even if the company was not. Elise was careful not to get between the werewolves and the skewers of meat. She filled up on the stuffed grape leaves and cheese pies.

Cabot yawned his way through repeating much of what

he'd told her earlier, only in greater detail. He ended with, "The teacher who told us that the kids were at the barn must have been a puppet working off a script. He handed us a flyer that had a map and everything. There were posters for the haunted house all over the school, so we didn't stop to think that it was odd that he gave the flyer to us."

"The chief of police is a puppet," she warned them. "He passed out silver ammo to all the men on the wolf hunt. He was so tightly scripted he barely knew what way was up. The head of the coven is a powerful witch. I'll have to be careful around her."

"I thought Grigori are immune," Seth said. "We are."

"We can be taken by surprise and held long enough to kill us. Nothing more than that, but still, a few seconds..."

"I should warn the Thanes." Seth took out a cell phone. He typed on the screen for a minute and then sighed and put it away. He took out a second phone.

"Two phones?" Elise asked.

"This one is Jack's." Seth tried to hand the phone to his cousin, but Cabot had fallen asleep sitting up. Seth pulled on the Thane's shoulder so he ended up slumped across Seth's legs.

Yes, the thirty-count box of condoms was complete overkill. She obviously misjudged the Thane's healing abilities.

Her dismay must have shown on her face.

"I'm his alpha." Seth patted his sleeping cousin on the head. "I can speed up his healing by strengthening his connection to the Source but I need to be in physical contact with him."

Which meant it wasn't going to be her and Cabot in the big poster bed. She was going to be spending the night on the tiny fainting couch. She salved her disappointment with baklava.

The prince tapped on Cabot's phone, unlocking it. "I don't have contact information for Isaiah or any of the Thanes that are with him. If I'm going to warn them, I'm going to have to use Jack's phone." He typed in a message. "Assuming the idiot will actually read anything from Jack."

He meant Isaiah.

She'd been surprised at how hostile the older werewolf had been toward the young prince. She assumed it was because Seth was protecting her against the Thanes. That Seth didn't have Isaiah's phone number indicated a deeper reason. "Why wouldn't he?"

"Because Isaiah hates me and Jack is mine."

"Yours?" Surely he didn't mean it the way it sounded.

"My heir. If something happens to me, Jack is the only—was the only wolf left of the Tatterskein bloodline. Heirs have a tighter connection to the Source than a normal pack wolf. It makes them higher rank because they're more dominant. Before I came to New York, Isaiah was the uncontested leader of the Thanes. His father leaves much of the day-to-day business of the Castle to Isaiah. There was an assumption that Alexander would shortly hand over New York to him. It was the entire reason for Isaiah's existence. His mother Raisa Artemyeva had been the result of a thousand years of careful breeding."

"The Wolf King has been breeding his own people like dogs?"

"He needs to. If he didn't strengthen the bloodlines, there wouldn't have been wolves strong enough to hold the more powerful territories. New York wasn't the first city Alexander had to hold himself. It was Athens first. Rome second. Paris third. London fourth. He was in Moscow before coming to New York. Each time he had to move and stand as the city's prince until he could breed a bloodline strong enough to hold the territory."

"I was taught the names of the cities he's held, but not why."

"The other failures weren't as public," Seth said.

It was a polite way to say that Pritt Eskola, the heir to the first prince, had gone feral after his uncle died. Eskola mowed his way through colonial New York. He'd killed nearly ten percent of the population, including his entire pack as they attempted to stop him. The deaths were later blamed on a yellow fever outbreak. Luckily Alexander got to North America before Eskola could lay waste to the entire continent.

The second failure had been under Alexander's close supervision and quietly eliminated. The two attempts had been a hundred years apart, which had always confused Elise in their timing. She realized now that the Wolf King had a house of cards; he had to maintain the strength of existing packs while building a new, stronger bloodline. This explained the arranged marriages and the fact that he often juggled brides from all over the world. Seth's parents were a prime example; his mother had been a careful blend of ancient bloodlines of Spanish princes sprinkled lightly with native Caxcan. Guadalajara might be only an Earldom, but the Wolf King had obviously bred it up so he could bolster old bloodlines without fear of inbreeding.

"He fathered Isaiah solely to become the Prince of New York?" Elise asked.

"That was his intent. The question remains if he was successful. Raisa had been the daughter of the Prince of Saint Petersburg and the granddaughter of the Princes of Istanbul and Kiev. She was fiery tempered and none of the Thanes could stand before her anger, except Jack's father, Anton. They were second cousins through Anton's mother." Seth patted his sleeping cousin's head. "After Raisa killed herself, though, it seemed like Alexander might have inbred her bloodline too much. It was obvious that Alexander was afraid that Isaiah would go feral; he sent Isaiah to Saint Petersburg to be changed by his grandfather."

What was the Wolf King waiting for? Considering that Seth became Prince of Boston at thirteen, Isaiah should be old enough to become the Prince of New York.

"Isaiah is what? Thirty?"

"Twenty-nine. Every year that Alexander doesn't hand over New York to his son, the more like a spoiled brat Isaiah acts. Lately, it's like he's only nine years old, jealous of every little imagined slight. Isaiah hates me. He hated that I was my father's heir when I showed up at the Castle and could meet his gaze. Then I became Prince of Boston at thirteen while he was still just a Thane at twenty-six."

Seth leaned over to press his face into Jack's shoulder. "I felt my entire family die. One by one. My mom. My aunts and uncles. My cousins. My little brothers. And then my father— which thankfully hit me like a freight train—so I didn't have to remember." He laughed bitterly. "And Isaiah's jealous of me. Jealous! The first few months, he'd pick fights with me because I didn't know how to use my power yet. I tried to get Alexander to stop him but Alexander would only say 'you're a prince, you stop him.' I figured out how; that's when Isaiah started in on Jack. And Alexander only said 'learn to protect what is yours.' I never thought Isaiah would actually let Jack die just to hurt me until Friday."

And Elise thought her family was psycho.

Seth rubbed his eyes. "I'm completely fried. There's no way I can drive back to the city. We'll go back tomorrow."

Elise nodded. It was too dangerous to keep the teenage prince in the line of fire. If he would only leave with Cabot in tow, then so be it. It only went to prove that God had a sense of humor.

12: DECKER

The house was silent and still.

Decker felt his heart go cold when he stepped out of his sleeping chamber and realized that his puppy was gone. He should have woken Joshua up last night and asked him plainly to stay.

It was night, as usual, but it seemed darker than normal.

He sat in the lone chair without bothering to turn on the light. Dawn was twelve long hours away. He couldn't believe that, at one time, he felt as if he'd never have enough time to do everything he wanted. Now he wished that he could sleep whole seasons away.

"Rally," he whispered to himself. "Rally. So maybe it's not to be with that puppy, but I could get another puppy."

But that was so unlikely that he couldn't fool himself into believing it. Werewolves guarded their children fiercely. They'd never let someone blithely take one away. Decker was over three hundred years old and he'd never heard of a stray puppy before. Even the young Prince of Boston had been snatched up by the Wolf King to be kept safe in New York City. Joshua was a rare, rare prize.

One that someone was desperate to capture.

"He really shouldn't be left running around the city alone." Decker stood and paced in the narrow cleared space in front of the chair. Joshua could have left minutes after sunrise and Decker wouldn't know. All he could know was that the boy left sometime during the day, which meant he could literally be anywhere in the world. Humans traveled at insane speeds this century. Zip.

Zap. Zoom. He could have taken a plane to the other side of the country. Or the other side of the world.

But Joshua had no money. Surely, an airplane ticket was more than a subway token. (Not that they used tokens anymore, it was getting harder and harder to keep up with the newest way to pay for things.) Joshua was penniless.

Unless he'd pinched Decker's wallet.

His wallet was still on the foyer table. Decker leafed through the bills, trying to remember how much cash he had the night before. There didn't seem to be any missing.

"Oh Joshua, if you were going to run, you should have taken money. A hungry wolf is a dangerous wolf." If one of the Grigori besides Elise—and perhaps including Elise—ran across him losing his temper in public, they'd kill him.

If the boy didn't want to stay with him, so be it. But if Decker honestly liked the boy, then he should protect Joshua by getting him to someone else to care for him. The wolves or the Grigori.

The wolves, he decided. He'd call the Wolf King's castle and let them know that one of their newborns had gone astray.

Decker reached for his phone and discovered it gone. "What? You leave the money but take the phone? That doesn't make sense."

He realized then that the urn full of coins was missing and his house keys.

"You only take keys when you need to get back into a locked house! He went out but he's coming back! Yes! Yes! Yes! He was probably hungry. He probably went out to get food! He's coming back!"

The happiness only lasted a minute until he realized that the boy should be back already. He'd told Joshua he'd take him out for a big steak dinner. If Joshua had gone out for food, he would have left hours ago, not shortly before sunset.

"Something's happened to him! I need to find him. Quickly. Elise can help me!" Decker reached for his phone again and then remembered that it was gone. No matter, he could use . . . No, the house no longer had a phone. Since no one called him, it seemed like an unnecessary expense. Besides, he hadn't memorized Elise's number since he only had to tap on her name. "Oh good God, why did they ever give up operators? You pick up the receiver and talk to a real, honest-to-God human being and she'd figure out what you needed. It was so simple, even I could do it!"

Someone started up the front steps. Keys jingled and he realized that his puppy had made it home. He shouldn't let Joshua know how worried he was. Decker headed for his chair. He'd act like he was patiently waiting. No, wait, what if something bad had really happened? Wouldn't it be better to show him how concerned he really was?

He was doing this frantic side-to-side step when the door opened.

His puppy looked scared to death. He walked into the foyer and thumped against Decker's chest with a whimper. Decker put his arms around the boy, who was shaking like a leaf.

"What's wrong?" Decker said.

Joshua whimpered something about possessed Vespa, universal law of probability, tissue boxes, Barbie dolls, giant ghost wolves and wrong-way streets. He ended quite clearly with "Red lights mean stop!"

"Yes, they do." Decker knew that much from simple observation. He didn't actually drive, but traffic lights hadn't changed for a hundred years. Even he had caught on to the regulations. What he didn't understand was: what was so upsetting about traffic signals?

Motion beyond the open door caught his eye. A purple-haired woman stood on the top step, eyes wide in surprise. Behind her was a willowy spirit guide.

He didn't know what they'd done to scare his puppy so badly. He wasn't about to let them continue. He hissed, showing his fangs.

The woman squeaked and ran. She mounted a purple motorized bike and sped away.

Interlopers taken care of, Decker focused on calming down his puppy. "There, there, have you eaten?"

Joshua pulled away to turn in circles. He seemed to be looking for a clear spot to put his plastic bags down. "Organic apple chicken sausage!"

Those four words did not go together.

"I promised you a steak dinner," Decker reminded the boy. "Are you hungry?"

Joshua dropped his bags. "Meat!"

Decker was going to take that as a "yes."

One steak dinner later, Decker had only a slightly better grasp on what was upsetting his puppy. It had been a traumatic day. As Joshua inhaled grilled meat, he leapfrogged through the events, looping back again and again to "the Vespa." Things got a little clearer when Decker realized that the said Vespa was the purple motorized bicycle, and not a giant Italian wasp.

The other recurrent comment was the lack of basic items in Decker's house. Toilet paper was cited three times before Joshua explained that he'd lost one of his grocery bags on Massachusetts Avenue. The packaging burst when it hit the pavement at high speed, toilet papering a block and a half of Cambridge.

That led to the mysterious outburst of "But I'm not doing that creepy funeral urn again! I'm done with that!"

Decker was sure that sooner or later, he'd know everything that had happened during the day. He wanted to focus on mending fences; the better to keep his puppy from roaming.

"As soon as you finish your pie, we'll go to a store and get everything a home needs." Anything to keep Joshua from disappearing again.

Decker wondered how Joshua had moved before he became a werewolf, because taking the boy to the store *was* like walking a puppy. A full tummy and the promise of toilet paper returned Joshua to high spirits. He led the way to a store by the name of Target. Joshua bounced with excitement. He cocked his head in confusion. He pounced on things that interested him. He did a little shift-shift-shift of the hips that would have been a tail wag if he had one. Decker struggled not to laugh out loud at times because he wasn't sure how the boy would feel once he was made aware of it. If it wasn't how he used to move, the boy might try to act more human.

And it was far too cute to put an end to it.

So he followed Joshua through the store, secretly grinning ear to ear.

Decker hadn't been in a large store for a very long time. He couldn't remember when he last ventured into a department store. Much had changed in the world since that time. It was like walking onto the surface of another planet. One with an artificial sun blazing with stark bright light. The new world stretched on and on under a metal sky with row upon row of shelving. It seemed to Decker marvelously bright and cheerful, but it could be just be the company he was keeping.

"I got garbage bags," Joshua was saying. "I had no idea how expensive they were. I got like seventy of them. I think that might only be enough to do like one or two rooms." He paused, head tilted, with a slightly worried look. "You're okay with me throwing things out?"

"Much of it is dross I should have thrown away long ago." At least everything they'd taken out of Joshua's bedroom had been.

Tail wag. "Good! Some hoarders don't want to let go of anything."

"I'm not a hoarder." Decker felt the need to clarify things for his puppy. "I had grown used to having people who would shift through my belongings, put away things that obviously needed to be kept, and do—something—with the rest. At one time, 'something' was to simply carry it outside and fling it into the midden or set it on fire. I know people now have rubber barrels and large square metal bins full of garbage, but I have no idea of how they become empty."

"Oh! Well, that makes sense." A bounce and tail wag. "Oh, wait, I'm not sure how that's done either." Unhappy puppy pout followed as Joshua realized that life wasn't as simple as he thought. "Back home, Thursday was trash day. I had to move the cans to the curb in the morning; because of the coyotes and raccoons and such, we couldn't put them out the night before. The truck came while I was at school. First thing I had to do when I got home was move the cans back to the garage."

"That seems fairly straightforward."

"Well, I don't know where my parents got the cans. They're special cans that the truck can lift with hydraulics and the name of the company is printed on the sides."

"See. This is the same kind of problem I had. The person who provides the can most likely only works daylight hours."

Tail wag. "You really do need my help."

Decker grinned. "Yes. I need to be saved from drowning in darkness."

Bounce. "I can use your phone to research it. On TV shows they always get a dumpster. You start at the front door and just work to the right, separating things as you go into keep, donate, recycle and toss. The tossed stuff goes straight out the door and into the dumpster."

Joshua was sounding Decker out for permission to get a

dumpster—if he could figure out how that was done. Decker
wanted to be as encouraging as possible. "Sounds like a good plan."

A total body wriggle. If he had a tail, it would be a blur
right now. Decker wondered what size of wolf Joshua was going
to be when he transformed. While Decker would love it if the
boy turned out to be a small bundle of fur, chances were his
wolf-form wouldn't be as puppylike as Decker would hope.

"Oh!" Bounce. Joshua pointed to a banner beyond the shoe
department. It read: Home. "We need towels!"

Decker smiled happily at the sign. *Home.* "Fetch some then!"

Joshua bounded into the section and pounced on sage green
towels. He only selected one of the largest to put in the cart.
That was a boy for you. Decker picked up enough to make two
full sets: bath, hand, and washcloth.

"I don't need..." Joshua stopped cold to stare at a mirror
in the shoe section beside them. It showed him standing alone
beside the cart. His head cocked in confusion as he realized that
Decker wasn't reflected in the mirror. Joshua looked at Decker
and then at his own reflection. He waved his hand in front of
Decker, and then walked back and forth between Decker and the
mirror. "That—that—that's seriously, *seriously* creepy."

Decker sighed. "Yes, that is a little hard to deal with at first.
Thank god I don't need to shave anymore, or I'd look like I'd
been in cat fights daily." He picked up a bath mat. "Which of
these shower curtains do you want?"

His puppy was oddly hesitant about picking up items that even
Decker knew he needed to lead a normal life. Decker plucked
up items that Joshua bypassed, like a matched bathroom set of
trashcan, soap dish, toothbrush holder, and some kind of odd
brush on a long stick that could be stored hidden inside a plastic
container. Decker wasn't sure what it was for but obviously every
bathroom needed one.

The next section was bedding. Pillows, sheets, blankets, and
something called "Aerobed" went into the cart. Around the corner
they hit the kitchen items. Decker stopped beside the display of
dish sets.

"These cost a lot of money," Joshua protested. "I can use
paper plates."

Decker wanted as much stuff as possible cementing the boy

into his life. He was going to build walls around Joshua using towels and sheets and dishes. It would be a gilded cage of things that belonged in the house and yet only Joshua would use. Decker wanted everything possible to keep Joshua from disappearing again. "A set of dishes would be cheaper in the long run."

"They're sixty dollars."

Which didn't seem like a lot of money compared to the Wedgewood china that Decker used to have.

"I want a home and a home has real plates," Decker pressed. The boy would be less likely to leave a house that felt like a home. His home.

"There are these!" Joshua picked up a cheap plastic dish sold individually. "I just need one."

Decker sighed. "If I hired anyone else to work for me, I still would have to buy things for them to use. In the houses I had before this one, I had a large household of servants. I supplied uniforms, dishes, bedding, food—everything."

"So you have dishes?"

Decker tried to condense a very long story. "I lost them."

"Well, I could use paper plates until we find them."

He had condensed too much. "Lost them as in my house was burned down."

"Oh, I'm sorry." Joshua paused and tilted his head in puppy confusion. "*Was burned down?* You mean—someone set fire to it?"

"Yes. Villagers don't come with pitchforks anymore, but the end result in terms of real estate has stayed the same. Saul—Elise's grandfather—helped me find this house after my last one burned. He felt responsible. Saul was young and felt that my employees should be warned of certain dangers. He didn't realize how badly that could go."

Joshua looked horrified. "One of your servants set fire to your house?"

"It's a long, long story—" Decker sighed as the puppy looked hurt. The boy had spent the day getting mere glimpses of larger pictures. Even though Decker would rather not explain in detail, he decided to make Joshua happy.

"It wasn't me that Saul was worried about—in terms of attacking my servants—but all the other monsters that I deal with on a regular basis. I help the Grigori track evil, which occasionally makes me a target. It is why my house is warded. Saul thought it was only fair that my servants should know what they might have to face. I had a beautiful young woman who worked for me. She had a very insane boyfriend—or better to say, a suitor who wanted to be more than just an acquaintance. My servant let slip the truth about my nature and he decided that the reason he was getting nowhere with his courtship was because I was obviously using my vampire powers to hold her in thrall. The truth was that she simply knew her worth and his lack of it but she was afraid of him, so she tried to scare him off by hiding behind me."

Joshua pretended to look at dishes. He was actually having an internal debate—accompanied by cute faces. The boy wanted to ask something but wasn't sure he wanted to know the answer. After several minutes, he asked tentatively, "Did you kill her suitor for burning down your house?"

"No." At the time, Decker had been disappointed that he didn't have the chance to do so, but now he was glad. Joshua obviously didn't want him to be a killer; relief flashed across his puppy's face. "Saul did."

"What! Really?"

"He was fond of my servant. She'd called him in a panic, and then went into the burning house to save me. She—she died. Saul made sure I was safe and then tracked down the idiot and killed him."

If Joshua had had puppy ears, they'd be drooping with hurt and dismay.

Decker patted him on the head. "It's okay. It was a long, long time ago."

"But you liked her and she died."

"Yes." She was just one of many, many people he'd lost over time. At least werewolves were long lived—if monsters didn't kill them.

Joshua tilted his head. "Is that why you only have the one chair? You lost everything when your old house burned down?"

"Yes."

"But you said that was 1959. Why didn't you buy more furniture and stuff?"

"I bought stuff. I have a house full of stuff."

"No! I mean things like dishes instead of record players and hula hoops."

"I thought—wrongly—that I didn't need them." Decker had

believed he didn't need dishes because he didn't eat. If he didn't eat off dishes, he had no need for a dining room table and chairs. Things somehow spiraled out of control from there. "I might not use these things for myself, but I need them, because I need people in my life."

Joshua considered the dishes on display and picked up a box of the simple but elegant white squares of china. Glasses and silverware went into the cart.

Decker glanced about trying to remember what was in his last kitchen for his servants' use. There had been pots and pans but currently his house did not have a stove. Oddly the store seemed to have no appliances. Joshua would need something to keep meat in. What did they call those things that replaced iceboxes? "Refrigerators. We should see if they sell them."

"Only little ones for dorms, but that's probably good enough." Joshua pointed at something no bigger than a hatbox. "Bethy has one in her dorms at college. She's supposed to give it to me when she graduates this spring."

Decker supposed that the miniature refrigerator would work as a stopgap measure. They would need to go shopping elsewhere for appliances and furniture.

"How are we going to get all this back to your house?" Joshua said and then with a little fear, asked, "We're not calling Winnie, are we?"

"Hansom cab." Decker slipped and used the old term. It got him an adorable tilt of the head. "I mean, taxi."

There were weird boxes around the next counter. He thought that they might be televisions until Joshua opened one up. They seemed to be breadboxes merged with a telephone. Joshua inspected them carefully.

"You want one?" Decker was surprised at how much these odd breadboxes cost. The cheapest was sixty dollars. What were they? The sticker on the shelf stated: Emerson 900 Watt Microwave.

"Yes," Joshua admitted guiltily. "I should have something I can cook food with. You don't have a range. I used the microwave at home—my parents' house—all the time."

Mystified, Decker shifted items in the cart around to fit the new box into it. If "home" had a microwave, then his house should have one too. Maybe he should buy two.

13: JOSHUA

They were halfway home in the taxi when Joshua realized that he'd forgotten paint. He whimpered—something he was doing distressingly often.

"Hm?" Decker leaned close so the driver wouldn't overhear them.

"I wanted to paint my bedroom. I forgot to look to see if Target carried paint."

The day had left Joshua feeling lost and confused even in the familiar surroundings of Target. All the store's departments had been in different places than the one in Utica. Tomorrow would be Monday. He wouldn't be getting up for school. He wouldn't be eating lunch with his friends. He wouldn't be going to the dojo after school. There would be no eating dinner in the living room with his parents while watching *Jeopardy*. As he thought of everything he'd lost, the universe seemed to open up wider and wider, and he felt even more adrift.

The TV shows on hoarding were all about people rebuilding their lives. They'd had their lives nuked in a totally different way; they were buried under the rubble of their own addiction. It gave him a framework. All the hoarder shows had the same formula. Declutter. Strip off any wallpaper. Roll on a coat of cheery yellow or calming blue paint (never white). Voila, a new life. Cue the weeping with joy.

The shows seemed to regard paint as some kind of magical elixir. Joshua had his doubts but he wasn't going to mess the formula. "I don't know a thing about painting a room. Do you?"

"No, painting is not my forte, at least not walls," Decker said. "I've painted pictures. In my time, gentlemen were expected to learn to draw and paint. I suspect because if you wanted to illustrate something you had in your head, you couldn't simply find the likeness in the Sears Roebuck catalog. You needed to draw it yourself."

Sears Roebuck?

Joshua dug his new pens and notebooks out of the shopping bags. He wrote: *paint, brushes, whatever. Watch some YouTube videos on painting a room. Pick up paint chips.*

"Paint chips?" Decker read over his shoulder.

Joshua blushed with embarrassment as he realized that somehow he'd scooted so close to Decker that he was nearly on the man's lap. Every time he stopped paying attention to what he was doing, he ended up leaning against Decker. It was some weird werewolf reflex. At least Decker didn't seem to notice. Joshua still had Decker's phone in his jacket pocket. He pulled it out, using the movement to casually slide away from the vampire. "Samples of paint colors. I've seen them every time I've been in a hardware store with my folks. They're pieces of paper with like a zillion colors. You can take them home. See how they look in your house."

A quick search brought up two hardware stores within a half-mile of Decker's house. "I can hit one of these tomorrow."

"I like most greens," Decker mysteriously stated. "Not crazy about the pale mint green that was popular in the fifties, but just about anything else is good."

"What?"

"Your favorite color. It's green."

"It is?" It kind of felt right and wrong at the same time.

Decker laughed. "You got green towels. Green sheets. All the shirts you picked out were green. It's not that hard to guess."

If it was not so hard to guess, why did he have to think about it? Was it really his favorite or was this some new werewolf preference? Why would werewolves have favorite colors?

Was he seriously overthinking all this?

No, he wasn't thinking enough. He had all these new weird werewolf quirks and no idea what triggered them. Decker said Joshua didn't have to worry about the full moon, but what if Decker was wrong? "After we get everything unloaded, can you show me the coal cellar?"

"The coal cellar?" Decker must have forgotten.

"You said—" Joshua remembered that they weren't alone. He glanced toward the cab driver, then leaned over to whisper. "You said we could use it as a cage for the wolf."

"I don't think you'll need it," Decker said.

"Why not?"

"Saul arranged for me to meet with the Prince of Boston when I moved from Philadelphia. It was the only way I could have stayed in the city."

"What was he like?"

"I told you about how most monsters don't have an off switch? How they're always on and uncontrollable because of that? You've seen those little bitty Christmas lights, the single white bulb?" Decker pinched his fingers together to describe tiny. "That's what most monsters are like, little lights, always on. Magically. Once you feel it enough times, you'll understand more. The potential. What you see is what you get. I made the mistake of taking the prince by surprise. He looked like a normal man. Tall. Black hair. Dark brown eyes. Not particularly strong or striking looking. But then, as I startled him, he turned on his power. He didn't change, not a single hair on his head, or even the color of his eyes, but I felt like I'd just touched the surface of the sun. He controlled all of Boston and most of the state and I could feel that. There's not an inch of his territory where I could go and stay hidden. He would know. That's why Saul had to introduce me. Otherwise the prince would have sensed my presence, assumed the worst, and hunted me down."

"So he seemed completely human—until he didn't?"

"Yes. If you're like the Prince of Boston, you control the switch, not the moon."

He remembered Winnie saying how Seth would check on her at night from New York City. Then there was that weirdness with the Wolf King *thing* that showed up at Sioux Zee's. No, he wasn't like that at all. He could be just like the legends. Decker certainly was conforming to the vampires in stories. "You go down for the count at sunrise."

"I'm a different kind of beast entirely. You have a reflection, I don't."

"Why is that? That doesn't make any sense."

"Like I told you. Logic is for men. Magic is for monsters."

14: DECKER

"I don't think this is necessary." Decker wasn't going to stop Joshua though. He knew what it was like to be scared of yourself. Or more truthfully, the monster within.

Decker had used the vacuum on the little room after Joshua had fallen asleep the night before but coal dust still lingered on every surface.

"This is good." Joshua stepped into the room. "I can put down my bed." He rubbed at his nose and sneezed into the crook of his elbow. "You can lock me in here."

"I'll stay with you." Decker swung the door closed behind him.

"I might hurt you." Joshua huddled in the corner. Scared little puppy.

"I doubt it." Decker made sure the door was bolted tight and then went to sit beside Joshua. "I know how you feel. Well—not exactly. My curse is different. Not better. Not worse. There's no way to compare the two."

Where was he going with this? He didn't know. He wasn't sure what to tell Joshua to make him feel better.

His puppy leaned against him. "How did you become a vampire?"

"I was a diviner..."

"A what?"

"Someone that uses a dowsing rod to find hidden objects. I could find things. I still can, not that I look often. It's one of the reasons I never bothered to clean up my house. No matter how messy it gets, I can find what I want. It's considered a gift from God. It's why the Grigori allow me to live. Why Saul believed in me. Why Elise trusts me in a limited fashion."

"Wait. Is that how you knew where the huntsman was in the park?"

"Yes. And it's how I found you yesterday. I had a sense that there was something I needed if I only looked for it. I zigzagged all over the Back Bay until I found you killing trees. Using my gift is a painfully slow process, which is why I needed your help to find Elise quickly."

"Wow. That's cool." Joshua sneezed again.

"It was a two-edged sword. I've always been able to find what I needed to live a life of ease. The gift, however, was considered by the ignorant masses to be black magic. I was hounded from one home to another. Then one day, the world changed, and I was caught up in it."

"What changed?" Joshua scooted closer. The puppy would have had his ears perked with interest.

"The Wolf King took residence in New York City."

"Huh? How did that make you a vampire? I don't get it."

"There is a basic truth about the werewolves that the Grigori hate to admit. For thousands of years, the Grigori killed all monsters, including werewolves. Despite their efforts, empires would rise and then fall into darkness, as monsters would spawn at the very heart of the capitals. Babylon was just one of many. Any time men gathered in numbers, breaches in the very fabric of reality would happen, as if the weight of so many souls in one place tore holes open and let in monsters.

"Then one day the Grigori realized that the werewolves weren't settling in towns; villages were growing up around the wolves and becoming cities. The Wolf King and his people are guard dogs. Their very presence protects the integrity of the world. Where there are wolves, breaches are rare, and when they happen, the wolves can close them. The truth was indisputable: humans need werewolves to prosper. So the Grigori made peace with the Wolf King, and his people were allowed to multiply freely in Europe and Africa and Asia."

"Not here?" Joshua pointed down at the cellar floor, meaning the United States.

"The Americas had not been discovered yet. As soon as the

colonies were established, the Wolf King started to tap alphas to guard the new land. He sent his wolves to Boston. Philadelphia. New York." He reached out to pat his scared puppy on the head. "See. Werewolves are good things. They keep the city safe. Everyone that can tell that you're a werewolf knows that. You don't need to be scared."

"Yay me." Joshua didn't sound happy. He put his head on Decker's shoulder. "There was a big guy at Sioux Zee's. He was scared of me."

"People are scared of police too."

Joshua sneezed loudly. In that split second of noise, he transformed. A wolf sat in his place. A very small black wolf puppy.

Decker stared at it in surprise. "That—that is unexpected."

The puppy whimpered in distress. Quiet at first and then growing in volume as it picked up its paws and stared at them.

"Hush. Hush. You're fine." Decker scooped him up. "You're fine. I'm here. I won't let anything happen to you. You're fine."

Something was very, very wrong. Decker knew that magic didn't follow the rules of science, but it seemed inconceivable that a hundred-and-twenty-pound man could become a twenty-pound puppy.

But he couldn't let Joshua realize that.

"There. See. You're fine." He couldn't think of any other words of comfort. He was a little too freaked out to think of anything. "Hush. I won't let anything happen to you."

Whimpering, the puppy burrowed into the space between Decker's arm and chest until his entire head was tucked into Decker's armpit.

"It's okay." Decker petted the puppy, trying to think of something sane and reasonable to say. After several minutes of silence, he took up his story. He might as well distract Joshua with his own tale of woe.

The Wolf King sent alphas to the Colonies. The prince that he sent to New York had been killed and his heir wasn't strong enough to take the alpha. Decker probably shouldn't mention that wolf or the following massacre.

"But—for some reason—the Wolf King decided that he would come to New York City himself. It was like rats fleeing a sinking ship; every monster abandoned its lair and fled before the Wolf King. I was on the road between New York and Philadelphia, running once again from people who thought I was the devil in flesh, when a wave of real monsters washed over the land. I'd stopped at an inn for the night. A vampire attacked in a feeding frenzy. Each person it fed on became a monster like it. It was a madness that grew like a fire, consuming everything until I was the last one alive in a small attic room. Only I wasn't like everyone else in the inn; I had my rare and magical gift. I could channel power. So when the monster tore open a hole into that monstrous realm, I could choose to shape the power that flowed out into a weapon or I could, for a time, close it off. I killed the vampires in the inn. God protected me—in that the last monster had fled into a coal cellar just like this one. When the sun rose and I fell senseless, I was hidden away until night—"

Decker paused as he realized a flaw in his plan that could be catastrophic. He'd assumed that Joshua was needlessly afraid and they'd leave the coal cellar shortly. He hadn't counted on Joshua changing and not being able to revert to human.

This could be a problem.

Joshua had never seen Decker senseless. Saul had described it as very unsettling. Joshua wasn't going to be able to cope with seemingly dead Decker on top of being stuck a puppy. Nor did Decker want to leave the coal cellar before Joshua had figured out how to change back. Despite his cavalier speech, he knew things went wrong with newborn werewolves. If Joshua lost control, the Grigori would come hunting his puppy, treaty or no treaty.

"Enough about me," Decker said. "We've determined that yes, you can become a wolf. Let's work on getting back to being a human."

For several minutes all he got out of Joshua were muffled whimpers. Decker couldn't tell if he was trying to change back, trying to talk, or just committed to freaking out in a very typically Joshua way (which thankfully was a very Zen peaceful but noisy way). Decker found himself thinking of funny things that the boy *might* be saying.

"*Why am I so tiny? This is so unfair! Not only am I a stuck being a werewolf, I'm a puppy.*"

It did not help that as Decker thought "puppy" Joshua wailed something that sounded remarkably close to the word.

"You're a very cute puppy," Decker said.

Joshua went absolutely still and silent.

Decker's sense of humor was going to get him killed one of these days. Teasing a werewolf while locked in a small dusty room was probably not a wise thing to do. He scrambled to think of a way to salvage that comment. "To me, you have always been a cute little puppy." No, that probably wasn't the right thing to say either.

Joshua sneezed again.

Decker found himself three feet off the ground with the head of a wolf the size of a draft horse wedged under his arm. He dangled there, too surprised to move. Not good.

With horses, you always wanted to control their head. He tightened his hold on Joshua's head.

The wolf shook him loose. Joshua sat back onto his haunches and banged his head on the coal cellar's roof. In the drift of loosened dust, Joshua lifted a paw the size of a dinner platter up to stare at it intently.

"This—this is actually a step forward." Decker lay on the floor, carefully not moving. "You've managed to transform again. So let's try for a human or at least human-sized."

Joshua sneezed. He became a human-sized wolf.

"Good! That's progress—"

Joshua sneezed again and became the draft horse wolf.

This was going to be a long night.

For the next two hours, Joshua was every imaginable size of wolf. Only his coloring stayed constant. Decker was starting to despair that Joshua would ever get back to normal. They were lucky that it was November and the nights were long. They still had hours before dawn, but time was running out.

Plan B. Set up the house so his puppy could survive the day without supervision.

"Enough of this! Let's go upstairs and clear the kitchen and unpack the new refrigerator and microwave."

Joshua was currently a draft-horse-sized wolf. He'd bumped his head on the ceiling again and was rubbing the spot between his ears with his giant paw. He paused to stare at Decker. "Hrm?"

Decker unbolted the door. "Since your bedroom is cleared, the next logical room to work on is the kitchen. I'm fairly sure there's nothing in the kitchen that I want. I should make sure before you pitch everything out. We have a few hours yet. We can clear it in no time."

It seemed like a brilliant plan until he reached the kitchen and picked up the first armful of clutter. There was no good place to put it down. He picked his way through the downstairs carrying the armful. Should he take it upstairs?

Giant wolf Joshua appeared with something in his teeth. He dropped it on the floor in front of Decker. It was an orange box that read: HEFTY EXTRA STRONG LARGE TRASH DRAWSTRING BAG.

"Ah, I see. Put it in a bag and then—then—put it outside until the dumpster comes. Yes. Very good." Decker puzzled his way through opening the box. When did boxes get this complicated? Inside was a thick roll of plastic. Individual bags peeled off the roll like layers of an onion. "How ingenious."

He fought the large slick piece of plastic looking for the opening. "I know there has to be an opening! The picture shows a drawstring bag! One of these sides must be it! No. No. No. No. No. Oh come on, one of them has to be the right one. There! Finally!"

Wolf puppy Joshua darted in and out between his legs, shoving stray items into the bag as Decker filled the first one. After they'd filled a bag, giant-size Joshua would carry it outside. (Decker didn't think it was wise for Joshua to leave the house but he had no way to stop that big a wolf. Luckily the driveway was shielded from view in the back.) They cleared the floor first and then worked on the counter.

What did living creatures need? Decker was no longer sure. Food. That was the easy one. Unearthing the kitchen sink reminded him that water was another must.

The faucets were smooth round knobs that the wolf wouldn't be able to turn without breaking. They'd gotten drinking glasses. Decker could fill them and sit them on the floor. The puppy could lap water from the glasses but not the draft-horse-sized wolf.

Decker eyed the toilet bowl in the downstairs bathroom. Most likely Joshua wouldn't want to drink from that. The toilet also brought to question how the wolf was going to relieve itself. Water in meant urine out.

They could lay down papers. They had rooms full of newspaper.

The puppy wrestled with the six-pack of paper towels.

"Here. I'll do that." Decker ripped open the plastic.

The puppy jumped up onto the counter beside the sink. It looked at him and then the faucet.

Decker put the paper towels on the cleared island. He went to the sink and gave the faucet an experimental twist. The pipes groaned. After a minute of coughing and rattling, rusty brown water poured out into the sink. "Oh. Dear. Maybe it will get better if we let it run. If you want some water, I can get a glass from the bathroom."

The puppy covered its eyes with its paws.

"What?" Decker cried.

The puppy sighed and looked pointedly at the paper towels abandoned on the island.

"I-I-I don't understand." Decker picked up the paper towels. "Do you want the paper towels or water?"

Joshua jumped off the counter and turned into a human. "You truly have no clue on how to clean, do you?"

Decker froze. Should he point out that Joshua was finally a boy? No. "People cleaned for me."

"How did you live alone for fifty-seven years without cleaning?" Joshua took the paper towels from him. "I'm seventeen and I know how! I started washing pots and pans when I was in first grade."

"When you take eating out of the equation, there is little need to clean."

"What about your clothes?"

"I do laundry. I wash my bed linens. I have a shower for when I get ichor or dirt on my body. Otherwise—I'm not a human, Joshua. I'm a magical being."

"If you say you're sparkly clean, I'm going to smack you."

"I do not sparkle." Decker leaned against the island to watch Joshua dampen a towel and systematically wipe down the counters. He could not stop smiling. His boy was going to be fine.

15: JOSHUA

Another late, late, late night with Decker. Another nightmare. Another morning with memories returning from the night he was attacked. This time of how the wolf stood over him, biting down hard, teeth grinding against bone, and then the sense of being lost in a flood, dark, hot and wild.

Joshua woke up burning in the sun that poured in through his bay window. They'd forgotten to buy curtains for his bedroom. The sun-rotten old ones had fallen down while they set up his air mattress bed.

They'd forgotten to buy an alarm clock. He had no idea what time it was except "day." It still felt like morning.

He wasn't sure what day it was until he started to count out from when he was mauled. That had been Friday. Saturday he'd been discharged from the hospital, fled his parents' house, and met Decker. Sunday he'd gone food shopping, won ten million dollars, talked to a dead woman, met the Wolf King, and spent three hours stuck as a wolf with a resizing problem.

It was Monday then. He was officially late for school.

He rolled onto his back, raised his hands toward the ceiling and stared at them.

Last night he had paws.

He was a werewolf.

A werewolf.

A werewolf.

A werewolf.

His arms started to get tired.

He'd probably been staring at his hands a lot longer than he thought. He was spectacularly not coping here. He didn't seem to be able to tackle his change head on. It was like jumping into a tar pit. It was too deep. Too dark. Too thick. There was nothing to hang on to. He felt like he was going to go under and never come back up.

What was he supposed to do now? He was a werewolf, but he didn't really know what that meant. What did werewolves do when they weren't out being wolfy?

He had thought picking a major to study in college was hard. He hadn't been able to answer that question either. What do you want to be the rest of your life? "Werewolf" was not one of his top ten picks.

He decided to focus on *Hoarders: Hipster Vampire*. It was something that he could wrap his brain around.

They hadn't finished in the kitchen. They'd cleared the floor and the counters but hadn't even opened the cabinet doors. He needed to clean all the cabinets and drawers so he could put away the dishes, glasses and silverware that they'd bought the night before.

Beyond that, everything became too much of a tar pit.

Right.

Get a dumpster. Deep clean. Paint some walls. Have a yard sale. Cry a little bit as someone (probably Decker) gently explained the facts of life. Done.

His stomach grumbled a bit. Oh yes, and go real food shopping. Decker had given him a fist full of fifties. With the microwave and mini fridge, Joshua could do more than just peanut butter and jelly sandwiches.

Which made him wonder what Decker "ate." And when. So far Decker had spent every waking moment with him, running around, buying things and then they would clean and plan until Joshua crashed out of sheer exhaustion. One minute they were putting the linens on his new air bed, talking about what they'd do the next evening, and the next he'd was waking up at seven-thirty (according to Decker's phone).

He had one vague memory of Decker patting him on the head. Decker did that a lot. He had large hands, compared to Joshua, that were cool to the touch. Joshua didn't want to think about how much he liked it when Decker patted him on the head.

Joshua tried to count sit-ups instead of thinking of Decker.

One sit-up. The man confused him the hell out of him.

Two. On one hand, Decker was rock solid when Joshua really needed someone to steady him. He made Joshua feel safe.

Three. The problem was that when he thought Joshua had both feet firmly under him, the teasing started.

Four. At least Joshua thought it was teasing. He couldn't be sure.

Five. It wasn't like Decker was hinting that he wanted something from Joshua. Every time he teased, he just took something Joshua said or did, and twisted it. Like last night at Target, Joshua had taken Decker's hand without thinking to pull him to the grocery aisles. Decker *smirked* at him and said, "Yes, I see the beef log. I'm sure it's tasty." Technically, Joshua started that...

Six. And when Elise told Joshua to keep his hands off Decker's sword. Decker made that sound sexual even without saying a word. Which was impressive. Maybe it was Decker's magical vampire talent...

Which would be a weird magical talent to have.

Joshua had lost count of the sit-ups. Where was he? Five?

Six. Decker had said that Elise was dear to him. He also said that she'd shoot Decker because she knew it really wouldn't kill him. She certainly acted like she'd cheerfully stab him many times.

Six. But then Elise warned Joshua not to hurt Decker. Which meant she thought he could. Hurt as in tear off Decker's head? Or hurt as in break his heart?

Six. Would she hold it against him that he wasn't gay and Decker was?

Six. Exactly how psycho was Elise? There was no question that she *was* dangerous. The question was *how* dangerous.

Six. Was Decker gay?

Joshua knew kids who thought it was hilarious when they grabbed their groin and said "suck me" when they weren't gay. Decker at least made everything he said sound funny. What if he was just joking about the homosexual stuff?

It was hard for Joshua to figure out because no one ever acted that way around him. His friends were all male, dorky, unpopular, and straight. The one obviously gay guy in high school hung out with a pack of girls. None of the girls in his grade ever gave Joshua a second look because he was so short and apparently "weird." He was never sure what he was doing that was so strange. Certainly, he'd tried hard to act like everyone else.

How many sit-ups had he done?

This was not working. Life had thrown him too many curve balls. He didn't even know which ones he should be juggling. The least important one probably was Decker's sexual orientation. The only thing Joshua knew for sure was that he couldn't go home.

And he was hungry.

A hungry wolf was a dangerous wolf.

It was really hard to write and walk.

Joshua could read and walk easily. It was a mile between his house and his school bus stop, so he always read as he walked. Going to school he normally brushed up for tests or finished any reading homework. (Really, with all the wonderful novels in the world, why did they always pick Godawful ones for class? He hated *Animal Farm* before he had to live it, thank you very much.) Walking back home, he read for pleasure.

Writing was a whole different matter.

He had to stop moving or his handwriting got so wobbly that he couldn't read what he wrote. While he'd gotten dressed he realized that the scary Wolf King manifestation had made him forget that Jack Cabot had gone to high school with Winnie. He felt like he'd wasted all that energy worrying when he knew that Winnie considered Jack "a knight in shining armor." Also he'd spent the twelve-plus hours with Decker without telling him anything constructive about the séance. Sioux Zee made it sound like the ghost's information was probably out of date, but Jazmin had thought his presence meant that it wasn't. Certainly the Wickers seemed to figure hugely into Jazmin's life. Were they the same Wickers chasing Joshua now? And where was the Prince of Boston? In New York with the Wolf King? If Winnie had told Joshua, he'd forgotten. All he could remember was that the prince peeked under her bed for monsters, or something like that. There were definitely monsters under the bed, but Joshua wasn't too sure about a Peeping Tom werewolf prince.

He needed to write everything down to keep it straight. His life had become worse than being thrown into the middle of a video game like *Call of Duty 4* without doing the tutorial.

He'd started with making a list on Decker.

Decker is a vampire. A freaky vampire. Other vampires were dangerous.

Decker had a scary giant sword. Someplace. It had disappeared after the fight with the huntsman. Decker had talked about channeling magic into a weapon. Maybe the sword only existed when Decker needed it—but then how did Joshua use it?

Decker had lived in Philadelphia before 1959. He came to Boston with Saul, and he was at least seventy years old despite looking twenty. What's that in dog years? (Joshua wrote that down, not as a joke but a question of how long he would live as a werewolf. Decker implied that the Wolf King was older than him.)

Decker slept—or something—sunrise to sunset. Where, Joshua was still unsure because the vampire could move freaking quietly. He'd judo-thrown Decker twice last night when the vampire startled him. Logically Decker's coffin was somewhere in the house and most likely the basement. When they went to the coal cellar, however, there was no sign of it.

Decker could lose control and that would be "bad." When and how were probably important questions. Joshua underlined the "loses control" part. Triggers would be good things to know.

He had run out of facts that he actually knew about Decker and detoured into myths. Decker didn't need an invitation to enter a public place, didn't seem to have trouble with garlic (they passed a bin of it in Target's grocery section), and so far hadn't reacted to a holy symbol (the cashier wore a cross). No reflection. Joshua circled that one with exclamation points because that one defied everything he knew about the universe.

Decker might be gay—maybe. Decker liked him.

Joshua had put lots of question marks next to the last one because he wasn't sure how much Decker liked him. Or in what way. Under it, he'd written, "He smells good" but scratched it out just in case Decker ever got hold of the list.

That was just about it. He knew next to nothing about the person he was living with. He didn't even know what Decker's favorite color was, just that the vampire was agreeable to painting the walls green if that was what Joshua wanted. And Joshua wasn't sure if it was the real Joshua that liked green or if it was the new improved werewolf part that was talking.

The blare of a car horn made him jump. He'd stepped out in front of a car. He jerked back onto the curb, blushing furiously.

He probably should be paying attention to where he was going. There was a lot more traffic in Cambridge and the drivers all seemed homicidal. He really didn't want to put "werewolves are nearly impossible to kill" to the test. Especially since Decker said it would still hurt a lot.

Which reminded him. He flipped to the page titled "*Things I Know about Werewolves for sure*" and wrote "*It still hurts even if it doesn't kill you.*" The list was depressingly short. Most of the things on it only raised questions instead of giving him answers. Things like: *Ferals are bad. Pack wolves are good. I'm a pack wolf.* That seemed to indicate then he was part of a pack. What pack? Winnie had said that the Boston werewolves were all dead. What pack did the werewolf that changed him belong to? Where were they? Not back home. He would have noticed a BMW i8 tooling around Sauquoit.

Joshua stopped cold as he suddenly remembered seeing the sleek black car.

They had planned to open the haunted house an hour after sunset. Shortly before people were supposed to start arriving, Joshua had to go pee. There was no bathroom or outhouse at the barn. All the corn had been cut down and the field was open to the sky, brightly lit by the rising moon. The only place for privacy was the trees that edged both sides of the cornfield. The road ran along the east property line, so he'd walked across the rough field to the other set. He was in mid-stream when the BMW growled slowly up the road, turn signal blinking, as the driver looked for the narrow break through the trees that marked the access road. When he found it, he pulled in and stopped, blocking the opening.

"Idiot," Joshua whispered. He was still peeing and didn't want to draw attention by shouting "Don't park there."

It was obvious later that the werewolf had deliberately blocked the escape, but at the time Joshua couldn't decide if the driver was just stupid or a self-centered prick.

A big African-American man unfolded himself out of the car, flexing as if stiff from a long drive. He took off his suit jacket and tossed it in through the open window. His business shirt, shoes and slacks followed.

"What the hell?" Joshua whispered as he zipped up. He couldn't even guess at what was coming.

Joshua watched in confusion as the man crouched on the ground, nearly naked. Then he stood, mouth open, too scared to move, as the man turned into a big grey wolf. It only took a few seconds. The transformation had taken just long enough to know that there weren't two beings moving through the moonlit night, that the man had changed to beast.

The memory fragmented. Bits and pieces followed.

There had been knives. They were like Elise's twin blades. They gleamed in the moonlight. Frank Cahill had them first, calling orders as if he was quarterbacking the fight. The linebackers piled onto the werewolf, trying to tackle it to the ground. Daphne kept screaming "Kill it! Kill it!" which sounded insane to Joshua. The wolf hadn't actually hurt anyone yet.

"Just run!" He'd planned to cover the retreat. "Get to the cars!"

Daphne pointed in Joshua's direction. "Cut him!"

For a moment, everyone went still and stared toward Joshua.

"Ilya!" the wolf shouted.

Joshua looked behind him, hoping that there was someone standing behind him. When he glanced back, the entire chaotic tangle of bodies was surging toward him. Joshua backpedaled, shouting wordlessly.

His memory tattered at that point. He remembered Chris swinging a knife at him as he grappled with D.J. The blade had hit with shocking force and blood rushed down his forearm. He clearly remembered thinking that he was going to die.

Joshua stopped on the busy Cambridge street corner. As college students brushed past him, he pushed up his sleeve. A long thin scar ran from his wrist to his elbow. He had a lot of scars; he'd lived a rough and tumble childhood. He knew all his old wounds and where he'd gotten them. This one was new.

Chris and D.J. had tried to kill him. He'd known them both since kindergarten. D.J. had held him down and Chris sliced open his arm to the bone. He should have bled out long before the paramedics arrived. They'd tried to kill him.

Then the werewolf tore Chris's head off.

Joshua whimpered. He needed something to eat. Now.

Fifty dollars bought less pie than he expected. To be fair, it was very good pie. The little café called Pesti Pie offered slices of pie and coffee. The wolf just pointed and paid and it was several slices in before Joshua could regain control. It felt very much like sitting in the backseat of the car, watching someone else drive. He experienced all the sensations but had no control of direction or speed. He managed to pause in the middle of a piece of salted caramel apple pie to establish control. He had already eaten a slice of butternut squash, caramelized onion, Gorgonzola, and walnut (which sounded weird but had tasted amazing) and a bacon, leek and Gruyere pie. Bacon pie. Why hadn't anyone thought of that before? He still had two pieces of banana chocolate cream to eat. Life was good.

Where was he going? Beyond just getting food? Oh yes, the hardware store. The magical paint formula.

He sat eating pie, watching painting videos and taking notes of things he'd need. He liked lists; they kept life neat and orderly. If it was on a list, it was already halfway conquered. There were lots of videos on YouTube but all of them were fairly boring. It gave new meaning to "watching paint dry."

Only after the pie was gone, the lists seemed complete, and he hadn't whimpered or growled for half an hour, did he try thinking about Friday night again.

He had come to with people lifting the wolf body off him. A female paramedic pressed a hand to his neck and shouted, "I've got a pulse!"

That brought a gathering of people looking down at him, all with flashlights that they shone in his face.

"What's going on?" he asked. "Why am I on the ground? What happened?"

"You're going to be okay," the paramedic said loudly and then murmured to someone that he couldn't see, "I can't tell how much of this blood is his."

"What?" Joshua cried.

"It's okay," she said as she examined his chest and stomach. "We're going to get you to the hospital."

A policeman crouched down beside Joshua. "Son, how many kids were here with you?"

"Where is here?" He could tell they were outside and it was night and the ground beneath him was painfully uneven. "Where are we? What happened?"

"He doesn't have any ID on him," the paramedic said.

"What's your name, son?" the policeman asked.

"I-I-I don't know."

"He might have a concussion." The paramedic focused even more light into his eyes. "Do you know what year it is? Who is the president?"

Joshua squinted against all the bright lights focused on him. "Why are you asking me? I don't even know what's going on!"

The paramedic turned off her light. "You've been hurt. We're taking you to the hospital." And then to the policeman, "He's not going to be able to answer any questions."

The night became another confusing jumble. Then later, the police came with photographs and questions. Who had been at the barn? Were there only ten kids there? Had he noticed any strangers? How did the animal get there? Did someone bring it? Who had driven the BMW i8?

All those questions, but they'd never mentioned the knives.

Did they not find the knives?

Elise had wanted to know how anyone managed to kill a werewolf. He should call her and tell her.

And go buy paint.

16: ELISE

The den of forbidden carnal pleasures came with a "honeymoon breakfast" brought to the room via a room service cart. The hotel made it seem like luxurious by providing a soft boiled egg in a hand-painted china cup and three pancakes. It cut corners by having only one piece of bacon and a single strawberry on each plate. It was not designed to satisfy three people, especially when one was a teenage werewolf who'd skipped two meals the day before.

"Are you sure?" the prince asked before attacking her plate.

"I normally just do a coffee and donut. There's a Dunkin' Donuts a few blocks down. I'll grab something there." It was almost a lie. Coffee was a must but she normally tried to make something for breakfast every morning. She couldn't stand cooking dinner just for one; it was too empty a ritual to bear. Healthy dinners were easy to come by eating out. Good breakfasts, on the other hand, were not. She suffered the silent emptiness of her studio apartment to make omelets with graviera cheese and *siglino* or occasionally *trahana* with feta cheese.

She could never understand why her mother spent so much time drilling Elise on how to live among other people and never explained how to be happy by herself. Maybe her mother didn't know. It would explain the hours at Decker's messy house.

Cabot and the young prince had given her the bed and slept on the floor as wolves. While she was in the shower, they'd changed back to humans. They still ate like wild things, ignoring

180

the silverware to use their hands. They used toast as scoops for the soft boiled eggs and tore the pancakes into quarters. After dunking the wedges into maple syrup, they licked their fingers clean. Obviously, wolves weren't taught all the basic living skills either.

"You should have some protein." Cabot held out his piece of bacon. "You didn't have any of the meat last night either."

Because she had both hands engaged in toweling dry her hair, she leaned down to eat it from his fingers. He watched her intently with his golden eyes, studying her as if she somehow confounded him. His fingers shone with bacon grease. She resisted the urge to lick them.

Remember: he was a wolf when you walked into the bathroom.

She licked the taste from her lips instead, prolonging the moment in her own mind.

He quirked up his left eyebrow even as he watched the slide of her tongue across her mouth. She blushed and turned away. The blush went hotter as she realized that the prince was watching Cabot watch her.

"I'm going to go get my donut," she said.

17: SETH

Something weird was going on between Jack and the Grigori. Seth wasn't sure he wanted to know exactly what. It made him feel guilty; if it weren't for him, Jack would be part of the New York pack like all the other Thanes. Wolves weren't meant to live in isolation.

Seth heard the hotel door close as he stepped into the shower. He realized that Jack had gone after the Grigori. He didn't want to think about why.

Refusing to think about his cousin, though, left his mind open to wallow in all his other problems. Samuels was dead. Joshua had disappeared without working knowledge on how to be a werewolf. Alexander had blown Seth's plans for returning to Boston out of the water. His territory needed him; people were dying. The king was right that just he and Jack couldn't handle the city alone. Seth had hoped Alexander would reassign some of the Thanes to Boston. Seth had already asked Samuels if he would be willing to be part of Seth's pack.

"Yes, sir," Samuels had said with his warm Southern drawl. *"I'm fixin' to have your back."*

Seth leaned his head against the shower wall. Grief formed a hard knot in his chest. Samuels had been a good man. He believed that the code of chivalry applied to the Thanes. Samuels had been kind to Seth not because he was a prince but because Seth had been only thirteen when he came to live at the Castle. He was the type of wolf that Boston needed.

Someone pounded on the hotel door.

Had Jack locked himself out of the room?

Seth reached out for his cousin. No. Jack was still down the street.

He turned off the water. The knocking continued. Being that the door was visibly in danger of breaking under the force of the blows, it was simple to guess that it was a werewolf on the other side. The Thanes were too afraid of Seth to beat on his bedroom door. It had to be Isaiah.

"I'm coming!" Seth dressed quickly. He hated being naked around Isaiah. The man was several inches taller than Seth. Isaiah used his height to subtly snub Seth. With no clothes to sacrifice, it was far too tempting to shift to wolf. Even Isaiah wouldn't play dominance games with him when Seth was a wolf.

Isaiah waited a minute and started to knock again.

Seth jerked the door open. "What?"

The one advantage to the bed and breakfast room was that it had a private entrance. Isaiah stood on the small wooden porch. He wore a different suit, shirt and tie than last night. The black Italian silk suit was the one Isaiah wore when nobility visited the Castle. It meant Isaiah expected to meet with someone he wanted to impress. It also meant he'd packed before chasing after Seth.

Isaiah stepped back out of striking range. "Give me the keys to the Porsche."

"No," Seth answered automatically. He paused to think up a reason. "I need a car to get home."

"Take the train." Isaiah held out his hands. "It's my car. Give me the keys."

If Seth went looking for Joshua, he'd need the mobility of a car. "It's a fleet car, just like the Bentleys. They're all registered to King Property."

"It's mine. I went to the dealership and ordered it."

But Alexander had paid for it, which was why it was registered to the motor pool.

"I'm not going to let you strand me here," Seth said.

"You can have the Bentley we drove up." Isaiah tossed keys to him.

Seth caught the keys. Last night, he'd been thinking of the amount of Jack's blood in the Grigori's Jeep, not safety protocols. He'd parked the Porsche in the end space; in plain view of the street. One of Alexander's big black Bentley luxury sedans sat beside the Grigori's Jeep. Isaiah must have driven around town until he spotted the Porsche.

None of the Thanes were in sight. The Bentley sat five comfortably. The Porsche carried only two. Isaiah made it sound as if they'd only brought one car.

"What else do you have here? One of the other Bentleys? Or one of the Escalades for off-road?"

"What does it matter to you?" Isaiah snapped.

In other words, they'd only brought the Bentley. Isaiah didn't care that three of the Thanes who came with him would be stranded wherever he'd left them. It meant that Seth should make sure that they weren't miles from nowhere.

"Where are the others?"

"Waiting at the hotel." Isaiah didn't even gesture to indicate where that might may be.

The Grigori stated that she hadn't been able to get two rooms in Utica since the area's hotels were overrun by people attending the funerals and big game hunters and the media. It was sad that Seth trusted the Grigori's word over his foster brother.

"How did you get a room?"

Isaiah snorted. "You call yourself a prince, but all you ever do is pretend you're a man. If you just let people know what you are, then you wouldn't be camping with your cousin and a Grigori." He made a show of leaning forward to sniff the air coming from the hotel room. "You didn't even get a taste of divine flesh? I would have thought with Cabot's family history, a *ménage à trois* would have been on last night's menu."

Did Isaiah want to be smacked into the next county?

"I'm married," Seth said coldly.

"Oh yes, what's her name?"

Fine. If Isaiah wanted to play petty games, Seth could play petty games. Let Isaiah keep the Bentley and all the responsibilities that came with it.

"I want the Porsche." Seth tossed the Bentley's keys back to Isaiah. "Did you find Samuels' body?"

Isaiah glanced away, refusing to admit failure. "We called the Marquis of Albany. He can find the damn needle in a haystack."

"Half the humans in the county should know what happened to it. The police. The reporters."

"The New Hartford police are under Wicker control. We had a long talk with the police chief. The Wickers kept him so focused on the hunt for Cabot that he hasn't a clue what's going on under his nose. He didn't know where Samuels had been taken. He said that normally any dog that bit a human would be taken to the Oneida County Department of Health for rabies testing."

Seth wondered if the man was still alive after Isaiah "talked" to him. "Rabies?"

"They're worried that the brat that Samuels changed might have rabies. Apparently, no one thought to start the kid on shots before he disappeared. If the boy had gone feral, rabies would have been the least of their concerns. It took us a while to find someone connected to the Department of Health. The damn thing keeps bankers' hours."

The offices would have been closed last night. Had Isaiah gone to bed instead of storming the county building? Seth glanced at his phone. The government offices would have opened an hour ago.

"What did you find?" Did Isaiah leave the place in one piece? How far behind the Thanes were the local police? Was that why Isaiah wanted to change cars? Had he run someone over with his?

Isaiah jangled the Bentley keys in his hand, glaring at the Porsche because he couldn't meet Seth's gaze. "I want my car."

"The marquis isn't going to take your shit either. I can hear this when you tell him, or you can tell me now, and I'll talk to him." Because Albany was old-fashioned and would ignore the less dominant wolf for the prince that outranked him.

Isaiah shot him an annoyed look and growled a curse.

"In your dreams." Seth shifted to force Isaiah to look him in the eye. "What did they tell you at the Department of Health?"

Isaiah growled. "The people there claimed that they don't have an in-house lab to do rabies testing, so their vet took emergency delivery of the body on Friday and should have prepped it for the New York State Diagnostic Lab at Cornell. The test needs to be done within twenty-four hours of the animal's death."

"And?" Seth trusted that Isaiah would have followed the lead, leaving a trail of destruction behind him.

"The vet's place was a madhouse. Samuels' body is missing, as well as the doctor and the technician working with him on Friday. The vet called his staff, told them to cancel all the Saturday appointments, but he never said anything about today."

The Wickers had obviously made it so that no one would miss the vet for days. How long before his staff decided to file a missing person report? Still, it didn't make sense.

"Why would the Wickers take Samuels' body? Their spells need material harvested from living bodies."

"You're the one that's been taught that drivel. You tell me."

It was one of the many sources of contention for Isaiah. Alexander felt that Seth needed to learn arcane matters but not Isaiah. When Isaiah riled against it, his father simply stated, "Seth is a prince; you are not one yet."

Yet. A word fraught with promises but no clear answers.

Isaiah's phone rang. He growled in annoyance. "What?"

"The Marquis of Albany is here." Seth's sharp hearing picked up Thane Silva on the other end. "He wants to talk to Seth."

"Seth?" Isaiah said.

"The Prince of Boston," Silva pointed out the obvious reasons. "The marquis can tell that he's here. Albany said, 'When Boston gets out of the shower, his highness needs to come see me.' He added in a 'please' as an afterthought."

Nothing of Isaiah.

Isaiah turned to glare at Seth. "We're on our way."

18: ELISE

Dunkin' Donuts was a few hundred feet down the quiet, tree-lined street. A hard frost still had a grip on the morning, limning the yards with crystalline beauty. Autumn was rushing toward winter solstice. The world was dying yet again.

It meant that the Wickers' blood magic would only be stronger.

Elise had to get her head back in the right place. Normally she didn't hunt sentient monsters. Humans usually cleared the area before the bullets started to fly. Sometimes it was via common sense—monsters liked dark, creepy places. Sometimes it was because the people were sensitive enough to pick up the evil radiating outward.

The Thanes could clear the deck of almost anything that the Wickers could throw at them, even puppets armed with silver bullets. The problem was that it would mean a high body count on the side of the human innocent bystanders. She had the advantage that, unless the puppet was tightly scripted, her own angelic glamour would make them hesitate long enough for Elise to counter in a hopefully non-lethal way. It hadn't worked on the police chief but it would probably work on anyone under his command.

With Wickers, it worked best to charge in and hit before the witch knew that she was in the area. She'd blown the element of surprise yesterday by rescuing Cabot instead of going for the kill on the driver of the red Bentley. If the puppets reported a beautiful woman flashing an Interpol badge, she was totally screwed. Worse, people had seen her Jeep.

Clarice guessed from the media feeds that there were multiple witches involved. So far, Elise had only spotted one. She didn't like the odds of this blind man's bluff, mostly because the Wickers had their blindfolds off.

Cabot was waiting for her when she stepped out of the Dunkin' Donuts with her coffee, bagel sandwich, and box of fifty Munchkins. When the bitter cold wind blasted over her, she felt a little guilty that she'd bought him only a light jacket. He was wearing it unzipped, though, as if he didn't even notice the cold.

"Wow," he leapt to help her juggle the door and the food. "When you go for a donut, you go for a donut!"

"I got these to share." She passed him the box of Munchkins.

"You are a wonderful person," he said with great sincerity and opened the box. "I love these."

"The glazed ones are mine."

"Yes, ma'am." He popped three powdered ones into his mouth, rapid fire.

She reached for one before he could inhale the contents. Their hands caressed inside the narrow space; his skin surprisingly warm. She jerked her hand back, blushing.

"Where's the prince?" she asked to cover her reaction.

"Taking a shower." He popped two more before closing up the box. "I wanted to thank you for rescuing me."

"You did that already."

He nodded, plowing on. "For the record, I normally wear boxers. They're more forgiving when you need to instantly transform."

She fully hoped that he wouldn't shred all three pairs of the underwear she bought.

"I really appreciate you taking care of me." He faltered. "But—but I'm a little confused by the box of Trojans."

Beware Greeks bearing gifts.

He had followed her to Dunkin' Donuts so he could have this conversation without Seth overhearing it. She wasn't sure, though, how he could be confused. It was pretty straightforward: a man, a woman, and a box of condoms.

"We don't do official knights and squires and things." He started to explain something but she wasn't sure exactly how it related to the box of condoms. "Samuels was my mentor, at least until Seth became prince. Samuels was higher rank; he was more dominant when I first became a Thane. I outranked him when my Uncle Gerald died and Alexander shifted me to Boston to be Seth's heir. Anyhow..." Apparently even he lost the thread of what he was trying to tell her. "Um." He tilted his head and gave her a puzzled look. "You fight with daggers, so you're a Virtue. Samuels always made it sound like Virtues were vestal virgins."

Samuels apparently never met her grandfather. To be fair, Saul had been a child of the sixties; he believed in free love. (Luckily for him, her grandmother had only been interested in having heirs to the bloodline.)

She kept it simple. "No. We're not."

"So—were the condoms—for me?" He spread his hands in confusion.

They stood in the silence for a minute.

"Yes." She was sure the embarrassed burn was hot enough to set her clothes on fire.

"Aaaaaand you?" He tilted his right hand into a point. At her.

The silence was longer.

She suspected that he'd stand there until she answered.

"We were going to be sharing a bed," she said in defense. Because that seemed too easily misunderstood, "I was entertaining—thoughts—" She wasn't sure how to finish that sentence. It was a shipwreck. No amount of bailing would help. "Yes."

"Us?" He spread his hands wide apart and brought them together, fingers entwined. He cocked his eyebrow again.

Amazingly, her blush could get hotter. Was he being purposely dense?

"Yes! I know your people must have sex!" Then it occurred to her that they might not be human when they did so. Had all the paintings in the hotel room been some kind of warning? "That—that—I mean—there's the younglings."

She'd confused him. He tilted his head, squinting as he tried to understand what she meant.

"I'm attracted to you!" she cried. "I wanted to have protection in case that attraction led to something."

"Protection as in 'condoms.' Not your knives or silver bullets?"

"Good God! Yes! I wanted to have sex with you!"

The result was much like she *had* hit him with a bullet. He stood, surprised into stillness, staring at her.

"Ah," he murmured. "Oh. Oh!"

"What?"

"I think a girl in high school tried to seduce me. I didn't get why she gave me one of those Trojan three-packs. She wanted to have sex."

Elise covered her eyes with her hand. No one ever warned her that werewolves were totally clueless.

"You and me?" He sounded like he was still having trouble wrapping his brain around it.

He shifted closer. Out of habit, she lowered her hand so she could track his movements. He read her body language.

"You're not going to stab me if I try and kiss you?"

"If I want to be kissed."

She'd confused him again.

He cocked his head to the side, squinting at her as if she was the most complex thing he'd ever seen. "You want sex but no kissing?"

She reminded herself that while he was extraordinarily good looking, he was a Thane. Alexander kept his Thanes on a short leash; it was possible that they were forbidden to sleep with humans and there were no female werewolves in their ranks. Asking him how many times he'd been with a female would probably derail the conversation.

"My family are born inhumanly strong and fast," she said. "I have the physical strength to stop normal men if I don't like what they're doing."

"Not a werewolf." He got that much. "So you reserve the right to get stabby."

"Yes."

"Fair enough. You've saved my life. Bandaged my wounds. Fed me. Gave me a safe place to sleep. Guarded me while I slept. Because of that, my wolf sees you as pack and is more than happy with the idea of skin time."

Skin time. The phrase jolted through her, reminding her of swimming at Ambelas Beach on Paros with her cousins. How free they'd been with each other in their swimming suits, and naked in the privacy of the family's villa. It had been the only time in her life that she didn't need to worry about someone taking casual touch as an invitation for sex. Suddenly she was hungry for that intimacy.

He cautiously moved closer to her. She steeled herself against the automatic reach for her weapons.

"It's okay," he murmured, shifting even closer. "I spent years wrestling with younglings. I know how to control my wolf."

She imagined him pinned to the floor with toddlers chewing on his ears. Not the most erotic image, but comforting. Wolf parents were famous for being protective of their younglings; if he couldn't control himself, he wouldn't have been allowed near unchanged children.

He radiated heat in the cold November air. He smelled of a forest full of autumn leaves and dappled sun. They both stared at his large hand resting on her hip. Then he leaned in to nuzzle into her hair. He had the gravity of the sun for her; she was drawn close to him without realizing it until they brushed together. He slid his hands to her back and then slowly eased her forward until she leaned full against him.

Her heart was hammering in her chest. It went against all her training to be within striking distance of such a dangerous creature, but it felt so right to rest against his strength. To be warmed by the heat of his body. To listen to his heartbeat matching hers.

He kissed her temple. He brushed his face against her cheek, his beard surprisingly soft against her skin. It reminded her that just an hour ago, he'd been a wolf, not a man. If she tilted back her head, he'd be able to kiss her freely. Deeply.

Did she want to be kissed? Stupid question. She dreamed of him kissing her, she wanted it so bad. Should she kiss him? He'd given vague promises to play nice but she would have little power to stop him if that was all lies. It was a bad idea, but being the good little soldier had only made her more and more miserably lonely.

She raised her hands to embrace him and tilted up her head for a kiss.

Her phone started to play Decker's ringtone. "I can promise you," her phone sang muffled by her pocket. "You'll stay as beautiful, with dark hair and soft skin...forever. Forever."

Elise swore and jerked away from Cabot. How was Decker calling her during the day? Wait. It must be the little mystery puppy, Joshua.

"What's wrong?" she snapped, angry because she was in the wrong place if he was in trouble. It would take hours to get back to Boston. She started for her Jeep despite the knowledge she'd never arrive in time. It was going to take her five minutes just to run back to her car.

"Is this a bad time?" Joshua didn't sound like he was in danger. He sounded like she'd just scared the shit out of him.

She reminded herself that he'd had his world turned upside down and shaken hard. She stopped walking since he didn't seem like he was in trouble. "Are you in danger?"

"No," he said. "At least I don't think I am. It's been a weird twenty-four hours. I'm a millionaire now. A millionaire werewolf. Shit. Where am I? Oh, I think I was supposed to turn at that last light. A lost millionaire werewolf living with a hoarder. A lost millionaire..."

"Why did you call?" It came out harsher than she wanted.

"Is this a bad time?"

Cabot's mouth flashed through her mind, inches from her lips. She closed her eyes, took a deep breath, and struggled for sounding calm. "No, it's not a bad time. What's wrong?"

"Oh!" Joshua gave a cry of dismay. "No! Not this place again! Stop it!"

"Is there someone there with you?" Elise knew it couldn't be Decker. No one else should know that the puppy was in Boston. She'd even forgotten to tell Cabot. She winced as she realized that her keeping the information from him probably wasn't going to go over well. She glanced back at the Dunkin' Donuts. Mr. Naïve translated her sudden departure as a desire for privacy. It was sweet of him to be considerate, but oh my God, the man needed hit with a clue-by-four.

And where the hell did the puppy get a million dollars?

Joshua dropped his voice to explain whom he was shouting at. "It's the wolf. It keeps looping back to this café that has amazing pies. I've already had fifty dollars' worth of pie and coffee. I need the hardware store."

Werewolves! Why was she getting so intimately involved with them? Obviously the only reason they survived as a race was because they were so indestructible!

Should she wave Cabot over and tell him about Joshua? No, one mess at a time. "Why did you call?"

"Huh? Oh! I wanted to tell you that Daphne had knives like yours."

Daphne? Elise swore as she remembered that was the name of the Wicker killed at the barn. "That's impossible!"

"They looked like yours," Joshua said. "At least, what I saw of them. A foot long and shining like—like—well, not like lightsabers—but gleaming. And the hilts were white like yours."

She swore. A witch that used blood magic couldn't even touch the daggers without being burned. The only way a Wicker would have angelic blades was because they'd killed someone in her family. Who did they murder?

Joshua ignored her silence. "The weird thing is: the police never asked me about the knives. I mean you've got ten dead kids..." His voice went ragged. "And—and—and the detectives never asked about the only weapons at the barn."

Her mind raced to when she last heard from various far-flung family members. The massacre was Friday night, so anyone she hadn't spoken to since Thursday could be the victim. That covered most of her family. She'd only talked with Clarice and Theodosia on Saturday while she was chasing after the hunts-man. When Decker hadn't answered his phone, Elise had called Theodosia for backup. Her cousin had been in Maine, checking into a wendigo sighting.

"Are you still there?" Joshua asked after she was silent for too long.

"Yes. Someone must have taken the knives before the police secured the crime scene." An unknown number of victims. Ten dead bodies. It would have been easy for a Wicker to walk in, take what they wanted and leave. No one would have been able to stop them.

As the sole survivor, Joshua must have been whisked away before the Wickers arrived at the scene. Since he was immune to their powers, they couldn't just walk him out of the hospital. They must have decided to wait until they could take him alone at his parents' home. With the knives they could kill him or any other werewolf that crossed their path.

Oh God, the prince! They'd lose Boston to a wave of monsters if he was killed!

"The Wickers killed a Virtue!" Elise called to Cabot. "They have angelic daggers! Go check on Seth!"

Naïve, yes. Stupid, no. Cabot instantly understood the danger; he raced back toward the hotel.

"Go check on who?" Joshua asked.

"I wasn't talking to you," Elise said.

"Oh, okay. Oh, thank God, I finally stopped walking in big

circles. Here's the hardware store. Hey, do you know what Decker's favorite color is?"

"What?"

"Well, I think that my favorite color is green. I'm not totally sure of that. I was wondering what Decker's favorite color was."

"I don't—" She caught herself before she snapped at him again. Lost puppy. "Why don't you ask Decker?"

"He's asleep. I'm at the hardware store now to pick up paint. I'm painting my bedroom green but I figure I should get the paint for the kitchen while I'm here."

Kitchen? Whose kitchen? Decker's house was a pigpen. *His* bedroom? She told Decker to take Joshua home, not keep him forever. It was doubtful the Wolf King would leave a puppy with Decker. Why would Decker be encouraging him to paint? How could he paint anything? The only space you could walk around in was the foyer.

"So do you know what Decker's favorite color is?" Joshua asked.

She would not scream at the poor lost puppy. She needed to get off the phone with him. She needed to call Clarice and find out which of her scattered family members was dead. "I don't know his favorite..." Actually she did. "Blue. His favorite color is teal blue."

"You sure?"

"Yes! Goodbye!"

19: SETH

Isaiah drove Seth across town. The Thanes apparently had bullied the staff of the historic Hotel Utica into giving them rooms reserved by other guests.

The Marquis of Albany waited in the elegant two-story marble lobby. He sat in a wing-backed chair, a cup of tea beside him. At first glance, Albany was a fragile old man; someone's grandfather waiting to be collected. He wore a brown tweed suit with leather patches on the elbows and penny loafers.

Arrayed behind him were a half dozen young men acting as his honor guard. As Seth scanned them, the males all dropped their gaze quickly. It was impossible to tell if any one of them was more dominant than the others. Since the marquis had lost all his sons in one disaster or another, these were most likely his grandsons and possible heirs; any one of them could become the next marquis. Albany had probably brought them so they could learn how to deal with Thanes by watching the old man do it.

The marquis stood as Seth and Isaiah walked up to him. He came to Seth's shoulder, seemed as if he'd only weigh a hundred pounds soaking wet, and smelled of pipe tobacco and age. His hair was pure silver but still thick and rough.

He was a Marquis at the heart of his territory and he radiated his displeasure. It chilled the air and deepened the shadows of the lobby. Albany loomed within his power, larger than life.

"Your Highness." Albany's voice held no weakness of age. It rumbled deep and rich with anger. "There are protocols for entering another alpha's territory. You don't sneak in behind their back and hunker down with Grigori unannounced."

Seth locked down on anger. He was only here because Isaiah—who could come and go as he pleased as a Wolf King's Thane—had done nothing to save Jack. It might be unfair for Albany to berate him, but whining about it would solve nothing. With the trail gone cold on Samuels' body, Isaiah was correct in calling in the alpha. Diplomacy demanded that Seth swallow his pride, apologize and then ask Albany's help.

"I'm sorry," Seth said. "My cousin had silver poisoning. I didn't know he was in your territory until I found him. Originally I thought he was in Ithaca, which is neutral ground."

"And the Virtue?"

Seth felt a blush start at the edge of his collar as he remembered Isaiah suggested that he and Jack should have had sex with the beautiful but dangerous woman. The Virtues were magical creatures, divine in nature. Albany could track Elise as easily as a strange werewolf in his territory. The old wolf knew that they'd spent the night together. Had he kept watch long enough to know that they only slept?

"She is hunting Wickers," Seth said. "She found my cousin and took him to an Earthblood spring. She saved his life but he was still weak."

"And now?" Albany asked.

Out of pure habit, Seth checked on Jack. His cousin held the Grigori in a careful embrace, seemingly about to kiss. The burn crept higher, knowing that Albany was fully aware what Jack and the Grigori were doing. "He's fully recovered."

"I see," Albany said dryly.

Seth felt Isaiah snort in irritation beside him. The honor guard all grinned with amusement. They were all in their twenties and early thirties; the youngest looked at least five years older than Seth. They thought it was funny that Jack was courting the Grigori. How could any of them know how hard it was for the man? To lose everything—family and pack—in a single day and left to be an anchor for a boy struggling with one of the most powerful territories on the planet? To be isolated for years, constantly badgered by Isaiah and his allies?

Seth growled as his control slipped. The flare of his alpha made everyone back away a step or two.

"Now, now." Albany pulled in his own power. "No need for a pissing contest."

"Wickers killed Thane Samuels and nearly killed Thane Cabot." Seth struggled to control his anger. "They've armed the police with silver and they've butchered humans in your territory to make snitches and God knows what else. They're standing and fighting and we don't know why."

"Wickers," Albany spat. "I hate the cowardly filth. They're harder to find than ghosts. You can't feel them moving through your territory. Not them. Not their puppets. They blend in with the masses. You can see their constructs only after the blood sacrifice has been made. The witches—the smart ones—slip away once their creations are fully active."

Isaiah had enough of being ignored. "Why didn't you come to Utica when Samuels was killed? Cabot was lying wounded in your territory for nearly a day and yet you did nothing."

"Thane Cabot is not my wolf. As was their right, the Thanes did not ask permission to enter my territory. I missed their arrival; something else had my attention. Nor did anyone call me; I learned of a wolf mauling in my territory via someone texting the news to one of my grandsons. By the news reports, all the children were accounted for and the wolf was dead—whoever he was. I had better things to focus on."

"What better things?" Isaiah sneered the question, his voice clearly implying that he doubted the reasons were justifiable.

Albany gave Isaiah a long stare filled with his power. After a minute, Isaiah dropped his gaze. Albany continued to stare as he took out a pipe and leather tobacco pouch. His hands danced through the familiar patterns of filling the pipe with tobacco and tamping it down.

Isaiah glanced back up, met Albany's eyes and looked down again.

Seth watched, amazed and a little confused. He'd never seen anyone whip Isaiah into place with such an outright display of dominance. There had been other meetings with other marquises; they'd always treated Isaiah with the respect due to a prince.

Isaiah browbeaten, Albany lit his pipe with a match. Rich-scented smoke wreathed Albany as he turned his gray eyes on

Seth. "I had a small breach in Cohoes. We were up and down and in and out of the Sprouts all around Van Schaick Island, killing melusine, until Sunday morning."

Seth nodded his understanding. Albany protected Boston's western boundary, so Seth had learned it in detail. The Sprouts were a multitude of water channels at the confluence of the Mohawk and the Hudson Rivers. Something about how the two rivers came together made the area extremely unstable. Over the last two decades, the Albany pack had lost a dozen of their wolves to the breach-spawned, including all four of the marquis's sons. A breach, no matter how minor, in that location would have had Albany's complete attention.

"We think the Wickers stole Samuels' body." Seth explained about the missing vet. "You should be able to spot a dead werewolf in your territory. At least, that's what I've been told."

"Yes." Albany sighed. "I've had to dredge up too many bodies out of those damn rivers."

"There's also a newborn loose someplace," Isaiah added.

"Hm?" Albany's eyes went distant as he considered his territory. He puffed absently on his pipe. "No. I would have noticed someone new added to my pack; I've spent the whole weekend doing head checks. There are only those of you here." He took the pipe out of his mouth and used it to indicate Seth and the Thanes. "And Cabot." This was a wave back toward Seth's hotel. "There was a puppy at the Amtrak station in Albany on Saturday but he was just passing through."

"Which way did he go?" Seth asked. He'd checked the train schedule yesterday. There had been six trains through Utica; the Empire Service, the Lake Shore Limited and the Maple Leaf had passed eastbound and westbound. Each train stopped at a dozen stations or more. Several of the stops gave Joshua access to other trains heading north and south. "Less than a hundred dollars" made most of the Northeast accessible to Joshua. But if Joshua had gone east to Albany, the choices started to narrow down. "South? North? East?"

Albany shrugged. "I gave him no mind. He wasn't mine and he seemed to be just passing through. I figured he was on his way to New York City. There is no reason he'd be heading to Boston."

The Lake Shore Limited was a straight shot to Boston. If Joshua was simply running blind, there was a one-third chance he went there. Seth glanced eastward. He desperately wanted Joshua in Boston where he'd be easy to find. He'd be the only werewolf in Seth's territory. Seth had been so focused on finding Jack that he'd ignored his link with Boston for days.

Seth closed his eyes and reached for Boston.

At one time his alpha had been huge and unknowable. Using it had been like peering through a straw to study his foot. Time and practice had expanded his ability until his territory felt like a second skin.

A hard frost had settled on Boston during the night but the morning sun was slowly warming the city. Millions of souls scurried through the streets and the buildings like ants, inscrutable in their coming and going. The pure humans remained unknown, simply warm bodies without gender or age. Darkness gathered around them. It pooled in the places of stillness. The faint weave of reality strained where it collected.

Seth could immediately tell something drastic had changed about Cambridge. The strain had lessened. The pools no longer ran as deep as the rest of the city. A single bright star moved among the human masses.

Seth focused tighter on Cambridge. A small male werewolf bounced through the aisles of a hardware store like an excited Jack Russell. He seemed to be loading painting supplies into a cart. Paint pans. Painter's tape. Drop cloths.

Was this Joshua? It seemed the right size, judging by the photos at Joshua's home: five foot two of solid werewolf muscle. Why would Joshua be painting? What would he be painting? Where did he get money to buy painting supplies? Who was this pint-size puppy?

Albany grunted. "How odd."

Seth opened his eyes, breaking his link with Boston. If it was Joshua, he was safe enough for now. "What is it?"

"I think it's your dead Thane." Albany pointed westward without explaining what was odd. "He's not far."

20: ELISE

"Nonononononono!" Clarice answered the phone instead of her normal greeting. There was some shrill alarm going off.

"Clarice?" Elise paced in front of the Dunkin' Donuts. She didn't want to lose her connection if something was wrong at Central.

"Hold on!" There the unmistakable low roar of a carbon dioxide fire extinguisher.

"What's on fire?"

"It's my coffee maker." Roar. "This is not my fault!" Roar. "I wasn't even touching it!" Roar. "Are you out? Please stay out. Oh, this sucks! Grandmother is going to take it away and not let me have another. I can't live without coffee!"

"Is it out?"

"Yes." Mystery sounds followed. Only after "Freaking hell, it's cold out" did Elise realize that Clarice was opening windows. The fire alarm went silent.

"Clarice? Clarice?"

Clarice sighed loudly. "Central. Report?" And a quiet, heartfelt, "Stupid coffee maker."

"This is Elise. The Wickers have someone's blades. Who hasn't reported in?"

"Um." Clarice typed on her keyboard, checking the logs of family members reporting in. "My baby sister, but Lissette never reports in. She doesn't see the point. Her last report was last Sunday. She was in West Virginia. She was trying to pinpoint rumors that there's some type of extremely large bear in the area. It might be an escaped pet—people keep the weirdest exotic animals—or some kind of cursed prince—although that's extremely rare these days. I suspect it's because there's a lack of princes more than anything else."

"Clarice! Focus!"

"I'm sorry. I haven't heard from Theodosia."

"I talked to Theo on Saturday. Anyone else?"

"I'm still checking. I think that's everyone but..." There was a minute of typing. "Oh no, Cade dropped off the face of the Earth two weeks ago."

"Who?"

"Cade!" Clarice typed furiously. "He's one of Solange's grandsons. He just finished his training in Greece. He wanted to bum around Europe before coming home. He's not active yet, so I wasn't keeping tabs on him."

Solange was their Grandfather Saul's youngest sister. She'd been eighteen and just out of training when Elise's great-grandmother had been killed. Like Elise had at that age, Solange hated Decker with a passion because she was too young to understand her mother's relationship with the vampire. Saul had moved Decker to Boston to keep the two separated. The rift in that part of their family never really healed. Elise barely knew the names of Solange's sons and daughters. Her grandchildren were completely unknown to Elise.

Clarice, though, as the main operator at Central would have talked at length with the boy, setting up everything from plane tickets to making sure there was a winter coat waiting for him at the safe house.

"Cade was supposed to fly home two weeks ago. According to his credit card statement, he was at Heathrow, then nothing. I'm checking to see if customs has him landing at Dulles. He wasn't hunting. I didn't think! I didn't think! Oh no!"

"He landed at Dulles as scheduled?" Elise guessed.

"Yes. He was supposed to take the train to a safe house and pick out his car the next day. He wanted a Mini Cooper. Stupid, stupid me was waiting for his call from the safe house. When I didn't hear from him, I just assumed he decided to live it up in Europe for as long as possible. I would. I miss Greece. The sun. The beaches. The brilliant white houses. All our cousins.

Remember that place called *ángelos loutró poulión*? They made the best elliniko cafe. There's only one Greek place close by and their 'Greek coffee' is only meh. It's like they never drank the real thing."

Elise would have interrupted Clarice but she could hear the furious clicking of keys. Clarice was searching madly for their cousin.

"I'm checking Dulles security tapes now," Clarice said. "Okay—he's off the plane at the gate. Oh Heavenly Father, watch over our beloved cousin and guard him from evil. He's walking. Walking. Walking. Escalators. Okay, here he is getting his weapon case. He's heading to the bus to the train station. Darn, going to need to get into the train station security system. Hold on."

While Clarice typed, Elise gave a heavily edited account of what she'd found in Utica. She shouldn't have bothered hiding her attraction to Cabot; Clarice connected the dots.

"Oh, he sounds sexy. I loved Grandpa Saul but I always thought it was a little creepy that Grandmother married her third cousin. Back in Greece, I always assumed I'd find a nice boy from another tribe. Yeah, right, all the angelic boys here in Philly." There were none. Their generation of East Coast Grigori had run heavily toward female. "The wolves have the right idea with arranged marriages. Okay, I'm in. Bus takes five minutes to get to the station, so 10:45 on October sixteenth. Yes, there he is. Walking. Waiting for the train to... Oh my god! Oh my god! Oh my god!"

"Clarice?"

Clarice whimpered. "He just stepped out in front of the train."

A Wicker must have caught him by surprise and in that moment of control, "pushed" him.

Clarice started to cry.

Elise forced herself to say, "What about his knives?"

Clarice sobbed for a minute before brokenly saying, "He set the case down on the platform. A man in a business suit picked it up and walked away."

Joshua was right. There had been angelic daggers at the barn on Friday. Since the police didn't report them, they were still in the Wickers' control.

21: SETH

"Not far" apparently was within walking distance as Albany led the way out of the Hotel Utica into the crisp morning. Isaiah ranged ahead, despite not knowing where they were going, in hopes that he would seem like he was leading. The honor guard straggled far in the rear. The Albany pack seemed to be setting a painfully slow pace until Seth realized that the old wolf wanted to talk and his grandsons were giving him privacy to do so.

"I inherited my alpha when I was young, just like you. Ninety years ago. I was sixteen." He didn't look over a hundred years old but neither did Alexander. "Albany had burned quickly through my family. All the Marquises of Albany burned out and died before they were thirty-five. My mother's people are from Tallinn; they're like granite. Her father lived to be a hundred and seventy. Alexander brought my mother here to America when she was twelve and changed her himself. The king was afraid that my father would die without an heir."

Albany waved his pipe toward the east. "It's the Hudson Valley. It mainlines the New York power straight up the river. When Alexander leaves New York, which is far too often, there are dangerous spikes in Albany."

"I don't blame you for—" Seth caught himself before dragging Jack into the middle of two alphas. Technically Seth was as guilty of missing Joshua in his territory as Albany was of not rescuing Jack when he was wounded. "I don't blame you for anything."

"This is not an apology, it's a warning. I'm probably the oldest living werewolf after Alexander. If the source does not kill you, it sustains you. I make no claim to genius but I have a certain advantage over most people; you've seen a hell of a lot by the time you get to my age. I was born when the Wright brothers were just getting the first plane off the ground. Most houses had no electricity, no running water, no telephone, or even indoor plumbing. The movies were silent, television was just a dream, and this newfangled Internet they have? Pure magic. I've seen massive changes."

"I don't understand," Seth admitted when Albany paused to puff at his pipe. "What are you warning me about?"

"Writing on the wall is too big to be read close up. It can only be read at a distance. Sometimes that distance is only gained with time. Things happen for a reason. We are not ruled by random chance. The hand of fate is upon us."

Seth had been told such drivel over and over again since his family was massacred. It never brought him comfort. "This mess is wholly of the Wickers making."

"They wish. Certainly, it smacks of them desperately grabbing at the reins, but the king has worked for centuries to sway fate in the direction that he wants. He sees the writing on the wall and reads it better than anyone because he has the distance gained by time. Everything he does, he does because he knows what is coming."

"He didn't save my family."

"He saved what he could. And he would have saved more, if your father hadn't fought him so. Alexander wanted all your brothers at the Castle. Because he'd lost his firstborn to the Wickers, your father refused."

Seth hadn't known. He stopped walking, rattled by the news. "If Alexander knew there would be a breach, why he didn't he do something?"

"He didn't know exactly when the breach would happen. Over time, you learn to sense it coming, but it always takes you by surprise." He waved his pipe at the maple tree they were standing under, the last leaves falling from its branches. "It's like winter. You know it's coming. You can see it in the bare branches. You can feel it in the air. When you get to a certain age, you can even taste it. But the exact minute when the snow will start to fall? No."

Seth considered the old wolf for a moment. What was the point of this conversation? Albany was setting a slow, leisurely pace to have it. What was so important?

"What should I be looking for?" Seth asked.

"I've watched for a hundred years as the king shuffled around his pawn pieces. Pulling a wolf from here and putting them there. Breeding this line with that line. Everything he does, he does for a reason. I can see the handwriting; I can guess what's coming." He paused to relight his pipe and waved the match in the direction of Isaiah. "Other people, they've got their nose against the paint. They have not a clue what letter they're staring at, let alone what the whole message says."

Seth snorted quietly. "The Thanes gossip about little else but what the king intends."

He started them forward again.

"The Thanes aren't even aware of the writing or the wall," Albany said. "Fate doesn't care about intentions. It happens. Alexander has been trying to create a bloodline to hold New York for longer than I've been alive. Eskola's line might have held if he hadn't been killed before his sons were of age. Alexander is a patient wolf but he decided to take the drastic course of standing direct stud for the alpha. He doesn't like to do that; he's a good breeder and knows not to inbreed too often. Isaiah's mother, Raisa, was the result of a hundred years of careful breeding, bringing together the strongest bloodlines and yet none that he'd bred himself into for generations."

"I know." Seth didn't add that it was ancient history.

"What you don't know is that everyone recognized that the baby was a failure the moment he came out of the womb. Raisa killed herself because she knew how she'd betrayed the king. Stupid girl. There would have been other children and one of them might have been what the king wanted."

Seth stumbled with surprise. He'd heard lots of explanations as to why Raisa had killed herself—she was unbalanced was the most given reason—but no one ever laid the blame on Isaiah before. "What?" And then the implication sunk in. "You think Alexander never intended to make Isaiah the Prince of New York?"

"Let me read the writing I can see on the wall." Albany waved his pipe, left to right, as if pointing out words written in giant letters. "Alexander gives mates to his princes as soon as humanly possible." He put the pipe back in his mouth. "Your father at twelve. You at thirteen. That is how it always goes. The oldest I've ever heard of, in a hundred years, is eighteen. The Prince of Los Angeles had ten older brothers but the alpha skipped them and settled on him. It took even Alexander by surprise. Part of it is simply to keep his princes from going off and falling in love with the wrong female. Wolves are stupidly loyal creatures; Alexander learned that lesson long ago. But if the prince is the result of a thousand years of careful breeding, you protect that investment of time by encouraging him to have heirs as soon as possible. If Alexander planned to use Isaiah's bloodline, he would have arranged a mate for the boy years ago."

Albany stopped Seth and turned the prince to face him. "Take care. There is something written bigger than what I can read. Alexander doesn't keep Isaiah close because he loves him; that is not our king. Alexander needs him. You have the strength to kill the man, and certainly he's stupid enough to tempt you to do so, but you must resist it."

Seth locked down on a growl of anger. "It wouldn't be a temptation if Alexander would just let me go back to Boston. I was supposed to go to Harvard next year. He says now that I'm to go to Columbia."

"Alexander is waiting."

"For what?"

"The writing on the wall to change."

22: ELISE

The wolves were gone from the hotel. Elise viewed the room with a mix of relief and dismay. Had Cabot taken his cousin back to New York? No, the Porsche had been in the parking lot, next to her Jeep. Were they coming back to the room? Probably, they'd left the donuts and Seth's suitcases. Considering the lack of hotel rooms, they might not have a choice.

Maybe she shouldn't have admitted that she was attracted to Cabot.

Actually, thinking about it, there was no "maybe." She should have kept her mouth shut.

She gathered her things. The most intelligent thing she could do was to see if she could get a second room.

"Sorry," said the owner who was manning the front desk. "We're full because of the funerals. The first one starts in an hour for Chris Barnes. Closed casket. They say that the wolf tore his head off. Poor kid. I swear, half the county will be at one funeral or another today."

The parking lot was full of families dressed in black. As far as she could tell, it was three sets of parents in their late thirties and a dozen sons, ranging from eight to seventeen. Various shades of red hair marked them as one extended family. The oldest boys were in suits, looking like they were going to a prom, not a funeral. They milled about the cars, talking about the cold and the chance of rain. Everything and anything but the reason they were gathered together.

It made her think of Cade. There should have been a funeral, all her cousins coming together in grief. What had happened to his body?

Seth had parked his Porsche next to Elise's Jeep. She eyed the low-slung sports car. Where had the werewolves gone? She'd forgotten to exchange information with them so she couldn't even call them. Nor could they call her. She wrote her phone number down and tucked it under the windshield wiper.

"Hey!" a woman shouted behind her.

Elise spun, hands going to her concealed weapons.

It was Joshua's sister. She was nearly Elise's age, which meant she was four or five years older than Joshua. She was all lean muscle and carried herself with the poise of a warrior. She'd pulled her blonde hair back into a too-tight bun. She wasn't the type of woman that needed makeup to be pretty, which was good, because she'd done a haphazard job at applying it. She wore black, although it wasn't clear if she planned to attend the funerals or not. Skin-tight yoga pants weren't normally considered proper attire to such things, even when paired with a black tunic sweater. The black Doc Martens combat boots finished the questionable ensemble.

Didn't U.S. Marshal Stewart say the girl knew judo? Joshua was a brown belt. His older sister most likely had a black belt.

Elise really hoped that the Wickers hadn't gotten hold of the girl. She would make a dangerous puppet.

"Where is he?" the girl snapped.

Elise moved back. She didn't want to fight Joshua's sister; the girl wasn't her real enemy.

The girl pointed at the Porsche. "Where's the guy who was driving this?" She stabbed her finger toward it three more times before managing to dredge up. "Seth! The guy from Boston. This is his car. Where is he?"

"How do you know Seth?" Elise was trying to remember the girl's name.

Joshua's sister threw her hands up in the air. "He came to my house and wrecked my bedroom!"

The girl's shouts and hand waving drew the attention of all the other hotel guests in the parking lot. "He's friends with my brother—or something. Scratch that, my brother doesn't know anyone who has girlfriends like you. All his friends are dorks. Oh my God, you're beautiful."

Bethy. Her name was Bethy and she obviously wasn't a puppet, just a loose cannon. Seth hadn't mentioned going to Joshua's house but it was simple enough to figure out. Sole survivor of a werewolf attack was going to be a newborn werewolf. As an alpha, Seth would be responsible for making sure said newborn wasn't dangerous.

Elise wasn't sure how she ended up Seth's girlfriend in Bethy's mind.

"I don't know where he is." Elise pointed at the paper tucked under the Porsche's windshield wiper. "I was leaving him a message."

"He took one of the pictures from our mantle. I realized it after he left. The little jerk."

The hotel guests obviously recognized Bethy from her parents' press conference. They pointed at her and whispered her name to each other.

Bethy ignored the onlookers. "I'm sick of people walking into our house and taking things! I want it back!"

The Wickers were the other people who had taken Joshua's things. Bethy might recognize the heart stone.

"Do you know what this is?" Elise took the silver moon out of her pocket and held it out so only Bethy could see it.

"That's Joshua's!" Bethy grabbed at the loop.

Elise jerked it out of reach. "I can't let you have it. It's evidence in a murder investigation."

"It was taken on Saturday. It has nothing to do with the barn."

"I didn't say it was part of the massacre. I'm investigating six murders elsewhere. What is it?"

"What?" Bethy put out her hand, palm up in a silent demand for the silver moon's return. "That's not possible. I saw it Saturday morning after we brought Joshua home from the hospital. Someone took it that afternoon."

Elise stepped back out of range of a quick grab and held up the loop. "What is it?"

"It's a rattle!" Bethy gave a "give me" wiggle of her fingers.

Elise swore. A baby rattle? Of course.

Bethy repeated the gesture, larger. "Usually it's in my mom's jewelry box, I saw it Saturday morning while my mom was picking out what to wear for the funerals. It was one of the things that went missing after Joshua ran away from home."

"Was it made for him?" Elise whispered. The crowd was drifting closer, curiosity drawing them in. "And how do you know he ran away from home? Who told you?"

"Porsche boy!" Bethy continued at the same loud volume. She seemed oblivious to the scene that she was causing. "After I talked with him I came into town and checked. Joshua's dirt bike is in the garage's storage shed. Why am I telling you this? You're probably a reporter and you're going to put this all on the news. Give it to me!"

Elise took a step back and shoved the rattle into her pocket. Bethy closed her out stretched hand into a fist.

One of the boys moved between them. The tween was dressed in a dark suit. His tie was askew and his shirt wasn't tucked in and his ginger curls looked like a rat's nest.

He held up a rose to Elise. "Here! Take this!"

"Huh?" Elise backpedaled more, thrown mentally off-balance by the boy's interruption.

He pressed forward, trying to force her to take the flower. Tears were welling up in his eyes. "Take it! Take it!"

She glanced around for his parents. They shifted forward, hands out reached, as if to pull him away. She'd been aware of the crowd moving toward her while she talked with Bethy but she hadn't realized that they'd surrounded her completely.

"Hold still, Grigori," one of the boys stated.

His power flashed through her. Every muscle stiffened in response. It felt like she'd been turned to stone. She couldn't even breathe.

"Take her," the warlock commanded. "Hold her tight. Don't let her go."

With faces full of dismay, the families grabbed hold of her. A score of hands tightened on her arms. Fingers clenched tight in her hair.

Close up, the warlock was clearly in his early twenties; too old to be part of the families he'd taken over. His auburn hair, though, made him blend in with them. She should have been able to recognize the Wicker. His Italian silk suit had been tailored expertly to his slim frame. Large gems flashed on his fingers. It was the classic warlock look; they had a need to be recognized as powerful.

The warlock pulled the eight-year-old boy to him, making the child a meat shield. "Where is the wolf?"

His voice was rich with his power. The answer rushed out of her mouth, spoken without her knowledge or consent.

"Which one?" She laughed as she realized he'd asked the wrong question. She took a deep breath of freedom as she managed to shrug aside his control. "Oh, you blew it."

He pulled the boy tighter against him. "You'll have to go through all these people to get to me. Tell me where the newborn wolf is. You're not here because of the massacres. You stopped my huntsman elsewhere. You know where the newborn went."

The warlock had talked to Stewart. Elise wondered if the U.S. marshal was still alive.

She didn't want to hurt these people but she couldn't buy her safety by telling the warlock anything. He knew she'd kill him the moment she got free. He and his coven had already killed nearly two dozen people. No court of men would ever convict him. No police would even arrest him. She and her family pledged their lives to fight evil like him; it was the only way they could gain heaven.

If she could stall, it was possible that more people would show up. Once the number was greater than he could control, the puppets holding her might slip free. They obviously wanted no part of this. They watched with mute terror, too strongly held to even protest.

"Why do you want him?" Elise said to gain more time. "Why did you kill so many people to get him? You have no hope of holding him. The Wolf King knows."

"Oh, let me tremble in my boots. Please. I've been dodging wolves my whole life. They're stupid animals, pure and simple. Your family has been pandering to them far too long. The time is at hand when we take what should be ours. Tell me where he is and I'll simply kill you. Otherwise I'm going to have to make use of you."

Make use. Such an innocent-sounding phrase for vivisection.

All over the city, the church bells started to ring. The funerals. No one would be strolling by to tip the balance. She was going to have to fight her way free. Most importantly, she needed to keep him from getting the rattle in her pocket. She didn't know what the Wickers planned to do with Joshua, but it was game-changing if the warlock was willing to risk so much to find him.

God, almighty, maker of heaven and earth, give me power to destroy this evil.

She shattered the knee of the nearest man on her left. He went down with a scream, the pain breaking the witch's hold on him.

"Kill her!" the warlock shouted, backing away, keeping his shield carefully between her and him.

Luckily none of the puppets were trained fighters. They tried to comply, but they had no idea how to kill a human outside what they'd seen in movies. She downed two more while they rained punches on her.

"Hey!" Bethy shouted as one of the men rushed toward Elise, butcher knife raised for a stab at Elise's throat. "No! Don't!" Bethy caught the man's knife hand and disarmed him. "Dumbass!"

The warlock had forgotten Bethy in the confusion and hadn't taken control of her. The one trained fighter had stood dumbfounded until the knife appeared.

"Run!" Elise shouted, hoping that the girl would escape.

The warlock pointed at Bethy. "You! Kill her!"

And lo, a miracle happened.

Bethy stepped forward, leg swiped the meat shield, knocking him to the ground. The field cleared, she grabbed the warlock and flung him hard.

Good God in Heaven! Joshua's sister was the one in a million who was immune to witches.

For one stunned moment, the warlock's hold was weakened on the puppets. They paused in their attack, loosening their grip. Elise ripped free her left hand and jerked her pistol out of its concealed holster.

"Kill them both!" the warlock roared from the ground.

Instantly the puppets tightened their hold on Elise. She couldn't raise her arm. She could hear Bethy swearing loudly as she struggled with their attackers. Elise didn't want to kill these innocent people, but she was quickly being left no choice. If they wrestled her weapons away from her, then they'd be able to use them on her and the werewolves. She pulled the trigger, firing blindly. Someone cried out in pain. Blood scented the air. She was able to raise her arm slightly.

"God forgive me and have mercy on their souls!" She pulled the trigger again and again.

The pistol kicked in her hand, booming loudly, as the puppets tried to wrestle it away from her. Bullets whined off the parking lot's asphalt. She had a dozen shots to hit something worthwhile, and then the gun was a useless hunk of metal. Five. Six. Seven.

Another puppet cried out in pain.

"Stop!" the warlock commanded. She felt his power pluck at her, quiet urges, easily ignored. He was trying to control too much with Bethy added into the equation. The puppets wavered and she managed to raise her arm enough. Her ninth bullet hit him in the foot.

Instantly the puppets scattered. They ran screaming.

Elise leveled her pistol at the warlock who was thrashing on the ground.

Even wounded, the warlock was dangerous. He held out his hand to Bethy. "Don't let her shoot me! I'm unarmed! I haven't done anything wrong."

"Like hell you didn't." Bethy wiped blood from her mouth. "What the hell is going on? Has everyone gone insane? What the hell are you doing?" This was to Elise. "You can't just shoot people. We should call the police."

Elise backed up to make sure that the girl didn't try to disarm her. Bethy didn't understand what was going on. "This man killed your neighbor, Joe Buckley. He cut Buckley's heart out while he was still alive. He's after your brother."

"He is?" Bethy cried. "Why?"

"I don't know." Elise only partially lied. She knew it was because Joshua was a werewolf, but why were the Wickers so intent on him? The area was filling up with wolves; it would be easier to snatch one off the streets in any other city in the world.

"Stupid ignorant bitch," the warlock snarled. "He's not even your brother. That stupid slut Alvarado ditched him with your family."

Elise opened her mouth to ask who Joshua really was when she remembered Cabot's conversation with Seth. "He's Ilya Tatterskein, isn't he?"

"He's the end result of two thousand years of breeding by Alexander," the warlock said.

The baby rattle was taken from the Tatterskeins' mountain lodge if the Wickers knew that it belonged to Joshua.

"What do you want with him?" Elise asked.

"The same thing that the Wolf King wants with him," the warlock said.

Ilya would have been Prince of Boston if he hadn't been kidnapped.

Several blocks away, the sirens of police cars wailed to life.

She realized that the warlock was playing for time. He planned only to tell her enough to keep her listening until new—heavily armed—puppets arrived. Even if she shot him now, there'd be Bethy to contend with. As far as the girl would know, Elise would have shot a wounded and unarmed man.

If she left him alive, she might have to kill police officers or be killed herself.

She took aim for a heart shot.

"I said you can't..." Bethy moved in to stop her.

A large black wolf streaked between them. It hit the warlock and blood sprayed across the cement.

Cabot! Elise jerked her gun up. She wasn't loaded with silver but she didn't want to piss him off by accidently shooting him.

The warlock looked like a ragdoll in the wolf's jaws as Cabot mauled the man. It was one thing to know an angry werewolf was dangerous, it was another to watch one tear limbs from a body.

And you wanted to sleep with Cabot? Seriously?

It was going to be really hard to kiss the man without thinking of the bloody muzzle of the wolf. All that blood.

When the warlock had been reduced to a half dozen pieces, Cabot turned toward the two men she'd wounded.

"Leave them; I need to question them." Elise reloaded. "Where's the prince? Is he safe?"

"He went someplace with Isaiah. I was looking for him when I heard gunshots."

Someplace close by, another siren wailed to life. Cabot wasn't the only one who'd heard the shots.

"Police are coming." She took out her hotel key and held it out to him. "They have silver. You can't be roaming the streets like that in daylight. Go get clothes on."

He growled, glancing toward the oncoming police and then her. "What if a Wicker is with them?"

"Then you'll hear more gunshots and you can come back. Go!"

Bethy pointed at Cabot as he stalked to the hotel room. "Did—did—did it just talk?"

"Yes, congratulations, your life just got a whole lot weirder."

23: SETH

Albany led them to a storefront a few blocks from the Hotel Utica. From what Seth had seen of Utica, they were in the business district of the city. (Albeit a very small area compared to New York City.) It was Monday morning, after the start of office. The streets were full of people.

One block back from what seemed to be the main drag, there was a low red brick building that clearly started life as a stable. The wide door that once allowed horses hitched to wagons to enter had been converted into a large window display. Gold lettering in an old-fashioned font arched across the glass, identifying the store as "Gold Coast Coffee, Antiques and Taxidermy." On the left side of the window display, bags of coffee were tastefully arranged between a bronze-plated antique cash register and balance scale. On the right was a pair of snowshoe hare jackalopes with deer antlers. The rabbits were locked in spar, their cannibalized horns inches from ramming into each other.

"Oh no." Seth's stomach gave a sickening roll. He didn't want to go into the store and find what had been done to Samuels' body.

Albany put his hand on Seth's shoulder. "That was what I was afraid of. There are humans inside. I can't tell if they're witch or puppet. They don't appear to be armed." He waved Isaiah toward the side alley. "Thane, take some of your people to the back door. We don't want them taking his body and running."

"Don't kill anyone," Seth added.

"It's the only way to be sure," Isaiah snapped.

"Don't. Kill. Anyone." Seth put his power behind the command.

"The prince is right," Albany stated quietly. "We need to find out how many are in the coven and where they holed up."

Isaiah growled but nodded agreement.

Seth hadn't been thinking about questioning anyone. He knew his foster brother; the Thane gave his wolf full rein far too often.

Albany kept hold of Seth while Isaiah took the Thanes down the side alley.

"Now is the time to be the prince you were born to be. If things go south, you'll be the one that needs to be strong for all of us." Albany patted him on the shoulder. "Good boy."

It reminded Seth of his vet, Dr. Huff. A wrenching home-sickness hit him. He didn't want to walk into this store and find a man he'd known and loved like an uncle butchered like an animal. Or worse, mounted like some hunting trophy. He didn't want to have to deal with possibly killing innocent people whose only crime was to be caught up in the power of a Wicker. He wanted to be home. Only he didn't have a home to go back to. All that was in Boston was an empty lot and the smell of soot and ashes.

Albany opened the door. Bells hanging above the door chimed. The warm smell of coffee blasted out into the cold street. The scent of dusty fur and dried skin followed, most likely too faint for a normal human to pick up. It raised the hair on Seth's neck. Growling, he followed the old wolf into the shop.

It was an assault on the senses. Every nook and cranny was filled with the bizarre and macabre. An anatomically correct science mannequin, its skin peeled back to reveal plastic organs. Ancient stuffed ferrets dressed in odd clothing. One ferret in a fez hat and blue bathrobe. A second dressed as a green beret soldier. The head of a third framed like a portrait with a tiara balanced between its ears. A duckling's head under glass. A songbird with parts of its body replaced with clockwork. A miniature skeleton riding a stuffed fancy chicken.

There were other, more normal things. Old farm equip-ment. Battered tin signs. A neon clock from the fifties. Gumball machines. An old jukebox. But the taxidermy nearly crowded them out of his awareness.

Why would you do this to another living creature? Killing

an animal to eat it, he understood. This was a mockery of the animal's existence. A demeaning of its life for eternity.

"Oh god, not Samuels," Seth whispered. "Not this."

"We'll put things right," Albany said.

The only clear area in the store was the barista counter. A young man stood behind it. He excelled at the squeaky-clean scruffy look of a hipster. His long dark hair was twisted up into a man-bun and his full beard was meticulously groomed. He wore a white linen shirt that showed off his sleeve tattoos and braided leather suspenders.

"I'm sorry, sir, but we don't allow smoking..." The barista trailed off as he noticed the number and mood of the wolves trailing in behind Albany. Even the supernaturally blind would notice the wave of anger coming off the pack. "Can I help you?"

"Alasdair Aillig Keir, the Marquis of Albany. Hold out your hand to me."

"Okay." The barista obviously thought that they were simply going to shake hands. He wiped his hands on a towel and leaned across the counter.

Albany gripped his hand, making the barista wince.

"Wow," the young man said. "You have a strong grip for someone your age."

"Which is?"

"What?"

"How old am I?"

"I don't know. Sixty-five? Seventy?" The barista tried to pull free. After the first tug, he looked to the nearest of Albany's grandsons. "Is he...?"

"He's deciding if he's going to tear your arm off or not," the grandson said.

The barista gave a nervous laugh and tugged harder. "Please, sir, let go."

"If he knew who you were, he'd never have shaken hands with you," Seth pointed out.

"I know," Albany said. "The other humans are in the back. The Thanes are screening them."

There was a scream from a back room. Something large hit the wall. Everything behind the counter shook at the force of the impact.

The barista's eyes widened and he tugged more frantically.

"You have something of ours here." Albany kept hold of him. "We're picking it up. You're going to stay right here, not moving, not calling the police. My grandson Daniel here is going to make sure of that. If you stay calm and quiet, you won't be hurt. Understand?"

"Not entirely," the barista said, too honestly. He winced in pain and changed it to, "Yes! Yes! I understand!"

"Shouldn't we question him?" Seth asked.

"If he didn't know we were coming, then he wasn't held long enough to learn anything useful. We need a puppet that's been held at least a day for them to know anything important. The longer they were held, the more they'll know. He's clueless."

Albany led the way through a door labeled "employees only" and down a dim hallway crowded with antiques. The smell of blood and death lingered in the darkness. It grew stronger as they entered the actual taxidermy workshop.

The space was an assault on Seth's senses. Plastic forms in the shape of dozens of mammals hung from the ceiling. Bare of skin, horns, ears, and tails, he couldn't even identify the animals that they were supposed to be. The beige color and the rounded forms made it seem like huge grubs were descending from the roof.

Birds in mid-flight were pinned to corkboards upside down, wings spread, wrapped in white paper to protect the feathers. The mounted heads of whitetail deer sat on the floor, waiting to be claimed. The workshop's harsh lights gleamed brightly off their glass eyes.

A coyote hung from two heavy chains by its spread back legs. It had been skinned down to its front shoulders. The skinning knife lay on the floor.

Isaiah had a man pinned to a bloodstained table. "What if I skin you?" he was growling as he choked the man. "What if I hang you up by your feet and peel you?"

"Isaiah!" Seth shouted.

Isaiah stopped choking the man long enough to point at the coyote. "Look at what they did to Samuels!"

"That's a coyote."

"Why else would they bring his body here? They used those chains and that knife and they hung him up..."

"Shut up!" Seth roared.

Isaiah snarled as he dropped his gaze.

"Where's the wolf?" Seth shouted at the gasping man.

"I don't know! I don't work weekends. One of the out-of-state hunters brought in the coyote this morning. He wanted it before going back home."

"He's in the next room." Albany pointed at a barnlike sliding door.

"That's the storage for the antiques," the man said. "We don't keep animals in there."

Seth grabbed the handle and dragged open the door.

A mutilated body lay on a table within, surrounded by a bizarre collection of ancient tools. It had been covered with a tarp at one point, but the canvas had been pulled aside to show the damage done. The large wolf had been skinned and beheaded. What was left wasn't even identifiable by scent.

Seth stared in horror at the body.

Anger came from deep inside him. He struggled to hold it in, to control his beast, even as his wolf fought to come raging out. It pressed his skin, hot and restless. It wanted to destroy everything in its path in blind rage.

He backed away from the body, hands pressed to his eyes to block out the sight, panting as he held in the wolf.

Around him, he felt the Thanes lose control. The scent of the Source grew heady. Fabric ripped loudly as one shifted to wolf.

"Stop it!" he shouted, putting power behind it. There were too many people here that the Thanes could harm, starting with Albany's grandsons. "Stay in control! You are the King's Thanes!"

Hoffman was the weakest of the Thanes. He was on his hands and knees, back bowed. He'd taken off his suit coat; his shirt burst open across his shoulders, showing off his tribal tattoos.

"Hoffman!" Seth roared.

All but one of Albany's grandsons had fled.

"Idiots!" Albany gestured at Isaiah who was closest to the body. "Cover that up!"

Isaiah snarled at the old wolf. "We need to give him a proper funeral."

"Fine." Albany brushed past him. He reached for the canvas tarp lying to the side. "There's no need to stand and gawk at him."

He tugged on the fabric. There was a loud metallic snap. Something flashed out of the carcass and lanced through Albany's heart. His grandson screamed as the old man dropped to his knees. An angelic dagger was buried to the hilt in his chest, its gleaming point sticking out his back, blood pouring down the blade and onto the floor.

Albany's alpha pulsed, furnace hot, through the room.

It hit his grandson and the man became the Source, blindingly bright, for several seconds. He howled wordlessly. The earth echoed the sound, magnified a thousand times.

The new Marquis of Albany transformed into large gray wolf. He smashed through the wall and ran.

Seth took off after him. The newborn marquis was close to feral. The man was lost in the Source, leaving the beast in control. Without the human wielding the magic, anyone that the wolf bit would become a feral. Each feral would need to be instantly killed, or they'd create more. It would be a quickly escalating problem. Seth had to catch Albany and submerge his wolf into the Source.

The Wolf King had taught Seth what to do when his Mexican grandfather died, but in the end, he wasn't needed. Seth knew what to do—in theory. He'd practiced on Cabot and a handful of Thanes pretending to be feral. Thanes were not scared animals. They never ran from him. They didn't have the potential of an entire territory at their call.

Seth chased after the wolf as it fled toward the crowded main street. The animal had the advantage of four legs and being in the heart of its territory.

Albany rounded the corner. A blue Ford pickup did a violent U-turn to follow.

"Look at the size of that wolf!" the driver shouted as the windows slid down.

"It's a saber-tooth!" His passenger was fumbling with a rifle.

Neither one seemed to realize that Seth was running beside them. The pickup was on a lift kit so he was mostly hidden from them.

The passenger leaned out the window with the rifle. "Hold it steady!"

Seth rammed his hand through the door's body and flipped the pickup. The truck went tumbling into the opposing traffic. The men's frightened screams and the desperate squeal of brakes and the loud crash of the accident behind Seth tore at him. He hated that he'd hurt the hunters, maybe even killed them. If they'd been loaded with silver and killed the new marquis, then the power would jump as far as it needed to find a new heir. Somewhere Seth wasn't, a different grandson would transform. He needed to protect this wolf to prevent that from happening.

Halfway down the block, disaster struck. A door to a law office flung open just as the wolf reached it. A man in a business suit walked out, talking on his phone. The beast and the human collided. They went down into a tumbling, snarling heap.

Two wolves scrambled to their feet.

The newly changed feral wolf was only the size of a German shepherd. It was a dirty yellow without any markings. It looked more like a rabid dog than a wolf. It crashed back into the building that it just exited as a human. The marquis charged down the street.

"Isaiah!" Seth prayed that the man was within earshot. "Isaiah! There's a feral on the loose!"

"We've got it!" Isaiah roared angrily somewhere behind him. "Just deal with the marquis!"

The Thanes had no hope of stopping the marquis. Isaiah clearly hated the reminder. They could, however, kill any feral that was spawned.

Albany darted down a narrow alleyway, across a back parking lot and leapt a fence. Seth charged after him. Beyond the area became more residential with single family houses mixed with two-story apartment buildings. The wolf wove through yards, through hedges, over fences. Every time Seth thought he could grab hold of the marquis, the wolf would dodge out of his reach.

The neighborhood ended abruptly in the large, busy parking lot of a strip mall. The anchor store was a huge supermarket.

"No, not toward crowds of people," Seth shouted.

Albany charged towards the grocery store. The glass door didn't open fast enough; the wolf crashed through in a spray of glass. Beyond were dozens of shoppers at the checkout lines. They scattered, screaming.

The wolf saw fleeing prey and charged after it.

"No!" Seth tackled the wolf.

They plowed through a display. The air went thick with the scent of Fruit Loops as cereal boxes exploded around them. They rolled, the wolf thrashing in Seth's hold, trying to break free. Under them, the loops crunched.

"Be human!" Seth shouted at the struggling wolf. He pushed the wolf down, back into the Source.

Seth was afraid it wouldn't work. In theory, a marquis at the heart of his territory was stronger than any Thane. The newborn lord, though, was lost in alpha amnesia; the human part of him had been swept away by the Source. With his humanity also went the ability to form a coherent resistance.

"You are human, damn it!" Seth shoved the wolf down, back into the Source. "Be one!"

The beast shifted to human. The new Marquis of Albany lay panting in the crushed cereal, gazing about in confusion. When Seth had inherited his father's power, it felt like he had just been born. He came to his senses in the throne room with no idea what had happened seconds earlier. His entire life wiped clean to a blank slate.

Seth kept hold of the man. "You're safe. No one is going to hurt you. There is no reason to run."

Albany looked to be in his early twenties. He had the old lord's grey eyes and strong nose. Instead of silver, his thick straight hair was dark brown. He panted with fear. "What? What's happening? Where am I?"

Seth glanced about. He hadn't seen the name of the store as they crashed into it. "A supermarket. Aisle five, Utica."

"Utica?" The lord pronounced the city's name like he'd never heard of it.

A police officer came around the corner, pistol leveled. Seth could smell the silver loaded in the gun. He locked down on a growl of anger; the officer shouldn't be able to guess that either of them were wolves as long as Seth kept his composure.

The officer barely glanced at them. His gaze darted everywhere, trying to spot the wolf he knew was somewhere in the store. "Where did it go? Where's the wolf?"

"Out the back!" Seth pointed toward double doors that led into the employees-only area of the store. Someone had fled that way; the doors were still swinging in their wake.

The officer stalked toward the door, gun ready. Seth kept still, not wanting to draw his attention back to Seth and Albany.

"My hands look so weird." Albany wriggled his fingers, staring at them with concern. "Are hands supposed to look like that?"

"Shh," Seth whispered. It was the first question Seth could

remember asking Alexander when he became the Prince of Boston. Lost in the amnesia, the wolf seemed to be the true version of his body. It made his long, hairless fingers seem alien to him. "Your hands are fine."

"You didn't even look."

Seth glanced at the man's hands. Five fingers, all where they were supposed to be. He held up his own hand, just like Alexander had. "See. Mine is just the same. This is the way you should be. Don't think about it."

Thinking could trigger a shift back to wolf. Seth could feel the animal within the man; close to the surface and restless. With the police so close by, Seth didn't want to risk the man transforming back to a beast. Luckily, most of the shoppers had fled the store, so there was no one to see that the man was naked.

Just like Seth, after the hands came the bare feet.

"My toes look weird too," the new lord said.

"They're fine." Seth hauled Albany to his feet. He needed to get the man to safety. Seth didn't know, though, who he was or where he lived.

"Why am I naked?" Albany asked.

Continued echoes of the worst day of Seth's life. In the beginning, Albany might be blissfully unaware of his grandfather's death, but slowly his memory would come back.

"Let's see if we can find you clothes." Seth guided him to the end of the aisle and scanned the overhead signs. Sometimes supermarkets carried T-shirts and underwear. The next aisle was canned fruit, dried beans, and pasta.

"Who am I?" Albany asked. "Where are my clothes? You know—it's illegal to run around buck naked."

"Yes, I know." They had to find clothes for Albany quickly. Seth could only keep control of his wolf through continuous physical contact. "You're the Marquis of Albany."

"What the hell does that mean? What's a marquis? What's my name? Why am I in a supermarket naked?"

A man came to a sliding halt among the broken glass of the front door. Behind him, the police squad car sat abandoned, lights blazing, radio crackling and hissing out reports of multiple wolf sightings.

"Boston!" The newcomer was another grandson of the old Marquis. "Oh, thank God! I was afraid Ewan had gone feral."

A name. That was a start. "Your name is Ewan." Seth pulled Albany into the first aisle, out of sight of the door. "Give him your clothes. We can't let him get arrested."

"Right." The newcomer started to strip off his clothes. "I'm Cameron Keir."

"Ewan? Ewan what?" the new lord asked.

Cameron gave Seth a bewildered look.

"It's alpha amnesia." Seth wondered why a possible heir didn't know this. Hadn't Albany braced his family for the inevitable? Or did the old wolf think he'd live for a dozen more decades? "He won't remember anything about himself for several days."

"Right. Sire told us. He expected the king to be here, making sure everything went right." Cameron stripped off his lightweight Giants football jersey and the long sleeved T-shirt under it. He pulled the jersey back on and held out the T-shirt. "Your name is Ewan Aillig Keir."

"Aillig?" Ewan shied away from the offered shirt. "You've got to be kidding. Who names their kid that?"

"It was the name of the first Marquis of Albany," Cameron explained. "It's a longstanding family tradition. Everyone gets tagged with it, in one way or another. It's my middle name too."

Seth intercepted the clothing. It could be simply the scent of another wolf, or there might be ancient history there. Alexander delayed returning from Belgrade because he was worried someone would kill the new prince. Seth traded the T-shirt for the gray polo he was wearing.

Ewan sniffed at Seth's shirt. He found it acceptable; he pulled on the polo.

The problem, then, wasn't the scent of another wolf.

"You're cousins?" Seth wished he knew more about the Albany family tree. All he knew was that most of Albany's obvious heirs had been pruned.

"No." Cameron pulled off his hiking boots. "He's my little brother. Everyone always thought the next Marquis would be me or my cousin, Dan. Ewan was always so quiet and agreeable; people didn't think he was strong."

"Was?" That made it sound like Cameron thought of his brother as dead. Was he planning something?

"They're going to have to change how they think." Cameron took off his belt. "Sorry about the shirt; Ewan hates my cologne.

He says werewolves shouldn't wear perfume. I don't wear it for him; my girlfriend loves it."

Seth tented the front of the borrowed shirt to sniff at it. The fabric smelled of amber, musk and citrus of some expensive cologne. Living in New York, Seth had grown used to the reek of perfumes. "You date a human girl?"

"No!" Cameron gave a surprised laugh. "She's part of the Syracuse pack. She just likes smelly things: candles and soap and all that crap. I know it's weird for a werewolf. She's quirky, but that's what I love about her. I want to marry her, but Sire wouldn't let me. Syracuse is just a barony. Sire..." Cameron's voice broke with grief. "Sire said that if I inherited the alpha, the king would simply dissolve my marriage. Alexander would shift my children to Syracuse pack to prevent them from inheriting Albany. Sire said it would be less heartache never to go down that road in the first place."

If that was really the case, then Ewan was safe with his older brother. Cameron didn't want the alpha and was strong enough to protect Ewan until he regained his memories.

Cameron stripped off his boots, socks, and blue jeans. "Should I give him my underwear too?"

"He can go commando." Seth was no longer sure which direction the bed and breakfast with the Porsche lay. "Where are the cars that you came in?"

"Across town at the hotel. I've got keys to the Land Rover. I'm not sure who drove the Phantom."

Nor did Seth know how to get back to the hotel where he'd met the old Marquis. They needed to get the new lord to safety. "Lead the way."

The rest of the Albany pack were huddled beside the cars when Seth reached the hotel. They were all older than Seth, some by a dozen years, but they seemed like a pile of unhappy puppies. Only one had the wherewithal to pace back and forth beside the pack's vehicles. Strong enough to ignore the comfort of the huddle, too weak to leave it by a dozen feet.

The youngest man staggered to his feet, tears streaming down his face. "Is it you then, Cam?"

"No, Keegan," Cameron pulled his sobbing cousin into a hug. He raised his voice to address all his family. "Ewan is the new marquis. He's got alpha amnesia. It's up to us to keep him safe until he's back on his feet."

"Ewan?" the pacer growled. "Ewan? We're screwed."

"Shut up, Danny," Cameron snarled. "You know he didn't choose it. The power goes to whoever can hold it."

The two were nearly equal in dominance. They glared at each other, neither flinching away.

Dan proved himself the weaker by dropping to pure logic. "It went to the closest person to sire when he..."

"It goes to the person who can hold it," Seth stated coldly. "There is nothing you can do to influence it. All the Wolf King can do is move people out of the pack, so they're not connected to the Source at that point. Ewan is the new marquis and that is the end of this discussion. Which one of you has keys to the Phantom?" Seth pointed at the Rolls Royce parked beside the Land Rover. He didn't want Ewan near the body which was best moved via the SUV.

"I do," Dan said.

Seth had hoped that one of the other men had the keys. It couldn't be helped. "Swap keys with Cameron..."

"Look, kid, we don't have to listen to you."

"Dan!" Most of his cousins cried out in surprise and fear.

"'This is not his territory," Dan snapped. "We're Albany. We don't have to obey some little kid."

Seth looked hard at the man, making him drop his gaze. "I am here as the King's stand-in to make sure the new marquis is safe. You will do what I tell you to or I'll make you."

"The king doesn't know yet, so you can't be here as..."

"Kneel!" Seth put power behind it.

Dan dropped to his knees, whimpering.

"Hey!" Ewan shifted between Seth and his cousin. "No. Don't. Don't do whatever you're doing. Stop..."

Seth stepped back to strengthen the impression that he was backing down. Ewan had the alpha instincts even-though he had no clue what was going on. He'd protect what was his. It came at a cost; as Albany's power flared to counter Seth's, the concerned look on Ewan's face gave way to confusion.

"Who are you?" Ewan scanned the parking lot. "Where are we? Who am I?"

"You're Ewan." Cameron put an arm around his little brother. "I'm Cameron. It's okay. We're going home."

"Every time he's stressed, it will make the amnesia last longer," Seth kept his voice low and nonthreatening. "He needs to be home, safe, surrounded by familiar things. We don't have time for fighting over who can tell who what to do. Someone needs to take the Land Rover and go to the coffee shop and get your grandfather's body. Now."

The Albany pack flinched back at the thought of facing their dead.

"Can't the Thanes..." Keegan started to ask.

"The Thanes are dealing with a feral." Seth glossed over the fact that Ewan created the feral. The man wouldn't be able to handle the guilt of knowing what he'd done. "Once it's taken care of, they need to focus on finding the Wickers."

"We should be finding the Grigori that did this," Dan growled.

"The Grigori didn't do this." Seth stomped on that. Even if Jack wasn't currently viewing the Grigori as packmates, the last thing they needed was a war with her family. "That trap was set by Wickers."

"That was an angelic blade..." three of the cousins started.

"With no Grigori attached. Each set of blades are made for the Virtue that wields them and the first strike the weapons make are into their own bodies. It's the magical wound that opens them to their Source. They *are* their blades. A Grigori wouldn't have left one of their blades unattended, where it could be taken or destroyed. They're irreplaceable. The Wickers must have killed a Grigori for their weapons. It's probably how they killed Samuels at the barn."

"Or the Grigori are working with the witches," Dan muttered.

Seth never thought he'd be glad for the last three years of dealing with Isaiah and the Thanes. It taught him how to calmly talk in the face of sheer stupidity. "The witches left the blade as a trap so we would attack our allies instead of coming after them. It's a false flag maneuver and needs to be ignored."

"A what?" Keegan asked.

"God, didn't your grandfather teach you anything about common political tactics? A false flag is a covert operation designed to appear as if it's committed by someone other than the people that actually carried it out. The Wickers obviously wanted any wolf that found Samuels' body to believe that the Grigori were behind his murder. They killed your grandfather simply to trigger a war between us and our allies."

"Then we should be looking for the Wickers," Dan said.

Seth clenched his fists tight to keep from smacking the older man. "It is vital that your grandfather is cremated as soon as possible. A witch can . . ." Then he remembered why his people always cremated their dead. "Get in the car. All of you. We need to go now and do this."

"Why?" Cameron at least pulled out car keys.

"With your grandfather's body, the Wickers can control the entire Albany pack. Come on. We have to hurry."

24: ELISE

"What the hell?" Bethy whispered for the third time. "You *were* going to shoot him."

Elise was glad that if the girl insisted on stating that over and over again, she was at least doing it quietly. Obviously she wasn't going to stop until Elise actually answered her. "Some evil cannot be contained. It can only be eliminated."

"You were going to *shoot* him!" Bethy whispered.

The emphasis had changed slightly. That was progress. Maybe.

"He was going to kill us. He killed your neighbor. The police wouldn't have stopped him. In fact, they would have helped him."

"Why?"

Why was Elise going to shoot him? She'd covered that. Why would the police help him? Being that they were standing at a murder scene, surrounded by officers, that wasn't a subject she wanted to discuss. Luckily the uniform nearest to them was busy throwing up. Cabot had done an impressive amount of damage in a matter of seconds. The warlock's head was a good twenty feet from his body.

"All the things people have told you are just legends and myths and make-believe are real," Elise whispered. "Except for the tooth fairy. It's totally creepy once you think about it in depth; some magical creature stealing baby teeth out of children's bedrooms in the middle of the night. I think that's made up; certainly I've never killed one. Whatever."

She was rambling because she was trying to vector possible attacks and counterattacks. The Wickers knew she was in the area, what vehicle she was driving, and where she'd spent the night. They'd also figured out they'd lost contact with the huntsman because she'd stopped it. They weren't sure where their construct had been destroyed; Clarice had sanitized the police reports on Saturday as soon as Elise verified that the bodies had been used as seedbeds. Nor had the Wickers realized that she was allied with the wolves. That, however, had just become obvious.

Even with the warlock dead, the Wickers had the upper hand. She needed to get one step ahead of them: figuratively and literally.

She needed to leave as soon as possible, but first, she should learn what she could of the dead man. Wickers never bothered with such things as driver's licenses and credit cards. There would be no ID on him. No sales receipts. No random slip of paper.

The warlock *had* left behind a littering of puppets.

One was curled on the ground, howling with fear. "Make sure he's dead! Make sure he's dead!" Another was unconscious, knocked out by Bethy. Neither one of those would be useful. She'd kept Cabot from killing them because they were most likely innocent of any true wrongdoing.

"You were going to shoot him!" Bethy had tenacity in spades, which might be the reason she was immune to Wickers' powers.

"Yes! He was a bad man," Elise whispered but it came out louder than she intended. The police officer erecting a tape barrier around the warlock's body glanced their direction.

She flashed her Interpol badge again. "I shot at the wolf. I think I hit it. It fled that way. I'm going to try tracking it."

She pointed in the direction that the puppets had fled.

Six black and white squad cars had responded so far to "multiple gunshots fired within city limits." All the vehicles had "City of Utica" written on their doors, not New Hartford. None of them seemed like puppets running on scripts. They did have silver ammo; they'd checked their magazines once they realized they were dealing with a wolf.

At the moment, she was safe from the Wickers. It would take the coven time to realize that the warlock had been killed. If the Wickers arrived while she was in police custody, it would be a death sentence.

"What the hell..." Bethy started loudly.

"Shush! Please!" Elise needed to find one of the other puppets. She scanned the ground. She'd shot at least one of them.

Bethy wouldn't be silenced, but at least she kept to furious whispers. "What the hell is going on? Who the hell are you? Interpol? *Interpol?* And what the hell was that?" She pointed toward the bed and breakfast. "That was not a wolf. I have spent the last two days learning everything there is to know about wolves. The average grey wolf is two and half feet tall and slightly over five feet long and weighs at most a hundred and twenty pounds. That *thing* was way too big to be a wolf!" She had learned everything. "And—and it talked!"

"I would have started with the talking." Elise shifted so it seemed that Bethy was pointing at her. "Don't bother telling the police about what you saw. They won't believe you. Hell, seven percent of Americans believe the moon landings were faked."

"If they won't believe me, why are you bothering to tell me that?"

"Because I don't need this becoming more difficult than it already is." Elise spotted blood drops heading away from the parking lot. She nodded to the officer nearest her and followed the trail.

For some odd reason, Bethy stuck to her side. Maybe because Elise hadn't actually answered her question.

"That man that just attacked us..." Elise attempted an answer that would rid her of the girl.

"The one you were going to shoot?"

"Yes, the very bad man who killed your neighbor and just tried to kill both of us. He was a warlock; a male witch. Witches never work alone. If there's one, there's always two to twelve more. I believe there were close to a dozen people in his coven, or at least, what's left of it. They're down at least three that I know of. There's also a woman driving a red Bentley and Daphne's supposed mother, the Wakefield woman that was at the press conference with your parents."

What was her name? Monsters weren't supposed to have names. Yet another reason Elise hated hunting Wickers. Monsters were supposed to be hiding in a dark hole with the bodies of their victims strewn clearly around them. Wickers walked in broad daylight and hid the bodies in shallow graves.

"Dahlia Wakefield. She's Daphne's mother and she drives the Bentley. She hates that she's stuck doing the grieving mother bit especially since she's angry with Daphne for screwing everything up."

"She told you that?"

"No. I eavesdropped on her before the press conference. It wasn't very hard; she doesn't seem to understand 'indoor voice.' No one is saying it but it's suspicious that Reed Wakefield and Daphne were both mauled to death, miles and miles from each other. Someone went through my parents' place, stole a bunch of stuff and killed my neighbor. My brother is missing. Someone is obviously after him. I have to suspect everyone."

Except Elise. Or maybe Bethy didn't have filters on what she told friends and foes.

"When a coven moves into an area, they pick out the best house for their needs and take it," Elise said. "The true owners are kept like dogs in the basement. That house across the road from the high school was too small for the entire coven. It was just a satellite residence. It gave them access to the school and a private backyard to do small creations. They would have someplace bigger, lots more bedrooms and more probably more land."

"This is not Saratoga Springs," Bethy said. "No one has money to maintain the mansions built back in the day. Most of them have been turned into offices or bed and breakfast places, just like the place you're staying at."

The blood splatters led to the corner and stopped. Elise swore, walking in a large circle, trying to pick up the trail.

Cabot caught up to them on her second pass. He wore a different T-shirt and second pair of blue jeans, so tight that she suspected he borrowed them out of Seth's suitcase. He padded up quietly in worn penny loafers.

Bethy didn't seem to notice Cabot at first. "Where are we going?"

"I'm tracking the puppet that I wounded."

"Puppet?" Bethy pretended to have a sock puppet on her hand. Cabot snickered.

Bethy jerked around to glare at him. "This is a private party. Get lost." Obviously she thought he was a random stranger just walking past.

Cabot questioned Elise with a raised eyebrow.

Elise shook her head. "He's with me. We—" She made it clear by pointing back and forth between her and Cabot who "we" included. "—are going to track the wounded puppet. You are not invited to this party."

"I don't give a shit if I'm invited or not," Bethy said. "I'm not completely following all the weird crap that just happened, but I got one thing straight. Some scary ass people are after Joshua and they seem to think you know where he is."

"Do you?" Cabot's voice went low and dangerous. Werewolves were famous for how protective they were of their young.

"I saved him from a huntsman." Elise didn't want to tell Bethy where her brother was. The woman couldn't keep her mouth shut to save her soul. "I hid him where he'd be safe and the Wickers wouldn't be able to find him."

"And you didn't think to mention it?" His voice still rumbled with menace.

"I was a little busy. Seems some idiot needed to be pulled out of a creek, patched up, fed, and given clean clothes and some place safe to sleep. Joshua's where the prince would be sure to find him, if he wasn't busy trying to find the idiot in the creek too."

"Fair enough," Cabot grinned sheepishly. "So he's safe."

"For now. It was him on the phone earlier. He remembered seeing the daggers at the barn."

"A hot chick like you gave Joshua her phone number?" Bethy snorted. "Not likely."

"Technically, no, I didn't give him my number. He borrowed my friend's phone."

Cabot snapped his fingers as he remembered something. "Speaking of phones, I left mine in New York. That's why I came back; I wanted to borrow your phone to call Seth and find out where he was."

She wasn't the only one letting things slip. Seth had tried to give Cabot his phone last night. The prince must have forgotten about it this morning. "Give me the room key."

As they swapped the two, Bethy lost patience with being ignored. "Where is my little brother?"

Elise wasn't about to tell her. Even if she didn't blab it to a Wicker directly, she could tell someone like her parents who weren't immune to the witch's Persuasion. The girl, however, wasn't going to leave them alone until she had an address. Elise's first thought was to send her to Wolf Castle but that wouldn't end well for Bethy. Annoying as the woman might be, she was an innocent in this. "In Philadelphia. 123 Elfreth's Alley."

Cabot recognized the address of Grigori Central. Confusion

spread across his face. He was trying to fit "where the prince can find him" with "Philadelphia." The wolf apparently thought that Virtues couldn't lie any more than they could have sex.

"Philadelphia?" Bethy didn't sound convinced. "Why would he go to Philly? How would he even get there? He was nearly broke."

"I sent him. I rescued him from a monster in Central Park in New York City." Since the Grigori weren't allowed in Manhattan, hopefully Cabot would realize that she was completely lying. She didn't want him muddling things by asking questions. "Afterwards I gave him money for a train with a map to my cousin's place."

Clarice could deal with the girl. Give her Greek coffee, lokma soaked with honey, and run her in circles. There were far worse fates.

Bethy had taken out her phone. She muttered as she typed in the address. "Elfreth. Sounds made up to me. Elfreth's Alley. Huh. What do you know."

There was weird loud groan, as if the Earth itself moaned in horror.

"What the hell?" Bethy said.

"The Marquis of Albany just died," Cabot said. "This is what happened when my grandfather died."

The marquis was ancient. What were the chances that his death was sheer coincidence?

"Call Seth." She turned to Bethy. "Give me your phone."

"Wait! What was that sound? Who died?" Bethy demonstrated why, despite her abilities, she had no place in dealing with the Wickers. She would burn up their time and attention trying to get her up to speed with no guarantee she wouldn't be a liability. At least she handed over her phone without more questions. "Who are you calling?"

"My cousin," Elise stated. "The one who lives in Philly."

"Hello?" Clarice answered the unfamiliar number without identifying herself.

"Αυτό είναι Elise." Elise used Greek since she was about to give her password information. "Οι αμαρτίες του πατέρα μολύνει το αίμα."

"Central," Clarice responded. "Report."

"The Marquis of Albany just died," Elise said. "I don't know details but I hate the timing. Cade's blades might be involved. Warn anyone in the area, the wolves might be on the warpath."

"Understood," Clarice said.

"I want to talk to Joshua." Bethy held out her hand for her phone.

Elise hung up and deleted Clarice's number.

"Hey!" Bethy cried.

"It's going straight to voicemail." Cabot tapped in another number. "He might have his phone off so he can dodge Bishop telling him to go home."

Elise handed back Bethy's phone. "I'm sorry that your family is caught up with this, but there's a dozen people dead here and another dozen dead elsewhere. Trying to explain all this so you can understand what's going on will take too much time. I need to find the person I shot, make sure they don't bleed out, and find out what they know about the witches before more people are killed."

Cabot growled and tapped in another number. The third number answered. "Tawfeek, its Cabot. Where's Seth?"

Elise couldn't hear the answer.

"I know where the Jensens live," Bethy huffed in annoyance as she realized that Elise had deleted Clarice's number. "You are such a bitch. Why are the pretty girls always such bitches?"

"Because we're sick of being 'pretty' like a piece of artwork!" Elise snapped and then paused as she parsed the rest of what Bethy's statement. "Who are the Jensens and why should I care?"

"Carl Jensen. The man you shot! He drives a blue Cadillac DeVille nearly as old as I am. It's got two hundred thousand miles on its V8 engine and is a complete gas hog. It was sitting here when I drove in earlier."

That would explain the lack of blood splatter.

"And you know where they live?"

"Yeah. I've driven them home after they've dropped off the DeVille for service. It's a fancy-schmancy place in New Hartford."

Would the puppets return home? There was only one way to find out.

Cabot held out Elise's phone, looking worried.

"What did you find out?"

"Wickers set up a trap. The marquis tripped it. It killed him instantly. Seth had to chase down the heir; he's sitting on him now. The Thanes are cleaning up ferals."

"They need help?"

Cabot shook his head empathically. "You shouldn't go anywhere near them right now."

Elise could guess the form that the trap took. "I'm going after the Wickers."

25: ELISE

Bethy was right about the DeVille and the fancy-schmancy house. It was a big two-story Tudor with a three-car attached garage sitting on five acres of wooded land. The Jensens had backed the DeVille through their flowerbeds to park it inches from the front door. All the car doors stood open. Luggage sat scattered around it. Obviously they planned to bolt, but something had stopped them.

Elise drove over the yard to block them in. She didn't want them fleeing until she could question them.

"Stay in the car," Elise told Bethy.

The woman ignored her, sliding out. "I'm not going to let you shoot the Jensens. Again."

Cabot growled softly, drifting toward the closed garage door. "Someone has been crafting here. I can smell it."

Anything could be in the house. Elise holstered her guns and pulled out her daggers.

Cabot sniffed loudly as he rattled the steel garage door to the two-car bay. "Locked." He leaned against it to listen. "Nothing is moving."

"Let's clear the house first." Elise turned and realized that Bethy had already charged through the front door. "Damn that woman."

"Hey!" Bethy called from the house. "Do you have a first-aid kit?"

Elise caught Cabot's amused glance. "What?"

He grinned sheepishly. "You're sexy when you're pissed off."

She blushed, not sure how to feel about the comment. Most

guys stopped finding her stunningly beautiful when she pulled out her weapons.

Bethy came to the door. "Well? I figure if you go around shooting people, you probably do have a first-aid kit in your car. Do you or don't you?"

"I have one." Elise ignored Cabot's snicker. "Who is in there and what are they doing?"

Bethy crossed her arms with a huff. "Mr. Jensen took a header in the kitchen from blood loss. Bart is having a meltdown. Johnny and Mrs. Jensen are trying to cope."

"Nothing else?" Elise asked.

"Like what?" Bethy clearly had no idea what the Wickers were capable of doing.

"Nothing...weird?" Elise didn't even want to try to explain constructs to the woman.

"Weird?" Bethy asked.

"Nevermind." Elise sheathed her daggers. She needed to get Bethy out of her life as soon as possible or she'd waste more valuable time trying to explain the impossible.

At one time, in the near past, the house had been the showpiece of a well-paid interior decorator. Winged chairs and leather sofas were artfully arranged around islands of large oriental area rugs that covered gleaming wood floors. The custom wood paneling, the chintz drapes, and paintings of fox hunts all harkened to an English manor lifestyle, not a backwater town in Central New York State. The rooms had been set to "autumn" with pumpkin scented candles and silk flower arrangements in shades of orange and yellow.

Sometime in the last week or so, chaos had blown through the house. Death lingered on the air; even the candles couldn't cover it. Bits of vines and dead leaves littered the floor along with long black zip ties. Judging by the number of cut restraints, the family had been kept hogtied in the living room when the warlock was too preoccupied to focus on them. Somewhere upstairs, the youngest wailed in long pent-up fear.

Carl Jensen lay on the kitchen floor. A bullet had cut a trail down the outside of his left leg. His wife Patsy was trying to administer first aid and failing badly while her eldest son shouted at her.

"We should call 911!" her son Johnny said.

"They will know then!" Patsy cried. "They will come and take us again."

"Not if I kill them first," Elise said.

Silence fell on the kitchen. The only sound was the wailing of the boy upstairs.

Bethy recovered first. "You can't just go around shooting people."

"Why not?" Elise asked. "I do it all the time."

"Are you some kind of sociopath?" Bethy cried.

"No, she's a law officer of the highest order." Cabot drifted in behind Elise. It surprised her how quietly he could move. Considering how his last brush with a Wicker in a kitchen ended, he was most likely spooked.

"Interpol?" Bethy said as if doubting the authority of the police agency.

"God." Elise put the first-aid kit down beside Patsy.

The woman flinched away. "Please don't hurt us. We didn't want to do those things. You got to believe us. Garland was a monster. He made us do horrible things. We were like remote-controlled toys to him and he took pleasure in breaking his toys. Please. It wasn't us. It was Garland."

"Yes, I know. That's why I shot him." Elise opened up her first-aid kit. It was a good thing that she'd restocked yesterday after dealing with Cabot. She would need to stock up again soon at this rate. "How long has ..." What was the name Patsy used? "How long has Garland been holding you captive?"

"Twelve days. We were at Sangertown Square to get snow boots for the boys. He walked up and looked at us and said 'oh, you'll do nicely' and that was it. He had us. We didn't even know that we should run from him. He seemed nice at first. It only seemed a little odd that we needed to leave with him."

Nearly two weeks? The Wickers had been in the area longer than she'd thought. Horrible for the Jensens but good news for her. They'd been held long enough to know useful information.

"How many are in his coven?" Elise cut open Carl's bloody pant leg, exposing the long narrow wound. Edges of the denim were stuck in the wound, embedded by the bullet. He was bleeding too much for just gauze. "Bethy, find me some clean towels."

"I'm not sure. They're all monsters." Patsy smeared her husband's blood on her face as she wiped at the tears running down her cheeks. "There was Garland and his mother and his uncle Reed. Reed is dead. There was a girl. Daphne. She's dead too. I'm not sure how she was related to Garland. The news is saying Reed was her father but that wasn't true. Her father was someone named Linden, who was killed when she was a baby."

"What's his mother's name?" Elise wanted to know how many Wickers were still alive. Bethy had said that Daphne's mother was Dahlia, or at least, the woman pretending to be the grieving mother.

"I don't know. We never saw her; he talked to her on the phone. Garland would mostly say 'yes, mother' and 'no, mother' to her."

"There's one in Europe," Johnny added. "Garland's brother or cousin. His name is Heath. First thing Garland did when he found out that Daphne had been killed was to call Heath and tell him to come back. They had a big fight on the phone. We couldn't hear what Heath was saying, but Garland kept shouting at him. He said that Heath had to be in Boston when they put the leash on the lost heir."

Cabot growled dangerously. If Joshua was Ilya Tatterskein, then he might have inherited Boston from his father, not Seth. "Where in Europe? Belgrade?"

"Yes!" the boy cried in surprise. "How did you know?"

"The Prince of Belgrade was killed by a large breach," Cabot explained to Elise. "The king left Friday morning to close it. None of this insanity would have happened if Alexander wasn't distracted."

The Wickers were on a tight timeline then. They needed to finish what they planned before the Wolf King returned to United States.

"What did he mean by leash?" Elise couldn't get the bleeding to stop. It soaked through all the gauze that she had in her kit before Bethy returned with a stack of folded bath towels. They were going to have to call 911 and get Carl to a hospital. Her window of questioning was closing quickly.

"I don't know," the boy said. "Please, I really don't. All I know was after Garland hung up, he kept shouting 'Not me! it won't be me!' And then...he...he...he made us...he made us do horrible things."

Elise didn't want to ask the nature of the acts Garland forced them to commit. Witches could dream up horrendous torture to display how complete their control was over their puppets. It made it less likely that the humans would disobey a command even when the witch didn't have full control over them. The historical records had given Elise nightmares when they covered it during her training. She didn't need new dreams.

"Daphne, Reed, Garland, Garland's mother, and Heath." Elise listed out the names they'd given her, starting with the Wickers that were safely dead. They still hadn't mentioned Dahlia. "Any others?"

"Rose," Patsy said. "She comes and goes. They're always saying that: where the hell has Rose trailed off to now? They treat her like she's some kind of bad weed. She's an older woman."

"She's at the Hillcrest Manor," the boy said. "It's a bed and breakfast. When Garland called his mother last, he told her that Rose and Cecily spent yesterday taking their dog to the vet to be tested for rabies and then getting it stuffed and mounted. Who does that to their dog?"

He misunderstood what had been done to the Thane Samuels.

"Is that all?" As if three wasn't enough to straighten Elise's hair. Four if Garland's mother wasn't Dahlia.

"I don't know," Patsy whispered. "I don't think so."

The boy shrugged even as he shook his head.

Elise changed the gauze for the stack of clean towels. "Here. Put pressure on this. Don't let up!"

She pulled Bethy into the living room. "He needs to be taken to the hospital or he's going to bleed out. Call 911. Once the ambulance gets here, don't let the kids out of your sight. Children often commit suicide after what they've been through, especially teenage boys. They feel like they should have protected their mother or siblings better. Make sure the people at the hospital understand that the family was held hostage for weeks."

"Me?"

"Yes, you." It would keep Bethy out of Elise's hair while she hunted for the remaining Wickers. "There was another family that Garland was holding. Find out what happened to them. They'll need intervention too if they were held more than a day or two."

She shouldn't have loaned Cabot her phone.

Somehow the Thanes decided that her number was his new contact information. The first call came as they were climbing into her Jeep. She frowned at the unrecognized number.

"That's Haji. Thane Tawfeek." Cabot held out his hand. He answered her phone with, "Cabot. Yes, for the time being, this is the number you can reach me at."

She was never going to be able to use her phone again. If he blithely assumed that a single use of her phone meant he could commander it, what else would he assume was his for the taking?

Garland's body after Cabot killed him flashed through her mind. He rendered the warlock into pieces in seconds. He'd obviously been trained to tear people limb from limb. Considering that anyone that he didn't kill instantly would become a feral werewolf, it should be no surprise. She'd been taught to kill humans but it was with blades and bullets. The intimacy of Cabot using his mouth unsettled her. It stressed how much faster and stronger he was than her. She shouldn't have told him that she was interested in him. At least, not until she knew she could trust him. He'd growled at her when he found out she knew where Joshua was.

He growled again, a dangerously loud noise in the tight confines of her Jeep. This time his anger was at the Thanes. "Yes, that's Seth's number but he's not answering his phone. Did you check with the Albany pack? Well, what did they say?" Cabot listened for several minutes before saying, "If Seth told them to leave him alone with the new marquis, then they should do it! Alexander sat on Seth for almost a month while he had alpha amnesia. Isaiah told them what? Oh, for Christ's sake, he can try to take Seth back to the city. No, I'd be happier knowing Seth was safe back at the Castle, it's just that I doubt Seth will allow that. If Isaiah doesn't want a public beating, he'd better give Seth at least a full day or two with the new marquis."

Cabot explained the fight with Garland and what they found out at the Jensens. "I'm heading to the bed and breakfast. The Jensens didn't know anything about what had been done with Samuels' body. The warlock that was holding them was trying to recover Joshua. The newborn. The warlock had made a huntsman that the Grigori killed and some snitches to spy on the boy's adoptive family. A pair of witches took Samuels' body from the vet's. We're hoping they're at the bed and breakfast with his skin."

Cabot listened, shaking his head. "The Wickers were in the area for at least two weeks before the Ithaca police called Bishop. They knew that wolves were incoming; they set a trap for both me and Samuels. They knew that Ithaca contacted the king; they had puppets there. The only reason they would let the information leak out was because they wanted it to. They wanted a Thane here. They wanted the newborn and for some Godawful reason,

Samuels' body. I think Albany might have been simply collateral damage—although they might have realized that we wouldn't be able to find the body without Albany's help. Certainly it means they've eliminated any chance for us to find them easily in Utica, but there's no way they could have predicted that Albany would be the one to trigger the booby-trap."

Cabot was right. The Wickers could have kept the Ithaca police department from calling the Wolf King. The Wakefields had planned on Joshua becoming a werewolf. They intentionally wounded the boy so that the Thane had no choice but change him to save his life. It was an insane plan requiring impossible timing. If they killed the werewolf too fast, then Joshua would have died of his wounds. It explained the anonymous 911 call so that the rescue teams arrived just as Joshua awoke. The EMTs were there to save Joshua's life in case the plan had failed.

It would have been a much easier task if the Wickers had been working with a willing subject. If the Wakefields had raised infant Ilya, they could have been able to condition him to be a sacrificial lamb.

The question remained, what did they plan to do with Joshua now that he was a werewolf? Elise could call Clarice, get her to focus her genius on the problem. To do that, though, she needed her phone back from Cabot.

He was gazing at her with a slightly sorrowful look. Her phone was nowhere in sight.

"What did you do with my phone?"

He patted at his pockets. "I was five when the Prince of Moscow sent his daughter Anastasia to Boston to marry my Uncle Gerald. She was thirteen, as headstrong as you'd expect a princess to be, and not happy about being sent to a country that didn't speak Russian. Because she was so young and didn't speak English, she lived with my family. My grandmother had been from Saint Petersburg and my father was fluent in Russian."

Elise wasn't sure why he was telling her this. Anastasia had been Joshua's biological mother, murdered by Wickers when she was just nineteen. Elise had known about the arranged marriage but she hadn't actually considered all the logistics. What were the wolves thinking, putting children that young into marriages? Shipping them off to foreign countries to live?

Then again, was it much different from her family? Elise flew to Greece when she was thirteen to take her vows as a Virtue and receive her daggers. Elise had pledged herself to God, not a boy on the onset of puberty, but she wasn't that much different from Anastasia. At least the other girl had the future of being Princess of one of the strongest territories in the world. It should have been a life of wealth and luxury with a large extended family. Elise had gotten a loft apartment, meals alone, and a depressed vampire as her only constant companion. Not to knock Decker, but he was a sad shadow of the man she remembered as a child.

Cabot was now checking the Jeep's various drink holders and change bins for her phone. "I don't remember what my parents told me but I distinctly recall asking my Grandmother Tatterskein why this strange girl had suddenly moved into the bedroom across the hall from mine. Nana said that Anastasia was the bride for the heir. Somehow, I decided that this meant she was going to marry me. To be fair, she was in my house, not Gerald's. I took some money from my dad's wallet and marched over to Macy's—scaring my family to death when I vanished without a word—to get an engagement ring."

How very sweet, but a little sad. Cabot had always been clueless.

It was also becoming obvious why Cabot didn't have his own phone on him. He'd gone back to patting his pockets. "It took a few months for me to get things straightened out in my mind. We settled on big sister and little brother. She didn't like Gerald at first; it was later that they fell madly and completely in love. Their fights at school until then were legendary. One time she flung this two-hundred-pound stone statue at him. Nearly killed him. It was one of the matched set of wolves that used to guard the front gate, so there's just this one wolf statue sitting there now. You remind me of her when you're angry."

Was this a good thing? Why was he telling her this?

"I think because she felt so isolated, she bonded closer to me than a teenage girl normally would. For the first two years, we were inseparable. I was jealous of Uncle Gerald when she finally fell in love with him. She knew I was feeling left out, so for nine months she made me part of her pregnancy. She took me to the sonogram. She let me feel it when Ilya started to kick. She even tried to let me pick his middle name, but Gerald wasn't buying Boba Fett. When Ilya was born, she made sure I was the first person to hold him after her and Uncle Gerald, even before my grandfather. Ilya was the tiniest thing I'd ever seen. She told me that I needed to protect him. That he would be my beloved baby brother just like I was hers. It was the first time I understood the term 'love at first sight.' Five days later, they were both gone."

The Wolf King hadn't sent a Thane to fetch Joshua, he'd sent the one person in the world who would move mountains to save him. Why hadn't Alexander told Cabot who he was looking for? Was it simply that the king had been distracted by the events in Belgrade or did he not want Cabot rushing blindly into danger? Certainly if Cabot had known it was Ilya at the barn with the Wicker, he wouldn't have played Rock-paper-scissors with Samuels. Cabot would have died at the barn instead of Samuels.

And she hadn't told Cabot where Ilya was. Still hadn't—not exactly.

"Joshua—Ilya—is in Boston. The Wickers sent a huntsman after him but we killed it. I have him where he should be safe from them. That's why the warlock came after me; he wanted to know where I had the boy hidden. I don't trust Bethy, though, to keep anything secret. She's a complete loose cannon with no clue what's going on."

"Who the hell is she?"

"Ilya's adoptive sister. She's doesn't know a thing about Wickers or werewolves. She's just trying to find her brother."

"Oh!" Cabot sat with a slight stunned look on his face as he thought back over the last few hours. "Okay. I couldn't understand why you were obviously lying. I thought you were trying to keep the information from me and doing a terrible job at it."

Note to self: subtlety was lost on the man.

"I'm sorry for being angry with you." He checked his door bin and found her phone. He held it out to her. "I'm sorry about your phone too. I lose mine so often that everyone is used to me improvising. They'll stop using this number once I call them with a different one."

"Apology accepted." She'd nearly pistol whipped a man yesterday for pointing a camera in her direction. Cabot had his heart ripped out at ten years old. She'd be a hypocrite if she couldn't forgive him growling a bit.

At least he demonstrated that he understood boundaries.

She pulled off the road into a cornfield before the driveway to Hillcrest Manor. According to the Jensens, the Wickers had taken over the bed and breakfast nearly three weeks ago. "How are we going to do this?"

"I'll scout ahead." Cabot pulled off his T-shirt.

"Oh, God," Elise whispered without thinking. After half a day, she'd gotten used to seeing him with clothes on. Shirt off was a whole different category of sexiness. Did he lift weights to achieve that chiseled physique or did it just come with the package deal? She'd never seen an overweight werewolf. Her breath caught as he undid his pants button.

"What?" He paused, hands on his pants zipper.

Elise stared at him for a minute before remembering what she was going to say. *You always considered your grandfather a pervert.* "I won't know if you run into trouble. No phone, remember?"

"Wolves can't use phones anyhow." He tugged his borrowed blue jeans down.

She blushed and looked away. *Wolves.* He's a wolf; only sometimes a stunningly sexy man. "Cars make effective weapons against Wicker constructs. I'll drive up."

"Be careful." He got out of the Jeep before stripping off his underwear. He tossed them onto the seat and shut the door.

She forced herself to watch him become a wolf; own what he was. He started to kneel. His body shimmered like the illusion that it was. The gleam became darker as his form blurred and changed shape. The color shifted from celadon to jade to obsidian. A wolf snapped into focus, larger than any found in the wild, covered in black fur.

See, he's not a human being. He's a magical being that just pretends to be human.

"I'll keep close to the driveway just in case." The wolf had Cabot's human voice. More proof that no matter the shape, his body wasn't true flesh and blood.

"Okay," she acknowledged only because she was on automatic. It was one thing to know that werewolves were magical creatures, quite another to witness a man that nearly kissed you reveal that his amazingly sexy body was all illusion.

You knew. You knew what he was. You saw him change before.

She started up her Jeep. Under the growl of the engine, she whispered, "Oh, will you just focus!"

❖   ❖   ❖

Topiary.

Why did it have to be topiary?

The bed and breakfast had been built in the late 1850s and styled after a big English manor. It was all pale limestone walls, banks of tall windows, and gray slate roof—even a cupola. The front lawn was massive and abnormally bare of trees and shrubs so that the visitor could be suitably impressed by the house.

Rambling like a flock of bored sheep, topiary meandered about the lawn, looking for something to kill.

There was a massive rabbit, a giraffe, and a family of elephants. The constructs must have originally been beloved evergreen sculptures and tourist attraction.

Elise paused the Jeep to stare at the topiary in dismay. "God, I hate Wickers."

Cabot appeared beside the car. He seemed to be laughing.

"What?" she snapped. There was nothing funny about this.

"The baby elephant! It's so cute!"

While the largest of the four elephants was bigger than her Jeep, the baby was the size of a Rottweiler. It charged around the other topiary as if on crack, its trunk upraised.

"It will not be cute when it's kicking our ass. They'll attack the moment we cross the patrol boundary that the Wickers set for them. It's probably a wide circle around the house, starting at the edge of the lawn." Otherwise, the topiary would wander off to attack neighboring herds of cows. The constructs weren't smart enough to differentiate between Grigori and Guernsey.

"There's a motor court around the side of the house," Cabot said. "It has a big wrought-iron gate. If we close it, they won't be able to get in."

"We'll have to be fast or baby elephant will get us." Hopefully the current movement of the other animals was indicative of their top speed.

"Race you!" He slipped away.

She couldn't see where he went. She had to trust that he was racing toward the motor court.

Trust. That was a word her family rarely used toward anyone, not even humans. Certainly never toward werewolves.

She floored the Jeep. When she hit the patrol boundary, the topiary turned and charged.

The rabbit outraced the baby elephant, coming in leaps and bounds that defied its root-bound origin.

"Come on," she growled at her Jeep, willing it to go faster.

The rabbit landed in front of her. It turned. Its face was a blank green mass of leaves.

"God in Heaven, hallowed be thy name!" She couldn't have stopped in time if she wanted to it. She plowed into it at full speed. She fought to keep her Jeep upright, but it rolled as the left wheels climbed the steep bulk of the rabbit. She felt holy power wrap tight around her as her Jeep tumbled across the lawn, the smell of bruised green and fresh earth filling the cabin. The rest of the herd came rushing toward her, a menacing rustle of leaves.

She landed passenger side down, airbags deployed. She clawed at her safety belt latch. She needed to get out before . . .

Her Jeep righted.

"Elise!" Cabot peered in the shattered passenger window at her. "Elise?"

Cabot had picked up her Jeep. He'd picked up a freaking car!

"Are you okay?" he asked.

"I'm fine!"

"They're coming."

She glanced in the rearview mirror. With the baby elephant in the lead, the other topiaries were nearly on top of them. The engine had stalled when she flipped. She dropped it into first, turned the key, and prayed. The Jeep roared back to life.

"Go!" She floored the Jeep.

Cabot dropped to all fours, turning into a wolf again.

The motor court had massive twelve-foot high decorative wrought-iron gates. Over-the-top impressive, yes, but probably not designed to withstand an onslaught of enraged topiary. She slammed on her brakes, skidding to a stop.

Cabot clanged the gates shut. "I don't know if they're going to hold; the lock is just for show. Papa Elephant is going to hit it full force."

"I'm on it." Elise shifted into reverse and quickly backed up so that the Jeep's back bumper pressed against the gates. Seconds later the elephants slammed into the iron bars. The Jeep shuddered and inched forward. "That will hold for now. We need to find the witch and kill her to stop them."

"They know we're here." Cabot leaned in the window to get his underwear. He didn't bother with the rest of his clothes.

"Works both ways. We know they're here too. This many constructs need to be mentally controlled within a short range." Elise undid the straps on the overhead gun rack and took down her shotgun. "We need to move before they can make and activate more constructs or call in backup."

"Shotgun?" He questioned her choice of weapons.

"Witch's greatest weapon is their mind. It's hard to think after you've been shot. It's easier to hit with wide-spread buckshot."

The door was locked and barricaded—not that it made much difference to Cabot. It was at once informative and intimidating to know how strong he could be. They entered via the back entrance into a huge kitchen.

The house reeked of fresh spilled blood. The Jensens had told Elise that the owners of the bed and breakfast had been an elderly couple, their son and daughter-in-law, and two young grandchildren. The Wicker must have heard of Garland's death and guessed that Elise would quickly discover their hiding place. She hoped it meant that the constructs had been a last-ditch defense but she knew better than to count on it. The Wickers understood that she was there to kill them. It was her sworn duty to God.

She stalked through the large kitchen, shotgun ready.

Cabot stayed at her side. "There are two witches upstairs. There's something else in the house. Something not mammal."

"Joy." The mind boggled as to what it could be.

The thudding outside in the motor court was a reminder that they had limited time before various reinforcements arrived.

"One is making a break!" Cabot charged through a large living room. The furniture was arranged into dozens of artful conversation groupings. He had to dodge around winged chairs and coffee tables.

Elise swore as she heard the front door open. "Cabot! Wait! Don't follow her!"

He collided with the baby elephant in the marbled foyer. Its bigger sibling wedged itself into the door trying to come through. Elise grabbed a heavy statue from one of the end tables. She flung it through the nearest window.

The witch was a young blond woman in a tight white sweater

and skinny jeans. Her name was Cecily if the Jensens were right about who was at Hillcrest Manor. Cecily turned at the sound of breaking glass. Her eyes went wide. Cecily pointed at Elise and shouted a command to the topiary. The giraffe swung its head toward the open window.

Elise shot the witch, hitting her square in the chest with the double-ought-gauge buckshot. Cecily went down screaming, blood instantly staining the white of her sweater. The giraffe froze, head inches from the window. Elise pumped the shotgun. She shot Cecily again as the witch tried to stagger to her feet. Once Elise was sure that Cecily didn't have the wherewithal to command the topiary, Elise drew her pistol. She took a careful aim with her Desert Eagle and made sure the witch was dead.

Clean death? Debatable. To the witch it wasn't any messier than being torn apart by a werewolf. Did she have any right to be squeamish over how Cabot killed?

"You were right; the topiary wasn't nearly as cute while it was kicking my ass." Cabot crawled out from under the mid-sized elephant that had managed to shove its way through the doorway. The baby elephant was frozen in place by the grand staircase. Mama blocked the front door.

Elise holstered her Desert Eagle. Picking up her shotgun, she pumped another round into the chamber. "All of the topiary seem to have been controlled by the dead witch. I think she was Cecily. The Jensens said she was a young woman. I think the Wicker upstairs is Rose."

Cabot sniffed. "You loaded with silver?"

"No. I locked it all up tight after Seth showed up."

"Damn, then Rose must have silver ammo." He pointed upstairs.

"I'll take point then."

"What?"

Elise drew her daggers. "I don't want to explain again to your people that I just happened to be covered in your blood."

"I heal," he stated firmly, but didn't charge up the stairs as if that settled the argument. Perhaps the elephants had taught him to listen to her.

"I can be bulletproof." She knelt down, daggers held point down.

"Really?"

"It takes a great deal of concentration. It's kind of like medita-tive prayer." Her cousins were better at it than she was. They teased her that she was from the angry side of the family. Apparently her mother was notorious for not being able to maintain the meditative state needed for the spell. If she didn't stay focused, the protective power vanished.

She lightly touched her dagger points to the marbled floor of the entryway. Leaves from the topiary covered the polished stone. She took a deep breath and struggled not to hear the loud rustling noise coming from upstairs or notice the muscles in Cabot's legs. Calm piety was what she needed to focus on. Another deep breath. "Blessed be the Lord, my rock, who trains my hands for war, and my fingers for battle; he is my steadfast love and my fortress, my stronghold and my deliverer, my shield and he in whom I take refuge."

Cabot stepped back as the power of the Lord settled over her. "Wow." He tilted his head. "Are those wings? It's kind of hard to tell. They're all ghosty."

She steeled herself against snapping "please shut up" since that would break the spell even as she formed it. "Amen."

She was halfway up the stairs, when the witch tried her first attack.

"Kill the werewolf," Rose commanded.

Elise's shield flared as the witch's power washed over her. "Never."

Rose gave a brittle laugh. "Do I detect feelings for the forbidden fruit? One has to admire your taste. Cabots are a wonderful mix of angelic and wolf."

Elise paused, surprised. She nearly turned toward Cabot but then caught herself. Focus! "Blessed be the Lord."

A bullet whined off her shield.

"My rock, who trains my hands for war, and fingers for battle." Elise started up the stairs again.

"Anton Cabot didn't have the full angelic glamour but he had enough to take your breath away." Rose's second and third shot ricocheted off Elise's shield.

"He is my steadfast love and my fortress," Elise growled.

Rose stood in the hallway. She seemed like a silver-haired grandmother except for the Glock in her hand and the massive rosebush lion at her side. The construct came rushing at Elise when she reached the top of the stairs.

"My stronghold and my deliverer." Elise sliced through the lion's left leg with both daggers. She sidestepped, letting momentum tumble the lion down the stairs to where Cabot waited. He could only slow the construct down but she only needed a moment.

"All that angelic sweetness wrapped in fur," Rose shot at Elise. "The sex must be amazing."

"My shield and He in whom I take refuge." Elise flung her right dagger.

It buried itself in the heart of the witch. The snarling and loud rustling downstairs went silent.

"Amen." Elise walked to the witch's body. She yanked out her dagger and cleaned it on carpet.

Only when she had all her weapons tucked away did she turn to Cabot. He was still human and covered with dozens of deep scratches that were quickly healing.

"Why didn't you tell me you're half angelic?" she said.

"Quarter angelic," Cabot corrected her. "You didn't know?"

"No!" she shouted.

"My grandfather—who I've never met—was angelic. It's why my father was a Thane."

"Your grandmother was Russian. Where did the name Cabot come from?"

"Lloyd Cabot was the Thane that the king married my grandmother to while she was pregnant with my father. Lloyd was killed in the king's service while my father was young. My grandmother works as the king's accountant for his Russian packs. She lives in Carnegie Hill on the Upper East Side."

"Why didn't you tell me?"

"We were kind of busy doing other things?" He echoed back her earlier excuse as to why she hadn't told him about Joshua. "My father was given the choice to be wolf or angelic at thirteen. He chose wolf. I chose wolf. Who slept with my grandmother has never mattered beyond that point."

"What was the name of the Grigori?"

"His name was Grigori."

"His first name!"

"Gavril. Why?"

"Because I wanted to know if we were related."

"I thought all Grigori were related."

"At first we weren't. Two hundred angels wed the daughters of man, and they all took more than one wife, as was the practice in those times. Our people all have one last name to reflect the fact we're descended from those the angels set to keep watch over mankind."

"That was an interesting way to 'keep watch.' Doesn't that make family trees confusing?"

"God, yes!" She didn't recognize the name so it meant that they weren't related for at least four generations.

"I'm sorry, I thought you knew. You knew my name when we first met. I just thought you knew *all* about me."

She'd thought she had. Was it because Gavril Grigori never knew he'd fathered a son? If Gavril didn't know, how did the Wickers find out?

"We should probably go," Cabot said. "If they called the police, they'll be here soon."

"We need information." Elise stalked into the nearest bedroom. "There is still at least one Wicker in the wind. Dahlia. Maybe two, if Dahlia isn't Garland's mother. The Wickers had something major planned, otherwise they would have fled the night you killed Reed Wakefield."

Luckily the bed and breakfast was devoid of the normal clutter of rightful owners. The Wickers had set up residence in hotel-sparse rooms. The two women had been packing when they'd been killed. Witches were clotheshorses; they had a massive amount of luggage. Elise emptied the suitcases onto the beds and sorted through the contents.

Cabot roamed through the room, opening up drawers and looking under the bed. "I'd always hoped we'd find Ilya alive but everyone always said that the Wickers took him to sacrifice him."

"They needed him as a werewolf, not a youngling."

Finding nothing of interest, Cabot moved to the next bedroom. "They couldn't have made him a wolf as an infant," he called from the room across the hallway. "Children go feral even when they're changed by alphas. That's why we wait until younglings are thirteen before making them into wolves. The magic overwhelms them if they're younger than ten or eleven. Alexander decided that we'd wait until thirteen just to be sure."

"If he'd been raised among wolves, then he'd recognize the Wickers as evil. He would have fled to Albany or the king, not to Boston where there's no werewolves."

There was a crack of breaking wood. "Oh, this has 'I'm important' written all over it!" Cabot called.

She hurried to see what he'd found. It was a large metal suitcase that had been padlocked into a closet. Cabot had simply torn the entire door frame out of the wall.

She tried opening it. "Locked."

"No problem." He tore the lid off.

There were ancient books and bound sheaves of paper.

Elise picked up one of the books. The lettering inside was all done by hand with careful spell runes illustrated. "It's their grimoire."

"What the hell?" Cabot flipped through the bound papers. "These are photocopies of wolf bloodlines. How the hell did Wickers get these?"

That explained how Rose knew that Cabot was angelic. "Who would have the originals?"

"Alexander." He continued to flip. "His are at the Castle. He's got one room just filled with all the records going back a thousand years or more. I think these are copies of the pack's ledgers. The king requires each alpha to record all births so he can keep track of family bloodlines. These are only the prince-doms. Boston. London. Moscow. Las Vegas. Los Angeles. And only for the last three hundred years or so."

"Three hundred?" She flipped to the inside cover of the gri-moire. "Oh shit."

"What?"

"This is the Monkhoods grimoire."

"Monkhoods. I know that name, don't I?"

"The Monkhoods nearly wiped New York City off the face of the map in 1702."

"*Those* Monkhoods! I thought they were all dead."

"Wickers are harder to pin down than ghosts."

Cabot turned sharply to listen to something she couldn't hear. "We really need to go. Now."

26: SETH

The city of Albany was a little exclamation point of skyscrapers in the middle of pastures. They rounded a bend on the NY Thruway after driving an hour in cow country and there it was, in its entirety. Seth hadn't realized that the state's capital was so small compared to New York City. It looked like it could fit in one block of Manhattan.

They stopped first at the pack's funeral home and met with the county coroner who was also the local wise woman. She signed off on death certificates for both the old marquis and Samuels, citing natural causes. It made Seth wonder about the Boston network that bypassed the official system. Who had signed off on his little brothers' mangled bodies?

Seth ordered the grandsons hostile to him to stay at the funeral home and oversee the cremations. He wanted a clear slate when they hit the family home.

Hundreds of years ago, the Court of Albany might have been well outside of the city but urban sprawl had grown up around it. "Wolf Road" was packed solid with strip malls, chain restaurants, and red lights. Set back from the road, protected by a high brick wall, and screened by evergreens, the pack's homes were invisible to the casual eye.

The Court was a collection of brick Queen Anne Victorians gathered around a cul-de-sac. They were big beautiful houses with all sorts of towers and attic gables and gingerbread trim.

The pack had felt the old marquis die. They knew from frantic phone calls that the new marquis was on his way home. They waited in the street to meet him, visibly distressed.

"Who are all these people?" Ewan cringed back.

"I told them not to do this." Seth struggled not to be angry. He needed to be the calm one.

"They're scared," Cameron whispered. "They need to see that we'll be okay."

"They have each other." Seth fought to keep his voice neutral. "This is not the time to be putting stress on Ewan. It will take him longer to find his balance."

Cameron nodded. "I'll deal with them. Ewan lives..." He stopped as he realized that everything had changed during the morning. "Oh! He'll take over Sire's place."

"Not yet. It needs deep cleaning, especially the bathrooms. The scent of another alpha in his sleeping space will unsettle him even when he doesn't understand what it is."

Cameron took a deep breath, bracing for the emotional landmines of having to clear out his grandfather's private areas. "I'll see to it. Ewan is in the bachelor house." He pointed at the house that they'd parked in front of. "Second floor. The bedroom with all the books."

Seth waited for Cameron to start the process of shooing away the pack.

"Who are they?" Ewan asked again, louder.

"That's your family. You know them all very well. You'll remember everything soon. Until then, you need to be patient."

The bachelor house had all the slightly chewed on marks of being home to male wolves too old to live at home with their parents but who hadn't found a mate yet. Decorations were nonexistent. The furniture was battered. The downstairs was crowded with games that could be played by teams. Darts. Billiards. Foosball.

The house had three bathrooms total. Ewan found and used all three without realizing that he was marking his territory.

Upstairs four of the six big bedrooms showed signs of being inhabited. Seth identified the owners by their scents. Cameron's room had a Giants poster and a desk scattered with engineering textbooks. The man seemed to be going to school at Rensselaer Polytechnic Institute. Seth wondered if it was where Cameron wanted to go or if he had wanted to go to MIT and wasn't allowed. Cameron seemed old to be college student; maybe he was a professor.

The other two housemates were the males that had quietly sided with the brothers; Seth hadn't caught their names. There was no sign of Dan and his supporter. They must live elsewhere. Seth felt relieved that Ewan could sleep without fear of attack.

Ewan's bedroom had floor to ceiling shelves crowded with books.

"Wow!" Ewan ran his hands over the spines as if they were made of gold. "I love to read."

"Yes. You do." That was obvious. "This is your room."

"It is? Awesome!"

Seth opened up drawers of the small chest looking for clothes and clues to who the inner Ewan really was. "Here. Get changed into your own clothes. You'll feel more comfortable. We need to get you reacquainted with yourself."

Ewan liked cotton boxer briefs, blue jeans and red flannel shirts. Ewan owned a wide range of books. He leaned toward mysteries but his collection was heavily seasoned with science fiction, epic fantasy, westerns and historical non-fiction. He liked Celtic Rock, which Seth hadn't known was a thing. It featured electric guitars, violins and bagpipes. Bagpipes?

While Ewan seemed willing to settle in and read everything in his bedroom, Seth moved them downstairs.

"Your grandfather might have explained things to you. He might not have. Either way, you're not going to remember anything for a while, so I'm giving you a crash course."

Seth put the empty rack on the billiards table. "This is your territory. The Marquis of Albany."

Seth picked up the cue ball and put it on the other side of the table. "And that is our king, Alexander. He's not contained within a rack. He controls the entire world. What I don't have here are all the other territories; all the other racks. Each territory— whether it's a marquisate like Albany or a little barony out in the middle of the nowhere like Juneau, Alaska—exists with or without wolves."

Seth put the solid yellow number one ball into the rack in the point facing the cue ball. "Over three hundred years ago, the king tapped your ancestor, Aillig Keir, to be the first Marquis of Albany. This morning, your grandfather died and you became the Marquis. Through you, all the other members of your family share the power that is Albany." Seth avoided the word "wolf" since sometimes newborns forgot the existence of werewolves. "It's a hierarchy of power. The king. You. Your family."

"I don't get it. How does the king figure into this? He's outside the rack."

"Because the rack is part of the whole that is the pool table. Think of all the green as one massive power source. The rack only limits what part of the green that the alpha can access. The king protects you from being overwhelmed by all the other green by limiting your connection to just this one area."

"Should I be taking notes?"

Yes? No? Seth hadn't written down anything his father told him. He'd been a quiet man, deeply etched by grief. Seth always sensed that if his father bothered to say anything that it was important. Alexander had merely told Seth to give a newborn alpha a sense of self, a structure to connect new power and abilities to. He'd warned Seth that people being what they were, there was no one-size-fits-all framework.

Seth compromised on, "If it makes you feel more comfortable, yes."

Apparently written words made Ewan more comfortable; the new marquis went off to find pen and paper. Then paper towels and another pen, as Ewan snapped the first one in two, causing a sudden flood of ink.

"You're stronger than you were before," Seth warned. "It's going to take a while for you to get used to that."

Time that Seth didn't really have to babysit a newborn alpha. He'd forgotten to tell Jack where he was going. He still had Jack's phone, so he couldn't call his cousin. Jack was in a car with the Grigori close at hand, traveling toward Seth. Maybe one of the Thanes had told Jack where Seth was headed.

For reasons Seth couldn't guess, Joshua was painting Decker's kitchen. Seth could understand the Grigori hiding a newborn wolf with the vampire; that made sense given all the available options. Painting the vampire's kitchen? That was a total WTF: vampires didn't eat.

"I still don't get it." Ewan's confusion pulled Seth back from Boston. "The king is the felt and the cue ball?"

"Here, give me the paper." Seth wrote down "King" and circled it. "See, this is Alexander. Under him are all the alphas." Seth created only four triangles under it. "There's you and your three nearest neighbors. To the east, Prince of Boston. Me. To the north is the Viscount of Burlington. To the west is the Baron of Syracuse. There are hundreds of other territories all around the world. Each territory has an alpha and we're all connected to the king. He is our alpha. We get our power from him."

"I thought we get our power from the territories."

"But he *is* the territory, just as you are Albany. He is the world. You are Albany."

Ewan frowned at the paper for several minutes. "Okay. Is marquis stronger or wimpier than barons?"

"Stronger. Much stronger. The order is King, Prince, Marquis, Earl, Viscount, Baron, Baronet."

"Wow, so Syracuse is a complete wimp?"

"Yes. But don't ever say that to the baron's face. Unless of course, he's being an asshole. Part of being a good alpha is learning not to be a jerk just because you can. You can't lead with fear. It gives too much free rein to your beast. Anger becomes your automatic response."

The doorbell rang. It was the three other Albany bachelor housemates with a stack of extra-large pizzas.

"I know how much newborns can eat." Cameron held the boxes out as an offering. "It's like they're black holes. Sire used to say that they were eating for two. I got Ewan's favorite. Paesan's."

The smell of hot cheese and savory meats made Seth's stomach growl. It was dusk and he hadn't eaten since breakfast.

"Please, we need to talk," Cameron said.

Seth wished he knew that he was doing this right. Alexander had only given him rough guidelines on helping a newborn alpha. He wanted to believe Cameron would keep his little brother safe. "Where's Dan and Keagan?"

"Keagan lives at the dorms at RPI. Dan is kind of married. He knocked up one of our second cousins in high school. That was back when our Uncle Wynford was heir. All of us had our lives put on hold after Uncle Wyn died. Dan and his wife have been on and off since then. She blames Dan for jumping the gun. She's worried that the king will move her and their boys to Boston. Nothing against you, but it's not home. Everything she knows is here in Albany. Dan will come around eventually once he realizes how screwed he would have been if he'd gotten the alpha."

Seth hoped that Cameron was a good judge of character. "Come in, but no 'you remember when' or 'don't you remember so and so.' Just keep to the moment."

Cameron glanced to his cousins. "We understand."

Ewan's favorite pizza had sausage, pepperoni, and meatballs smothered under cheese. Hidden jalapenos were little notes of heat nearly lost under the mountain of meat. The cousins turned out to be named Drustan and Tadhg.

Cameron waited until they were on their second slice of pizza before launching into the real reason the bachelors had showed up in force. "Thane Silva called asking if you were safe with us. I told him that you were. They're still hunting Wickers in Utica. He made it sound as if they intend to drag you back to New York City, whether you want to go or not. They can't really do that, right? You're a prince."

No, Isaiah couldn't make Seth do anything directly but he could threaten to create massive collateral damage. "The king ordered them to make sure I'm safe from the Wickers."

"Wickers wouldn't be so stupid as to . . ." Cameron stopped in mid-sentence. His eyes went wide. "Shit! I just remembered! Aren't you like just fifteen? What the hell are you doing in the middle of this mess?"

"You're fifteen?" Ewan cried. "I thought you were like twenty-five."

"I'm sixteen. I'll be seventeen at the end of the year."

"Seventeen is still—wait—how old am I?" Ewan asked.

"You're twenty-one," Cameron supplied. "You're the bachelor house baby."

"I'm twenty-one? I'm an adult then. He's just . . ."

Cameron caught Seth's flash of annoyance. "Ewan! Don't— Don't go there. Please."

"But he . . ."

Cameron held up a hand to try to ward off Ewan's attempts of finishing the sentence. "Please. Please."

Drustan distracted Ewan with another piece of pizza.

"Why are the Thane being such jerks?" Tadhg was the eldest of the four and thus the one most likely to view Seth as a child. "If you get an orphan puppy dropped on you, you don't pull the crap they're doing. They tried to trash talk to Sire about you when we first showed up at the hotel. The phone call was more of the same. What the hell is that about?"

"When Isaiah becomes Prince of New York..."

"According to Sire, that's an 'if' he becomes." Tadhg proved that the cousins had all overheard the supposedly private conversation.

"In this case, it's 'when.' New York doesn't have a pack beyond the Thanes. When Isaiah or anyone else becomes prince, the only people he'll have at the start will be Thanes that the king gives him. As luck has it, the ones that will most likely stay with the king are the most dominant Thanes. His lawyer Bishop. Devi. Nakamura. Beridze. Cook."

"Oh, I see," Cameron said. "Low rung people get an instant kick up to top rung the moment Isaiah becomes prince."

Seth nodded. "But only if Isaiah asks for them to stay as part of the New York pack. If they remain with the king, then they'll shift to wherever the king sets up residence next—which might be Tokyo or Karachi."

"Where?" Drustan asked.

"Pakistan." Seth wondered if their grandfather had taught them anything. In his defense, the old marquis probably had focused on his sons who were now dead. "It's on the coast of the Arabian Sea."

"Talk about leave everything you know behind!" Drustan muttered. "I'd suck up to Isaiah too."

Tadhg smacked his cousin.

"Ow!" Drustan grabbed another piece of pizza and moved out of range. "You don't have to be a jerk to suck up to someone. There's suck up and then there's suck up. You set your limits and keep to them. Have your principles. I thought the Thane were supposed to be the best of us. The all-stars. The king's voice."

"The ones he actually sends out to be his voice, yes," Seth said. "They're all handpicked and trained. They're top rung. They'll go with the king when he shifts residence. There's about a dozen, though, who were yanked out of their pack because the king didn't want them taking the alpha. Samuels was one; he was fine with the demotion. Some of the others are bitter because they could have been top dog."

"They're not even near the top anymore," Cameron said.

"Exactly," Seth said. "None of the Thanes at Utica have ever been sent out as the king's voice. They normally do things like work the carpool, clean the Castle, take suits to the dry cleaner, and guard the doors."

"We're not going to let them take you," Tadhg said firmly. "This is the safest place in the state beyond the Castle. We need you here. They would never try this if Ewan was up to speed."

"I'm Ewan in this story, right?" Ewan tapped his chest.

"Yes," they chorused.

He pointed to his brother and cousins. "You're Cameron, Tadhg, and Drustan and our family sucks at naming people. You," he pointed at Seth. "You are really scary when you're mad. And I'm not following this at all. What's your name again?"

"Seth Tatterskein. I'm the Prince of Boston. Your neighbor."

Drustan snorted at Seth's choice of words. "Sire always said that you should keep a close eye on your neighbors. When their shit starts to fly, you're the first to be hit."

"Drustan!" Cameron smacked his younger cousin. "How long will Ewan be this way?"

"It depends," Seth said. "If we keep him from being stressed out, maybe a week or two. My grandfather died last Wednesday. His heir only suffered a few hours of amnesia."

"What about breaches?" Tadhg asked. "We always have more when the king is out of the country. We had one just this weekend. My little sister Bryg was dragged under and nearly killed. Sire always finds the breaches and closes them. How soon will Ewan be able to do that?"

What did Seth tell them? That he had no idea because the king never let him near one?

"I don't—I don't know how long it will take him to learn how to close them. It took me two months just to be able to pinpoint them on a map."

"Close what?" Ewan said. "What are we talking about?"

The three cousins looked horrified. They'd lost fathers, mothers, brothers, and sisters to the monsters spawned by breaches.

"What are we supposed to do?" Cameron asked.

Seth wished he could offer his help but he was running blind in Albany. "Until Ewan can handle it, the king will close any breaches that open."

"But he's in Europe!" Drustan cried. "How soon does he get back?"

Alexander couldn't be in two places at once. If he had to choose, the king probably would protect the two million people of the Serbian city over the tens of thousands in Albany.

"I don't know," Seth whispered.

27: DECKER

Decker woke knowing he'd made a horrible mistake.

He'd forgotten what it was like to be alive. To move around while he was awake instead of lolling in his bed, wanting oblivion to take him again. To live instead of merely existing.

He'd forgotten how quickly he became hungry. For a decade, he only had to feed once every week or so. The months he mostly spent sleeping, he could go for weeks. On top of being wounded, he'd spent the nights cleaning and shopping. He'd burned through his reserve.

He had to feed. Now. Before he lost control completely.

He hurried upstairs. He needed Elise. She would keep humans safe from him if he lost control. He didn't want Joshua to realize how weak his control...

He stopped in the kitchen door, surprised. Joshua had obviously spent the day painting.

Nude.

Well, not completely nude. He was wearing white briefs and a pair of blue jean shorts that were threatening to fall off. It showed off the fact that his martial arts training had given him chiseled abdomen muscles. Sweat gleamed on his bare skin. The dark stubble on his jaw suggested that he'd forgotten to shave in the morning. Thankfully he'd covered the wide front window with newspaper, or the entire neighborhood would have been treated to a show.

He turned, saw Decker, and blushed. "I was going to wait for you but I was impatient to see what it looked like. I was just going to do a little. What do you think? Elise said your favorite color was teal blue. Is this okay? It's called ocean blues. I thought it went well with the white cabinets."

"What happened to your clothes?"

"I kept getting paint on me and then I stepped in the paint pan." Joshua pointed at one of his sneakers, its sole covered in teal paint. "I'm starting to see why my mom never would let me—Decker?"

Without realizing he was even moving, Decker had crossed the room and wrapped himself around Joshua. He tasted as good he smelled.

"Did—did you just lick me?" Joshua asked.

Oh damn it all. This is not good.

"I'm hungry." He forced the words out. "This is very bad."

Joshua shifted into a now familiar judo hold, but he didn't follow through. "We agreed on no biting!"

"Joshua, I'm sorry," Decker panted, trying to keep hold of the urge to feed. "If I do not eat, now, I will kill the first human that I cross paths..." He was suddenly on the floor with Joshua straining to hold him pinned. This close, he could not help but feel the power inside the warm body. "This is really not helping."

"Will you kill me if I let you feed?" Joshua growled.

Could he keep in control? "I-I-I think—I think you'll hate—feeding—"

Joshua tightened his hold to punishing. "Focus, Decker! Will you kill me?"

The monster wanted it. "You will hate..." Me.

"But you'll lose it if you don't?"

"Yes." He was almost losing it now. "I—I—" Couldn't think of another answer.

"So? Do it." Joshua let go.

Decker had him in his arms, nuzzling into Joshua's neck, before he could stop himself. The scar from the werewolf attack was at the juncture of Joshua's shoulder and neck. It hadn't been a ragged wound of a mauling, but one bite, done with almost surgical care.

"Hey! Hey! What are you—? Decker!" Joshua yelped as Decker's hands moved by an instinct he couldn't control.

He could sense the power locked within the werewolf's skin. Deep as an ocean, warm, smelling of green. He wanted to wallow in it. Needed to. It was full of dappled sunshine and dark shadows and soft fur. He licked his way to Joshua's mouth and kissed him hard and drank deeply. He was vaguely aware of

Joshua's fingers tangled in his hair. Decker half expected Joshua to tear his head from his shoulders, or at least rip his hair off his skull. The werewolf could; he had the strength. Instead Joshua whimpered and moaned and strained against him. Power flooded through the connection, dark and wild.

He hoped he would be able to stop with just a sip, but his body drank until he was full. Satiated, he slumped against Joshua.

Joshua gazed at him with full golden wolf's eyes.

"Oh, Joshua, no," Decker whispered, fear filling him. Was the boy going to transform? Decker had never fed on a wolf before. Had he stripped away Joshua's control? The window was right there; Joshua could be in the street, killing, before Decker could even try and stop him. "Stay with me."

Joshua blinked and his eyes returned to their human brown, but filled with confusion. "What—what the hell was that?"

Decker laughed with relief. "I told you that you would hate it."

Joshua stuttered for a full minute trying to make words come out before he cried, "I thought you were going to bite me! Drink my blood! That's what vampires do!"

"I only sink to that level if I lose total control." His limbs were refusing to move. Joshua was going to hate him for this. Decker could see it on his face already. "I'm sorry. I didn't want to. I should have gone out yesterday. Killed something."

"But—but—did you have to—you know—touch me?"

Thank God he had only touched. There were worse things his body could have done once it slipped free of his control. "Life essence is strongest during sex and death." He could have killed Joshua.

"Oh God, don't say sex." Joshua pushed him off. "I need to go shower."

Decker laid on the plastic dropcloth, limp with magic-fed euphoria, even as Joshua crawled toward the stairs. He'd screwed up horribly. Joshua was going to hate him. Joshua might never want to see him again.

"You could have warned me!" Joshua called back. "We could have had this conversation days ago!" He deepened his voice to mimic Decker's. "Oh by the way, you might want to keep me fed or I'll try and jump you!"

Decker covered his mouth to keep in the laughter. But if he didn't laugh, he was going to weep his soul out. Not that either would help at this moment.

28: JOSHUA

What was that? What the freaking hell was that?

Joshua huddled in the scalding hot water, not wanting to think, but not able to get past the echoes of something rolling through his body. When Decker had talked about power and light bulbs and the surface of the sun, it had all seemed metaphysical and stupid and relating to someone else but not him. Not him. That wasn't him.

It was the wolf.

But he was the wolf.

But that wasn't him.

He'd known that he was feeling weird around Decker. His tablet was full of stuff leaking out that he didn't want Decker to know about. That he smelled good. That smell made him want to be close to Decker. To roll. To wallow.

And Decker had reached through Joshua and tapped something huge within him—something that he didn't even know was there. Tapped and opened the valves and poured it through him.

And the wolf enjoyed it.

The wolf had moaned and opened his mouth wide and thrust his hips in an effort to feel more of Decker. The wolf had raised his hands, grabbed hold of Decker's hair and pulled him closer. The wolf wanted more.

Joshua had been merely been along for the ride.

Decker had warned him that he would hate it. Joshua felt so stupid. He'd thought it would be painful and bloody and he had the possibility of dying—nobly protecting the lives of others—but actually dying. He'd asked that stupid question about being killed.

And afterwards, Decker had laughed at his stupidity.

Decker knew he'd hate it.

Decker probably thought he was a stupid, stupid little homo kid.

And now he was being a stupid little emo kid. Sitting in the shower, crying his eyes out.

The water started to run cold. He didn't feel better. Cleaner.

He turned off the water and woodenly toweled himself off.

What was that? What had Decker tapped into? He couldn't feel it as strongly as when Decker was—was—doing *that* to him. But it was as if he'd been blown up like a huge balloon and now was walking around, aware of the emptiness inside of him.

No, not empty.

Dormant.

A forest at dusk instead of full day.

There had been sunlight and the smell of green.

Was green his favorite color? Really? Had he even ever actually had to sit and think about it? No one ever asked. At least, he couldn't remember anyone ever asking him. It wasn't a question people asked boys. It was a girl thing.

Decker thought green was Joshua's favorite because he'd bought all green shirts at Target. But for back-to-school shopping two months ago, Joshua had bought all blue shirts.

His favorite color had been blue.

What the hell was that?

He went to his empty bedroom and sat on his airbed. *This is my life. One big vast emptiness. No family. No friends. No future. Not even a favorite color. The wolf took everything. I have nothing.*

He felt utterly lost. He hated the feeling. He'd been happy all day. The paint had transformed the kitchen and family room that had been filled with trash just the day before. He'd been looking forward to moving on to painting his bedroom. He and Decker planned to buy a couch and TV tonight. The man hadn't seen a movie for forty years. There were so many things Joshua wanted to share with him. All the *Hobbit* and *Lord of the Ring* movies alone would take a week to get through. Decker was going to be so blown away by all the special effects.

Was he really excited about sharing the movies with Decker? Or was it the wolf who wanted to be with the vampire?

Oh God, he was freaking whimpering again.

If he sat here alone until sunrise, then he would be utterly alone afterwards.

He couldn't call his folks. Ignoring the entire werewolf issue, there was no way he was going to talk about sexual orientation with his parents. Ditto for his handful of close friends. Elise had sounded like she was too busy trying to stay alive to deal with his petty problems.

Which meant that the only person in the world safe to talk to was downstairs.

This was going to be so embarrassing.

If Decker made a single freaking joke, he was going to beat the snot out of the vampire.

Decker sat on the floor of the kitchen, hands pressed to his face.

Joshua stood at the door, not knowing what to say. *Not that. Or that. Nor that.*

He scanned the freshly painted family room. He'd done it first in forest green. He didn't know how it made him feel. Part of him thought that the color was calming and restful. That it made the house a safe retreat from the world. He suspected, though, that was the wolf. The real Joshua probably didn't give a shit what color the walls were.

"What was that?" Joshua finally decided was a safe thing to say. "The green?"

"It's the source of your power." Decker's voice was ragged with emotion. The vampire sounded as if he was close to crying. "A werewolf's bite is a magical wound. It connects you to the pack's magic. That's why it isn't a disease that can be cured. I've never heard of anyone being able to seal off a soul once it's been opened to a power source. Trust me. I've spent hundreds of years searching for a way to free myself from my curse. If it were possible, I would have found it. The only reason I still exist is I've always been too much a coward to kill myself. It's probably why I can't keep my mouth shut; I keep hoping I'll piss the wrong person off enough that they'll put me out of my misery."

"You really want to die?"

"I have been very happy the last few days. To have you leave—I could not bear that. Not after remembering what it's like to be truly alive. I've been so lonely since Saul died. Please don't hate me."

"I don't hate you," Joshua snapped. "I'm pissed. I didn't want—I'm not gay."

"I know. I have teased you, and I'm ashamed now. It seemed harmless, since I thought nothing would ever come of it. And now those thoughtless jests poison everything. I'm sorry. I did not want to hurt you."

"I think Joshua likes you. I know the wolf likes you a lot. Why? And how do I know when it's me and not the wolf?"

"I don't know. My friendship with the Grigori and the hours I keep mean I rarely cross paths with werewolves. They're all early to bed and early to rise people; it's the Puritan influence on Boston."

"Someone has to know."

Decker sat quietly on the floor, thinking. After a minute, he said apologetically, "The royal vet."

"The who?"

"The prince maintains a doctor to take care of the pack. She's the royal vet. If anyone is going to know anything, it's Dr. Huff."

"You're taking me to a vet?"

They took a taxi to Watertown. The offices were closed when they reached it.

"Great," Joshua growled.

"She's the royal vet. She'll see you, no matter what time of day it is." Decker got out and paid the taxi driver.

"You're kidding."

"No. The prince paid for her training and bought this building for her. She cannot refuse you."

The vet looked barely old enough to be a doctor, although it might have been the long pigtails, black eye shadow and lipstick. She glared at their hands, then their feet, then out at the curb.

She scowled up at Decker. "Where's your pet?"

Decker tilted his head slightly to indicate Joshua.

"Oh!" She smiled brilliantly and patted Joshua on the head. "Who in the world are you? Such a little cutie! Good boy! Good boy!" She scratched him behind his ear, which felt ridiculously good. "Come on in."

Dr. Huff led them through her living room, full of chrome and black leather, pushing aside her small pack of mismatched dogs. She had a three-legged black lab that was gray around the muzzle, a pit bull missing an eye and a little Jack Russell terrier that seemed to have springs built into its feet. By a side door, she paused to get a large cookie out of a big clear jar.

"Here." She handed him the cookie.

It was a very good cookie, although very savory, as if it had bacon mixed in with the sweetness.

She took out another, broke it into three pieces. "Sit. Good boys. Stay." She tossed a piece to each dog.

"Did you just feed me a dog biscuit?" Joshua said.

"I bake them myself." She led the way through the side door, calling, "A hungry wolf is a dangerous wolf!"

There was a waiting room that smelled of disinfectant with pictures of dogs and cats and various illnesses each could get. Joshua slowed down as he took in the various magazines scattered on the side table, a wall of flea and tick medication, and a poster that stated "Get your pet microchipped!"

"W—w—wait," he cried. "You're a real vet?"

"Of course I am. You don't think the prince would trust his family to a quack, do you? Here, take your shoes off and step on the scale."

It was a low, wide scale meant for large dogs. Joshua eyed it for a minute before sighing and taking off his shoes. "Is this totally necessary?"

"Yes." She noted his weight on a form. "Good boy!" She handed him another biscuit. "Now your height."

Joshua stared at the cookie. The first one had been good. He wasn't sure he wanted to eat another now that he knew what they were. "What is in these?"

"Things to keep werewolves happy and healthy." She nudged him toward a wall-mounted height rod. It looked identical to the one that his pediatrician used. "They're also good for dogs, but I balance them for werewolves."

"How can everyone just look at me and know I'm a werewolf? I don't look any different!"

She noted his height. "This job requires a degree of awareness. Psychic. Spiritual. Supernatural. Whatever you want to call it. It's why the prince chose to send me to school and not any other of the fifteen hundred applicants for his scholarship."

She noticed that he was still staring at the biscuit. "Eggs, milk, bacon bits, maple syrup, whole wheat flour, and oats." She patted the stainless steel table. "Hop up. You radiate 'I am magic' now to anyone that can sense that kind of thing. Those of us with experience with various magical creatures can tell what kind of being you are. Good boy."

This was because he'd eaten the cookie or scrambled up on the table or both.

"Please don't do that." Joshua glanced at Decker and it worried him that the vampire wasn't smirking as usual. Decker was still looking freaked, which was at once unsettling and reassuring. Decker was really scared that Joshua would leave, which might mean that he was deadly serious about killing himself.

"Sorry." She caught herself before scratching behind his ear. "It's been a few years since I had a wolf patient."

"Why? What happened to all the wolves in Boston?" He flinched as she tapped his knees with rubber mallets. "And do you need to do that? You haven't even asked why I'm here yet."

"You're a wolf in Boston." She took his hands and looked at the fingernails on his right hand. "You're now my patient. I need to get a baseline of what is normal for you before someone drags you in here half-dead and wanting me to treat you for God knows what. It takes a lot to bring a werewolf down, so when one comes to me, they're very messed up. Unfortunately, there is a shitload of weird stuff in Boston these days that the Grigori can't keep up with, so I want a complete workup on you. Especially if you're with him. You are Silas Decker, aren't you?"

"I didn't realize I was known," Decker said.

Dr. Huff snorted and switched to Joshua's left hand. "Oh, please, you've been in Boston longer than I've been alive. People talk, especially about potentially dangerous neighbors. If it makes you feel better, people are glad that Boston had a backup plan now that the shit has hit the fan."

Joshua jerked free his hand. "What do you mean by that? 'Especially if you're with him.' What shit and what fan?"

She stopped and stared at Joshua. "Oh. Oh dear."

"What?" Joshua asked fearfully.

"You—you weren't raised by wolves?" Dr. Huff said.

"No!" He was fairly sure she meant werewolves and not literal wolves.

"Oh my!" She glanced at Decker. "Where the hell did you find him?"

"Back Bay Fens. Killing trees."

"You mean the huntsman was after him?"

Decker nodded.

"Oh, good God!" Dr. Huff said. "Do you even know the first thing about taking care of a puppy?"

"Hello!" Joshua cried. "I'm still here! What shit? What fan? How do you know about the huntsman? It wasn't on any news-feed. And don't call me a puppy; I'll be eighteen in four months. I can take care of myself."

Dr. Huff gave him two cookies. "A puppy is a werewolf under the age of eighteen. Although I suspect you're actually a newborn. Werewolf families normally isolate newborns for a month. You're a lot stronger than you think. You can kill someone if you hit too hard. You must never hit a human."

"I know. It's why I left home. I wouldn't—hit that is. The first thing they tell you in martial arts is not to strike out in anger. Next year I would have gone to college." The hurt of that failed dream made the wolf whimper. "I would have left home then."

She huffed. "You might be able to take care of yourself if you were still human. You don't know anything, however, about werewolves. Worse, you can't go on the Internet and look it all up. Which is why you're probably here. You've got questions that Decker doesn't know the answers to, but he does know I'm an authority. Which is amazingly clever, but I suppose to live as long as Decker has, you need to be intelligent."

"Thank you," Decker said. "I think."

"Can you take off your shirt?" she asked Joshua.

"What happened to the wolves in Boston?" Joshua tried to ignore Decker as he stripped off his T-shirt. At least the vampire was pretending to study a poster about heartworms. "Is that the shit you're talking about? That the prince's family was killed?"

"Yes." She inspected the wound where the werewolf had bitten Joshua. "You were changed two or three days ago? This is a classic bite that wolves use to change their younglings to wolves. This here." She traced the arch of the bite. "Misses all major arteries. It's on the left side so the wound doesn't affect the dominant arm. Upper torso so the newborn has no difficulty walking afterwards. You were changed by someone who knew what they were doing and took a great deal of care doing it. But you don't know who, or you'd be with him, not a vampire."

Elise was right that the werewolf must not have chosen him at random.

"Three years ago, the Wolf King demanded that the Prince of Boston send his oldest son, Seth, to New York City to live. No explanation. The prince had to pull all of Seth's medical and school records to go with him, which is how I know the nitty gritty. The prince was furious but he had no choice. Two weeks later, every wolf in Boston and half the Grigori were dead. The Grigori that survived brought me Seth's uncle, Anton Cabot. I couldn't save him."

"What—what killed them?"

"A large breach had been torn open down in the subway tunnels. The wolves and the Grigori managed to keep the city from being overrun but at a horrific cost. The Wolf King came with his Thanes to clean up the few that the prince and his wolves hadn't killed before dying. Since then, Boston has been a very dangerous place to live. If it weren't for the Grigori, the streets would be littered with dead."

She examined his eyes closely, which let him study her. She was older than her first impression, her hairstyle and clothing making her seem younger. She was probably closer to his mother's age than his older sister.

"Why did you come see me?" she asked.

He blushed hotly and looked away. He hadn't realized that he would need to actually say anything to get answers. He wasn't sure how to ask questions without dying of embarrassment. "My favorite color used to be blue, but now it's green—because the wolf likes green."

"Okay," she said, sounding slightly mystified. "Please don't break my table."

He'd dented the stainless steel top with both thumbs. "Sorry. The wolf likes Decker. A lot. Really a lot. I want to know why."

"Oh!" She patted him on the head and then caught herself. "I'm sorry. I can see where this could be a problem. There's multiple layers of attraction there. Vampires are devourers. They feed on life essence. Pack magic is extreme life essence—it's why they're so difficult to kill. You two are the North Pole and South Pole of a magnet; his nature calls to your wolf. Add in that canines like to roll in dead things and wolves are like monkeys in that they need physical touch to stay emotionally healthy, and you're fighting a stacked deck."

✧   ✧   ✧

Dr. Huff had given them a pamphlet titled "Care and feeding of your puppy" with a picture of a dark haired boy and girl on the cover. "I know it's a decade away at least before I get the next round of puppies, but I thought I'd put it together so I wouldn't forget anything. Seth is going to have enough on his plate and I don't know anything really about his wife."

"Wife?" Decker and Joshua both echoed.

"Alexander arranged a marriage for him years ago. She's from the San Diego pack. I've tried to contact her vet, but I need to go through her parents and apparently things are not going smoothly there. Dominance is a huge issue with werewolves and it relates to how connected a wolf is to the territory. When Alexander arranged the marriage, he changed the girl's territory from San Diego to Boston."

"What difference does it make?" Joshua asked.

"Boston is the second most powerful territory in the world. San Diego is a marquis but not a particularly strong one. It's like giving a half-grown wolf to a pair of Chihuahuas. I have no idea what Alexander was thinking. But until Seth and his wife move back to Boston, I only have stuff like this to do as part of my official duties."

Joshua started reading the pamphlet as they waited for the taxi to arrive. It stressed the "proper feeding of puppies" and went on at length about the amount of meat that werewolves needed in their diet.

It made Joshua want steak just reading about what he should be eating.

They detoured to Home Depot to buy a stove and a full-size refrigerator. It was going to be a week before the appliances could be delivered. Since all he had to cook with was a microwave, they bought a little tabletop charcoal grill, a huge bag of charcoal, lighter fluid, and matches.

"Please don't burn the house down around my ears," Decker pleaded as they carried their purchases toward the exit. "I've done that. It's not pleasant."

"I'm going to cook in the driveway." Joshua took out the phone to summon another taxi.

Decker glanced outside at the dark rainy night. "Might I suggest we stop at a restaurant?"

29: JOSHUA

Joshua dreamed of darkness.

Not at first.

The night started with erotic wolf-driven dreams featuring Decker. The vampire alternated between prey to be stalked and a soft plushie toy to be chewed on. The wolf had enjoyed Decker's feeding. It had plans that required Joshua's involvement.

He woke up, bed covered in black fur, biting at his pillow as he humped his airbed. "That wasn't me! It's him! It's him! It's the wolf." He bolted from his bed, wanting to put distance between him and the dream. His face burned with embarrassment despite the fact there was no one to witness the physical evidence of attraction. He limped to the bathroom. "Stupid wolf."

He considered a cold shower. No. He needed more sleep. He splashed cold water on his face and crawled back into bed.

He dreamed then of the darkness.

He walked through unfamiliar streets. It might have been Boston proper, which he'd only seen from across the Charles River. The buildings were taller and denser than in Cambridge. He was hunting something, although he wasn't sure what.

He came to a park filled with manicured lawns and a careful scattering of trees.

"Please!" someone cried faintly in the darkness. "Please!"

He followed the sound across grass. He came to a shallow kidney-shaped wading pool roughly the size of football field. He tried to read the signs around it but the letters crawled away, refusing to be deciphered.

I'm dreaming. Oh God, this better not be another sex dream. "Decker, is that you?"

"Please! Oh Gods! Please, no!" A man wailed. It wasn't Decker's voice.

Joshua crept forward. "So is this a sex dream or something scary thing I forgot?"

He doubted that this place was something he'd forgotten like the events at the barn. He'd never been in this part of the city. This was nothing like the park he'd been in on Saturday night. That place had been barely controlled wilderness. Here the grass had been cut and trampled nearly to the point of death. The pool was made of cement like an oversized birdbath. The trees were carefully placed and manicured like giant bonsai plants.

"Please! Just let me go!" the man pleaded nearby.

The only thing besides grass and trees were two bronze statues of frogs sitting at the edge of the pool. Both were the size of a large man. The one on the right leaned his head on his fist, gazing down at the water in deep thought. The other sat on a tackle box, a fishing pole in hand and a can of googly-eyed worms beside him.

"He'll know! He'll stop you!" the thinker frog cried without moving its lips.

"We want him to know." The fisherman stayed frozen in place even as it answered. "We want him to try and stop us."

The thinker frog screamed.

There was a weird deep groaning noise from the wading pool. It sounded like metal strained to the point of breaking. The dark waters stirred. The surface lifted, as if pool been covered with black plastic, and something underneath surged upward. A massive creature pressed its face against the wet black. The groaning grew louder.

Joshua backed away from the pool.

With a weird metallic shriek, the surface tore and darkness flooded out. It blasted over Joshua, hot as a monstrous breath from a massive animal. It swept Joshua off his feet and he went tumbling through the dark...

Joshua woke up burning in sunlight that poured in through his bay windows. They hadn't replaced the rotted curtains in his bedroom. With the memory of the black crowding close, he was glad that they hadn't. It felt so real. Even lying in the bright sun, it felt like he'd be lost in the darkness if he just closed his eyes.

Didn't the ghost say something about drowning Boston in darkness?

He rolled onto his side to fumble through the clutter beside his airbed. He'd moved the charger for Decker's phone upstairs. He'd moved a lot of things to his bedside. At some point he needed to put something beside his bed to act as a nightstand. Along with some curtains; he was starting to feel crispy.

He found his notebook first. Decker had pinned a stack of fifties under the pen. Did the vampire have Scrooge McDuck's money vault in the basement someplace? Joshua yawned, flipped the page and wrote: Still Need.

Nightstand. Curtains. Alarm clock.

Decker's phone said it was ungodly early after being up most of the night cleaning and dancing around personal issues. The wolf *liked* Decker. Polar opposite magic attracted. The wolf was yin to Decker's yang. God, that sounded dirty.

It sounded like something Decker would say.

Joshua rolled onto his back, eyes closed, phone pressed to his chest.

Darkness groaned as something strained to break through . . .

He opened his eyes.

The nightmare felt so real. Werewolves had bad dreams like everyone else. Right? He had those weird nightmares about the massacre. The football team chasing him through the playground. Being Clark Kent at the baseball game. This was just more weirdness because his brain just couldn't take all the creepy strangeness.

What if it wasn't a nightmare? What if it was somehow real?

He should call—someone—and warn them—or something.

He used the Find My Friend app to cyberspy on Elise. She was in Albany for some reason. A hundred and sixty-six miles. She'd snapped at him the last time he called her. He forgot to tell her about what the ghost actually said. He'd rambled on and on to Elise about lottery tickets and paint colors and pie . . .

Thinking of pie was a mistake. His stomach rumbled, reminding him that it'd been hours since he'd eaten and that there was raw steak in the mini fridge.

"Oh, come on! I can't be that hungry."

Decker had made good on his promise. He'd taken Joshua to an amazing steakhouse where waiters brought swords full of meat, saying he could eat all that he wanted. They stayed until nearly midnight. He shouldn't be starving after all that!

His stomach grumbled loudly that it was empty. Food. Now.

Still need: an umbrella or raincoat.

It decided to rain while he took the small grill out of its box and assembled it. Since the grill had a lid, he didn't pay much attention to the light drizzle. Something about being wet, though, kept triggering his transformation. He was a boy then a puppy, then a boy again, and a puppy again, and back to boy as he positioned the grill in the driveway and filled it with charcoal. (Luckily the driveway doglegged between the house and the garage in back, so he was safely out of sight.) Every time he turned into a pint-size wolf, he'd have to go up onto the back porch and shake dry until he was dizzy.

"Oh God, why does everything have to be so hard anymore?" He whimpered once he got back to boy. "I just need to get this damn charcoal lighted!"

At least—but strangely—his clothes were always dry once he got back to human. It didn't make any sense. Where the hell did they go when he was a wolf? How did they come back and not be wet or inside out? Even the lighter was still in his jean's pocket.

He made the mistake of trying to walk down the back steps while still dizzy. He went end over end and landed at the bottom of the stairs as a puppy.

Tent. Now.

He went back up to the covered porch—shook until his fur was dry—changed into boy—waited until he wasn't dizzy—and collected one of the large canvas tarps he was using as paint drop cloth. He carried it out over his head, shielding him from the rain.

He tied one end to the dumpster and the other end to the garage door.

"One outside room: check."

In theory he knew how lighting a grill worked. He'd seen his dad do it dozens of times. (His parents claimed that there was some weird accident when he was four which triggered their insistence that he didn't start any fires, be it indoors or out.)

Several minutes of holding flame to the black bricks of charcoal resulted in nothing but burnt fingertips.

What was he forgetting?

Lighter fluid!

He dashed back into the house. He'd left the bottle of fluid next to the salt and pepper. The wolf decided to grab the steaks while he was in the kitchen.

"I don't know." He put the steaks on the ground beside the hibachi so his hands were free for the lighter fluid. "I think that the coals have to get all white before I can put them on. I am talking to the wolf. I don't think the wolf cares. I think the wolf would be happy to eat these raw."

Did he just wiggle his butt at that idea in a close approximation of tail wag?

"We are not eating this raw!" he cried.

We? We?

"There is no 'we,' there is only I!" He fought the safety lock on the fluid and sprayed the black bricks liberally. "This is my life. I am not going to let you take over—more than you already have." He closed the cap on the fluid. "I am not eating these steaks raw. I am cooking them until they're medium rare." He took out the Zippo lighter. "And I am not having sex with a . . ."

A massive fireball of flame whooshed upwards and set the tarp on fire.

"Oh no! Not good! Water! Water now!"

He ran in tight circles. He hadn't bought a garden hose yet. He wasn't even sure if there was an outdoor spigot. The tarp was burning; still tied to the dumpster full of old newspapers and the ancient garage filled with God knows what. He hadn't looked in it yet.

"Look what you made me do! I promised Decker that I wouldn't set fire to his house! We have to stop it!"

The wolf took over. They dashed into the house. The wolf grabbed the narrow mop bucket, darted into the powder room and flung the tank lid onto the floor.

"What are you doing? Did you break that? That's porcelain! China! Like a teacup." No, he didn't want the wolf to think the toilet was some large watering dish. "It's glass you pee into, not drink out of! Don't set fire to the man's house and break his toilet too!"

The wolf dipped the bucket into the full tank.

"Oh! That's brilliant! Great thinking!"

They ran out into the driveway. The entire tarp was ablaze and an orange tabby kitten was trying to steal his entire package of steaks. The wolf growled at the thief. The wolf started to put down the bucket to rescue the meat.

"No!" Joshua shouted. "Focus! Put out the fire! We'll deal with the kitten after the fire is out."

Three fast trips and he had the fire out.

The kitten was trying to drag the five pounds of steak into the bushes.

He snatched up the steaks and the kitten. It hissed at him and latched claws and teeth into his hand. "Ow! Ow! Ow! I'll give you something to eat, just not my steak!" He carried kitten inside with his steak and opened a can of tuna fish. "There!"

He held out a little bit of the tuna. "Yes, it's very yummy isn't it? I like tuna too, but Dr. Huff says I should eat steak. Red meat for werewolves, not fish. Want more? You need to stop hissing at me. There. Yes. See. Be nice and you—ow, ow, ow! Okay, I'm feeding you more!"

30: SETH

Ewan played bagpipes.

He played them badly.

It was a fact that Seth first became aware of at seven-thirty in the morning when a loud mysterious "*squawwwwkk*" bolted him awake. He fell from his makeshift bed on the couch in a tangle of blankets.

"Ewaaaaannnnnn!" one of the cousins called in annoyance.

Another "*squawwwwk*" answered the complaint.

"What the hell was that?" Seth shouted as the cousin didn't seem alarmed or surprised.

"Oh, shit, he woke Boston!" Drustan whispered as Seth started up the stairs.

"Bagpipes, your highness," Cameron called. "Ewan! It's dawn!"

"Sorry!" Ewan said. "I couldn't sleep and I found this under my bed. It's so cool that I play them." There was another loud squawk that Seth now recognized as a single reedy note played on a bagpipe. "At least I think I can play them. Can I? Oh! Cool! We have a dog!"

The cousins were gathered in the upstairs hallway, various levels of undress for sleep. Ewan had a bagpipe tucked under his left arm. They turned toward Seth. Shock went over Cameron's, Tadhg's and Drustan's faces. Cameron and Tadhg jointly shoved Ewan back into his room and blocked the door. Drustan retreated into his bedroom.

"What? That isn't our dog?" Ewan asked from behind the wall of his protective family. The bagpipes gave a disappointed sigh.

282

"Your highness?" Cameron's voice shook.

Seth had transformed when he'd been startled awake without realizing it. He hadn't accidentally changed for years. "Sorry. It just—just—startled me."

"It's okay," Tadhg edged back more despite Seth's apology. "We're all used to Ewan's blasted bagpipes."

"Did the dog just talk?" Ewan asked.

"Since we're all awake, how about we do breakfast," Cameron said. "There's an IHOP right on Wolf Road. They're doing all you can eat pancakes this week. That is, if you like pancakes, your highness."

"We're taking the dog to breakfast?" Ewan cried with delight.

The IHOP was a surprisingly busy diner with laminated menus filled with pictures of glistening breakfast food. The booth came preloaded with coffee, sugar, creamers, an assortment of jams and two bottles of syrup. The cousins were well-known; food started to arrive within seconds of them sitting down. Pancakes first; hot, fluffy and as large as the platter. Sides of bacon, eggs, and hash browns were added at surprising speed considering all the wolves had said to the waitress was "the usual."

"You tip well, don't you?" Seth guessed at the reason for the good service.

"Extraordinarily well," Drustan stated with pride. "We take care of our people."

Seth was finishing his second stack of pancakes when his phone rang. He had turned it back on when the Albany pack reported that Jack had been trying to get hold of him. He left it on after calling Jack back on the Grigori's phone.

"I need to get this." Seth got up from the booth to put distance between him and the Albany pack. He wanted privacy as he fought with whoever was calling, be it Bishop or one of the other Thanes.

He was out the restaurant's door before he realized it was Dr. Huff calling him.

His yearly checkup was in December, the day before his birthday. Why would she be calling now? Was she in danger?

Seth focused on Dr. Huff's place. Her office was filled with people moving about with dogs on leashes and cats in carriers. He found Dr. Huff via her signet ring. She paced behind her desk, headset in hand.

He answered his phone with a tentative hello.

"Your highness? This is Dr. Huff," she started out using his formal title instead of his name. It meant that she was calling as the royal vet, not his family doctor. "I thought I should call you and tell you that I examined a newborn werewolf last night."

"Joshua?" Seth switched focus to his brother. The boy was running in frantic circles in Decker's driveway, while something burned overhead. What was Joshua doing?

"Yes! Joshua," Dr. Huff said. "Silas Decker brought him in. The man does not know how to raise a puppy."

Seth frowned as Joshua dashed in and out of Decker's house with a bucket. For some odd reason, he was using the toilet's tank as a watershed. "Was Joshua hurt?"

"No. He's perfectly healthy, just very confused. He had questions about being a werewolf that Decker didn't know the answers to. I have to admit bringing Joshua to me showed a great deal of intelligence. I spent the night reading up on infection vectors. From what I can tell, Joshua could bite the man without fear of creating a feral. The original bite that made Decker a vampire acts as a vaccine against the magic of the werewolf bite. Texts also suggest that Decker has a healing ability on par with a werewolf."

The fire was out at Decker's house with the exception of a small hibachi in the driveway: the apparent source of the flames. Joshua was wrangling a kitten that was trying to steal Joshua's breakfast. That the kitten was still alive spoke volumes of Joshua's control of his temper.

"How safe is Joshua to the general populace?" Seth asked. "We normally isolate newborns until they have control of their wolf."

"He's a sweet little puppy," Dr. Huff fell into the voice she used with her patients. "A very good boy. No snarling. No nipping." Her tone went back to pure business, which meant the news was not all good. "But he's resisting integrating with the wolf. He sees it as a dangerous separate being. He's managed to keep it in check for several days, which is impressive, but it's going to lead to more trouble down the road. He won't be able to stay human under stress. The more times he loses control to the wolf, the harder it will get to regain power. It's a cascading problem."

"I know."

"The Grigori keep a strong presence in Boston. They'll be closer to him than you. And if he loses it badly enough, they will consider him feral."

"I know."

She was calling Seth because he was the Prince of Boston. By the Wolf King's law, puppies were the responsibility of the alpha whose territory they were in. It didn't matter that Joshua was a year older than Seth. Dr. Huff was well aware that if Joshua was a very strong dominant connected to the Boston Source, there wasn't anyone but Seth that could control him.

"I'm dealing with a disaster," Seth explained. "The king is in Belgrade. The Marquis of Albany was killed by the Wickers. I'm sitting on his heir until I'm sure he's safe."

"Oh gods," she whispered, clearly shocked. "I understand. You're needed there. I think Jack would be fine, if there isn't a dominance issue. From what I can determine, Joshua is a strong dominant. I would advise against sending a random Thane to deal with Joshua; most are going to be too heavy-handed to deal with a puppy that wasn't raised by your people. Scaring him will only make the wolf more unmanageable for him."

At the moment, the only Thanes available were Isaiah and his lackeys. Seth didn't want any of them in the same state as his brother.

"I'll come to Boston as soon as I can," Seth promised. Somehow.

"He should be safe with Decker," Dr. Huff said. "The vampire might not know how to raise a puppy, but he's a powerful ancient creature. The Wickers will not cross him lightly, even if they knew where to find him. I've been royal vet for ten years and I only know Decker's place is somewhere in Cambridge. It's one of the better kept secrets in Boston."

He, Jack and the handful of others had been told the location of Decker's residence because they were possible heirs. His father hadn't shared the information beyond that. Seth knew that the decision wasn't easy for other people to understand. Dr. Huff was one of the outsiders that they rarely kept secrets from. With Joshua as her only patient beyond Seth, she probably expected to be told his street address.

Dr. Huff wasn't immune to the Wicker's powers. It was one of the reasons she wasn't told in the first place.

"Since Decker submitted to my grandfather's rule, he is considered under our protection. Something like him could only be safe if his resting place is kept secret. The question is: would the Wickers have to fight him to gain Joshua?"

"I believe so. He seems genuinely fond of the boy." She hesitated before adding, "Your grandfather mentioned once to my predecessor that he found Decker 'comfortable' to be around, thus the reason he allowed the vampire to stay in Boston. There seems to be a universal compatibility there. The polarity of magic attracts, not repels."

It would explain the massive cleaning and painting Joshua was doing at Decker's house. Vampires didn't use kitchens but growing puppies did. Ignorant of all things related to werewolves, Joshua wouldn't realize he couldn't stay with Decker.

"Okay, I'll..." The restaurant door banged open and people came screaming out. "Shit!" Seth hung up without saying goodbye. He shoved his way through the flood of humans. What the hell happened while he was gone? He could hear the loud growling and snarling of a large upset wolf.

The Three Musketeers were standing back, staring at their booth, as it shook and quivered.

"What the hell is going on?" Seth roared.

"Ewan's stuck," Cameron said.

"What do you mean he's stuck?" Seth peered under the table.

The massive wolf wedged upside down in the tight space peered back. "Help."

"He was asking about the black dog at the house. We told him that we were all werewolves including him..."

"Oh God, no, you shouldn't have told him that! Not here!" But they had. Seth knew from experience that the natural reaction to being told you were a werewolf was to see if you could transform into a wolf. The only puzzling part was how Ewan ended up wedged under the table, upside down. "How did you...? Never mind." Seth grabbed the edge of the table and ripped it from the steel posts.

"Our food!" all four cousins cried as Seth flung the table aside.

"We're leaving!" Seth caught Ewan by the ruff of his neck and pulled him to his feet. "Be human!"

"I don't know how to... omph!" He turned into a man as

Seth forced his wolf back into the Source. "Oh, this is how I ended up naked in Utica!"

"Yes." Seth pulled off his shirt and put it on Ewan. "Cameron, you're driving. You other two, clear a path. Nothing stops us."

Out they went, a hopefully unstoppable juggernaut, as the police cars came screaming into the parking lot.

31: JOSHUA

The charcoal lit.

The fire put out.

The kitten fed.

While he was waiting for the charcoal to be ready, the whole "clothes were someplace else while he was puppy" started to creep him out. They smelled. Not in a horrible stinky way. The scent reminded him of dried leaves and sunshine. It made him think of his backyard on a warm afternoon during the autumn. Normally he'd find it a pleasant smell.

He'd taken clean clothes out of his mom's dryer, put them into his backpack and left home. They should smell of soap and dryer sheets and his sweat. Until he started to turn into a wolf, they had.

Once he thought about it, he started to imagine monster fleas and ticks crawling around on his back, or something worse. Something weird and alien. Flesh-eating mold. He decided that it was time to change into his new clothes.

Decker had bought a trashcan for the bathroom but not Joshua's bedroom. His new clothes created a ton of litter that the kitten thought made great toys. Bags from the underwear. Tags from the shirts. Weird stickers on the jeans. The kitten tried eating the plastic bits and pieces. Joshua shoved all the litter into one of the Target shopping bags and added *trashcan* to his list of things he still needed.

His new clothes felt scratchy and stiff, especially the underwear.

He decided to wash everything he wasn't wearing. Decker mentioned that he had a washing machine in a laundry room off the kitchen. Joshua kept dropping clothes as he carried them downstairs. When he bent over to pick the fallen item up, something else would tumble to the ground. It threatened to turn into an endless bad juggling act. Seriously, he needed a laundry basket before started wolfing out and sending his new clothes to the mystery forest.

He put his clothes on the kitchen island, added *laundry basket* to his list and played "what's behind this door" to find said washer.

Washing machine.

Decker had to be joking. He used that? It looked like some kind of medieval torture device. No, not using that.

Dryer.

Decker's boxers were hanging on the clothesline that was strung up higher than Joshua could reach. No. Just no.

Laundromat. Even if Decker bought a new washer and dryer, Joshua still would need clean clothes long before the machines showed up. Surely with Harvard and MIT nearby, there were coin laundries. He carried his new clothes back upstairs for safe keeping in his room, growling.

Luckily, it stopped raining. The coals were ready for the steaks. He put the meat on the hot grill and prowled around the yard, making notes.

Rake. Extension ladder. Work gloves. Weedeater.

Decker's house wasn't the only one on the block with a tower and attic windows and all sorts of old gothic vibes. His place, though, was the only one that looked Addams Family spooky. Everyone said that Decker's home was safe because it was warded, but the Wickers probably only had to look at it to know a vampire lived there. The entire house needed to be painted. The leaves raked. The gutters cleaned out. The weeds trimmed.

A yard gnome would help brighten up the place and make it a little less suspicious. Maybe more than one. An entire mob of yard gnomes, glaring at people as they passed by. *"Move along, nothing weird here to see."*

Okay, maybe gnomes wouldn't help. Joshua crossed them off his list. He'd have to see what the hardware store had to make the house more welcoming.

He flipped the steaks and argued with the wolf. "Wait! Wait! You're as bad as the cat! I don't want the meat raw and cold in the middle! I don't care that you don't care! We're eating them medium rare! I have better things to do than to stand here fighting with you! I should be figuring out what the ghost meant. I should be trying to figure out if my dream meant anything important."

He should have talked to Decker about the ghost.

They'd gotten a lot of work done the night before, all while carefully avoiding any conversation about what had happened between Decker and the wolf. Instead they talked about the world at large.

Decker proved to be woefully ignorant about almost everything about modern-day life. He lost contact with the world shortly after he moved in. The ancient television they'd unearthed and hauled to the dumpster had died in the late sixties. The dozens of magazine titles trickled to a stop by the seventies. The mountain of newspapers gave out a decade later. Even the junk mail started to peter off as the world moved on to spam emails.

Decker knew nothing about computers or the Internet or even how his cell phone worked beyond accepting incoming calls. The microwave utterly mystified him.

More alarming, his mailbox—a rusted out tin box sitting on the front porch—had been stuffed full with utility shutoff notices. Nothing had been paid since August.

"Saul had someone that he trusted to pay those things," Decker explained. "I think he died. Everything just stopped being taken care of. That usually means the person doing it died." Decker sighed and added wistfully, "It happens more often than I like to admit."

Luckily buried in among the magazines and newspaper was enough bank account information that Joshua was able to set up online payments for the gas, electric, and water before they could be turned off. He needed to go to the bank and deposit more money before the next month's bills were due.

Decker needed him. It was becoming more and more obvious. Technology had outstripped the vampire's knowledge. Nor could Decker take care of the outside of the house during the night; it would draw too much attention. Paying someone else to take care of the yard work required someone awake during normal business hours. Everything from arranging for the dumpster delivery the day before to depositing money into Decker's bank account needed someone like Joshua to deal with it.

But it was more than that. Decker seemed positively fragile emotionally since the feeding. He broke down weeping twice. The first time while Joshua was playing the 45 record of "Stay." Joshua wasn't sure what triggered Decker the second time; he glanced over to discover the vampire wiping tears off his face. It was for Decker's sake more than Joshua's that they danced all around the issue.

Would Decker really kill himself? The layers of clutter spoke volumes on how apathetic the vampire had become over the years. In all the chaos, there had been no sign of any other people. When had Elise's grandfather died? Did the hoarding start with Saul's death? How long had Decker been alone? Thirty years? Forty?

Sometime while Joshua was distracted thinking about Decker, the wolf got the steaks off the grill, into the house, and eaten one. The kitten was lapping up the bloody juices from his plate.

"Oh geeezzz! Both of you are nothing but trouble."

He gave the plate to the kitten to finish and got out a clean one. After the second New York strip steak, Joshua felt a great deal saner.

Cat litter. Cat food. Cat dish. Cat everything. Assuming that Decker would let him keep the kitten.

It was one thing to paint the kitchen without talking to Decker. If the vampire really cared what color the walls were, he would have painted years ago. It was quite another thing to bring an animal into the house. (A second animal into the house if you counted the wolf.) His parents' cat, Charmin, was actually Bethy's, but she couldn't take him to college with her.

Joshua really would like to keep the kitten. A pet implied a certain permanency.

Considering Decker's state of mind last night, he would probably agree to anything to keep Joshua from leaving. Somehow that didn't make Joshua feel better.

Still need: doorbell.

Winnie stood on the porch when Joshua opened the front door to leave for the hardware store. She squeaked in alarm and danced backwards. "I'm sorry! I'm sorry! I rang the doorbell!"

"You did?" Joshua pushed the button a couple of times. Nothing. There could be several things wrong with it, but since it was half a century old, he might as well replace as many pieces as he could. He took out his shopping list and added doorbell button, chimes, and transformer to his list. He'd also need a tester and some screwdrivers. "It doesn't work."

"I would have sent in Fred to get you but the house is warded."

The spirit guide loomed in the shadows of the porch, bent nearly double as he hovered protectively behind Winnie.

"He's not around, is he?" Winnie peered in through the open door.

"Decker? I think he's asleep, or whatever he does during the day."

"Most night creatures are dormant during the daylight hours." Winnie put her fingers to her purple lipstick lips but caught herself before she actually chewed on her purple-painted nails. "It probably would seem like he's hibernating."

Joshua blushed furiously as the wolf made him step back into the house, eager to find the man deeply asleep. "I'm leaving!" He stepped back outside and slammed the door shut. "Stupid wolf."

Winnie scurried down the steps to the sidewalk, putting distance between her and the angry werewolf. "I'm sorry! I—I can go with you." It wasn't so much an offer as a question. She pointed to her Vespa to make it an offer. "I can give you a ride."

"No!" He didn't want to get on the scooter ever again. "I was going to walk." He felt bad for obviously scaring her. "You can come with me. I'm going to the hardware store."

She brightened. "Okay."

They started to walk with Fred drifting behind them. The spirit guide's presence made the hair on Joshua's neck stand on end.

"I'm sorry I didn't come by yesterday," Winnie said. "I tried to do another session to find out more about Jack. Marie popped in and took me off for an eating and shopping binge. She's figured out credit cards. Luckily she hasn't figured out about taking the tags off yet; I took all the clothes back. Which is a real shame; she has amazing taste. I just wouldn't be able to pay the minimum on my credit card until we cash in the lottery ticket. I have no idea when Granny will let us do that, so—back the clothes go."

It took Joshua a moment to remember that "Marie" was the ghost of Marie Antoinette, Queen of France, who was haunting Boston for unknown reasons. Winnie been kidnapped as the ghost took possession of her body and her credit card.

"She did leave me a note." Winnie took out a paper receipt

from a local bakery for a whopping sixty-three dollars. Something was written on the back in elegant cursive script.

"Is that French?" he said.

"Yes, it took me all last night to make sure Google Translate wasn't mangling the meaning. It says that I should find another lover since Jack has taken refuge in the arms of another woman, one much prettier than me. She recommended the clerk at the bakery. I'm not sure if that is supernatural knowledge that he's a good match, or she just wants better access to cake."

Joshua wasn't sure how to respond. "I'm sorry?"

"Oh, it's good news, except the sixty-three dollars part. Jack is alive."

Who was Jack again? Oh yes, the wolf that sent him to Boston—or at least—he thought the wolf meant Boston but it really meant New York City. He was losing track of all the weird players in the new life, most of which he hadn't actually met, like Marie, Jack, the prince and technically, the Wolf King.

The wolf snarled at the thought of the Wolf King.

"Hush!" Joshua snapped. Winnie edged away from him. "Sorry. And I'm sorry that Decker hissed at you the other day. The Wolf King and everything..." Meaning her driving. "I was kind of freaked out."

"No! No! I think it's sweet."

Sweet? Sweet? What did that mean? He growled with annoyance.

"I brought brownies." Winnie held out a large Tupperware container filled with dark cake-like bars that smelled heavenly.

"I just had breakfa...oh, these are good! Mmmank mmmou." The wolf filled his mouth before he could turn the brownies down. The wolf was a serious black hole when it came to food.

The brownies lasted until they reached the hardware store. He grabbed a cart. There was candy and chips by the checkout counter right inside the door. Winnie threw one of each kind into the cart. Considering he'd already growled at her three times, he decided it was probably a smart thing for her to do.

"I need to get a bunch of stuff." He pulled out his list. "I'm hoping I can get it all here."

There were discounted Halloween decorations, and everything needed for fall cleanup and winterization in the first two aisles. Employees were setting up displays for Christmas lights in the third. The thought of missing the holidays with his family made the wolf whimper. He hurried around the corner into the laundry aisle. There were hampers, mesh bags, clotheslines, pins, hangers, folding drying racks, and plastic laundry baskets. Simple unadorned stuff to make his life easier without all the messy emotions that an imploded life left behind.

The garden hoses were in the garden section. Next to them were the statues of gnomes and a vast array of frogs. He had no idea that frogs were so popular. Only the one that was the size of a bulldog was realistic. The rest were weird cartoon versions doing all sorts of unlikely things.

"I had this weird dream last night." The garden statues reminded him of his nightmare. Winnie might know if the place was real. "I was at this park someplace in Boston. At least, I think it was Boston. But there was the shallow pool with frog statues. One was thinking and the other was fishing."

"That's the Frog Pond. It's in the Boston Common. It's my second favorite part of the park. Third. Second. The swan boats are my favorite, definitely, even though they're horribly touristy. My mother used to take me on them when I was little and tell me the story of ugly duckling who grew up to be a beautiful swan. It gave me so much hope. But the Frog Pond is second favorite. In the summer, you can wade in it and play in the sprinklers. In the winter, you can ice skate and drink hot chocolate. They floated jack-o-lanterns in it for Halloween."

Joshua shivered as he remembered that the last jack-o-lantern he'd seen had been the Huntsman's head.

Winnie didn't seem to notice. "It was magical. They light the pumpkins up and float them out into the water. The statue of the ducklings from *Make Way for Ducklings* are adorable but just there's not much to that. A mother duck and eight ducklings. She's fairly big, large enough that you can sit on her. You could trip over the babies if you weren't paying attention."

"So there's frog statues at the Frog Pond?" Joshua tried steering the conversation back to his dream. Not that he really wanted to talk about it; it was upsetting that he'd dreamed about someplace that was real. How did he know that the wolf hadn't taken him out for a walk in the middle of the night? Judging by the black fur in his bed, he'd spent part of the night as a wolf without realizing it.

Oh God, what if he'd molested Decker?

We can check on him when we get back! Tail wag!

"No!" Joshua snatched up a bright pink flamingo and shoved it into his cart.

Winnie eyed him uncertainly. "There are a whole bunch of bronze frog statues, all in silly poses. My favorite is Joann, she's wearing a snorkel mask. The fisherman is Tommy and Angela is the thinker. It's definitely my second favorite place. Least favorite? The graveyards. They used to hang 'witches' there." She used her fingers to form the quotes. "As if they could! No, the women they hung were all people like me. Sad to say, we tend to be restless spirits of the creepy kind when we're murdered."

"They don't talk?" Joshua struggled with the idea that "Angela" had a male voice in his dream.

"The ghosts?"

"The frogs."

"Not unless they're possessed—which considering how close they are to the graveyard—is a distinct possibility. We should go check."

"We are shopping!" Joshua waved a second flamingo at her. He was not getting on the Vespa.

"After we take everything back to Decker's. We can take the subway. It's on the Red Line."

He should find out why he was dreaming of places he'd never been. He wasn't sure which was worse, suddenly having weird true dreams about talking frogs or being a sleepwalking werewolf. If it was the latter, he'll need to figure out some way to keep the wolf locked in the house at night.

Winnie wouldn't come into the house. They'd called a taxi to haul everything back to Decker's. She used the mailbox as an excuse to stay outside and install it. Afterwards she carefully swept all the dead leaves off the porch, positioned the welcome mat, and danced the flamingos around the yard to find the spots for them. No matter where she placed them, the bright pink bird statues looked like they were trying to run away.

He'd had second thoughts on the flamingos, the doormat (it said "Wipe Your Paws") and taking her to the Frog Pond with him. After she'd been so patient, though, he felt he should leave the statues in place and let her act as native guide.

✧   ✧   ✧

"The Frog Pond" was a cement kiddie pool. It looked exactly as it had in Joshua's dream. If he was a character out of *Lord of the Rings*, he could probably tell if a wolf had stalked through the park the night before. Instead he could only stand staring at the pond, wondering. Prophetic dream or sleepwalking wolf?

The pool was set in a long winding depression within the park so all the land sloped down to a wide sidewalk that ringed the pond. The rain clouds reflected in the still water. Because of the reflection, it was impossible to see the bottom. There were wooden placards lined up down the middle of the pool, giving a proper sense of how shallow the water was. It seemed ankle deep. The signs stated "No Wading" with a picture of dog to indicate they meant pets too.

"Isn't it wonderful?" Winnie skipped across the brick sidewalk to wrap her arms around the neck of large bronze frog statue in the thinking pose. The frog was almost as big as Winnie. "They'll drain it, clean it, put up barricades and make it an ice skating rink in a few days. It hasn't been cold enough yet. In the spring they have a carousel. When they light the carousel up at night, it's magical."

Magical. That was what he was afraid of.

Joshua crept forward to poke the fisherman frog. It was solid cold metal. It looked exactly as he remembered it from his dream. Even the bronze worms in the can at it the feet had the same googly eyes. How did he know? Had he been here when he was young? Certainly there were spots in his memory still missing from the amnesia. His parents, though, never left Central New York. If it wasn't within a two-hour drive, it didn't exist.

"Have the frogs ever talked to anyone?" Joshua asked.

"No."

Even if he lost total control of the wolf, how did he explain the talking statues? The creepy black thing in the water?

"The prince used to live a few blocks from here." Winnie pointed off to the right. "They had a row of big beautiful four-story houses, all side by side, taking up the entire block. Bay windows in the front. Little private walled-in backyards. You'd never know by looking that wolves lived there. So quiet, clean, and orderly. They'd lived there since God knows when, like the 1640s. Not in those exact houses. I mean the first houses were probably little log cabins. The Pilgrims landed in Plymouth in 1620. The brownstones were only a hundred and fifty years old, give or take a few decades. The princess would often bring her younglings down to play in the pond in the summertime. It was kind of funny but a little sad too. As soon as they arrived, everyone would get the feeling that they should go."

"Why?"

"Because most people could sense that the children weren't entirely human. People are like herd animals at the core. They feel safest when everyone around them is just like them. Scientists call it the reptile brain but it's more like zebra brain. Run from anything that isn't four-legged and striped. If you can't run from it, try kicking it to death."

That would explain his childhood.

He stared at the water reflecting the dull gray sky. Not that he wanted the frogs to start talking to him, but he wanted to understand how he had dreamed of a place he'd never seen before. Everyone kept talking about breaches. Maybe that was what the black thing was in the water. A hole in reality that was letting a monster into their world.

Next thing he knew, he was ankle deep in water, snarling at the bottom of the pond.

"Oh geez!" Joshua shouted at the wolf. "What the hell are you doing? You didn't even take off our shoes!"

The wolf didn't listen, splashing about to pounce on every shadow, snarling in anger.

"The Central Burying Ground is over by Boylston Street." Winnie ignored Joshua to point south toward a baseball field. "I usually avoid that. The swan boats are across Charles Street." This was to the west. "The *Make Way for Ducklings* statues are over there. My mom used to take me on a boat ride and then we'd have high tea at Bristol Lounge at Four Seasons. They have fifteen different types of teas and just wonderful pastries."

The wolf stopped snarling. "Pastries?"

"Scones and finger sandwiches and...are we going for tea?"

The wolf had bounded out of the pond, caught Winnie's hand and was squishing in the direction that the wolf thought the Four Seasons must lie. "Apparently. We'll come back later."

"That's probably a good idea."

The coin laundry fascinated Decker. After a long but uneventful afternoon exploring Boston Commons, Joshua had talked Decker into an evening of doing wash at a nearby laundry. The vampire kept opening and closing the lids of the washers. Luckily the only other customer was a college student who sat with headphones on, listening to music while reading a textbook.

"You don't need to light the water heater or engage the agitator mechanism or hand feed the clothes through a wringer?" Decker complained earlier that they didn't need to go out to do laundry. He owned a washing machine and he'd only crushed his hand once on the wringer torture device.

"No, it does all that automatically." Joshua suspected that Decker's real objection to the laundry was that it seemed a step toward Joshua moving out of the house.

"We must get one of these," Decker stated firmly. "Do they sell them for private use?"

"Yeah. We could have gotten them at Home Depot, along with the refrigerator and the range." Joshua winced as he remembered how much those two appliances had cost Decker.

"When we are done here, let us go and get them."

Joshua told himself that Decker actually needed a new washer and dryer. "We'll have to move the old machine out and make sure there's the right connections. Power. Water. Maybe paint the laundry room."

It was a dreary little cave. So far the magic formula of clean and paint was producing better results than tackling the weirdness head on, à la the Frog Pond or the conversation with the ghost.

"What color do you want to paint it?" Joshua was sitting on one of the washing machines, hemming his blue jeans by hand. He'd bought the shortest inseam that he could find without shifting into the boy's section but the legs were nearly a foot too long. He dug through his messenger bag to find the paint samples that he'd picked up that morning. He fanned the papers across the lid of the machine containing his sheets and blankets. (He really should have washed them before using them but now was better than never.) "I think the teal blue is too dark. It should be something bright, like yellow. Or whatever this is. Filtered Sunlight. Maybe not. Beacon Blue? It's not as dark as what I used in the kitchen."

"I said I like green." Decker was staring at the dryer that Joshua had just started with his underwear and socks. He opened the door and stuck his hand into it.

"Oh, just let it run!" Joshua cried.

"So it blows hot air over them until they are dry?"

"Not if you stop it! Gee, how do you start it?" Joshua studied the dryer's controls from where he sat. "Oh, hit that button there!"

"This one?" Decker pointed at the wrong button.

"No, the other one. Yes. Hit it. Hit it!"

Decker grinned at him slyly, his brown eyes lighting up with merriment. "I'd hit that."

Joshua pursed his lips together to keep from smiling. "Not funny." Not in the light of what had happened yesterday. How did Decker do that anyhow? Had he spent hundreds of years practicing every possible double entendre? How did he even know that one?

Sorrow filled Decker's face. "I'm sorry. That's a bad habit of mine: talking."

The wolf had reached out and caught Decker's hand before Joshua could think of a safe response.

Joshua looked away as embarrassment burned up from his collar. They froze in place, holding hands, both studiously ignoring the fact that they were. Decker's hand was larger than his and cool to the touch.

"It's okay," Joshua forced out, then added truthfully, "It was funny."

Decker patted him on the head. "I will be more careful with what I say."

The wolf wiggled with happiness and let Decker escape to restart the dryer.

Joshua focused back on sewing the hem and explaining his afternoon. "High tea at the Bristol Lounge had all this really good finger food, little sandwiches and stuff, but it was all just one bite. Winnie said she was on a diet but I think she was just being nice—and cautious—and let the wolf eat her share too. We went back to the park afterwards. I thought Winnie could maybe talk to the ghosts in the area, see if they knew anything, but she said they were too scary to deal with without safeguards. We poked at all the frogs, but none of them said anything. The wolf kept wading in the pond. I couldn't keep him out of it."

"Saul told me that dreams cannot be taken literally, especially when they are prophetic." Decker took off his long wool coat. "The speakers were probably not frogs but people you do not know. Any image your brain supplied would be wrong, so it substituted in an obviously wrong picture, one with allegorical references. The fisherman being a hunter. Killer. The contemplative frog being a peaceful person, innocent of actions that warrant whatever the fisherman does to him."

Decker laid his folded coat behind Joshua. He did it without teasing. It was simply that the vampire took good care of his expensive clothes. It was the wolf that tilted slightly, so he could smell Decker better as he brushed past.

Distracted, Joshua accidently stabbed himself with the needle. "Ow. Stupid wolf!"

Decker caught his hand and peered closely at the welling blood. Joshua blushed at the touch of his cool fingers, expecting some innuendo about sucking. Decker surprised him with a very concerned, "Those aren't silver are they?"

"What? The needles?"

"Silver is poison to you. You have to be careful with it." Decker picked up the package and read the label. "It doesn't say."

"I'm pretty sure needles are stainless steel."

"They look like silver." Decker took his hand again to examine it with medical care. "I don't know much about sewing; I've always used tailors. I know at one time needles and such were very expensive. A man had to give his wife a special allowance just to cover the cost. They called it pin money."

Decker had given Joshua the money to buy the needles, pins and thread to hem up the jeans. The man was concerned enough, though, not to make the obvious connection. Not that he had to; Joshua had made it without help. This time the burn of embarrassment reached the tips of Joshua's ears.

"I'm pretty sure needles are stainless steel." Joshua eyed his finger. The blood was gone and there was no sign of the pinprick. He became aware that with both their heads bowed over his hand, their foreheads nearly touched. "It's fine."

"I think you're right. They must be steel." Decker let go of his hand.

"Saul had dreams that came true?" Joshua sat on his hand to keep it from taking hold of Decker's again. *Stop that!*

"No, one of his cousins. From time to time a divine ability appears in the Grigori bloodlines. Traditionally, that Grigori does not become a Virtue but serves in the Central Office, coordinating the others as a Dominion, even though they are nearly as strong as Powers. Elise's cousin Clarice is such as person."

Joshua made note of the various Grigori ranks to ask about later. He wanted to stay focused on the Frog Pond. "What about were-wolves? Do the other wolves dream about places they'd never been?"

"I don't know enough about their magic to say."

"Maybe I'm not a pack wolf. Maybe I'm some kind of weird monster that will go all evil on people come the first full moon. When was it again? Shit. Tonight." He glanced at the college student who would be in harm's way if he wolfed out completely.

"You may think that the wolf is controlling you. This—" He tapped Joshua on the temple. "—is what controls you. And this." He spread his hand over Joshua's heart, making it flutter oddly in his chest. "And, unfortunately, this." He poked Joshua in the stomach. "Always remember that a hungry wolf is a dangerous wolf. Okay?"

"The pizza dude should be here any minute." Joshua focused back on hemming his blue jeans. "I don't know how you can say I'm in control when the wolf keeps pulling stupid shit like attacking the pond."

"I think the dream scared you more than you know. You went with Winnie because you were worried. When you discovered that the pond was a real place, you had still no idea why you dreamed about it. You had gone to do something. You wanted to do some-thing. The wolf merely acted on your desires."

"To attack the pond?"

"Well, you've established beyond a doubt that there is nothing in the pond."

"Woot woot."

"Yes." Decker paused to consider the phrase before repeating it. "Woot woot."

Joshua wasn't sure if Decker understood what he meant. "Okay, sure, the wolf accomplished something . . ."

"You accomplished something. You are the wolf. The wolf is you."

"Oh! Pizza!" Joshua waved to the deliveryman that arrived holding a thermal bag.

For the next ten minutes the bag, then the box, and then the first three slices of pizza totally fixated Joshua's attention. The deliveryman was apparently paid because he disappeared. Joshua was licking the grease from his fingers when he realized that Decker was watching him with delight.

"What?" Joshua braced himself for an innuendo.

"You take such joy in eating."

Joshua squinted as he parsed the words. No. Nothing kinky about them.

Decker picked up Joshua's shortened blue jeans and started to carefully sew stitches into the hem where Joshua had left off. "Dr. Huff said, though, you should eat meat."

"This is sausage, pepperoni and Canadian bacon. Besides, when we have pizza delivered, there's no waitress that keeps coming back and asking if you're sure you don't want anything. You really don't eat any real food?"

"I throw up real food. Sometimes immediately. Sometimes after few hours of feeling horrible. You only throw up so many times before you give up. I can taste food but then I need to spit it out. Does not make me a delightful dinner partner. Besides, your body stops wanting it, so it stops tasting as good."

"That sucks." Food only tasted better since he became a werewolf. It was the only plus he could think of. He ate a little slower, trying to remember what they'd been talking about when the delivery guy walked in. The Frog Pond.

"There was nothing in the pond. What do you think my dream meant then? What was the scary black thing that came out of the water in my nightmare?"

"The blackness might have represented a breach. You don't know what one looks like, only that it generates monsters."

"What exactly is a breach? Someone—I think it was Dr. Huff—said it was a tear in reality."

"Exactly. What an average person sees is merely one layer of reality. Even in this realm, there are many things that they can't perceive. Ghosts and spirit guides and many specter monsters are unperceivable to a normal human."

"Like Fred." Joshua stretched his free hand high over his head to indicate the tall willowy spirit guide.

"Yes. Magical wounds like the bite of the werewolf or a vampire creates a hole into another realm. It is the source of our power. Yours is not the same as mine. A breach is a tear without a living focal point. Any creature it brushes against, it corrupts. Anything that animal then bites becomes corrupted too. It's a wave of evil, killing everything in its path."

The washing machines with his shoes started to spin up to drain. It rattled ominously. He and Decker stared at it.

"Is it supposed to do that?" Decker asked.

"I think my tennis shoes are making it unbalanced." The wading pond had made his shoes smell weird. The wolf had tried to throw them out. Joshua didn't want to lose the few things he had of his old life. Washing his shoes was a last-ditch effort to save them from the wolf. The drawback was that he was stuck in socks until they dried. "It will automatically stop if it's too unbalanced."

He finished the pizza as they watched the machine finish the rinse cycle. When the lights went out, he fished out the mesh laundry bag with his shoes in them. He sniffed them.

"Well?" Decker asked.

"I think it worked." He wasn't growling at them like before. "The cleaning mama website said to stuff them with dry towels and put them in a load with more towels."

"Wouldn't the towels then smell like feet?"

"I'll wash them afterwards." He pulled out the jeans he'd worn that afternoon. They also smelled clean. He tossed them into a second dryer. "Because I'm totally clueless, I had a completely useless prophetic dream—which I suppose makes it a normal nightmare."

Decker thought for a moment before shaking his head. "No, not useless. You've discovered you have a very rare gift. In time you will learn how to properly use it. It is like any skill, it takes practice. It took years for me to hone my ability."

Joshua swiped the payment card to start both dryers. The tennis shoes started to quietly thump as the tumbled about the drum.

"I finished this pair." Decker held up the pair of jeans he'd been hemming.

"Great! Thanks!" Joshua started the empty washer, poured in the liquid laundry soap, and added both pairs of shortened jeans and all his T-shirts.

Decker had rescued the paint samples from the washer's lid. "Let's use this color for the laundry." He held up the light green named Seedling.

"Are you sure?"

Decker reached over and tugged on the collar of Joshua's green shirt. "I like you in green."

The wolf drifted closer to Decker, licking his lips. Joshua blushed as he remembered the other dreams he had last night; the ones where Decker was some kind of chew toy. *Stop it. Stop it.*

Luckily the phone started to play "Für Elise" in Joshua's pocket.

Decker had insisted that Joshua carry it since he didn't have a clue how to use it beyond answering incoming calls.

"What is it doing?" Decker asked after Joshua took the phone out of his pocket.

"Elise texted me." He read it aloud. "Ask Decker if he remembers the Monkhood Coven."

"The Monkhoods?" Decker repeated. "Oh good God, I thought they were all dead."

"Is that a yes?"

"It depends on what she wants to know. They were infamous in their time, much like Lizzie Borden or Jack the Ripper. They are the true reason I became a vampire, but I never met any of them personally."

Joshua typed in "he recognizes the name but isn't sure he knows anything useful."

The phone played "Für Elise" again, this time as Elise called them.

Joshua answered with a cautious "Hello?"

"Let me talk to him!" Elise snapped.

Joshua tapped the speakerphone icon. "He's right here."

"Tell me everything you remember of the Monkhoods. You were alive then, right?"

Decker looked surprised at the phone. Joshua wasn't sure if it was because he didn't realize that it had a speaker or because of what Elise asked him. "Everything?"

"Everything!"

Decker slowly spread his hands as if *"Everything"* was too big to wrap his brains around. "The Monkhoods were a powerful English coven, reportedly from Bristol. They fled England at the time of the Great Purge that the London pack carried out after the Great Fire of London in 1666. The Monkhoods had started the fire. They made a scapegoat of Thomas Farriner who owned the bakery where the fire started. They'd also taken the Lord Mayor as a puppet and kept him from starting the firebreaks. It allowed the fire to claim most of the city. The Wickers hoped that in one act they could rid city of both the werewolf prince and the London-based Grigori tribes."

"The Great Purge was the first time that the Grigori allied with the werewolves instead of simply coexisting under the terms of the peace treaty. The Monkhoods settled in Salem in 1667 and quietly started to eliminate all the people who were resistant to their powers. It came to head during the witch trails in 1692. It was claimed later that the Monkhoods had lost control over the events, that the Puritans took the ball and ran, as Saul liked to say. Either way, the Prince of Boston went to war against them, forcing them to shift to New York City when I was ten years old."

Joshua took a deep breath as he realized Decker was over three hundred years old. He looked twenty, which was probably how old he was when he was made a vampire.

Decker didn't notice Joshua's dismay. "New York had been New Amsterdam and property of the Dutch until 1664. Since we did not have the Puritan influence of the Massachusetts Bay Colony, most divines lived well. Cotton Mather had little influence until the English took over. Things quickly changed after the Monkhoods arrived. They turned humans against anyone not of their coven, much as they had done in Salem."

"Why didn't the Prince of New York stop them?" Elise asked.

"The Wolf King had made Barnabas Tatterskein Prince of Boston in 1640," Decker said. "He was a wise old man when he forced the Monkhoods out of his territory. Alexander hadn't made Wolter Eskola Prince of New York until 1690. Wolter was barely twenty when the Wolf King shifted him out of the Gelderland pack, along with a half dozen cousins and one older brother as reinforcements. Wolter was too young to recognize the dangers that the Wickers represented."

"You were there when the Wickers killed Wolter. Right?" Elise said.

"I wasn't," Decker said. "The Wickers had moved against me. I believe it was to keep the prince from asking my help in finding them. I'd fled the city just two days before he was killed. I was halfway to Philadelphia when the Wolf King's arrival emptied New York of monsters."

"Close enough!" Elise said. "Did anyone ever find and destroy their spell books?"

Decker shook his head. "No. New York City was not what it is today. It was possible for a determined force to search every inch of it. The Wolf King is nothing but determined."

"Were the Wickers all killed?" Elise said.

"I believe so," Decker said. "One or two or maybe three had been torn to pieces in the process of trying to capture Wolter's heir when they killed the prince. There were so many pieces it was difficult to tell how many witches were killed. The Wolf King had all the boats locked down until they could be searched. The wolves scoured the area on foot for days in all directions. It's unlikely that any of the Wickers escaped."

"So most likely the grimoires were well hidden someplace where they could have been found by another coven?" Elise said.

"Yes. It was even possible they'd left a copy hidden in Bristol. It was an unthinkable distance when I was young. If the Prince of London hadn't searched Bristol closely, any cache could remain hidden for years."

Joshua startled slightly at the name "Bristol." He'd eaten at the Bristol Lounge that afternoon. Was just a weird coincidence or something more?

"What the hell is that thumping noise?" Elise asked.

"My shoes," Joshua said. "They're in the dryer."

"Where the hell are you?" Elise snapped.

"At a laundry," Joshua said.

Elise cursed. "You're supposed to stay at Decker's house because it's warded. The Wickers can find you if you're running all over the city."

"I'm not running all..." Joshua remembered where he'd been most of the day. "We're just on the next block. We'll go home when my shoes are dry."

"Why the fuck did you wash your shoes?"

The wolf growled in anger. Joshua wasn't sure if it was because the wolf didn't like Elise shouting at him or if because it was remembering why the shoes smelled.

"The wolf wanted to throw them away," Joshua said. "Because they smelled bad to him."

There was long silence on the other end of the phone.

"Hello?" Decker tapped the phone, accidently turning off and on the speaker.

"Don't." Joshua blocked him from doing it again.

"Fine," Elise said quietly. "Finish your laundry. Go home. Don't. Leave. The. House."

She hung up before Joshua could argue with her, which was probably a good thing. It also meant that he had promised nothing.

32: SETH

"I'm making a list." Seth had pulled Cameron into the kitchen for a semi-private conversation as the other two Musketeers coached Ewan through transforming into a wolf and back. In hindsight, IHOP had been a mistake, but they'd gotten safely away. Lunch and dinner had been catered by Cameron's mother. "It's a list of dos and don'ts. I need to leave for a little while."

"Why? Thane Silva said they're still dealing with puppets."

Dinner had been five quarts of homemade potato salad, fifty pieces of fried chicken and two dozen ears of corn on the cob. Seth wasn't sure if this was a huge miscalculation on what her sons could eat or if the leftovers would be gone by morning. When Cameron's mother dropped off the food, she'd said that the Thane had called the main house while they were at the restaurant.

"I know what Thane Silva told your mother." Seth didn't bother to explain that the Thane routinely said one thing and did another. "There's a newborn puppy in my territory. He's totally alone. I need to go check on him."

"The newborn from Utica?" Cameron asked.

"Yes." Seth didn't want to explain further. He didn't want the information to leak back to Isaiah. One disaster at a time. "He went all the way to Boston and stopped. I didn't realize it until I talked with your grandfather yesterday."

"What about Ewan?" Cameron asked.

There was a startled yelp in the living room and a loud crash. Seth ignored it.

"Ewan's doing better than I was after a week." Ewan had familiar people and places surrounding him. Seth had been stripped of everything except Jack. He wrote *"Don't take Ewan out in public again"* at the top of the list. "My biggest concern was that he was safe from the other heirs. After living with you for a day, I'm no longer worried that one of you will kill him."

He added *"Don't leave him alone with other heirs"* just to be sure.

There was another yelp and crash from the living room.

Cameron glanced toward the noise, worry on his face. "Are you sure he's going to be okay?"

"The important thing is to not put him under stress. The amnesia means that the wolf is more in control than normal. It's closer to the Source than Ewan is, so it can easily tap his power. Anyone that angers him will be dealing with an alpha wolf, not Ewan. None of you can control it. It's unlikely that he'll kill any of you; the wolf is protective of those it loves. Everyone else is fair game."

"So basically he's like a newborn?" Cameron's father had been killed shortly after he'd turned eighteen. It had fallen to Cameron to shepherd his younger brothers and sisters through their change. Between his experience and strong dominance, he was a good candidate for taking care of Ewan. It was the only reason Seth felt like he could safely leave.

"Yes. One that can kick your butt, but a newborn." Seth wrote down *"no arguments with each other."*

Speaking of newborns—Seth checked on Joshua. His older brother continued to confound him. Joshua had gone to the hardware store again, this time to buy flamingos for Decker's yard. Afterwards, he'd taken the Red Line to Boston Commons and waded about the Frog Pond. What in God's name was he doing? Why flamingos? Why had he gone wading in November? Why did he leave the safety of Decker's house?

Jack had caught up to Seth late last night. With the Albany pack in mourning, Jack didn't press for Shelter and Assistance. His cousin checked into the hotel across Wolf Road from the Court. In the morning, Jack retrieved the angelic blade from the pack's funeral home. He and the Grigori spent the rest of the day buying clothes (Jack was wearing Seth's), restocking the Grigori's first-aid kit, and using their respective world-wide contacts to try and track the surviving Wickers. The coven had vanished out of Utica. The Grigori were currently combing international flights, looking for anomalies that would suggest someone had flown unreported out of Belgrade since the massacre on Friday. Seth wasn't sure how this would help find the coven, but he supposed any lead was better than none.

Aside from Joshua being a newborn, the fact that the Wickers were still looking for him was alarming. It was becoming more and more clear that Seth had to do something about his brother. Quickly.

"I won't be gone long." Hopefully. "If I have to, can I bring the puppy back to here? It would be best that he has other wolves around."

"We have younglings here at Court." Cameron didn't want to say no. The man understood how dangerous a newborn could be. "We have a hunting lodge near Saratoga Springs. Maybe it would be best to take both your puppy and Ewan there."

"That sounds good." Seth still had Jack's phone which tracked all the Thanes, even Isaiah. The king's son was in Utica. According to Jack, the Thanes had dealt with nearly two dozen ferals in Ewan's wake. Isaiah followed up by killing all the puppets that he could find in case they were running on scripts. Isaiah should have run out of people to kill. Why was he still in Utica?

Whatever the reason, it only reminded Seth that he couldn't let Isaiah anywhere near Joshua. "I'm sorry about having to ask for help. I'm not sure what else to do with the puppy while I'm here shepherding Ewan."

"It's no problem! You're just a kid. We shouldn't be putting all this on you. We have a younger brother who is fifteen. Sorley. When your family was killed, Sire went to Alexander and asked that we could foster you. Sire thought it better here with kids your own age than at the Castle, surrounded by men. The king said he needed you in New York."

It was the first Seth had heard of the request. Considering how long he had amnesia, it wasn't surprising that he didn't remember Albany's visit to the Castle. Considering the amount of time that Alexander spent training Seth on being a prince— lessons that drove Isaiah mad with jealousy—it wasn't surprising that the king refused the offer.

"When Sire realized you were in Utica," Cameron continued, "he demanded to see you so he could talk with you. We couldn't help but overhear what Sire told you about Isaiah and the whole writing on the wall stuff. What he didn't tell you is that he's fought with the king—as much as anyone can fight with

Alexander—about sending wolves to Boston. It didn't have to be you. It could be anyone. Things would be better in Albany if Boston had even a handful of wolves to keep the area stabilized. Sire wanted Thanes to be stationed there. The king refused."

Seth felt a stab of guilt. In the last three years, Albany had lost a dozen of their people. How many of those were because Seth hadn't gone home? "He says that he doesn't want anyone in Boston until I take residence, but he won't let me move back. I've spent that last three years going to summer school so I could graduate early. I thought I'd be able to go to Harvard next fall, but he says—he says I'm to go to Columbia instead."

"Four more years," Cameron whispered like it was a death sentence. Considering the effect on Albany, it was.

"I'm sorry." Seth silently vowed that it wouldn't be four years. Somehow he'd get back to Boston.

"It's not your fault. Sire always said that the king knows things and sees things that we can't even begin to understand. Not that it didn't make Sire angry, but he accepted that the king was doing the right thing."

Seth locked down on a growl. He'd heard the same mantra over and over again for the last three years. Meanwhile his family was dead, people were dying in his territory, and now to discover that his neighbors were being killed off too. Why? Why wouldn't Alexander let him go home? What had Alexander meant by "needed"? It wasn't as if Seth did *anything* in New York City except endure Isaiah's torture.

"You can bring your puppy here," Cameron said. "Anytime in the future, if you need someplace to chill, we're cool with you coming here. Anytime. We'll even get a bed so you don't have to sleep on the couch. We had one but it got broken."

There was another crash in the living room but this time followed by laughter.

It was not hard to imagine how the bed had gotten broken. Seth and his brothers were constantly breaking their furniture when he was little. His mother called them *demoledores*.

He fought a wave of bitter sadness. His younger brothers were a pile of ashes and a collection of gravestones over empty graves; there was no bachelors' house in the future of the Boston pack.

Cameron was watching him, concern plain on his face.

"I'll—I'll keep it in mind." Seth was glad his voice didn't break. "Thanks."

33: ELISE

Elise was going to hell.

She just knew it.

There was a long line of people who were going to send her there. There was the Wolf King who would tear her head off for taking Seth to Boston instead of somehow getting him back to New York City. (How she was supposed to do this with someone that could toss pickup trucks around, she didn't know.) There was her Grandmother Marion, who would beat her for getting involved with the wolves in the first place. Her cousins were going to kill her for putting Decker at risk. And Decker...

Decker wasn't going to blame her. He was just going to stop waking up. He'd done it once before. His furnace had failed last winter and she'd had to break into his sleeping chamber to get him out of the house long enough for the boiler to be replaced. She'd thought it was just the cold that made him lethargic. Lately, though, she could barely get him out of the house to feed. He'd slowly gotten quieter and reluctant to do anything.

Decker had been at a laundry with the puppy. He'd been talkative and cooperative on the phone. Obviously the puppy had made him happy for the first time in a long time. Maybe even since her grandfather had died.

As they drove across Massachusetts, it dawned on her that Decker had been her only friend since she'd been assigned to Boston. He was the only person that she saw on a near daily basis. He'd been utterly dependable when it came to helping her hunt down and kill monsters. She never had to worry that he'd do everything possible to keep her safe. She'd discounted it all because he was the family's pet vampire. The truth was, he was a handsome, intelligent, and charming man, totally able to hold a conversation while looking at her. A highly embarrassing episode proved this was true even when she was naked. (Yes, she was covered in mud but that wouldn't faze most men. In fact, it would probably make things worse.)

The Decker she knew as a child wasn't the same as the one she found when she returned to Boston. He was like a brilliant light that was slowly dying. How do you tell if it's truly fading or if it's just your eyes?

She'd accidently given Decker something to love and now the wolves were going to take it away. Seth was going to drag his newly found brother back to New York where he would be safe within the Wolf King's Castle. Decker was going to be heartbroken. It was going to break him at last.

It was horrible to know that something was irreplaceable in your life only after you'd lost it.

It was like some nightmarish disaster moving at glacial speed. They'd left Albany after breakfast. It was a three-hour drive from Albany to Cambridge. They'd arrive before long before sunset. Decker wouldn't have a chance to say goodbye to Joshua.

She drove just under the speed limit watching the clock on her dashboard tick off the day. Sunset was at five-thirty. If she could delay the wolves a few hours, Decker might be awake before they took Joshua.

Despite her delays (one stop for gas, twice to use the restroom) they arrived before noon.

"How about lunch first?" she suggested. "Joshua is probably still asleep if he's keeping Decker's hours."

Seth closed his eyes and concentrated. "Yeah, he's asleep. Let's go through a drive thru."

Elise was hoping someplace sit down and slow service, but she'd take any delay.

Seth volunteered to fetch food from the McDonald's on Massachusetts Avenue since it didn't have a drive thru. He came back with five large bags of food.

"I got some for my brother," Seth explained as he handed one of the bags to Cabot. "Newborns are always hungry."

Elise noted that the prince had chosen the most possessive way he could to indicate Joshua.

"He's at the vampire's?" Cabot cried as she turned onto Garfield Street.

"Decker's house is warded," Elise snapped. "A Wicker wouldn't be able to spawn a construct into it."

There was a dumpster in Decker's driveway. She stared at it in confusion. Where did that come from? She backed up and went looking for a legal parking space. The nearest was two blocks away.

There was a pair of flamingos in the yard, wading through the dead leaves. There was also a new mailbox and house letters and a welcome mat. The coco fiber rug had little dog prints surrounding the words "Wipe Your Paws." There were new curtains on all the downstairs windows, shielding the view into the house. The doorbell was still broken.

"Ilya's asleep." Seth pointed up to the tower room. "Upstairs."

She found her front door key and let them in.

The house was freaking spotless. The living room was not only cleared of all the rubbish, it was also freshly painted in a rich moss green. The wood floors gleamed. The house no longer smelled of dusty old newspaper. Pine scented the air.

"We used to come and stand on the sidewalk," Cabot whispered. "To see where the vampire lived. This isn't how I imagined it. I thought there'd be coffins and bats."

Seth bounded up the stairs. Elise went after him, feeling sick in her stomach. If Joshua had transformed Decker's life this much in such a short time, it was worse than she thought.

At the bedroom door, Seth paused and laughed.

The room was emptied, scrubbed clean, and painted. Joshua was sprawled face down on a queen-sized airbed, covered in sheets and blankets, with a ginger tabby kitten sound asleep on top of him. By his head were graph paper and Post-it notes detailing out an elaborate plan he was making with Decker.

Close beside the bed was an old leather-bound book: *Les Trois Mousquetaires.* Decker had been sitting and reading after Joshua fell asleep.

I'm so sorry, Decker.

34: JOSHUA

"Joshua. Hey!" Someone patted him on the head. "Come on, wake up."

He yawned, rubbed his eyes, turned his head and looked at his alarm clock. It read eleven-fifty-eight. Last time he remembered, it was seven in the morning. "Oh geez, I just got to sleep!"

Sunlight was seeping through the curtains. He started to pull his blanket over his head to go back to sleep when several things filtered in. First was that Trouble was pinning down the blanket and pulling hard would launch the kitten across the room like an orange nerf ball. Second, that the voice belonged to Elise. She was a crazy woman with many, many weapons, none of them off limits for making him aware of how pissed off he was making her by ignoring her.

Third, was she wasn't alone.

Trouble squeaked in surprise as he was launched across the room.

Showing amazing reflexes, the teenaged stranger caught the kitten before Trouble hit a wall.

"Ow! Ow!" the boy cried as the kitten latched on with teeth and claws.

"Sorry! Sorry!" Joshua tried to spring to his feet but the blanket wrapped around his legs and he went face down. "Oh damn."

Talk about great first impressions. Who the hell were these guys?

Joshua untangled his legs and went to rescue Trouble—or the

boy holding the kitten. It was slightly unclear which one needed to be saved. "Sorry about that."

He pried Trouble from the teen's hand and it was like touching the Green. The kitten let go of the stranger's hand and climbed Joshua's arm with needle-sharp claws.

"Ow, ow, ow, Trouble!" As the kitten stood on his shoulder and hissed at the stranger, Joshua touched the boy's wrist again. Green.

He placed his hand on the boy's chest.

... he stood in a dapple forest, the sunlight shafting down through leaves far overhead ...

Joshua lifted his hand. Put it back.

... ferns grew green and lush and there was a trickle of water someplace close ...

He lifted his hand again. Put it back.

... a dark beast moved in the shadows ...

He jerked back to hide behind Elise. "Oh my God, Elise! They're werewolves!"

Elise pressed her hands to her face. "Yes, they're werewolves. You're a werewolf too. Remember? This is the Prince of Boston, Seth Tatterskein, and his cousin, Thane Cabot."

"Holy shit," he breathed. Why were they here?

The prince lifted up a McDonald's bag. "We brought breakfast."

Somehow Joshua doubted it was going to be that simple.

Last year for homecoming, he had a serious crush on Judi Miller. He'd made the mistake of telling three of his best friends he was planning on asking her out to the dance. In his defense, he'd told them in order to ask advice on how to approach her. Most of the girls in their grade, he'd known since kindergarten. The phrase "familiarity breeds contempt" worked on both sides of the possible relationship. Judi had moved into the area when they were sophomores.

Mark tuned out the discussion because he was having a text fight with his own girlfriend. George wanted to know logistics— how was Joshua going to "take" a girl to the dance when he couldn't drive? Joshua honestly didn't see the problem since Judi drove a red Mustang. It turned out that there were dozens of weird traditions centering around the gifting of flowers, meeting the parents and taking pictures that Joshua hadn't been aware of. Lance said nothing but occasionally looked seriously pained by the discussion.

It turned out Lance knew that Judi was a lesbian because he'd caught her making out with his sister.

Joshua ate the Big Mac meals (Seth bought him three for some reason) lost in a horrible wave of déjà vu.

Cabot seemed fascinated by the house. He kept opening doors and peering at what was behind them. Since some of the doors triggered avalanches of Decker's belongings, the conversation kept getting derailed with unburying the Thane.

Seth wanted to know about Joshua's SAT scores, what clubs he belonged to, if he'd been an officer in any of the clubs. That was what started the déjà vu feeling. Seth was stuck on logistics related to school—but to what end Joshua couldn't figure out.

Elise was acting like she had a lesbian sister.

"Why—why are you asking me about my high school? Shouldn't we be talking about the barn? The wolf that attacked me? Daphne? Why was she there? Who was the wolf?"

The werewolves glanced at Elise.

"We know most of that," Elise admitted slowly. "The wolf that changed you was one of the Wolf King's Thanes. He and Cabot were sent to your school to find you. They'd split up. Samuels went to the barn, Cabot to Daphne's house. The witches that were part of Daphne's coven—she was a witch—nearly killed Cabot."

"Wait—wait—wait." He was completely right. It was one of *those* conversations. "Me? They went to my school to find me? Why?"

"Because you're my brother," Seth said.

"What?" Joshua said.

"Because you're my brother," Seth repeated.

Joshua turned to Elise. "What?"

"You were adopted."

"You're my brother," Seth said again, like it was the sanest thing in the world.

Which it wasn't.

"And my cousin," Cabot added.

Joshua sputtered for a minute as his entire world was rewritten. He'd asked his parents hundreds of times if he was adopted. They'd always said no. He didn't want to believe that they'd lied his whole life but it had been impossible to ignore the he was the only short person in his family.

Speaking of which, both Seth and Cabot towered over him too.

"How the hell did I end up so short?" Joshua asked. "Was my mother a midget or something?"

"She was short but not that short. You probably weren't fed enough meat as a youngling." Cabot opened the big hall closet full of eBay items. "He has a Partridge Family lunchbox. Why does a three-hundred-year-old vampire have a lunchbox?"

"Hey!" Joshua leapt to rescue the lunchbox. "That's the eBay stuff. Those are going for a hundred dollars. Don't mess it up!"

Elise winced again.

Joshua carefully put the lunchbox back into the closet. "If I eat a lot of meat now, will I get taller?"

Seth glanced to Cabot, who shrugged. "Maybe. Normally we do have a growth spurts after being changed, but we usually go through the ritual at thirteen."

"Ritual?" Joshua asked. "There's a ritual?" If there was, he was still missing a lot of his memories.

"It's like getting married," Cabot said. "You can do the whole three-hour Catholic wedding or you can go down to the justice of the peace."

"What?" Joshua cried.

"What he means is," Seth said, "the bite is the only necessary part of the change. We've made it more elaborate. Think bar mitzvah."

"We're Jewish?"

Elise rubbed at her face. "We woke him up and dropped a mountain on him. It's going to take a while to sink in."

"It would help if people would just tell me straight out instead of talk around the issue. I mean, if the girl is a lesbian, just tell me instead of saying I shouldn't get my hopes up."

"What?" they all asked.

He turned to Elise. "What are you not telling me?"

"They want to take you to New York City," she said, "to live with the Wolf King."

He was out the back door before he even realized that he was going to bolt.

Joshua had spent most his life running from bullies. He'd gotten very good at it. Mapping escape routes was essential and he did it without thought. He was out the back, up the garage wall, across its roof and into the neighboring yard with a high fence in a flat out run.

Any escape plan was always weighted by the seriousness of the beating that the bully was probably going to deal out.

Being chased by the girl's lacrosse team because you walked into the wrong locker room? (Yes, reading while walking had its dangers.) It depended on if they grabbed their sticks or not. No? Take the beating in the most private place you can reach. Being chased by the three Roberts brothers and their five friends, all of whom will probably end up in jail on manslaughter charges someday? Run like body organs were at risk—because they probably were.

Joshua ran as he tried to figure out the risk level here. He wasn't even sure why he was running. He was fairly sure they didn't want to hurt him. Seth was being friendly in a "dog at the shelter who really wanted to be adopted" kind of way. Which was kind of sad. Cabot? Cabot seemed to be there because Seth was there in a bored older sibling kind of way. When the older sibling was Bethy, that kind of setup usually ended badly for everyone. So Cabot was the dangerous one.

And since Joshua was a werewolf now, Cabot could beat the snot out of him without fear of doing lasting harm.

Avoid Cabot at all cost.

Like now.

Joshua jerked to a halt, caught Cabot as the man reached for him, used Cabot's momentum and flung him with everything Joshua could summon.

Cabot went impressively airborne.

He came down a wolf.

"Oh shit! Now he's mad!" Joshua took off running. He might have accidently triggered the dog and ball response; Joshua ran, so the wolves were now chasing. Maybe he should have sat and talked his way out of this. Talking, though, had never been his strong suit, hence his vast experience at running.

He was running out of known escape routes and he'd lost track of Seth. When escaping bullies, it was always important to know the location of all possible attackers. Maybe Seth wasn't chasing him. Doubtful. The whole dog and ball thing.

Speaking of dog, Cabot was closing on him again, snarling.

Joshua jerked to a halt, turned and yelped. Cabot was freaking huge as a wolf.

The bigger they are, the harder they fall. Fear sent Cabot flying even further this time.

Out of known escape routes and running blind on the campus of Harvard—which was all open lawn and little walking paths. Lost, lost, lost—and the wolves had grown up in Boston. Not good. So not good.

Where the hell was he going anyhow? He was in his pajamas and barefoot. He needed to loop back to Decker's for clothes and Elise was probably still there. She had that "I don't want to get involved in this mess" vibe going on. From what he could tell, she didn't like him either.

Wolf!

Airborne wolf!

Was that still Cabot? Or had that been Seth?

What was he going to do? Bullies were normally not physically fit. Flat-out running usually got rid of most of Joshua's attackers within a half-mile. Lacking that, reaching a teacher or his house normally ended the chase. There was no teacher. Home was no longer safe. A police station would get him sent back to Utica.

Cabot suddenly slammed into him from his side. He didn't see the wolf until he was pinned to the ground. Massive jaws flashing toward his face.

"Cabot!" Seth roared.

The wolf yelped and jumped off Joshua.

Seth pointed at Joshua as he scrambled to his feet. "Sit!"

Joshua's body sat.

He sprang to his feet.

"Sit!" Seth pointed down.

Joshua's body sat again.

"Stay!" Seth growled.

"I'm not a dog!" Joshua snapped.

"No, you're a wolf." Seth sat down beside him. "A Boston wolf. And that makes you my responsibility. I know what it's like to be jerked out of your home. I fought the Thanes that Alexander sent to fetch me. I didn't want to go. But going was the right thing to do. I would have died with my family, and Cabot would have gone feral and countless humans would have died before Boston was fixed. If it could have been fixed. Even with me alive, the city isn't safe."

"And New York is? I've heard the stories about the Wolf King and his Thanes. The king scares the shit out of me! Look at me! I'm a bully magnet. You want me to go live in a house with a bunch of macho buttheads with fur? I'm staying here."

"With a vampire?" Cabot slunk back. Somehow, he seemed smaller than before. At a glance, he would have passed as a big black dog.

"Yes, with Decker. I like him. He likes me." Decker needed him. "I feel safe with him." Joshua pointed at Cabot. "You do not make me feel safe."

Cabot growled at him. "You have no idea what's going on. The Wickers kidnapped you once. You're coming with us to..."

"No," Joshua said.

"You don't have a choice!" Cabot snarled.

"I'm not going!" Joshua shouted.

"Cabot," Seth snapped, and his cousin—their cousin—sat back down. "He's dominant enough to talk back to you. Isaiah would hate him even if he weren't my brother. He'll try to kill Joshua first chance he gets."

The scary thing was that Cabot nodded to this logic. "I'd kind of like to see him throw Isaiah a couple of times."

The look Seth gave Cabot made the Thane duck his head and whimper. "I thought about taking him to Albany but we can't leave him there, not with Ewan still coping with alpha amnesia. It would be better if we just leave him here with Decker."

"The Wickers..." Jack started.

"If we can find the Wickers and eliminate them, then he can stay."

35: DECKER

Decker woke to the sound of people talking in his house. Normally, not a good sign. Strangers usually came with pitchforks and torches. No smell of smoke though, just cooking steak.

"Trouble!" Joshua's shout filtered through the flooring from the direction of the kitchen. "Drop it, Trouble!"

Male laughter followed. Deep voices. Adults. More than two. Decker cautiously made his way upstairs.

There were two black wolves of Boston in the kitchen with Joshua and Elise. They were in human form but Decker recognized what they were. As there were only two in the world, they had to be the young prince and his cousin. The prince sensed him coming before Decker reached the kitchen; he was watching the door. The Thane noticed him because of the prince's focus. Cabot shifted slightly to protect his cousin. The two gave him hard, silent stares.

"Decker!" Joshua cried when the boy spotted him. He bounced across the kitchen to pounce on him. "Life has been weird today. Well, more weird than normal. The big news is that I really was adopted and my biological father was the Prince of Boston. Who was also Seth's father, which makes him my half-brother, and—" He paused, thinking hard, as he pointed at the Thane. "I'm not sure how Cabot is related to me."

"My mother was your father's oldest sister," Jack Cabot stated as he continued to stare coldly at Decker.

Decker's dismay must have shown on his face because Joshua said quietly, "I'm not leaving. I don't want to live with the Wolf King."

321

"I'd rather him stay with you as long as you'll allow it," the prince added.

Relief flooded through Decker. He knew, though, that the prince did not have final say; the Wolf King did.

"But Seth wants the Wickers..." Joshua trailed off.

"Dead." Seth knew how dangerous the Wickers were. "It's not safe for him to leave the house while they're alive."

Elise and the werewolves explained that they'd lost track of the Wicker that fled Utica. They knew that one or more were still alive. The freed puppets reported that the Wickers had been focused on something in the Boston area. The details were too vague for even Clarice to pinpoint their lair. They needed Decker's ability to find the coven and kill them.

His puppy didn't like the idea of killing people. He edged closer to Decker. "Can't we just turn them over to the police or something?"

"No," Elise said. "God wants them dead, else he would not have put me in their path."

"That's one way to see it." Joshua leaned against Decker. Elise made the boy nervous and the whole situation obviously made the wolf unhappy.

Decker patted him on the head. "You can stay at the house while we hunt."

"No!" Joshua grabbed his arm. "We're a team! Like the Avengers."

The Avengers? Well, he did fight with a sword like John Steed. "Does that make you Mrs. Peel?" he asked Joshua.

The boy tilted his head in confusion. "What?"

"Obviously before your time," Decker murmured.

Joshua tilted his head the other direction. "You seriously don't know who the Avengers are?"

"Apparently not," Decker said.

"Hold on." Joshua dove across the kitchen. Maps covered the island's countertop. He dug through the papers until he found his tablet. "Let me add it to my list."

Cabot peered over Joshua's shoulder as he wrote. The Thane read aloud, "Amazing wonderful things that I must share with Decker?"

Joshua glared at the Thane. "Yeah. You have a problem with that?"

"I don't," Decker said. "I'm touched. I'll have to make a list. Amazing wonderful things that I must share with Joshua."

Joshua wasn't sure if he was teasing. "Like what?"

"Like *The Avengers*." Decker hastily explained the version he meant, since Joshua obviously had never heard of it. "It was one of my favorite television shows back when my television actually worked. I had a thing for Emma Peel." Elise reminded him of the delightful Mrs. Peel; not that he'd ever admit it to her. He wasn't sure if she'd take it the right way. She was already giving him the oddest look.

At least the prince had stopped giving him a cold look.

Cabot tapped the maps spread out on the countertop. They stepped down in scale, starting with New England as a whole and ending with Boston proper. They represented the prince's territory as defined by human borders. "The puppets think that there might be a Wicker here in Boston, creating constructs for their end game."

"It's a two-step process," Elise said. "The first is weaving together the inert materials. The vines. The totems. It can be made days or even weeks ahead of time if the Wickers have access to large refrigerators like florist shops or meat packing plants."

"While the constructs are still inert, I won't be able to spot them." Seth swept his hand over the map of New England to emphasize how large his territory was. "Since the constructs can shift through the source of blood magic, they can teleport from any location to any place. The Greater Boston area is most of the eastern third of Massachusetts. The Wickers could be literally anywhere within a hundred miles of here and still be considered 'in Boston.' I won't be able to spot the constructs until they become active."

"Wait!" Joshua cried. "Is that how the huntsman followed me to Framingham? It teleported?"

"Yes," Elise said. "If you hadn't gotten on another train, it would have caught you there."

"And teleported you back to the Wickers in Utica," Seth added.

"Garland controlled the huntsman," Elise explained. "While it was active, he had a mental connection to it. I've been told it's a very limited vision telepathy, so unless something comes into view that the Wicker can identify, the witch doesn't know where the construct is or who it's interacting with. Since the spell is controlling the huntsman's movements, keeping it on target, Garland must not have seen anything he recognized except me."

"He knew you?" Joshua sounded dismayed. Elise must have told the boy that she'd killed Garland.

"He had to know she was a Virtue." Decker tried to soften the news. "A beautiful woman with twin daggers is a dead giveaway." Oh, he shouldn't have used the word "dead" as Joshua looked more dismayed. He patted Joshua on the head to comfort him.

"Either the huntsman didn't see you or Garland didn't recognize you and your sword." Elise meant Decker.

"What sword?" Cabot asked.

"The sword I used to kill the huntsman." Joshua tried to measure out the length of the blade by holding his hands as far apart as he could. He was still inches short. "It's creepy and red and..."

"Can we focus here?" The prince tapped the maps. "Once the constructs go active, I will be able to spot them, but that's too late. The Wickers are invisible to me. Their power isn't from an outside source. Decker, we need you to find them."

"I can do that." He'd do anything to keep Joshua safe. "I'll warn you, though, my way is tedious."

"It's better than sitting and waiting for them to strike," the prince stated.

36: SETH

Ilya.

Ilya!

Seth let the Grigori ride shotgun so he could sit in the back with his newfound brother. He'd had spent a lifetime daydreaming how things would be different if their father had been able to save Ilya as an infant. (Anastasia had to die for Seth to be born. Everything after that, however, was fair game.) Every time Seth got blamed for fights his little brothers started. Every time he had to fork over a beloved toy because he was the oldest. Every time he sat through a boring business meeting in the name of "one day you'll be prince," he'd dreamed about not being the firstborn. Not being heir. Ilya would be the long-suffering eldest son.

He'd imagined his older brother would be taller, impossibly patient, and very mature.

Joshua wasn't the Ilya that Seth had expected. Certainly he wasn't taller and he didn't have the mythical patience that Seth had imagined him to have. (Decker was correct: his method of finding things was tedious.) In certain ways, Joshua seemed much younger than Seth. Maybe because Joshua had grown up as the baby of his foster family instead of the heir. It could be because his life hadn't gone down in flames at thirteen like Seth's. Nor was he constantly under pressure from all sides to be the prince of one of the most powerful territories in the world. It could even be that he'd grown up in a tiny rural town instead of Boston or New York City. When Seth changed schools at thirteen, he'd noticed that the Manhattan kids seemed more mature than those of Cambridge.

Seth had been worried since talking with Joshua's foster sister, Bethy. She'd made Joshua sound like a coward, running from all fights. An easily frightened child made for a weak wolf.

Yes, Joshua ran from fights. His bolt from Decker's house, however, had been sheer tactical genius. If Seth hadn't been the Prince of Boston, he wouldn't have been able to keep track of Joshua as the boy charged through Cambridge.

Nor was Joshua weak. He'd gone toe to toe with a Thane. A Thane! He could look Seth in the eye while he steadfastly refused to be called Ilya. Seth didn't think even Jack could do that. (Seth wasn't sure; Jack rarely said no to Seth.) Joshua would be Seth's heir if he was part of the Boston pack. Only Joshua wasn't.

Alphas anchored newborns to their territory when they changed a child. Samuels had been part of the New York pack. It had been a miracle that Joshua hadn't gone feral. As default, though, Joshua was packmates with Isaiah and the Thanes.

It was a small but important detail; one that the king could easily change. Alexander moved wolves from pack to pack all the time. Until he did, though, Seth wouldn't be able to sense where Joshua was outside of Seth's territory. Even within it, Seth could only track Joshua because he was a magical creature like Decker and Elise. Seth had felt Jack get stabbed from a thousand miles away because they were packmates. Seth would have no idea if Joshua was attacked, wounded or even killed.

How soon would the king return from Belgrade? A few weeks? A few months? Seth had been lost for nearly a month after he became prince. He'd been far from his territory, the Castle had been unfamiliar, and Isaiah had made his life hell, all of which slowed his recovery. The Prince of Belgrade might be facing the same problems.

When Alexander got back to the United States, would he shift Joshua to Seth's pack? Seth needed an heir who could take Boston. Jack stood as his current heir but it was understood that anything that killed Seth would have to go through Jack first.

It would be logical for Alexander to shift his brother into Boston's pack.

Alexander didn't always do what seemed logical.

The old Marquis of Albany told him that Alexander was

waiting for the writing on the wall to change. What did it say to keep Alexander from moving wolves to Boston?

Seth knew there were wolves that were unhappy with their current situation. For three years he'd trailed in the king's wake, visiting territories scattered over the world. He'd met teenagers in remote locations who wanted to live in big cities. Young people who wanted a wider choice of mates. Wolves stuck near the bottom of a dominance ladder filled with people that they didn't like.

Boston could take them all. Yet Alexander left the city unprotected.

Why? The king never explained himself. Until Seth talked with Albany, he'd assumed it was simply because he was waiting for Seth to get old enough. Now he wondered. Yes, he was "married" but Alexander hadn't brought the girl to the East Coast. Seth thought it was because he was only sixteen and there were no other females at the Castle. Isaiah's mother had been very young and that ended badly. Yet Anastasia had still been sent to Boston six years later when she was just thirteen. (That ended badly too but for vastly different reasons.)

Watching his long-lost brother bounce about the backseat of the Bentley, Seth wondered what the king knew that he didn't.

His brother had questions of his own. "So this Green." Joshua tapped his fingers against Seth's shoulder. "That's like some forest we're connected to?"

"Yes, it's our Source. All magical beasts channel power from another realm. An invisible layer."

"The Kleenexes, yes, Winnie explained that. She says you spy on her when she's sleeping. How do you do that?"

"Who?" Seth asked.

"The Wise Woman's granddaughter?" Jack asked from the front. "She has a big plant spirit guide and loves the color purple?"

"Yeah! Her!" Joshua said. "So how do you spy on her?"

"I don't spy." The Wise Woman lived in South Boston. How did Joshua even meet her? "At least not in the way you mean. She must be aware of my scanning the city for monsters. If she's using a plant spirit guide, then she's feeding off a power in harmony with ours. I can sense her just as clearly as she can sense me; which is to say not very much at all."

"But you're in New York when you're doing this—not spying—stuff."

Decker smothered a laugh. Joshua's look of worried confusion gave way to amusement. Seth found himself smiling with them. The two were a regular Key and Peele together. Seth was starting to understand why Dr. Huff thought werewolves were universally compatible with the vampire. He was comfortable to be around. Maybe it was why their grandfather had allowed Decker to settle in Boston and protected him all these years. Or maybe it was because his grandfather saw the handwriting on the wall. Did he know that Boston would need the vampire someday?

"Seriously, how does it work? Winnie talks about boxes of facial tissues. Decker says its Christmas lights and the surface of the sun. I see a forest! And…and…wolves who aren't there!"

"What?" Seth said.

"When I was in the hospital, I saw Cabot. Sort of. I had a vision of him. He told me to leave—to run. He told me to find you. That's why I came here. I thought that the Prince of Boston would be in Boston! How the hell was I supposed to know to go to New York to find Boston?"

All focus in the car went on Jack. Their cousin said nothing.

"Jack?" Seth said.

"Yes, I could have phrased it better," Jack admitted quietly. "But I thought I was just delirious from the silver poisoning."

Joshua was now locked on Seth, expecting some kind of explanation. Seth had nothing. If Seth could talk to Jack through the Source, he would have done it to save Jack's life.

Seth fell back on his training. "We are the Source. We can perceive it because it's as much a part of our bodies as our nose and eyes. We can control it with mindful exercise as much as we can control our breath."

"This!" Joshua shoved forward his right hand, fingers splayed. "This is not forest!"

"Yes, it is." Seth pressed his fingers against Joshua's and went to the verge of shifting form. His brother jerked away his hand, eyes wide. "The moment you were bitten, no part of you remained human, not even a single strand of your hair. You became completely and wholly the Source. Most people transform to wolf when they're changed."

"But—but—but…" Joshua said, "we aren't trees!"

Seth had never questioned what he was taught. He'd grown up with the knowledge so basic to his day to day life that he hadn't thought to question it. He stared at his hand. Maybe he should. In the meantime, he could only repeat what he'd been told. "We're like the flame of a candle. We wouldn't exist without the Source. It fuels us. We burn bright, able to heal from almost any wound, take any form, radiate light and heat further than we can reach with our bodies..."

"Really? Like flashlights?" Joshua pointed his finger like he expected light to beam out of the tip. He frowned in fierce concentration. Decker had both hands over his mouth but his eyes danced with merriment.

Seth rubbed at the bridge of his nose. He hadn't thought teaching a newborn would be this hard. "Only in a manner of speaking. It's an analogy! My scanning for monsters is a form of radiation. Metaphorically. I'm in New York City but my thoughts can reach Boston."

"Which way?" Jack called from the front. They were at a T in the road. Seth didn't recognize the area but a quick check with his power showed that they were in Brookline. They had been slowly winding their way around Boston, supposedly triangulating on the Wickers. It was good that Decker had warned them that it would be tedious, otherwise Seth would suspect that the vampire was leading them on a wild goose chase.

The car was silent as Decker focused on his power. "Try left."

Jack growled softly at "try."

"I'm sorry," Decker said.

It took hours and hours, meandering back and forth, slowly working their way south of Boston on the network of back roads that started out as cow paths. Just as Seth was sure that Decker was completely misleading them, the vampire murmured, "We're close. Stop the car."

They were at the far edge of the little town of Milton. The road they were on was marginally two lanes wide with trees pressed close on either side. Jack pulled off the asphalt onto grass. On the right was a house screened by the trees. Across the road was an old stone wall, barely two feet high outlining a large yard. A white colonial house with a classic symmetrical façade sat back from the road a good fifty feet. A lamppost at the edge of road illuminated its driveway.

Decker got out of the car, leaving the door open.

"The colonial?" Seth whispered.

"It's a Georgian," Decker whispered back. "Named because they were popular during the reigns of King George the Second and his son, George the Third. And ... no." He walked out in the middle of the road. They spilled out of the car to follow him. The moon was full in the clear sky, softly lighting the night. The werewolves' breaths misted in the cold air.

"This way." Decker pointed beyond the Georgian's driveway. In the pool of light thrown by the lamppost, there was low sign that read Thatchwood Nursery and Florist.

"Oh God in heaven," the Grigori breathed.

Seth closed his eyes and expanded his awareness of the area. Both houses were empty despite the late hour. If he had to guess, the Wickers had taken the entire neighborhood hostage. The driveway for the nursery was actually around the corner on a side street. It consisted of small house, a large barn, and a giant greenhouse. Dozens of people moved about the buildings. He hoped that it was merely one or two powerful witches with a host of puppets. He could be wrong.

In the greenhouse and hidden among the saplings of the nursery were large constructs.

"Decker?" Joshua called quietly.

Seth opened his eyes. The vampire had vanished soundlessly from their side without them noticing. "Shit."

"Where did he go?" Jack whispered.

"It will be all right," Elise said with quiet confidence. "He can be like darkness when he wants."

She was right. Seth could barely pinpoint the vampire drifting through the night. Joshua whimpered quietly with worry.

"He's fine." Seth patted Joshua on the shoulder.

A minute later, Decker returned without a sound. Was he actually floating to be so quiet? The vampire pointed at their black Bentley. "You said that the remaining witch drove a red car like this one?"

"Yes," Elise said.

"It's parked behind the house. You can't see it from the road. The engine is still warm. I can't tell how many witches are here, just that the only ones near to Boston are in this area."

Seth focused on the car in question. It seemed to be another Mulsanne extended wheelbase like the king favored; it was nearly two feet longer than most luxury cars. "He's right. It's a Bentley."

Where was the witch? Jack had described her as a tall brunette wearing a red fox jacket. He scanned the people within the buildings but none seemed to be in a fur coat. He reported what he could pick out. "There's about thirty people there. I can't tell how many are witches. There are massive constructs that haven't been activated with a blood sacrifice yet. I could have spotted them from Boston if they were. I think they're rooks."

"Rooks?" Joshua growled softly.

"Defense constructs. Very big. Very destructive. Very hard to kill. Imagine giant wooden octopus turtles."

"Are you trying to hurt my brain?" Joshua growled louder.

"It's okay." Decker patted Joshua on the head, quieting him. "We'll explain everything. Later."

Jack put a hand on Seth's chest and tried pushing him toward the car. "I am not going to let you go in there. It would be suicide. We're too few to take that many."

Seth steeled himself against letting his anger slip. Joshua knew how to fight but he hadn't been trained to kill. The stress of a violent fight would unleash his wolf. (Joshua was barely in control of it now.) Anyone Joshua bit without killing would become feral. It would be Utica after the marquis died all over again.

"We have an hour, at most, before I will not be able to function," Decker added. "Whatever we decide, we must do so quickly."

Ocean bordered Seth's territory to the east and south. The only people he could call for help other than the Thane were the Viscount of Burlington and Marquis of Albany. The baron did not have wolves to spare and Albany had already lost too much to the Wickers.

He didn't want Isaiah meeting Joshua. In the confusion of pitched battle, it would be too easy for Isaiah to kill Seth's newfound brother.

"Please, Seth," Jack begged.

"Fine," Seth said. "We'll fall back and call Isaiah. Let's take Decker home. I can keep watch on the Wickers now that I know where they are."

37: ELISE

"The king always said," Cabot said from the shadows. "That if we needed to fight a Grigori, never to do it during the daylight, when they had time to prepare."

After dropping Decker and Joshua safely in Cambridge, they'd driven back to Milton. Seth had directed Elise to a secluded area within the Blue Hills Reservation to wait for the arrival of the Thane. An ancient stone observation tower loomed over the parking lot and picnic shelter.

Elise had followed a trail deeper into the woods to find a clearing so she could pray. She spent the hours in prayer that full vestment needed. As the power had settled upon her, she'd grown aware that Cabot waited at the edge of the glade. Still. Silent. Watching. Learning the truth about her. Wrapped in the quiet strength of the Lord, she could calmly recognize it was the same as when she had forced herself to watch him change shape. To acknowledge his inhumanity.

She rose from her kneeling position, feeling feather light. Her daggers gleamed like captured stars within her hands. The power flared out around her as radiant ethereal wings. "The Wolf King speaks with the voice of experience. The Thanes are here?"

"Not yet."

Elise loved the calmness of full vestment. The world no longer chafed at her, she could see the law and order of God in all the chaos. The universe was clear, bright, and sharp to a razor's edge. She was a wondrous, cutting weapon within it. She'd been put into place to cut out the disorder that evil wrought.

Glorious as she felt, it scared her slightly. It would be so easy to lose herself. She'd been given valium once in ER while they set her broken arm. (She refused to let them put her under; it was far too frightening to be unconscious around so many strangers.) The drug had given her the same peaceful feeling. She recognized then how addictive vestment could be. There were others that retreated fully into the power. When she'd met them after her epiphany, it was terrifying to realize how empty they seemed beyond the holiness.

Cabot gazed at her with wide eyes, seemingly caught between awe and concern. "Is it like my wolf? Where you're never sure where you end and it starts?"

"The wolf is yours and yours alone. I have no claim on this power. I can only open myself to it and allow it to enter."

"With us, that is how ferals are made."

"Your Source is life, which is chaos in nature. It grows where it will, where it can. You can't give it control and expect anything but chaos. Holiness is order. It is laws put upon life so it does not destroy itself by its chaos. Cancer is when the chaos turns the body against itself. Law keeps all in check, even if it is by means of destruction."

"You are the destruction."

"Yes, the Virtues and the Powers." Dominions like Clarice were touched by God but hadn't taken their vows. They chose not to open themselves to God's power. In most cases, the risk of being overwhelmed was too great.

Virtues were detectives, living among humans, seeking out evil and surgically destroying it. Powers sterilized an area, leaving it to God to winnow out the good and evil. Elise deemed the situation too delicate to call in a Power and Clarice had agreed with her. A Power might kill the Thanes despite the political mess it would cause. The decision left her without backup from her family.

"I've never had to fight a Rook before," Cabot said. "I don't think any of the others have either. Seth says that Rooks are specifically meant as defense against wolves."

"Yes. They can deal out massive damage and are highly resistant to your bite. I will be able to withstand some of their attacks but not all four of them at once. You will need to keep the others off me as I go for the kill shot on one."

He drifted closer. "I will protect you."

She thought he might stop out of the reach of her gleaming daggers. Instead he slowly moved within her personal space. The vestment made her hyperaware of the heat of his body. The supernatural strength within his tall form. His breath against her upturned face.

"What are you doing?" she whispered.

"I'm letting my wolf know you completely," he murmured.

They drifted together without her being aware that she'd moved. With the calmness that came with vestment, she could see the angelic perfection in his face despite all its roughness. The symmetry of its lines. The rich gold of his eyes.

To her relief, he still took her breath away with his rugged looks. Since the vestment protected her from all glamour magic, it was Cabot alone that made her heart race.

He leaned closer to kiss her.

There was a loud snap of static electricity and a visible spark that flew between them as their lips nearly touched.

She burst out laughing. "Sorry. That's a drawback to vestment; I'm carrying a serious positive charge. In training, my cousins and I would play tag and zap each other."

He grinned. "A kiss would be worth a little pain." But then his grin vanished and he turned his head, listening. "That's the Porsche's engine. Isaiah should have been here hours ago. He must have waited until someone brought him the second set of keys from the Castle."

The moment was gone, which was probably for the better.

There were five Thanes with the king's son. They'd expected four. The fifth was the Chinese-Canadian Felix Leung who apologized for the "kerfuffle." (He didn't explain further, leaving Elise clueless as to what exactly was a kerfuffle. He might have been alluding to how long it took the Thanes to arrive.) They'd arrived in three cars. Isaiah alone in the Porsche Boxster. The five others were divided between two black Bentleys. They were all dressed for a business meeting in black suits and polished dressed shoes.

With the knowledge of Cabot's true breeding, Elise couldn't help but eye the men for evidence of further intermixing with the angelic line. Isaiah had struck her as a handsome man on their first meeting. Now that she looked for the signs, she found them. Isaiah had the telltale symmetry of features and the eye color normally only achieved with colored contacts. Was Alexander purposefully breeding his wolves to the angelic bloodlines in secret? Was that why Gavril Grigori had nothing to do with raising Anton Cabot; Gavril didn't know that he had a son?

"Have you heard from the king?" Seth sat on the hood of Elise's Jeep as if it was a throne. They'd talked at length on how to handle the incoming Thanes. Step one was to see if Isaiah had been more successful at reaching his father than Seth.

Isaiah snarled at the question. "Bishop called me to remind me that your safety took priority over everything else. I told him that I couldn't be expected to babysit you if you keep running away."

The fact Isaiah was in the Boston area was evidence that his answer hadn't gone over well.

"The Wickers that killed Samuels are here," Seth said. "I'll go back to the Castle once they're no longer in my territory."

Cabot had managed to get Seth to agree to this earlier once he pointed out that Seth would be blind to the witches outside of Boston. Cabot promised to go with his cousin to New York at that point, eliminating all the reasons for Seth could have for not returning with the exception of Joshua. Elise suspected if they didn't kill the Wickers in this battle, Seth would drag his brother off to safety. The promise, though, was to be a carrot for Isaiah.

"So all we have to do is tear a few heads off and you'll be a good little puppy and do what the king commanded of you?" Isaiah looked at Elise meaningfully. He was implying that he'd kill her.

Cabot growled but didn't shift his position.

"You're to cooperate with the Grigori," Seth said coldly. "You'll need to work together to kill the Wickers' constructs."

"We need her with seven Thanes here?" Thane Silva sneered. He included Cabot in the count.

"A Rook killed four Thanes in 1871 outside of Chicago," Elise said. "A surviving Thane destroyed the Rook by setting it on fire and running. The entire city went up in flames. There are four Rooks within the greenhouse."

Elise carefully kept out of range of the Thanes. She trusted Cabot to protect her back but he needed time to react. "There are thirty people inside. We've killed five Wickers. We know that one was in Belgrade as of Friday but we haven't been able to track him. We think there's a witch named Dahlia here; her car is behind the house. She's a tall, middle-aged brunette that posed as the mother of the witch that killed Samuels. She's the right age to be the mother of the warlock that attacked me but it's possible that there's a third witch someplace. The rest of the humans are most likely puppets."

Isaiah growled with annoyance. "How do we know any of the coven are here? It could be all puppets. This is obviously a trap designed to kill werewolves. The Wickers could have put all the puppets on script, armed with silver. Why should we fight it at all?"

"The puppets don't have guns," Seth stated calmly. "I checked."

"Wickers usually don't arm puppets if they expect to lose control of them," Elise said. "A silver bullet is just as deadly to a witch. Rooks take a great deal of focus to control; if the Wickers activate the constructs, they'll have to release some or all of the puppets without a suggestion in place. Something as counter to self-preservation as fighting werewolves would take hours to put into place. After the horrors that the Wickers subject their puppets to, they will seem the more dangerous monster to their captives."

"The Rooks aren't activated?" Leung asked.

"It's a trap without teeth at the moment," Elise said. "But it would only need a knife stroke to set them in motion. We'll be blind to who the witches are until the blood sacrifices start."

"This isn't our fight," Silva growled. "The Grigori should just handle it."

That brought Seth off the Jeep in a roar of anger. "They killed Samuels! They butchered him like an animal. They murdered Albany! They nearly killed Cabot. They've sent a huntsman after the newborn that Samuels made. How is this not our fight?"

"The puppy is right; it is our fight," Isaiah agreed using the most derogatory term he could for the prince. He pointed at Seth. "But you are not to be part of it."

"I will not fight unless provoked," Seth half-promised to stay out of harm's way. "You'll be without your phones as wolves. I need to stay close so I can warn you of danger."

Elise could tell that the wolves hated the idea as much as she did. They'd discussed strategy prior to the Thanes' arrival.

She and Cabot couldn't sway the young prince. Isaiah glanced at Cabot as if expecting him to object. Cabot shook his head.

"Whatever," Isaiah said. "I always hated Boston anyhow."

The gibe landed. Seth winced as he recognized the truth of the taunt. If Seth was killed, the city would vanish under a wave of monsters. "I'll be careful."

"It would be better if you weren't even here," Leung said. "A trap for werewolves in your territory? Who do you think it's for, eh? The Thanes? No. You. Traps don't always work the way you think. These Rooks might be here just to distract all those who would protect you."

The prince looked anywhere but at his cousin. "We all recognize that it's a trap. I'm the only one that can see all the pieces and anything that the Wickers might add to it once you attack."

They'd looped around and around this before the Thane had arrived. They couldn't risk the prince, but at the same time, their success depended heavily on his ability to see everything in his territory. As a compromise, they'd worked out a way for him to stay out of the fighting and still communicate with them.

"The longer we wait, the more chances there are that they'll realize we're here." Isaiah took off his suit jacket. The Thanes followed his lead and started to strip. It was an education on how the werewolves were as perfect in body as Grigori were in beauty. The men were all equally muscular; the only real difference was height and color of their skin.

A minute later, they were all large gray wolves, nearly indistinguishable from each other. Cabot stood apart, black as ink.

"Let's do this." Isaiah bounded away. The other wolves followed.

"Stick to the plan!" Seth called after them.

Cabot paused at the edge of the parking lot to make sure that Elise was coming.

Only the calmness of her vestment let her race after them despite her reservations about the other Thanes. The nursery was a half-mile away through the wooded park and across paved back road. Several acres of saplings surrounded the buildings that made up the florist's greenhouse, separate storefronts, equipment shed and joint business offices. A large gravel parking lot backed the buildings. The red Bentley sat nose against the large century-old barn, hidden from the main road.

As they reached the parking lot, her Jeep's horn blasted twice.

"They've activated a rook," Cabot growled.

"We must have tripped an alarm." Elise spotted a surveillance camera mounted on a light pole. "Damn it, I hate tech savvy witches."

"Stick to the plan," Cabot called.

Isaiah forged ahead. "Find the witches. Kill them. They should be easier to find now; they'll be covered with blood."

"We were to fight as a team!" Cabot shouted after the king's son.

The giant construct came smashing through the wall of the greenhouse. It was a twenty-foot-tall wooden Frankenstein's monster of plants joined together by magic. The wickers had hollowed a massive oak tree, studded it with flails and filled the cavity with woven climbing rose vines. At the very center would be the sacrifice, pulled into the oak by the roses even as his heart gave its last flutter of life. That fist-sized muscle remained the only vulnerable point of the construct despite the fact that the human was no longer alive.

"Here comes another one!" Cabot shouted a warning as they charged the first.

"Leave this one to me." Elise drew her daggers. "The Lord is my rock and my fortress and my deliverer!"

The vines whipped toward her as she charged the rook, too many and too fast to dodge. They tore at her flesh as they attempted to bind her. They withered as they were coated with her blood.

"My God, my strength, in whom I will trust." She dodged the spiked heads of the flails as they swung at her. She heard Cabot snarling as he fought the incoming rook, protecting her back. "My shield and the horn of my salvation, my stronghold. I will call upon the Lord, who is worthy to be praised; so shall I be saved from my enemies."

She slammed blades into the heart of the rook, one foot apart. "Amen!"

Her daggers flared to unbearable whiteness. She carved the compound of two equilateral triangles, one with each dagger, creating the Seal of Solomon hexagram. She felt her vestment swell with power in the presence of the holy symbol. It flooded over her and into the rook, funneled by the blades. The massive construct shuddered, brilliance leaking out of every crack, as God's might filled its hollowed center.

She jerked free her blades as the construct went up in a roar of white flames.

A third rook had lumbered out of the greenhouse while she had been focused on the first. It had been programmed to kill werewolves so it joined with the second rook in fighting Cabot. The two massive constructs had the black wolf pinned to the ground and were beating him with their flails. He was making horrible yelps of pain.

"Cabot!" she cried. Despite the calm of full vestment, her heart pounded with fear. A normal human would die from the damage that Cabot had taken already.

"I got this! Ow! Go for the kill! Ow!"

The Porsche came racing down the street, skidded into the driveway and roared toward the rooks pinning Cabot.

"Seth!" Cabot yelped. "You promised!"

The Porsche smashed into the nearest rook, knocking it off its root-like feet. The car accordioned from the impact.

"My God, my strength, in whom I will trust!" She charged, reciting the attack psalm. Why did she agree to this chaos? So many people would die if the prince was killed!

A massive black wolf exploded out of the crushed Porsche. "Isaiah, you shit, you didn't stick to the plan!"

Immediately the prince was wrapped with vines. He went down snarling.

"My shield and the horn of my salvation, my stronghold!" Elise slashed the vines holding Seth, freeing him. "I will call upon the Lord, who is worthy to be praised; so shall I be saved from my enemies."

She drove her blades into the heart of the upright rook. "Amen!"

"The last one is coming!" Seth shouted as the construct went up in white flames. "Isaiah! Get your ass back here!"

"Seth, get back!" Cabot cried as the prince tried to free him from the toppled rook.

"I'll free him!" Elise dodged a spiked flail. "Seth, get back before you're trapped again."

"Isaiah!" Seth roared. "Freaking hell! We're supposed to fight as a team!"

Elise slashed at the vines holding Cabot. She'd forgotten to track the fourth rook. A flail hit her full in the shoulder. Even muted by the vestment, the blow sent her tumbling.

"Elise!" Cabot shouted.

The prince leapt forward to yank her out of the way of a second blow.

The rook that Seth had knocked down had regained its feet. The two constructs chased Seth as he pulled her to safety. "The Wicker realized you're the biggest danger here. She's changed the rooks' target to you. Isaiah!"

This time it brought the Thanes running. The grey wolves were covered in the blood of puppets.

"We killed everything!" Isaiah cried. "The witch isn't here!"

"She's here!" Elise shouted. "The rook couldn't have changed targets otherwise. You missed her!"

"Buy her time!" Seth backed out of the fight. "Keep them off her! I'll scan for the witch."

Elise rushed through the attack psalm as fast as she could. Her focus needed to be true as her pronunciation. The tangle of wolf bodies, swinging flails and whipping vines fought for her attention. She was aware that Seth kept back out of the fight now that Isaiah was engaged in the battle.

With the seven Thanes intercepting the vines and flails, she was able to kill the remaining two rooks quickly.

"The witch is in the barn," Seth reported. "I don't know how you missed her. She just started a fire. There she is! Stop her!"

Dahlia Wakefield had used their distraction to run to the Bentley. The big car roared to life. The reverse lights flashed on. Leung raced to intercept it as Dahlia punched the gas pedal. Wolf and several tons of metal collided in a horrible meaty thud. The Bentley won the encounter. It flung Leung to the ground and rolled over his body. The Thane yelped in pain.

The Bentley slewed sideways. Dahlia worked the shifter, mouth set with determination, not even glancing toward the oncoming werewolves. The woman had courage, Elise gave her that. Courage wasn't enough.

Silva hit the side of the car, shoulder first like a linebacker. He caught the undercarriage with both hands and heaved. The big car groaned as he rolled it onto its roof.

"Don't kill her!" Elise shouted. Their last chance at finding out the coven's plans was about to be torn limb from limb.

"Don't kill her!" Seth echoed Elise, making it a command that the wolves had to obey.

"Not all of us are Grigori's lap dogs!" Isaiah snapped.

Seth snarled wordlessly at his foster brother. It was deep-chested dangerous sound.

The werewolves obeyed. They shifted to human form so they could safely manhandle Dahlia without making her feral. The witch was pulled from the wreckage by Russo. He held her pinned to the ground. Seth knelt beside Leung to check on the fallen Thane.

Leung murmured, "I'm fine. Just give me a minute to shake it off."

Elise started with the questions that she thought that the witch might actually answer. "What do you want with Joshua?"

Dahlia laughed. "Why should I tell you? You're going to kill me regardless. I've had a Grigori death sentence on my head since I was five."

The Grigori only killed witches who did blood magic, which meant that Dahlia had made her first human sacrifice at five years old. The idea boggled Elise for a minute.

In her silence, Isaiah inserted a threat. "We can make you wish that we would just kill you." He snapped Dahlia's left wrist to illustrate his point. The woman screamed with pain.

"Isaiah," Cabot growled a warning. His gaze was on Seth. The prince looked younger than sixteen in his shock and dismay. Cabot didn't have the dominance to stop Isaiah.

"What do you want with the newborn?" Isaiah ignored Cabot, taking hold of the woman's other wrist.

Seth winced but did nothing to stop Isaiah. "The newborn" was his brother and his responsibility.

"The king keeps you ignorant of everything, doesn't he?" The witch gasped. "Has he told you why he hasn't given you New York? New flash: you're a big disappointment to daddy dearest."

Isaiah snapped her other wrist, making her scream. "What about the boy?"

"We were going to take you eighteen years ago!" The witch gasped and sobbed. "Then we learned that you were useless to us. Not worth the bother. We needed someone strong, and you're just a weak, disappointing worm..."

Isaiah shattered her arm and dislocated her shoulder.

"Oh, grow a spine!" Elise trusted the vestment to keep her safe from the Thane. She pushed between Isaiah and the Wicker. "She's lying to you so you kill her quickly. They're masters of manipulation."

"We're immune to her powers," Silva said.

"Not if you believe simple lies." Elise decided that to move on to other, less dangerous questions. Seth had said that his foster brother might hurt Joshua. If the Wicker continued to enrage Isaiah, the possibility would become certainty. "Who is still alive in your coven?"

The witch sobbed in pain. "No one. They're all dead. You've killed them all."

It was an obvious lie since "Heath" was last in Belgrade.

"Where is Heath?" Elise asked.

Dahlia threw her a frightened look.

Elise nudged her broken wrist. "Where is Heath?"

Dahlia wet her mouth and possibly lied with the truth. "Belgrade. He was to open a breach and then wait for the Wolf King."

"I know he was there. He came home..."

"No! He's still in Belgrade. You'll never find him. Not even the Wolf King could find us. We waltzed all around him for twenty years. Unseen. Phantoms."

"Where's Thane Samuels' skin?" Seth said.

"My new coat?" Dahlia said. "I left it in the barn. It suddenly got too warm for fur."

Dahlia must have doused the building in accelerant as a fire was raging inside.

"Oh shit, it will burn." Cabot took three running steps before realizing he'd be leaving Elise and Seth alone with a witch and Isaiah. He jerked to a stop.

"Let it burn," Isaiah said.

"We need to be sure she isn't lying," Elise pointed out.

"I'll get it!" Hoffman raced off. Silva followed after him.

"What did you mean?" Isaiah lifted the woman up to snarl in her face. "Why were you going to take me? You were honestly going to take the king's son out of the Castle?"

Honestly? Who did he think he was talking to?

Dahlia whimpered in fear and pain. "The Monkhood coven had been chased from their homes in London, from Bristol, from England, and then out of Boston. They were tired of running. Their plan was brilliant but flawed. They'd staked everything on the wrong wolf. A leash won't control a feral. Pritt Eskola wasn't strong enough to take New York. Linden found their grimoire with all their well-tested spells against werewolves. We could do it right; we just had to be sure to take the right wolf. That he wouldn't go feral on us. We thought you were a golden opportunity. The king's own son. His first male child born for centuries. Who could ask for more? We had to be sure. We were nearly as disappointed as the king when we learned how stupidly weak you are..."

Elise realized that Dahlia was either stalling for time or baiting Isaiah. If it was the latter, she succeeded. With a snarl of anger, he tore her throat out in his bare hands.

"Damn it, Isaiah, we didn't learn what they were trying to do!" Seth cried.

"She wasn't going to tell us anything useful." Isaiah flung Dahlia's body aside. "She was dead the moment we showed up. Letting her rant just allowed her to spit in our faces."

With a loud "whuff," the barn exploded.

"Shit!" Seth cried. "Hoffman! Silva!" Fire was the one of the few things that would kill a Thane.

"We're here." Hoffman came stumbling back with Silva. Both Thanes were covered with soot and coughing. "Samuels' skin might have been in there, but there was too much smoke. We couldn't smell or see a thing."

"The damn bitch poured gasoline everyplace before setting the fire." Silva paused to kick Dahlia's body. "The explosion was a big kerosene heater that just went up."

Isaiah waved at the huge plume of black smoke rising from the barn. "We're going to have firefighters here shortly."

"Is there anything still moving?" Elise asked Seth.

"Everything is dead," he said.

She let go of the vestment. Pain washed in from where the flail had hit her in the shoulder.

Cabot caught her as she staggered. He'd transformed into human sans clothing. It felt wonderful to lean against his strong body. "You're bleeding! A lot!"

She looked down at herself. The thorns had torn open her clothing and sliced her arms and legs. Blood gleamed red against the whiteness of her skin. "Oh. That. It looks worse than it is. It heals quickly."

"Good." He looked worse than her with massive bruises on every part of his body. "I was worried."

She found an unbruised spot on his shoulder to lay her head

on. It felt like finding the eye of the storm. The rooks blazed about them, waves of heat coming from the holy fire, blasting back the chill of the late autumn afternoon. The king's son had discovered the crumpled Porsche; he howled in anger. The Thanes sulked in circles around the prince and Isaiah, whining complaints that they should be fleeing the scene. Yet she felt calm and safe.

What she felt toward Cabot wasn't glamour. If it was, there'd be no room for this moment. She would feel desire, not relief that they both survived. This serenity might even be love.

He kissed the top of her head. She looked up into his golden eyes.

Yes, it could be love. What a frightening thought. Allies with benefits had been simple and doable. So far, it had been a possible one-night stand that never came to pass. She could have walked away and never have seen him again. He would have been an embarrassing memory. Love? With a Thane? What a mess.

He lowered his lips to hers. Even though a cold logic whispered that she was walking straight into an emotional minefield, she kissed him.

38: SETH

Isaiah wouldn't shut up about Seth wrecking his Porsche. They were hiking back through the forest to where they'd left the cars. Behind them, sirens from fire trucks drew closer, responding to the thick, black smoke rising from the barn. Isaiah sent all the Thanes ahead so he could continue his whine-fest without witnesses.

"Four months!" Isaiah shouted as he pointed back to where they'd left the crumpled wreck of his sports car. "It took four months from the time I ordered it until it arrived at the dealership."

"At least you can get a new one!" Seth snapped. "If I lost Jack, there would be no getting another cousin."

"It was my car! You had no right to take it from the Castle!" Isaiah stabbed his finger toward Seth. "This wouldn't have happened if you kept your hands off what is mine!"

Seth slapped his hand aside. "It wouldn't have happened if you'd done what you were supposed to do! You knew that Jack was hurt! With the king in Belgrade, you were supposed to keep track of all the Thanes! You ignored the situation until after I took the Porsche. You were supposed to work as a team with the Grigori. If you'd done that, I wouldn't have had to use the Porsche against the rook."

"We were here for the Wickers," Isaiah said. "The constructs were nothing but a distraction that we ignored."

"You could only ignore the rooks because the Virtue was killing them," Seth growled. Said Virtue looked like she'd been dragged through a mile of barbwire. "She couldn't take the brunt of all four at once. You were supposed to protect her."

345

"That was your plan, not mine," Isaiah stated. "I don't risk my life protecting anyone."

"We're not at the Castle. This is my territory. You do what I tell you to do!"

"I'm so sick of the 'I'm a prince' swagger," Isaiah said. "No one cares."

"I'm sick of you being an asshole because you aren't a prince. I'm betting the voices in your head sound like a whiny little girl. Boo hoo hoo, daddy hasn't given me a pony."

Isaiah roared and threw a punch.

Seth jerked back out of range. He could whip Isaiah back in line with dominance but he was tired of pulling punches. The wolf in him wanted blood. Twice Isaiah had nearly gotten Jack killed. "Really? Really? You know that you can't deal it out at my level. You're just a Thane. I will wipe the floor with you. Daddy's not around to stop me. I will happily beat the living shit out of you if that's what you want. Just bring it."

Isaiah caught himself and backed away, growling. He probably remembered last time they'd fought; Seth had thrown him through the north wall of the library. He'd been in a great deal of pain for a day and a half as all the various broken bones healed. "You've had it so easy. It was all just handed to you."

"My entire family was killed!"

"You had a family! I never did. I have a king, not a father. My mother killed herself when I was a month old. Cook is the closest thing I ever had to a mother and you know how warm and cuddly he is. You had the entire package most of your life! I went to your house for your third birthday. The cake. The ice cream. All the presents. Cabot playing protective big brother and your little brothers under foot. It was heaven. You know why I was at your house? So Cabot's father could take me to Russia to live for a year. I don't speak Russian! I'd jump through hoops to call home to speak to anyone that understood English, and not once during that entire year, did my father talk to me. All my life I was told I'd be the Prince of New York. I'd have a wife and kids. I'd have packmates close as brothers. What have I gotten? Shit. I've gotten shit! And every day I'm not made prince, the whispers over how I'm a disappointment grow louder. Do you think I couldn't hear Albany? A damn marquis. I should have been able to make him crawl and beg for forgiveness. Instead it's me that had to back down!"

"Your life is shit so it makes it perfectly fine to attack an orphan half your age?"

"You're a fucking prince. Suck it up."

"Act your age!"

They'd reached the cars. The Thanes had already rinsed off blood, dressed and divided into the two Bentleys. Hoffman, Leung and Tawfeek were in the front car, Silva and Russo were in the back.

"You're going back to the Castle." Isaiah pointed at the second car. "Get in."

Seth didn't want to get into a car for four hours with Silva and Russo. They were nearly as bad as Isaiah. Nor did he want to go back to the Castle yet; he'd promised Ewan that he'd return. He should see Joshua before heading back to the Court of Albany. He didn't dare take Isaiah to Decker's, nor any of the Thane he controlled. The vampire's resting place was a family secret; one Seth would keep even if his brother wasn't hiding at the house. Dahlia had driven Isaiah to new heights with his jealousy. Anything that belonged to Seth wasn't safe from his foster brother.

"We'll take the train." Seth pointed to the Amtrak station in Westwood just five miles away. "The Virtue can drop us there."

Isaiah glanced at Cabot and Elise as if he was considering threatening them to force Seth into cooperating.

"Oh, fucking hell, Isaiah!" Seth shouted. "You told me to take the train in Utica. All the Wickers are dead. I'm in my own territory and I have Jack with me."

"Fine. Go!" Isaiah flung out his hand to indicate that Seth should lead in the Virtue's Jeep.

As long as Isaiah didn't follow him onto the train platforms, Seth would be able to get to Cambridge and then to Albany. Seth waved Jack and Elise to the Jeep. He would explain the plan once they were in motion. "Let's go."

They were within a mile of I-93. The Thane should have taken the exit before the train station to head southwest to New York City. The big black cars didn't move out of the passing lane to exit. They passed under the sign reading: UNIVERSITY AVE MBTA/ AMTRAK STATION RIGHT LANE. Elise turned on her right turn signal and started to shift across the five lanes. The second sign appeared another hundred feet or so down the road. The Bentleys stayed in the fast lane.

"Where the hell are they going?" Seth tapped on Jack's shoulder. "Call Isaiah."

Isaiah's phone went to voicemail.

A moment later, Jack's phone rang.

"It's Leung," Jack passed the phone to Seth. "Isaiah's making him do the dirty work."

Seth glanced behind them. Both of the Bentleys were still in the far left lane. Seth answered Jack's phone with, "Where are you going? You missed your exit."

Thane Leung didn't bother to repeat the message. In the background, Isaiah murmured something so low that the phone didn't pick it up. "Your highness," Leung translated it to something politer. "With the king out of the country, Albany is at high risk of a breach. The more wolves in the territory, the more stable it will be."

On the surface, the statement seemed entirely innocent and true. Seth knew his foster brother. Isaiah was heading to Albany for revenge. Cameron and his cousins weren't equal to the Thanes. Ewan was the only one that could stand up to Isaiah. The price for doing so would be steep. Every time that Isaiah triggered Ewan's instincts to protect his pack, Albany's Source would wash away all the memories that Ewan had recovered. Instead of taking a week to recuperate, Ewan could be lost until the king returned.

"Leave Albany alone!" Seth ordered. "Just go back to the Castle."

Another murmur was translated as "Your highness, please, let us handle this. The king ordered you back to the Castle."

"Albany wasn't dead when the king gave his orders!"

"Stop being a pompous little ass!" Isaiah obviously had snatched the phone from Leung to shout at it. "For once, do what you're told!"

"I can't trust you to do the right thing," Seth said. "So I need to do this myself."

Seth glanced back at the Bentleys as Isaiah snarled a string of curses that ended with the line going silent. A phone sailed out of the passenger's side rear window of the lead Bentley.

"Ooooh, Leung just got that phone," Jack cried as the rectangle of glass exploded into a billion pieces before being run over.

The lead Bentley swung into the fast lane and raced past the Grigori's Jeep. Seth braced, anticipating the big car to sideswipe them. Hoffman was driving, hunched over the steering wheel as if he expected Isaiah to hit him from the back seat. Leung was looking out the rear window at his new phone disintegrating. Tawfeek looked like he wanted to be anyplace else but the back seat. He gave a small apologetic shrug as the Bentley roared past. Isaiah glared ahead, ignoring Seth and the Jeep. The second Bentley pulled into the left-hand lane, following the first. Thane Silva was behind the wheel. He held up his middle finger as he drove past.

"Still exit?" the Grigori asked as they were nearly on top of the decision point.

"No. We're going to Albany."

The Grigori swung back onto the highway. As they drove toward the turnpike, Jack tried to get one of the Thanes to answer his calls.

"Haji is in with Isaiah." Jack rationalized why they were ignoring him. "The bastard isn't going to let Haji answer his phone. Russo is with Silva. They must figure if there's a shitstorm over this that Isaiah will take the brunt of it."

"They're right," Seth said. "Alexander won't bother to find out who was in what car. Isaiah is highest dominance; he decides which way they jump. Alexander has never punished Isaiah for what he's done to me in the past. Isaiah must think that he won't get in trouble for this."

Jack sighed as his call went to voicemail once again. "And if no one dies, he won't. Alexander doesn't care about intentions, he only cares about end results."

"If there's a breach, someone will die," Seth growled. "It could be as bad as three years ago."

"What are you going to do about Joshua?" Elise asked.

Joshua was ignorant of dominance and strong enough to challenge a Thane. He'd trigger everyone's kneejerk reactions, even Jack's. Worse, Joshua wouldn't stand and fight, he'd run. His brother was good at running. Seth wouldn't be able to protect the Albany pack if he was constantly needing to chase after Joshua.

"Decker is asleep," Elise continued. "Joshua won't want to leave without saying goodbye. If you leave him in Boston, I'll keep a close watch over him."

Seth hated the fact he had been too angry to say goodbye to his family. He'd spent the morning whining about how unfair it was that he had to go to New York alone. He'd fought with his brothers over things he wanted to take, stupid things that the king would have bought replacements for. A video game console. A remote-controlled car. He couldn't even name all the useless things that he stuffed into boxes that morning. It'd been too painful to unpack. Every bit of it reminded him that he'd made his little brothers miserable, ruthlessly taking favorite toys, hours before they were killed. He deeply resented that Alexander tore him away from his family.

Joshua had already fled his foster parents' house without saying goodbye. He'd spent the week making a new home. Cleaning. Painting. He even got a pet. If Seth tore him away from all that, he'd hate Seth.

"The Wickers are dead..." Seth started.

"The ones we know of are," Elise cautioned.

Seth shook his head. "Decker's house is warded. Its location is the best kept secret in Boston. We're the only ones that know where he lives..."

"The wise woman, Sioux Zee, knows where the house is," Jack reminded Seth. "She did the wards when Decker moved in."

Seth locked down on a growl of frustration. Did these two want him to drag Joshua into the middle of a fight with Isaiah?

"She's kept her silence for half a century," Elise said. "She can be trusted. The problem is Joshua himself. He doesn't stay in the house at all times."

Seth checked on his brother. "He's there now. He's asleep."

"I've told him to stay in the house," Elise said. "You might want to stress that."

Every other time Seth had checked on Joshua, he'd been out roaming the city, going as far as wading at Frog Pond.

If they detoured to Cambridge just to explain to Joshua face to face, Isaiah would have an hour or more to terrorize the Albany pack.

"I'll call him," Seth said.

"Hm?" Joshua answered the phone with a sleepy grunt.

"This is Seth. I need to go to Albany for a while."

"Hm?" Joshua gave another grunt.

Seth paused and checked on Joshua again. Yes, he was in human form, but his connection with the Source blazed stronger than normal. Seth was talking to the wolf. "Be a good boy and stay in the house. Stay. Stay."

"Hm."

Seth took that as a "yes" and hung up.

"You're kidding," Elise said. "Stay?"

"I'll call him again when Joshua's actually awake."

39: JOSHUA

Joshua dreamed Seth had called him. His little brother explained that he needed to go to babysit four Mouseketeers. The mice were extremely cute; they looked like Mickey Mouse except they wore clothes. They lived in a big brick Victorian with lots of cool games. Darts. Foosball. Billiards.

As the mice played, a big bad wolf arrived. It stood outside the house, huffing and puffing. Joshua knew that while the house was made of bricks, the mice would need to leave sooner or later for cheese pizza, cheese nachos, cheese fries and beer. It worried him. (It also confused him. If the mice needed a babysitter, how could they order beer?)

He woke up holding his cellphone. According to the log, Seth had called him. Joshua had apparently answered. This put talking in his sleep to a whole different level. Was Seth really going to Albany to babysit beer guzzling mice? It was all very mind boggling.

The most surreal aspect of his dream was the part that didn't change when he woke up: he had a little brother. "Little" being subjective: Seth was taller and stronger than him. Seth looked and acted like a prince. Unlike his sister, Seth actually seemed to want Joshua as his brother.

Bethy wasn't really his sister. That was a surprisingly painful realization. She'd spent most of his life torturing him in some way or another. Flushing the toilet when he was in the shower. Short sheeting his bed. Taking him on snipe hunts. Taking him out trick or treating when he was too young to go alone only to take half his candy because she was too old to get any herself.

He pressed the palms of his hands into his eyes. Was she happy now that he was gone? He wasn't sure if he wanted her to be happy or sad.

Why had his parents lied to him for his entire life? He'd asked so many times if he was adopted. The answer had always been a firm "no." Sooner or later he would have found out; he needed a social security number to go to college. When were they going to tell him? He was nearly eighteen. Did they plan to tell him on his birthday? What kind of sucky present would that be?

His stomach growled, reminding him that a hungry wolf was a dangerous wolf.

With everything else going on in his life, Joshua failed to wrap his brain around the passing of time. He'd somehow noticed but not really *noticed* the huge displays of canned pumpkin and cranberries and bags of stuffing all through the supermarket until he was at the cash register. He'd been counting the fifties that Decker had given him when the clerk suddenly thumped a massive frozen turkey down onto the belt.

"What's that?" Joshua asked even though he technically knew what it was.

"It's a turkey." The clerk pushed buttons on her cash register, presumably charging him for it.

He eyed it, feeling like somehow he was being pranked. "I—I—I mean—why—why—why is it there? I didn't—I wasn't going to buy..."

"We're giving out free turkeys. You bought enough to get a turkey." She finished typing. Her screen showed that it weighed twenty-five pounds and he wasn't being charged for it.

"What am I going to do with a turkey?" he asked.

"Cook it. For Thanksgiving."

And then all the cranberries and stuffing and pumpkin hit him straight between the eyes like a bullet. Thanksgiving. He hadn't even thought about it. His family always went to his grandmother's, just like the song, over the river and through the woods. It was one of those great-and-horrible-at-the-same-time family events that always made him feel like he was adopted.

Because he was. Not that anyone ever admitted it.

He'd spent every Thanksgiving of his life stuck at his grandmother's house. He never had anything to do but watch the Macy's
parade—because everyone else was—or slip off to another part of the
house and risk being tortured by his bored cousins. Usually it snowed
or rained, making the outdoors forbidden territory lest he track in
mud. They weren't allowed to eat anything in case it would ruin their
appetite for the feast, but his grandmother could never correctly
estimate the cooking time for the turkey. Early afternoon became
late afternoon and sometimes early evening before they sat down
for dinner. In the meantime, Bethy would throw fits, saying that her
stomach hurt, and get snacks, which she would then lord over Joshua.

A sudden wave of homesickness hit him and he started to
whimper.

The cashier and the bagger both froze, gazing at him in round-
eyed in surprise.

Embarrassment began to burn its way up Joshua's neck. At
least he hoped it was a hot blush and not fur. "I don't know how
to cook a turkey."

"Turkeys are easy," the cashier said. "Just get one of those bags.
And remember the junk inside."

Bags? Junk? He didn't want to spend the time to ask her what she
meant. He just wanted to escape before the whimpering got worse.

The turkey lurked on the kitchen counter.

Decker appeared behind Joshua like magic as usual, nearly
getting judo thrown. Again. "I thought we were over that." Decker
meant being thrown.

"I'm jumpy. You should make more noise."

"Click. Clack. Click. Clack," Decker said.

"What the hell are you doing?"

"It's footsteps. Like on the radio."

"No one does radio plays anymore."

Decker sighed but moved on. He pointed at the massive frozen turkey lurking on the countertop. "What is that and why is
it making you jumpy?"

"It's a turkey."

"It is?" Decker poked the plastic covering of the frozen bird.
"They've certainly changed since I was human."

"I don't know what to do with it."

"Don't you normally cook turkeys?"

"No." Joshua felt the homesickness well up again and this time there was no stopping it. Which was how Decker ended up on the couch, holding a wolf puppy, while the turkey continued to lurk on the kitchen counter.

In the end the turkey was banished to the freezer until he figured out what to do with it.

The turkey lurked in the freezer for a whole week. He could sense it lurking from the moment he woke up until he went to bed. There wasn't any place in the whole house where he couldn't pick up its presence.

Just when he thought he'd managed to ignore it, the compressor on the refrigerator would kick on or the ice would drop in the icemaker and he would be made aware of it again.

On Friday, it got worse.

He got a second turkey.

"What's this?" Dr. Huff pursed together her black lips and eyed the plastic bag on her receptionist counter. At their feet, a pit bull was desperately trying to get Joshua's approval, much to his owner's concern.

"It's a turkey." Joshua pushed the plastic bag toward her, leaving a wet trail of condensation.

"No, no, I'm a vegan." She pushed it back toward him. "You need to eat meat to stay healthy. A turkey is good for you, especially the dark meat."

"I've got two now. This one is fourteen pounds and the one at home is twenty-five pounds. What am I supposed to do with them? And why do they keep doing that?" This was with a glance down at the fawning pit bull. It was completely ignoring his owner pulling at his leash.

"It's a dominance thing." Dr. Huff took a dog biscuit out of the glass jar on the counter and fed it to Joshua. "And you should cook the biggest turkey for Thanksgiving." She petted him on the head as he started to whimper. "Oh, it's okay. Call your brother and invite him to dinner."

He swallowed down the cookie. "Brother?"

"Seth. You have his number?" When he nodded, she scratched him behind his left ear. "Good boy."

✧   ✧   ✧

Joshua was finishing the third pint of Ben & Jerry's ice cream—this one Pumpkin Cheesecake flavored—when Decker came up behind him quietly announcing "Click clack click clack." Joshua grunted around the spoon in acknowledgment of the vampire's presence moments before Decker wrapped himself around Joshua.

"Seriously?" Joshua complained. "Can't you just walk harder?"

"It's funnier this way." Decker rested his chin on the top of Joshua's head.

Normally Joshua would be slightly pissed about the full body hug, but at the moment—with the poultry positively *looming* beside him—he needed the comforting. Or perhaps more accurately, the wolf needed Decker close.

The little pamphlet on "puppy care" that Dr. Huff had given him stressed that he should expect having an overriding need to be in physical contact with "his pack members" during periods of stress. It also warned that the wolf had a very liberal view as to who qualified. The hug worked like a very good drug on his nerves. He relaxed back against Decker even as embarrassment burned its way up his face.

At least Decker never teased him. "I thought you took care of that."

This was in regards to the second turkey that was currently lurking on the countertop where the first one had sat last week. There wasn't room in the freezer for it. Yet.

"I got a second turkey," Joshua mumbled around the last spoonful of pumpkin cheesecake.

"And some ice cream." Decker picked up the three empty containers. "Gilly's Catastrophic Crunch? Two Wild & Crazy Pies? Cotton Candy?"

"I got the ice cream earlier. I wanted to see what these flavors tasted like. I never had them before." One of the unexpected bonuses of doing his own food shopping: buying *anything* he wanted. Seriously. Ice cream at his parents' house was chocolate or vanilla. Usually fat free. He'd had no idea of the range of flavors available until he hit the frozen food aisles at the store that lived up to its name of "supermarket." He couldn't decide what flavor he wanted, so he went with "all of them." He still had Red Velvet Cake and Triple Caramel Chunk in the freezer.

The thought of another pint of ice cream made him made him whimper.

"You don't have to keep the turkey." Decker turned Joshua around so he could pat Joshua on the back while rocking him.

"Oh please, don't rock. I think I might hurl."

The rocking stopped and the patting turned to a back rub. "You can throw the turkeys away if they upset you."

"My mother would kill me for throwing away that much good food."

"She—," Decker said tentatively, "—wouldn't know."

Which was really the root of the problem. His parents didn't know. They didn't know where he was or if he was okay or anything. He hadn't called them. He had no idea how the conversation would even go but he was fairly sure it would involve questions like "where are you now?" and "when are you coming back?" and most importantly, "what do you mean, young man, that you're not coming back?"

He'd always been the good kid. He'd always done what his parents told him. He always told them where he was going and he always got home before his curfew. He couldn't imagine telling them that no, he wasn't returning.

Not even for Thanksgiving.

He tossed the spoon in the vague direction of the sink and clung to Decker, whimpering louder.

How do you tell your parents "Thanks for raising me but I'm really someone else's kid"? He knew his dad wouldn't take that as an answer; there were too many lawyers on his side of the family. His dad would want to take it to court and fight it out. Let a jury decide.

He was fairly sure the werewolves didn't have lawyers. The wolves just killed people that pissed them off. How could he explain how much danger his parents were in while making it seem he was perfectly safe? He had no idea. He couldn't even explain why he ran away from home in any way that didn't make him seem like a nutcase unless he lied. A full week of wracking his brain and he'd still hadn't come up with a reasonable lie. All his parents knew was that a large dog had plowed through the prom committee. How did he explain that it had been a werewolf? That he was now a werewolf? That at any possible moment, he might turn into a tiny puppy or a horse-size wolf?

Okay—that last one would be fairly obvious three minutes into any reunion—especially if Decker wasn't there—and he wouldn't be if it was during the day...

The whimpers became a keen.

Deep breaths. Deep breaths. He was seconds away from being stuck a puppy the rest of the evening. With a gallon of ice cream in his stomach, that couldn't be good.

"You're fine. Everything is going to be all right," Decker murmured, carefully rubbing his back. "And please don't throw up on me. This is my favorite shirt."

"What am I going to do?"

"Do what makes you happy."

"I don't know what that is."

"I will throw away this turkey so it's not you throwing away food."

"No! Then I would have eaten all the ice cream for no reason."

"Then I'll put it in the freezer."

"It won't fit!" There were two more pints in the way.

"I will make it fit. Go sit in the living room and watch some *Avengers*, and I will take care of the turkey."

So Joshua sprawled on the recently delivered leather sofa with his kitten and watched the old British TV show on the new eighty-four-inch screen. Whatever Decker did, he did it quietly and quickly, as he came into the living room before Mrs. Peel had affixed the red carnation on John Steed's jacket.

"What did you do?" He didn't even bother to disguise the fact that the puppy wanted in Decker's lap. He scooted over until he was tucked under the man's arm. The wolf was instantly happy.

"I took care of it," Decker said.

"Did you throw away my ice cream?"

"No."

"The turkey? I wanted the turkey."

"I made it all fit."

"How?" Joshua had tried for ten minutes before realizing he would have to actually eat an entire shelf of ice cream for the turkey to fit inside.

"Elves and magic," Decker said.

They watched for several minutes while he dealt with the concept that somehow Decker had bent time and space to fit the fourteen-pound turkey into the crowded freezer. Part of him wanted to go see how and the other part dreaded finding out that something else—not ice cream or turkey—had been tossed in the name of ultimate happiness.

"What am I going to do?"

"Cook the turkey. Eat it," Decker said. "Isn't she wonderful?"

"Yeah, Mrs. Peel is hot. Dr. Huff says I should call Seth and invite him to Thanksgiving."

"That would be an excellent idea."

"You really think so?"

"I spent a long time thinking that I needed a good reason to be friends with anyone. In the end, I had no one. It was slowly killing me but I couldn't see any way out of the grave I climbed freely into."

Joshua liked that Decker needed him as much as he needed Decker. It made him feel like he mattered. Perhaps that's why Decker was so patient with him when he was losing it to the wolf; Decker wanted to be needed too. That was a good thing—right? Or was it a sign of that bad relationship they called "codependence" that everyone talked about but never explained?

Joshua wondered if he should look up the term or avoid enlightenment like the plague.

"If you need a good reason to be friends with Seth," Decker said, "then remember he is the Prince of Boston. He will be living somewhere nearby in a few months. And he is, and always will be, your brother."

"Right. Is it okay with you? Do you mind if I invite him over?"

"This is your home."

"It's your house. I just live here."

"There is no 'just,' Joshua. It's our home. And if you want to invite someone to dinner; it's your right."

"You bought the house. You've lived here for fifty years."

"Yes, this was a house. A house I was dying in for fifty years. You are what makes it a home."

If was really unfair of Decker to say something like that while Joshua was still feeling so raw. Without warning, he was a puppy scrambling into the man's lap.

At least he didn't throw up the ice cream.

Joshua had had a brother for only two weeks now. He still wasn't sure how he felt about it. His relationship with his older sister—adopted older sister—had been extremely rocky. In fact, he was fairly sure that Bethy could barely tolerate him. She might love him—maybe—in some twisted obligatory way. But liked him? No. In the seventeen years that they'd been siblings, most of their conversations were as short as possible and conducted with growling and snarling on her part. (And she wasn't even a werewolf.)

Joshua couldn't imagine calling Bethy on the phone and just talking. He couldn't remember a conversation that didn't start with a question like "where is" or "what did you do with," that wasn't seasoned heavily with insults, and that didn't end with a physical threat.

What did siblings talk about when they weren't trying to beat the snot out of each other? Joshua had no idea.

The weird thing about talking to Seth was that the moment the phone rang, he could *feel* Seth's presence, like his brother had stepped through the ether and was there in spirit. Which meant that Seth already knew how Joshua was feeling even without him saying anything. Which was really, really freaky weird.

"Joshua! What's wrong?"

"People keep giving me turkeys," Joshua said. "I have two now and I think I'll probably end up with a third one in the next week or so."

There was a moment of silence and Joshua felt Seth expand his awareness, apparently scanning the house for living birds.

"Turkeys?" Seth asked after a minute. "Are we talking turkey turkeys with feathers and stuff, or dead turkeys?"

"Dead turkeys. Frozen turkeys. Big ones. They're kind of freaking me out."

"Oh!" Seth made the connection. "The first Thanksgiving alone! Yeah, that's a hard one. I'll warn you now that Christmas is harder."

Joshua whimpered.

"So you have turkeys." Seth looped back to the start of the conversation and put it on track. "Can I come up for Thanksgiving dinner?"

Joshua eyed the phone. He'd thought he was calling Seth instead of the other way around. "I don't know how to cook."

"Neither do I. It will be an adventure."

"In food poisoning," Joshua muttered.

"Ah, the joy of being werewolves is that we don't get poisoned. We can eat five-day-old sushi and not get sick. The king hasn't returned from Belgrade but Isaiah finally went back to the Castle.

With him gone, Ewan is safe. I'm packing up here. I need to get back to school. I've missed three weeks. New York is crazy on Thanksgiving Day with the Macy's parade. Do you mind if I come up the day before? It's a school holiday."

"As long as we don't have to watch the parade on television."

"God no. I'll bring some movies. Is Jack invited? It would be nice."

Cabot probably followed the same love/hate algorithm that Bethy employed but what was Thanksgiving without a cousin to torture you?

"Yeah. Sure," Joshua said.

"Cool. I'll see you Wednesday after next."

40: SETH

Seth hung up his cell phone. He stood for several minutes holding tight to his awareness of his brother. At the time, he'd been so sure that leaving Joshua in Boston with Decker was for the best. It was nerve-wracking to sense how alone his brother was and how far, far away. Not another wolf for hundreds of miles. If something happened, it would take Seth hours to get to him. Decker slept all day. The Grigori wouldn't be able to control the wolf.

Seth had been scared when Joshua called him. He'd been afraid that something had gone wrong. The feeling had deepened when Seth reached out and felt how rattled Joshua was. Over turkeys! He'd been thinking that since Joshua was seventeen they were on equal footing, but the call reminded him that the boy was a newborn. The months after being changed from human to werewolf, it felt like being strapped into a rollercoaster blindfolded. The wolf took you for an emotional ride that you were rarely in control of.

Seth couldn't imagine dealing with the wolf all alone; it had been hell even with his parents riding curb on the worst of it. It was, however, the mess he'd left his brother in. He'd felt so guilty that he'd pushed Joshua into agreeing on a longer visit than just dinner. Judging by the way that Joshua was currently dashing in frantic circles about Decker's house, he'd only increased his brother's anxiety.

After ping-ponging about Decker's house, his brother collided with the newly awakened vampire. Decker must have forgotten to announce his presence; he went flying across the living room. Luckily the vampire hit the couch instead of the television. Seconds later, puppy Joshua scrambled into Decker's lap to be held.

That was the other troubling thing. How was Joshua getting so small when he changed? Most newborns transformed into human-sized wolves. Pack wolves only grew larger after months of practice strengthened their connection with the Source. Joshua seemed to be able to change back and forth without any damage to his clothes. One moment he'd be fully clothed; a moment later he was a puppy. His speed of transformation was simply breathtaking compared to even the Thanes. When he changed back, he was clothed again. Where the hell were the clothes while he was a wolf?

And could Seth do that? He'd been taught to strip down before changing. What if all this time, he could skip that part?

Jack appeared at the door. "I've got the train tickets." He picked up the unease that Seth was radiating. "Are you okay?"

"I got a call from Joshua."

"Did something happen?"

"It's just the normal newborn joyride overloaded by the very real problem that he's alone; without the people that raised him or us there with him."

"Isaiah has spent the last two weeks proving you right," Jack said to soothe Seth's guilt. "He came here to harass the Albany pack out of revenge. He had the perfect excuse that he and the Thane were making the alpha more stable until Ewan was able to handle it. He knows that keeping you here was screwing up your schoolwork so he stayed until he got bored. You couldn't have protected both Ewan and Joshua. If you'd sent Joshua to the Castle, Isaiah would have found out, and then you would have had to choose which one to save."

"I feel like I chose Ewan over my brother."

"I hate to say this, but you had to. Ewan is marquis. If Ewan goes down in flames, he takes all of Albany with him. Joshua might be your brother but in the grand scheme of things, he's not that important."

Seth could sense that Decker had gotten Joshua calmed down and back to human. They were sitting together, talking, while watching something on the television. It was a comforting tableau but it didn't erase the knowledge that, as Prince of Boston, Seth should be the one making sure that one of his packmates was safe.

Only Alexander wasn't going to let Seth move back to Boston to live. While dealing with Joshua, Seth was starting to understand why. Seth might have all of Boston's power to tap and years of experience—but he also would be expected to face any emergency that cropped up while Joshua could run from the danger. ('Flee' seemed to be his brother's gut reaction.)

Bringing Joshua to the Castle, though, was a recipe for disaster.

Isaiah admitted that his jealousy was deep rooted in the fact that Seth had all that Isaiah wanted. Loving parents (ignoring that they'd been murdered.) A happy childhood (that went down in flames when he was thirteen). A close-knit extended family (who were all dead now.) Being a prince was simply icing on the cake. Isaiah would be jealous of any addition to Seth's supposed bounty.

It would only be a matter of time before Isaiah hated Joshua for his own sake. The boy technically still had his loving adoptive parents. He could theoretically return to his happy childhood home. As Seth's heir, Joshua would be Isaiah's equal. Isaiah might grow to hate Joshua even more than he hated Seth.

"How is he?" Jack broke Seth's silence.

Seth checked again on his brother. A bowl of popcorn had been made but the scene was much the same. Joshua was leaning heavily on Decker's presence to stay calm. "Fine. I'll feel better once I see him."

Jack cocked his head in confusion. He held up the train tickets to New York City. "You want to go to Boston?"

"He invited us to Thanksgiving dinner," Seth said.

"Did you call Belgrade?"

"Alexander won't care." Seth hoped he wouldn't. "All the Wickers are dead..."

"We think."

"There's no active constructs in my territory. The Grigori haven't found any sign of survivors. I'll promise not to do any monster hunting or stick my nose into deep holes and what not. You'll be with me. Joshua's got a black belt or something in Judo. And there's Decker. So it's not like I'm going to be alone. Alexander doesn't celebrate Thanksgiving any more than he does Christmas or Easter. Cook will probably be making something like bratwurst and sauerkraut or haggis on Thursday instead of a turkey."

"And Joshua is going to cook this turkey that we're going to be eating?"

"Hopefully," Seth said. "We could always order lots of takeout on Wednesday night and have leftovers as a backup plan..."

"...if we don't burn down the house."

41: ELISE

Elise was sitting on her couch, staring at her ceiling. She'd taken the day off to deal with all life's little needs. Yes, there was evil that needed to be slain, but she was out of clean clothes, her toilet needed scrubbing, and the dust bunnies were approaching epic size. She liked that the world seemed safe enough to focus on herself, but it left her feeling hollow. It was the closest she got to a holiday. Shouldn't she do something fun? What did she like to do for fun?

It left her floundering in the realization that when she became a weapon for God, she'd abandoned all that made her human. Her life revolved around killing. She did what was needed to strengthen her body, care for her weapons, and know her terri-tory. Humans had interests and hobbies and things they did for sheer joy. What did she like to do?

Joshua and Decker were doing superhero movie marathons. She didn't like the fake reality of movies since seeing *Old Yeller* as a child. She'd spent a week crying over the ending. Her mother finally pointed out that the dog was acting as much as the humans in the film. Elise looked it up. She discovered to her dismay that the dog's real name was Spike and had appeared in dozens of other movies and TV shows. All that crying over a dog that got up and bounced away after the cameras stopped rolling! Feeling betrayed, she resolved never to watch another movie. Maybe she should give them another try.

Elise's phone played Cabot's tone. She blushed as she thought of what she *really* would like to do for fun. There was small hope of that; Cabot was three hours away. Their relationship hadn't progressed beyond their first kiss, mostly from lack of being in the same state. She'd dropped the wolves off in Albany two weeks ago. Cabot and Seth were guarding the new Marquis of Albany from Isaiah and the Thane. She'd driven home to Boston to keep an eye on Joshua. (As a weird side-effect to babysitting the newborn werewolf, she'd gained five pounds. The boy had excellent taste in junk food. He always had the best pizza, donuts, pie and ice cream.)

She picked up her phone to see what Cabot had texted her.

The message asked, "What are you doing for Thanksgiving?"

"The same thing we do every night, Pinky," she muttered. Her family didn't take holidays because monsters never rested. Christmas was something she saw other people celebrate on television shows. It made her sympathize with Jewish children. Thanksgiving was the worst because every store and restaurant closed down while all of New England attempted to be someplace else. The highways would be gridlocked from New Hampshire to Connecticut, starting Wednesday and continuing until late Sunday.

She texted back, "Saving the world."

"Seriously? Need help?" was the immediate reply.

For some reason, that made her grin widely.

"I can't leave Boston..." She wasn't sure how to explain. "...because evil. I'm planning to just lurk in the shadows like normal."

"Like Batman?"

"Batgirl."

"I stand corrected. So, no plans other than terrorizing small monsters?"

"Why? Is this a trap?"

"Want to do Thanksgiving with us?"

She frowned at the screen. Us? Surely he didn't mean with the Wolf King. She typed in and erased "huh?" and "what?" and "who?" before sending "At the Castle?"

"LOL. No. Decker's."

Decker's? She struggled to pair "Vampire" with "Thanksgiving Dinner." Two weeks ago it would have been a laughable impossibility. The house had been a crowded tomb that smelled of dust and moldering newspaper. There had been embarrassing testaments to her boredom when she'd visited as a child. She built a book fortress in the library when she was four. At five, she created a diorama of plastic cowboys tying Decker to a stake as their "Indian" counterparts built a bonfire of matchbooks. (At least she showed some restraint and hadn't used the matches to set the house on fire.) When she was six, she'd scrawled "Decker is a monster" in crayon on every scrap of paper she could find in the living room.

It slightly freaked her out when she walked into Decker's. With the exception of the TV, the leather couch, and the two stools in the kitchen, the first floor was completely and totally empty. It seemed like she'd walked into the wrong home; a stranger intruding on someone's privacy. All she had known of Decker had been thrown away, along with all her childhood rebellions. What did Joshua think of the diorama? Did he even realize she was the one that made it? Its absence made her feel like she'd been forgiven of petty sins but slightly lost as to where she fit into Decker's life anymore.

The kitchen now sported a huge double-oven gas range and a side-by-side refrigerator. The scents of Joshua's last meal always hung heavy in the air. Steak. Tuna salad. Hot buttered popcorn. Still, she couldn't imagine eating Thanksgiving at Decker's. Who was going to cook the turkey? Her? And where were they going to sit? On the floor?

As if guessing her concerns, Cabot texted, "We plan to bring folding tables and chairs in one of the Land Rovers if Joshua doesn't get anything by Thanksgiving."

She smiled at her screen. Cabot might be naïve but not an idiot. She loved that about him.

There she went, using the "love" word so casually.

"So, want to eat with us?" he texted.

It would be a step toward fitting herself into Cabot's life and back into Decker's. "Yes."

42: DECKER

The prince was coming early for dinner and staying the night.

The statement filled Decker with quiet terror. He was careful, though, to keep his fear from Joshua, who was seriously not taking the holiday well. They sat on the sofa watching cooking videos, calmly discussing logistics, while Decker tried very hard not to panic.

The prince was sleeping over.

"You really think we should get beds? It's just one night." Joshua cocked his head back and forth as he made adorable faces at the list he'd written out.

"At Thanksgiving. Then there's Christmas. New Years'. Easter. Besides it's always good to have a place for unexpected guests to sleep." Not that Decker had had such guests for three hundred years, but that was beside the point. "We can get the beds at the same place we bought this sofa and your bedroom furniture."

The prince was going to be playing house with Decker's puppy.

It meant that Seth was worried about Joshua and was rethinking leaving him in Boston. The prince was young. He had made a snap decision. Seth had had time to reconsider.

At best, this was just a prolonged visit to see how well Joshua was really doing. Pretenses can be kept up during a few hours but not a few days. At worst, it was to break the news that Seth had decided it was better for Joshua to move to New York. Or it could be something in between, where Seth was going to watch and judge and make a decision later.

Whichever it was, this had to be the best damn Thanksgiving ever.

If Decker told Joshua all this, however, it would only make Joshua lose control to the wolf. The boy was in grief over losing his adoptive family but he wasn't ready to interact with them. He couldn't just leave them in the dark. (He could. Decker actually thought it might be better if Joshua didn't contact his adoptive parents. The boy was still a minor. If the couple attempted some legal means to force Joshua to return to their home, things could get messy. The adoption hadn't been legal. It was possible that the couple could be charged as accessories to kidnapping. Annoying wolves was not the safest thing to do.) Joshua would be happier, though, if he knew that they knew he was fine.

"We should go out shopping," Decker said. "Call a taxi."

"W-w-what? We just made popcorn."

"We'll get beds, a table and chairs, a big roasting pan, and a Christmas card."

"A Christmas card?"

"When I was human, there was none of this calling people on the phone. We wrote each other letters. Humans had been doing it for hundreds of years. A perfectly fine method of communication. It's sad, really, that it's totally fallen out of practice. At least, I assume it has, as we have not seen anything like stationery in all the shopping trips we've done. I've noticed, though, that Christmas cards are still quite popular. We'll send one to your family with a letter inside explaining how happy you are."

"That's a great idea!" Joshua hugged him hard, wriggling in puppy joy.

"Hurry. Hurry. Call the taxi. Time is short if we're going to get the furniture in place before your brother and cousin arrive. I'll go get some money."

In short order they were at the very bizarre furniture store in Natick where they'd bought the leather sofa. Really, he didn't understand how modern man thought. The place was like a circus train collided with an entire steamer filled with custom-made furniture. Hundreds and hundreds of pieces of furniture, none of them like the one beside it. The selection was stunning because somewhere out there was an entire warehouse of copies, just waiting to be stuffed in a truck and dropped into place within hours of making a selection. (They'd gotten the sofa delivered the next morning by paying extra.) The mind reeled.

And some of the fabrics? Who in God's name would want them in their house? Had the entire race gone colorblind since he became a vampire?

"What do you think of this?" Decker pointed at what looked like a very ugly print to him.

"Do you really want another couch for the living room?" Joshua wrinkled his nose at it. "I can sit on the floor."

If Joshua sat on the floor, he'd probably end up in a puppy-pile with his brother and cousin.

Decker wanted to avoid that. "What about two leather chairs that match the sofa?"

"Oooh, that would be nice."

Then the fabric was as ugly as Decker thought.

They found the chesterfield chairs and immediately attracted the same sales person who had handled the purchase of the sofa last week.

"We'd like two of this one." Decker pointed at the one that Joshua was sprawling in. "Tomorrow if possible."

Her eyes went wide but she kept a smile plastered on her face. "Rush delivery is more," she reminded him. "Much more, this being the holiday season."

"Please. It's a family emergency."

She laughed. "Just found out that you're hosting Thanksgiving dinner, huh?"

"Yes, we'll need beds and a dining room table too."

"Ah, out-of-town family. The best kind." She led the way to the tables. "They go away when the weekend is over."

"Hopefully." Decker was willing to let the prince move in, if that was what it took.

Joshua eyed the table that Decker pointed out; little puppy dog tail droop. "It's huge."

Decker patted him on the head. "The thing about families is that they grow." And a huge table would indicate that the prince would always be welcome to come and visit. Anytime. Just that he needed to leave his brother when he left. "Besides, a little table would look wrong in our big dining room."

Joshua lowered his voice. "It's expensive."

"Money is one thing I have lots of. If I ever manage to run out of what I have, I can always find more."

"You mean?" Joshua held up his hands as if he was holding dowsing rods.

"Exactly."

"Is that where you got all your money?" Joshua whispered.

"Yes. I've been sitting on a small mountain of cash. All I've spent it on for decades has been taxes, gas, electricity and occasional small repairs on the house. I want to use it now to make this a happy Thanksgiving."

The welling of tears in Joshua's eyes was the only warning Decker got before he found his arms full of puppy. Luckily no one was looking in their direction. The saleswoman had been busy copying down the numbers of the table and various chairs.

Decker unbuttoned his overcoat and tucked the puppy inside the wool, hidden from sight.

"We have these in stock," the sales woman announced. "You want this and the leather chairs and you said something about beds?"

"Yes, two queen beds and mattresses. We have two men coming. A brother and a cousin."

"Ah, I see. Beds are—" She glanced around for Joshua.

"He's in the restroom," Decker lied. "Lead the way. He'll be along, wagging his tail behind him."

43: JOSHUA

How did people cook before YouTube?

Joshua typed in "how to cook a turkey" and discovered that the search engine believed there were hundreds of thousands of videos on the subject. That was a lot of turkey. Within a page, however, the simple directions fell to the outlandish. One video explained how to cook the turkey in a beer keg. Another method was using the exhaust of a Lamborghini sports car. Another video showed how to dig a big hole, build a fire, and then bury everything, turkey and all.

He went back to the first page of hits and started to watch the top videos.

Turkeys—he had. Some of the things that he didn't have were obvious. Stuffing apparently required bread cubes and butter and chicken broth. Mashed potatoes needed potatoes—of some sort. His grandmother boiled potatoes and whipped them with a hand mixer while adding milk and butter. His great aunt always complained, saying she should use a potato ricer. His mother, though, used a box of instant flakes. He didn't want to attempt the real potatoes—his grandmother's were very hit or miss—but there was suddenly something very wrong with the world when he wrote "*instant potatoes*" onto his list. It made him think of Wickers for some reason. He shuddered, crossed out the words and merely wrote "*mashed potatoes.*" He had a few days to practice cooking them.

Cranberry sauce was a must. As were biscuits and strawberry jam and pie. They had to have pie.

It made a lot of food for three people but at the same time, it seemed a very lean Thanksgiving dinner. There should be veggies.

373

Something green. Maybe. He was cooking for werewolves. Did Seth eat vegetables? One video mentioned turnips and another talked about Brussels sprouts. People actually liked those? His family always made a green bean casserole with cream of mushroom soup and fried onions sprinkled on top. Was that too redneck for Seth?

His mom always made a "traditional" Jell-O salad for all holidays that was a cloudy pinkish orange color. The flavor, though, wasn't orange; it was something else. He'd never watched her make it; he had no clue what she put into it to get to look like that. There were always nuts on top—weren't there? He flailed for a while making random stabs at Jell-O recipes but found nothing that sounded close.

Which looped him back to what he should do about his family.

He and Decker spent nearly an hour looking at Christmas cards after picking out the furniture and paying a small fortune to make sure they'd be delivered during the weekend. Joshua thought that anything that had a baby in a manger should be avoided. Santa? Christmas trees? Presents? They reminded him of the one year that Bethy stole everything out of his Christmas stocking before everyone else woke up and left a lump of coal. (She gave it back after he was reduced to tears. She never understood that he was mostly upset by the idea that Santa thought he was bad. He'd spent months in trouble that year because "he kept getting into fights" as bullies refused to leave him alone.)

Angels made him think of heavily armed Elise.

Snow scenes made him feel bleak.

In the end, they went with a card of a ginger tabby kitten that looked like Trouble.

If his parents were going to get the card before Thanksgiving, he needed to mail it soon, which meant he had to write the letter that would go inside of it. The problem was he had no idea what to say.

The letter wasn't going to write itself.

Reluctantly he sat down to write it.

Dear Dad and Mom.
Dear Mom and Dad.
Dear Mom and Dad and Bethy.
Dear Mom, Dad and Bethy. How are you?
Dear Mom, Dad and Bethy. I am fine. I will not be coming home for Thanksgiving. Or Christmas. Or ever.

Dear Mom, Dad and Bethy. I am fine. I'm having Thanksgiving with my real family this year.

Dear Mom, Dad and Bethy. I am fine. I miss you very, very, very . . .

Dear Mom, Dad and Bethy. I picked this card because it looks like my new kitten, Trouble. Decker picked a stupid wolf card but I told him it wasn't funny. You wouldn't understand.

Dear Mom, Dad and Bethy. I love you all so much. Even Bethy. I miss you every day. I hate not being able to tell you where I am or how I am or what has happened to me. I've become a . . .

Dear Mom, Dad and Bethy. I know you must be worried about me but you shouldn't be. I am fine. I know this must be very hard for you to understand, but it is the truth. You had no way of knowing this but I had been kidnapped as a baby and my real family has been searching for me all these years. I am sorry, but I will be spending Thanksgiving and Christmas with them this year. I miss you. I would call but I know that you would tell me to come home and I don't want to do that. I love you so much, I couldn't bear to tell you no. So I'm not going to call. I will let you know exactly where I am on my birthday. I know this must be hard on you, but know that I am safe and loved where I am right now, and please be happy for me. Always yours, no matter what, with love, Joshua.

Joshua leaned against Decker's back, reading over his shoulder as the vampire wrote out the letter in elegant calligraphy. "That's perfect, Decker. It's like you read my mind."

"I just listened to your heart." Decker put down the pen among all the crumpled and torn pieces of Joshua's attempts. "You'll have to copy it into your own handwriting."

"Thanks. You saved me."

Decker reached back to ruffle Joshua's hair. "Any time."

On Monday morning the weather report announced that a Northeaster was sweeping in from the ocean and would be hitting the area late Tuesday night. (They probably announced it earlier but Joshua hadn't checked the news since Friday morning. It had been a hectic weekend of cleaning and painting the two bigger bedrooms for Seth and Cabot.) He stared at the television, feeling his stomach drop. The weatherman gleefully described sleet changing to snow then ice and back to snow for an impossibly slick commute on Wednesday morning. The bulk of the storm, however, would come as a polar vortex sweeping in from the west to collide with the Northeaster. By Thursday night, a blizzard of epic proportions would lock down most of New England.

He thought of the letter he'd sent his parents. The one they'd be getting today. He told them he'd be spending Thanksgiving with Seth and Cabot. If he didn't, it would be as if he'd lied.

Well, lied more. Or something. After he mailed the card, guilt started to eat at him for all the things he didn't tell them. It felt like lying by omission. He knew that they'd be worried about the massive wound on his shoulder; it had completely healed before he even reached Boston. They'd wonder if he had warm clothes to wear; he'd only taken T-shirts and a light jacket. As a werewolf, he was always plenty warm.

He hated the fact that they'd probably keep worrying about him despite the card just because he hadn't told them everything. But "everything" would have made him seem a total nutcase. If he'd told them the truth, they'd have stormed Decker's house and dragged him away to some shrink. That would go so well: a know-it-all doctor trying to cure him of his delusions. Joshua wondered what the shrink would make of a horse-sized wolf having an anxiety attack.

Still he hated all the lying he had to do to his parents. He'd always taken pride on how truthful he could be with them. He picked up his phone, thinking he could call Seth and make sure he was still coming. If the roads were going to be bad, maybe Seth shouldn't come. It seemed wrong to urge his younger brother to risk his life just so Joshua could stop feeling guilty about telling his parents he was spending Thanksgiving with "his family."

His phone chirped and a text from Seth appeared on the screen.

"*Take turkey out of freezer and put in fridge! Now!*" An entire row of "!" followed.

His first text ever from Seth was some kind of weird turkey emergency. "*What?*" he typed back.

"*Turkey needs to thaw,*" Seth texted. "*Cook says you need to move turkey to fridge now or it still be a block of ice on Thursday.*"

"*Okay. Did you see the weather report?*"

"*Hold on.*" A minute later. "*Ouch!*"

Joshua frowned at the screen. What did "ouch" mean exactly? "*It will be dangerous to drive.*"

"Don't worry. We'll be there."

"Okay." And then because that seemed too plain. *"I'm look-ing forward to it."*

"Same here, bro."

Bro. Joshua stared at the screen. *Bro.* No one had ever said "Bro" to him before. That Seth said and meant it as "brother" freaked Joshua out. Bethy never called him "bro" or "little brother" or any cutesy term like that. Booger Face was the closest she got to it.

But then Bethy hadn't wanted a brother. (She'd told him that many times.) And Bethy had never lost one before—and Seth had lost three.

Maybe having a brother was actually going to be cool.

It snowed.

It sleeted.

It hailed.

It did things that he didn't know the words for.

He became addicted to checking the weather.

Seth might say he was coming but Joshua started to seriously doubt him. When the governor declared a state of emergency and shut down the turnpike on Tuesday, Joshua gave up hope.

He went to the refrigerator and stared at the turkey lurking within. "You planned it this way, didn't you? You're some kind of evil anti-holiday god. You want me to be miserable. I didn't ask for this. I never wanted to be a werewolf. I had my life planned out. I was going to college. I had lots of friends. Okay, not a lot of friends, but they were normal and I could call them during the day when I was upset and not have to wait until the freak-ing sunset! And I had parents. I really, really love my parents. I don't care that they're not my biological parents. They did the best they could and that I wasn't really theirs never mattered. My God, they spent more money on buying me than their pickup and Dad loves that pickup. And I've ruined Thanksgiving for them and probably Christmas too."

The turkey lurked and the electricity flickered.

"What? On top of being totally alone all Thanksgiving, you're going to make it impossible to cook too? Well—fine—I'll show you!" He snatched up the turkey and ran to toward the front door. He'd just freaking fling the damn thing as far as he could throw it. As a werewolf, he should be able to clear the neighbor's house.

He had to stop at the door to juggle the turkey while getting all the locks undone. He never understood why Decker insisted on so many freaking locks. It always took forever to open the freaking door. It just made him so freaking mad!

He got the last lock undone, flung open the door, and nailed Cabot in the face with the turkey.

"Ow!" Cabot staggered backwards. He caught the turkey before it hit the ground. Blood trickled out his nose as he stared at the frozen bird. "What the hell?"

"Seth!" Joshua leapt at his brother.

Seth caught the wolf puppy and carried him inside. "Obviously I should have called but I was afraid we wouldn't make it, so I figured we'd just show up. I hope you don't mind that we came a day even earlier than we agreed."

"Why did you throw a turkey at me?" Cabot complained. He stomped his way toward the kitchen, carrying the turkey. "It's still half-frozen. You could kill someone with this!"

Seth settled onto the couch with Joshua in his lap. "Maybe it's one of those Martha Stewart recipes; a very elaborate seasoning process. Take it for a walk. Show it the town. Buy it a few drinks."

Joshua was too happy to see them to be embarrassed yet.

Cabot wedged the turkey back into the crowded refrigerator. "No need to worry about the blizzard; he's got enough food in here to feed an army of werewolves." He opened the freezer and laughed.

"What?" Seth asked.

"There's like fifteen pies in here. Pumpkin. Cherry. Apple. Peach. Blueberry. Dutch apple. Key lime. Banana Cream. Turtle cream? Fruits of the forest? What the hell are those? Wild berry blast with lemon crust? Where did he find all these? Southern pecan. Coconut meringue. Lemon grove meringue. One. Two. Three... I stand corrected. There are fourteen pies."

"Sounds wonderful to me." Seth patted Joshua on the head, making him wag his tail. "Good job! I love pie."

"Me too. Obviously it's a family trait," Cabot said. "Well, they're not going to do us any good in the freezer. I say: let the baking begin! What kind should we make first?"

"Leave the pumpkin for Thanksgiving dinner," Seth said. "I say apple, peach, and pecan."

"Which one of those?" Cabot examined the range, looking for the oven controls. "I like peach the best."

"Make all three!" Seth said. "Fourteen pies. Five days. That's an average of three pies a day. Besides, I'm hungry."

Joshua leapt from Seth's lap, over the back of the couch and landed as a human, able to do such things as operate an oven. "I'll do it. I've got some chicken pot pies and frozen French fries too and extra chicken gravy. I can make those too."

Cabot stared at Joshua. "Seriously, how does he do that?"

"Do what?" Joshua glanced to Seth who was shrugging.

"Your clothes," Seth said, which didn't explain anything.

"What about my clothes?" He was wearing blue jeans and one of the green shirts that the wolf liked. He'd been feeling stressed out so he'd picked clothes that would comfort the wolf.

"We take ours off." Cabot leaned against the kitchen island. "Shirt, pants, underwear. Everything goes."

"Do they get lost sometimes?" Joshua had given up on washing his clothes every time he transformed. He was growing used to them smelling of deep woods. He'd never considered that they might not return. He was usually too worried about whatever triggered his transformation—and sometimes crushing Decker.

"If we don't take them off, they get ripped to shreds," Seth said. "Kind of like the Hulk. Boom! Hulk smash."

Joshua shifted, trying for big. He went too big and bumped his head on the ceiling. He transformed back to human. He was still clothed.

Cabot jerked back, swearing. "Seriously! How is he doing that?"

Seth spread his hands. "He's shunting the extra mass to and from the Source. I think he's somehow storing his clothes along with whatever mass that he exchanges."

"You guys change size." Joshua had seen Cabot, at least, in "big dog" and "super scary wolf" mode.

"Yeeeeeaaaah." Cabot made the "yes" sound like a "no."

"It would be cool if we could figure out your clothes trick," Seth said.

"I want to know how you can talk," Joshua said. "When I try to talk as a wolf, even I can't understand what I'm saying."

Cabot snickered.

"It's easy to learn," Seth said. "I'm surprised you didn't figure it out already, but our dads showed us. Food first!" He pointed at the kitchen. "Everything is harder to do if you're hungry."

44: DECKER

Five thousand dollars' worth of seating and the wolves were in a puppy pile on the floor. Decker decided that he should be happy that at least they weren't gnawing on the expensive leather.

The three black wolves were nearly equal in size. He could tell them apart only by the fact that the prince and his cousin were wearing boxer shorts. The prince's were red plaid while the Thane's were dark blue. The underwear was never intended to be worn by werewolves; an extra hole had been torn for the wolves' tails. The rest of the visitors' clothes were scattered about the living room. Whatever triggered the disrobing had ceased to occupy the wolves' attention and they were now watching a movie and giggling like little boys. The movie had a bunch of men dressed as knights pretending to ride horses while men ran behind them clapping coconuts together.

Joshua was tucked between the two others. The message was clear; the prince had come to protect his brother.

Decker carefully considered everything he could say to announce his presence. He settled for "Click clack click clack" and sat down on the couch where there was plenty of room for Joshua to join him.

"Decker!" Joshua leapt up and landed in Decker's lap. Thankfully between floor and couch, he shrank to puppy-size. "I can talk! The quick black wolf jumps over the lazy Grigori."

"Wonderful." Decker hugged him. "I wouldn't say that around Elise though. She might hurt you. Pride might be a sin but that doesn't seem to stop the Grigori."

"Ah, right." Joshua settled onto Decker's lap, much more relaxed than he had been last night, but clearly not totally back to an even keel. Decker had felt horrible having to abandon his boy at dawn when Joshua seemed close to losing his sanity. Decker's cursed existence only felt like a curse when it affected the ones he loved.

"Seth brought lots of cool old movies with him," Joshua said. "We're watching—what are we watching?"

The Seth wolf gave Decker a level, calculating look and then focused back on the television. "*Monty Python and the Holy Grail.* Our father loved comedies. We'd watch his favorites every year during the holidays. It was our family tradition. His copies were burned with our house, but I've bought my own."

Puppy ears drooped a little. "My grandmother would put on the dog show after the Macy's parade. She breeds Jack Russell terriers. I was the only one that they liked. We didn't do anything together as a family except talk about stupid stuff like—like—a whole hour of talking about stinkbugs. After dinner, it would be grandpa's slide shows of their trips to dog shows all over the country. Which wouldn't be so bad but grandpa always cuts people's heads off when he takes their pictures."

"There's Easter," Decker promised lightly. Joshua would be eighteen then and his parents wouldn't be able to turn to the police to control where he lived.

Seth looked up again, this time worried, but he said nothing. Two little lost boys. One helpless to save the other.

45: ELISE

Cabot had called to say they were eating in the afternoon but let slip that none of the wolves had ever cooked a turkey before. At one earlier point, during an odd conversation about a carton of milk that had gone bad in her refrigerator, he also admitted that werewolves didn't get food poisoning. Between the two facts, she decided it would be in her best interest to be there when the three wolves started to prepare the food.

As added insurance, she made two plates of deviled eggs to take with her.

What she hadn't considered was how to get the eggs to Decker's. They were slippery little things, skidding about on the plates. With the streets basically sheets of ice, she didn't want to be distracted by little egg bombs pelting her as she dodged bad drivers. (As it was a holiday, it was guaranteed that she would pass at least one car spinning out of control.)

Tupperware would work—if she owned any. All the stores were closed. She stood at her counter glaring at the eggs. What could she use as a carrier?

Half an hour later, one facial tissue box mummified in aluminum foil and filled with deviled eggs, she was ready to go.

"You haven't started the turkey yet, have you?" she texted Cabot.

"Just finished breakfast and cleaning up. We'll tackle the turkey next."

She had to hurry then.

383

She jerked open her apartment door and Joshua's sister Bethy stood in front of her, hand upraised to knock. "What in God's name are you doing here?"

"You!" Bethy pointed at her fiercely. "You know where my brother is."

Elise stood there a moment wondering if she could get the girl tied up and stuffed into a closet before the wolves started their turkey cooking attempt. Unlikely. Bethy was a black belt in God knows how many martial arts. "How did you even find me?"

"I took pictures of your and Porsche boy's license plates. A friend of mine ran them for me at the DMV. The Boxster was leased by some real estate company in Manhattan."

Which would seem like a dead end for someone who didn't know about the Wolf King.

Elise pulled shut her door and made sure it was locked.

Bethy shifted to block her escape. "We're not going anywhere until you tell me where my brother is."

"I'm going to see him right now. You can come with me."

Bethy frowned at her like the invitation was a trap. If they didn't get there soon, it might be.

46: JOSHUA

Three werewolves stared at one very naked turkey.

"There. Not so brave without your plastic covering, are you?" Joshua poked at it.

"Do you always talk to your food?" Seth had opened the box of oven bags and was examining the contents in confusion. They had assembled everything to prepare the turkey on the kitchen island from the turkey itself to various raw vegetables to a ten-pound bag of flour.

"Only when said food has been terrorizing me for weeks." Joshua picked up the plastic oven bag. It unfolded and unfolded to a huge size. "So we just stick the turkey in this and cook it?"

Cabot picked up the turkey and shook it at Joshua. "Stuff me! Stuff me! Gobble, gobble, gobble."

"That's your job, Cabot," Joshua said.

Seth found the cooking guide. He pointed at Joshua. "Preheat the oven to three hundred and fifty. Jack..."

"Yes, sir?" Cabot made the turkey salute with its right wing tip. Something slithered out of the body cavity and dropped to the ground. "Sir, I think I just shit myself!"

"What the hell is that?" Joshua laughed.

"Those are my privates, private!" Cabot cried.

"I think that's the neck and the giblets." Seth pointed at the sink. "Jack, its pissing blood everywhere. The recipe says to rinse it off and pat it dry."

"Yes, sir!" Cabot made the turkey salute again and then turned it upside down to stem the flow of blood. Something else fell out of the neck opening and landed with a wet splash on the tile floor.

"Cabot!" Joshua laughed harder.

Jack glanced down at the bloody objects on the floor. "I think those are the giblets. That other thing is either its neck or turkeys have bigger dicks than I thought."

Trouble came streaking around the corner to leap on the bloody bag.

"No!" Joshua cried.

He and Seth both leapt to grab the giblets and collided. Seth kicked the neck in the scrabble and it went skidding across the floor, leaving a blood trail behind it.

"Not under the fridge!" Joshua shouted even as the column of raw meat disappeared underneath the big refrigerator.

Seth shouted something like "grab that" and then suddenly the room was filled with a haze of white flour.

"Trouble! Trouble!" Cabot shouted, dancing about, looking for someplace to land the turkey while trying to herd the ginger kitten with his feet. Flour drifted down like dry snow.

The doorbell rang.

"Get him!" Cabot cried. "I think we need that for the gravy!"

Joshua and Seth lunged again and collided again.

"You get him, Joshua!" Seth cried, rubbing his temple and backing away.

The kitten was greatly hampered by the number of feet trying to block him and the fact that the giblets package was the same size as he was. Still he growled angrily as Joshua caught him and attempted to gently wrestle the bag away.

"We will give you lots and lots of turkey later," Joshua promised. The paper bag squished wetly in his hand and the smell of blood filled his senses.

. . . wetness sprayed his face, blinding him. He blinked rapidly. Tasted the blood. Realized what just covered him . . .

"Joshua?" Seth crouched beside him.

Joshua realized that tears were pouring down his face. "The blood," he whispered. "There was so much blood."

He went to wipe the tears from his cheeks but Seth caught his hand.

"You're going to make a mess." Seth kept hold of Joshua's hand holding the giblets. "It sneaks up on you when you least expect it. One minute you're fine and the next you're lost in the grief." He patiently wiped Joshua's face with his shirt cuff. "It will hurt bad for a while, but it gets better. You just got to hold on and be strong."

"Cabot," Elise's voice came from the other side of the kitchen counter. "What the hell are you doing?"

Cabot turned, still holding the turkey, covered head to toe in flour. "What does it look like?"

"Like you're doing some kind of odd Mexican tag team wrestling, which is why I asked."

"Si," Cabot said in a Mexican accent. "I am El Hijo del Thane and this is my partner, El Pavo Desplumado!" Cabot had the turkey shake a naked wingtip at someone behind Elise. "She should not be here. This is not the right time for visitors."

Elise leaned across the counter and looked down at Seth and Joshua. "Oh. I see. Let's go."

A familiar, annoyed "What?" came from the dining room. "We just got here."

Joshua whimpered as he realized who was with Elise. It was his sister, Bethy.

"I'm not leaving until I see my brother!" Bethy said.

Seth stood up and Cabot put the turkey on the counter.

Bethy was about to meet his protective new family in the worst possible way.

"I'm fine!" Joshua cried. "It's okay. Just—just—just get the damn turkey into the oven. I don't want to see it again until it's cooked."

Everyone stood around and glared at each other. Joshua was sure the damn turkey was snickering. He got up, threw the giblets into the sink, and scanned the counter for the oven bag. It looked like it had snowed in the kitchen; flour coated everything.

"Stop playing with the turkey and rinse it," he snapped at Cabot as he swept flour off the countertop. What did he do with the bag? There were two in the box. "We need to make the stuffing. Somehow. I had a recipe writ—writ-writ..."

He sneezed.

Bethy leaped back swearing in surprise.

Elise blocked her from running. "You wanted to see him. There he is."

Bethy was the only one looking at him. Everyone else was

glaring at his sister; ignoring the draft-horse sized wolf in the kitchen.

"Oh freaking h-h-h—" Joshua sneezed again.

Seth leaned down and picked up the puppy. "Jack, get the turkey in the oven."

"Will do." Cabot continued to glare at Bethy.

Joshua was sure that the turkey was gloating as Seth carried him upstairs to hide in his bedroom.

47: SETH

Seth's father had always told him that as prince he'd need to be the bedrock for his pack. He never told him, though, how to put his people back together once they'd come undone. Seth sat on the floor of Joshua's bedroom, holding the whimpering puppy and feeling useless. Had he done the right thing leaving Joshua in Boston? What should he say to Joshua about the massacre? He knew from experience that nothing anyone said actually helped ease the pain of losing everything. It seemed wrong not to say anything; maybe that was why people kept saying all the stupid stuff to Seth when his family had been killed.

What should he do?

The first time Seth had seen his brother was in this room. It had been empty except for an airbed. It didn't even have curtains. Three weeks had made a world of difference in the bedroom. It now held a queen-sized platform bed, two nightstands, a dresser, a chest of drawers, and a computer desk all in a dark thick Asian style. A large oriental rug, floor length curtains, fantasy prints of dragons, and a variety of lamps completed the bedroom into a comfortable space.

It was a far cry from the tiny closet-sized room that Joshua used to have at his adoptive parents' house. Seth knew first hand that a big private space and a big bed did little to repair a hole left by being torn away from your family.

"I'm sorry," Joshua whimpered. "I didn't see it coming. I was laughing at Cabot and all of the sudden I was back at the barn, covered with blood. But I was coping! I was! I really hate this part of being a werewolf. Everything will be fine and then something happens and it's like someone else steps into my skin and I'm *this!*"

It wasn't clear if "this" was being a puppy or whimpering loudly or both.

"It gets easier," Seth said. "You get to recognize when the wolf is about to take over and head it off. Give it time."

"God I'm so tired of the waiting. Wait until you can drive. Wait until you can go to college. Wait until you can leave all the bullies behind. Wait until you grow up enough to do everything you want to do."

"Yeah, I know. Same here." Seth realized that he hadn't thought about college for days. He'd been fixated on going to Harvard since his family died. He'd even gone to summer school to graduate early. "College" one time meant returning to Boston and truly start being a prince. He'd been furious when the king declared he'd go to Columbia in New York City instead. Then all the chaos with the Wickers happened, and college became unimportant in the grand scheme of things.

The puppy scrambled out of Seth's arms to trot to the bed. "I love my parents, but the longer I've lived here in Boston, the less I want to go back to their house. I like having a bed that I don't need a ladder to get into." The puppy leapt onto the mattress to demonstrate. "And that little railing—the one the keeps you from falling to your death in the middle of the night—always made me feel like I was still in a crib. My desk was under my bed and if I stood up wrong, I'd hit my head."

Maybe Seth was wrong about the worth of a bigger room and bed.

The puppy bounced up and down on the mattress. "It rocks that I will never again have to eat liver and onions again, or hamburger slop or the kitchen sink."

"Hamburger what?"

"Oh its browned hamburger with cream of mushroom soup and mixed vegetables. The kitchen sink is what my mom calls putting all leftovers into a soup. She usually makes it on Wednesdays because Thursday is trash day. I like to keep all my food separated and eat one thing at a time. It's a little OCD of me..."

"It's a Tatterskein thing. Our father always ate everything

carefully separated like that." It was a habit that enraged his Mexican mother. "Jack does it too."

"It's genetic? How weird but awesome. I'm not going back to my old school. Not even the teachers were nice to me." The puppy flopped down onto the bed and sighed deeply. "Why is Bethy even here? She doesn't even like me!"

Seth thought of his first meeting with the woman. After beating him with a bamboo sword, she'd broken down and cried over her missing little brother. "No, I'm fairly sure she loves you very much. She drove through a blizzard and cornered a Grigori Virtue just to see you. People don't do that when they hate someone."

"I guess. Thanksgiving at my grandmother's always was horrible. It was more than not being allowed to eat all day until the turkey went on the table, or having to watch the dog show or my grandfather's endless collection of bad pictures. It always seemed that no matter how hard I tried, my grandparents and aunts and uncles always acted if there was something wrong with me. I always felt worthless by the end of the day."

Seth didn't know what to say. He couldn't imagine a life where everyone stood against him, including his family. It was hard enough when it was just Isaiah and a handful of the Thane.

"The last few days have been great. Thanks for driving up early." The puppy jumped from the bed and landed a boy. "Alright. Let's do this. Deep breath!"

"Are you sure?" Seth asked.

Joshua laughed. "No. I'm good, but my wolf? I'm not sure about him. I'm still trying to make peace with him. We're happy though that Bethy came to see me. She might have planned to take me home but I don't think she'll try to drag the wolf to her car. Although I wouldn't bet on it; she's kind of fearless."

"I gathered that."

"I think my wolf can handle Bethy. I mean, I don't think he'll hurt her and certainly he's not going to let her drag us back home."

Seth floundered for something constructive to say.

"I miss talking with my folks," Joshua said. "But really it's like I've just gone to college a few months earlier than planned. I wanted to move away. I couldn't wait until I could. We're not going to let anyone move us out of this house. We like it here."

Seth looked away, feeling guilty. He'd been debating for days if Joshua should be moved to New York for his own safety. He thought that Joshua needed him nearby. Teaching him. Protecting him. Healing him.

This wouldn't be an issue if the king merely let Seth move back to Boston.

Joshua needed Seth, but moving him to New York would be the same as the king refusing to let Seth move back to Boston.

It was a weird and uncomfortable feeling for Seth to realize that he felt the same as Alexander. That the king was keeping Seth close at hand to teach him, protect him, and possibly heal him. At the time, Jack had seemed like an adult to Seth when they lost everyone they loved. In truth, Jack was only a few years older than Joshua was now. It would have been unfair to the grieving man to strand him alone in Boston with a newborn prince. Nor could Jack fully be Seth's "father" because he had to obey Seth, not the other way around.

Seth felt like he'd just taken a giant step sideways mentally to view the world from an entirely different angle.

"Hey." Joshua put a hand on Seth's head. "Are you okay? I feel a little guilty dragging you here to Boston instead of being with your foster dad."

Surprise forced a laugh out of Seth. Dad? The king? "He's still in Belgrade. Bishop says that the new prince is having trouble carrying the alpha." It was probably going to kill the man in a few years. The king was setting up a marriage to guarantee that the bloodline continued. "Besides, he doesn't do Thanksgiving. Most holidays to him are artificial things, made up by men to support a culture he doesn't see himself as part of."

"So I didn't take you away from anything?"

"No." Just a horde of people gathering outside the Castle to watch the Macy's parade, reminding Seth that he no longer had a family. That wasn't really true. He had family. He had Jack and Joshua, and a wife that he'd never bothered to contact. He wasn't even positive he knew her name. Come to think of it, Alexander would probably bring her east in a year or two, so Seth could father children. Was he ready to be a father? He didn't feel ready. He didn't even know how to be good brother to Joshua.

One thing he was sure of: forcing Joshua to move to New York would make him miserable. It was obvious that much of his happiness was tied to making this place his home. Since his safety at the Castle was questionable, it wasn't worth the tradeoff.

Besides, with Joshua in Boston, Seth would have a good excuse to visit the city often. He could keep the bedrock that the king provided him while using the trips to start to rebuild everything he'd lost.

It was a tiny baby step and yet it felt like a giant leap. Joshua gave him a base camp to finally move forward. Tomorrow, he could show his older brother the city and they could lay plans to rebuild their pack.

"Great!" Joshua grinned. "Let's go make sure we have a dinner to eat tonight. And I'm making an official house rule: snacking is allowed."

48: ELISE

Bethy's reunion with her brother could have gone better.

Elise sighed as she thought of a dozen ways she could have prevented the disaster from happening. She'd let own emotions distract her. Nothing could be done to change the past. She could only hope now to salvage the future.

"There, you saw him, we should go." Elise caught the other woman by the arm. She triggered some automatic defense reflex and ended up on the floor. Oh yes, black belt in judo. Elise was batting zero today.

"What the hell!" Bethy danced away from Elise. "What the hell! What—what—what was that?"

"That was Joshua." Elise didn't add in that he was Bethy's brother, not with Cabot looking so pissed off. She wasn't sure if he was mad at her or the unruly turkey. She got off the floor and distanced herself from both of them.

"That was a-a-a..." Bethy sputtered, looking for a word to describe Joshua's wolf.

Don't say monster! Don't say monster!

"...freaking big...something! What was that?"

"A werewolf." Cabot picked up the turkey, glared at it, turned in a full circle and put it back down. He glared harder at it. "Joshua is a werewolf. It's what he was always supposed to be."

"What?" Bethy cried.

"Joshua was born to a long line of werewolves." Elise really hoped that this was the right thing to do. Telling the woman the truth might get messy. Elise couldn't imagine any other way to recover from Bethy seeing Joshua transform, not if Joshua wanted future contact with his adoptive family. "Cabot is Joshua's cousin through his birth father and he's also a werewolf."

"Wait," Bethy cried, holding up a finger. "He's the talking wolf that tore the ginger-haired jerk apart?"

It took Elise a moment to remember that the warlock in Utica had been a redhead. Bethy had seen Cabot kill a man. Maybe Elise shouldn't answer that question.

Unfortunately, Cabot answered for her. "Yes."

"And Porsche boy?" Bethy pointed upstairs.

"Seth is Joshua's younger half-brother." Cabot picked up the turkey, started for the sink, stopped, and put it back down on the counter again. "And yes, he's a werewolf too."

"So all that craziness back home, that was because Joshua has always been a werewolf, which is why he's always acted so dorky growing up?"

"That's a fairly accurate summation," Elise said.

"Ooooooooookay." Bethy stared at the floor, apparently rethinking Joshua's entire childhood. "That. Makes. Sense."

It did?

"Right." Bethy took out a scrunchy hair tie. She twisted her long blonde hair up into a bun with practiced ease. "I came here to make sure my brother had a good Thanksgiving dinner with his family, and that's what is going to happen. Not the family I expected but his family nonetheless. You." She flicked a hand at Cabot. "Get out of the way. Shoo. Shoo."

Which of course confused Cabot. "What?"

"You obviously have no idea how to cook." Bethy whipped a santoku blade out of the knife block. She picked up one of the onions and reduced it into thin, equal slices. "If you want to be useful, rinse out the turkey, pat it dry and put it in the roasting pan until I'm ready to stuff it."

Cabot gave Elise an odd bewildered look.

"I have never cooked a turkey." Elise didn't want to cook this turkey, despite having spent the last twenty-four hours bracing herself for the possibility that she would need to. Wrestling with a naked dead bird was not on her list of fun things to try.

"I thought I wanted to go to culinary school so I spent a year working at the Tailor and the Cook. We started doing all organic turkey dinners in October. Two months of turkey. I never wanted to see one again. I decided to go into pre-law like my grandmother wanted me to."

Cabot picked up the turkey and carried it to the sink. Good man.

This might not be a total disaster after all.

"What can I do?" Elise asked.

Bethy snorted as she diced celery. "Find out what else needs to be cooked. Turkey and stuffing is obvious by what Joshua has out on the counter. Knowing *my brother*, he has detailed lists someplace."

The emphasis was impossible to miss. Bethy wasn't giving up Joshua as her brother simply because his birth family was present nor because he was now a werewolf. It was a determination that Elise couldn't help but admire.

Elise found the lists beside the refrigerator. She read it with growing dismay. "He planned the turkey, stuffing, mashed potatoes and gravy, sweet potatoes casserole, green bean casserole, corn on the cob, peas, biscuits, baked macaroni and cheese, baked beans, cranberry sauce, pickles, black olives, three types of pies and 'Mom's mystery Jell-O salad' but that has a question mark beside it. All that for four people?"

"You've seen us eat." Cabot came to murmur in her ear.

She blushed hotly as she remembered him eating bacon and wanting to lick his fingers afterwards. "Did you bake the pies already?"

"Yes and no. We've baked six pies so far but we ate them all. There's nine more in the freezer."

"Six pies? Six?" Bethy cried. "And you've eaten them all? This morning?"

Cabot laughed. "Since Tuesday."

"Okay." Bethy pointed at Elise. "Pies need to go into the oven immediately. After we get the turkey stuffed and in the oven, we can work on the side dishes."

The prince and Joshua came downstairs as they were stuffing the turkey.

Bethy greeted Joshua with, "Hey, dumdum, you could have at least asked me for money and a ride to the train station instead of just disappearing."

"Yeah, yeah, that would have gone over *so* well," Joshua

said. "You probably would have sold me to a circus or a zoo or something."

"How much do you think I could get?" Bethy asked.

Joshua twiddled his nose at her, which seemed to be the end of the jibes. "You got the pies in? Good. According to the cooking bag instructions, it will take three hours to roast the turkey."

Elise expected Seth and Cabot to bristle at Bethy acting like a drill sergeant but they cheerfully followed orders. It dawned on her that the wolves never had to cook anything in their lives. They'd gone from their mothers' house to the Castle. It made her wonder how the wolves had expected to actually make all the dishes. None of the recipes were complicated but the sheer volume of food was daunting. Sweet potatoes needed to be washed, boiled, mashed, and mixed into a baking dish with brown sugar and butter. The giblets needed to be cooked, cooled, and readied for the gravy. The Jell-O salad recipe needed to be investigated and debated since Joshua didn't know exactly what was in it. He'd bought boxes of nearly every flavor of Jell-O and planned on winging the salad. (The mystery flavor turned out to be apricot mixed with crushed pineapple, cream cheese and Cool Whip. Most of the recipes they could find called for diced dried apricots but their mother never used them nor had Joshua bought any, so that ingredient was ignored. The recipes all stated "refrigerate until firm" so it was questionable if it would be ready for dinner but they made it nevertheless.)

The kitchen held endless surprises for Elise. She knew perfectly well that less than a month ago it had no appliances, dishes, pots, pans, or cooking utensils. Judging by Joshua's lists, he'd spent the last week buying every imaginable item for the dinner down to multiple serving platters, utensils, and pre-printed place cards.

Surprising too was that Joshua, Seth and Bethy accepted Elise as part of their oddly-joined family. Joshua apparently saw her as Decker's niece or something. Seth appeared to be happy for Cabot. Bethy seemed as immune to jealousy as she was to a Wicker's power. For the first time in years, Elise felt like she belonged. It was a joy to be with people, to hear the warmth of their laughter, to be working on a feast that they'd eat together. Despite her misgivings about eating Thanksgiving with the werewolves, she was glad that she came.

49: DECKER

Decker decided that the saying about old dogs and new tricks had to apply to him. It was the only way to explain why he found it so unsettling to wake up to a house full of people. He should find it normal since he once had servants that lived with him. The fifty years of isolation had marked him deeper than he thought.

Everyone was carrying bowls and platters from the kitchen into the dining room. The table had been set for six, obviously with much thought put into the sitting as there were place cards to make sure people sat in the proper seat. The cards were in Joshua's careful handwriting.

As Decker stood in the shadows, he watched people come in, put down the bowl they were carrying, and rearrange the cards. Cabot shifted Seth to the head of the table and put himself next to Elise. Seth moved Joshua to beside him. A girl that Decker didn't recognize flipped a card with "Bethy" written on it, wrote Elizabeth, and switched places with Seth. The mystery guest was Joshua's adoptive sister. Elise came in, eyed Cabot's card beside hers and went back into the kitchen.

Joshua came in carrying a bowl filled with steaming mashed potatoes. "Oh geez, guys! Who messed with the name cards?"

"I didn't," Elise called from the kitchen.

Bethy carried cranberry sauce and thumped it angrily on the table. "You sound like Grandma. Let people sit where they want. And why do we have six place settings? Who is Decker?"

"I'm Decker." He put a hand on her shoulder.

It turns out that Bethy had the same reflex as her brother.

"Bethy!" Joshua helped Decker off the floor and then gave him a suspiciously snuggly hug—as if he was moments from becoming a puppy. Joshua had been fine early in the morning, before sunrise forced Decker to his sleeping chamber. Apparently the addition of his sister had him rattled again.

"I'm Silas Decker," Decker introduced. "Welcome to our home."

Bethy frowned as she glanced at first Joshua and then Seth. "Wait. I thought—who exactly are you?"

"He's my friend!" Joshua growled. "And I live here with him."

"Decker is a trusted friend of our family," Seth said quietly.

"He's not a werewolf then?" Bethy asked.

The silence was deafening.

"No," Elise said finally.

"What?" Bethy picked up that something was loudly not being said. "Didn't he know?"

"He knows!" Joshua cried. "Can you just stop asking questions? My life is weird now. I don't want to talk about it. It's one of the reasons I didn't want to go home for Thanksgiving. You know how they get! Do you have a boyfriend yet, Bethy? What are you going to major in? Culinary? Why would you want to do that? Oh, pre law now, I'm so glad you came to your senses. Which law school have you applied to? When are we going to get our great-grandchildren?"

"All right! All right!" Bethy cried. "I get it. Fine, I'll stop asking."

"Can we just eat?" Joshua still hadn't let go, keeping hold of Decker like he was a lifeline. "I'm hungry."

There was a silent agreement among everyone (but Bethy) and the sitting ended up with Joshua at the head of the table with Seth to his right and Decker on his left. It meant that everyone but Bethy was mostly happy with the arrangement. Joshua filled up a plate but when Bethy was distracted, placed it in front of Decker.

Decker eyed the plate. Did Joshua really want him to eat the food? He would, but he was not looking forward to how sick it would make him feel. Joshua caught his eye and shook his head. Okay. So the plate was just to make it look like he was eating. Werewolves were fine for big sister but vampires were not. Or more likely the puppy was out of the bag, but Joshua was desperately trying to keep everything else hidden.

Decker had forgotten how to hold forks and knives. As he fumbled with the utensils, someone tangled their legs around his.

He glanced across the table at Seth. The prince gave him a warning look. Decker realized it was Joshua maintaining his contact with him while seemingly focused on filling his plate with food.

Bethy proved to be determined. "Am I not allowed to ask any questions at all or can I at least ask what you think you're going to do about school? You wanted to go to college. You scored amazing on your SAT. You're just going to give that up?"

There was an uncomfortable silence as the prince communicated with his cousin via eye contact.

"His father left me as trustee to his estate and legal guardian of any children that survived him," the Thane finally said cautiously. "I plan to enroll Joshua in a private school here in Boston."

The Thane was shouldering the responsibility of possible broken promises. Unsaid was what the prince planned and what the king allowed might be two different things. Still, it meant that the prince intended for Joshua to stay in Boston. Decker felt like leaping to his feet and bounding about the room, shouting with joy. He controlled the urge and merely grinned with happiness.

The conversation shifted to the weather which apparently worsened during the day. Bethy would need to sleep over; the question was where.

Decker sat grinning, pushing food around with his fork. He could not remember being this happy for a long, long time. He thought he could live by himself, but that had left him alone with death. This is what he needed: other people to surround him with life.

50: JOSHUA

Best. Thanksgiving. Ever.

The evil turkey was reduced to bare bones. His mother would have immediately cooked it down for soup. Joshua happily stuffed the picked clean carcass into a bag and took it out to their garbage cans. Once the dishwasher was stuffed to the brim and all the pots scrubbed, they collapsed in the living room to take turns playing a party video game. Decker was hopelessly lost, unable to follow the frantic motions on the screen. Elise had never played the game before, and thus was not much better. Bethy and Seth squared off as if they had something to prove. They laughed and laughed and laughed until Joshua's wolf popped out in sheer joy, like some weird furry jack-in-the-box. (Bethy jumped and cursed each time the wolf appeared. It made her, however, admit that Joshua couldn't attend his old school.)

"What are you doing for Christmas?" Bethy growled after losing to Seth. "Are you coming home then?"

Silence fell on the room.

"No," Joshua said. "I can't, not until my birthday. When I'm eighteen, I'll go home to visit. You know Mom and Dad; if I go back any sooner, they'll get lawyers involved, and they can't afford that."

"We can host Christmas here," Decker said.

"Good idea," Cabot said. "But we're not having frozen poultry that can be used as projectile weapons."

"Ham." Decker smiled hugely. "A nice Christmas ham."

401

"I get out of school a week before Christmas." Seth seemed excited by the idea. "We could come up and get a real tree at Bog Hollow."

"Bog Hollow?" Joshua laughed. "That sounds like something out of a horror movie."

"It's a cranberry bog that does cut-your-own Christmas trees in the winter," Seth explained. "They have hayrides and the best hot chocolate. We used to go every year to get a tree off them. We'd always get the seven-foot-tall tree because our house had really high ceilings, even higher than Decker's."

Joshua's family had always cut one of the small trees that grew where their backyard abutted state land. It wouldn't seem like Christmas without the scent of fresh pine. A real tree would make both him and his wolf happy.

Life was good but fleeting. Bethy had told their parents that she was stuck in Syracuse because of the weather. As soon as the roads reopened, she needed to drive to Saratoga Springs for a postponed Thanksgiving with their grandparents. Elise planned to leave before midnight. Seth could only stay until Sunday morning. The wolf was going to miss his brother and cousin horribly. (He could tell because it popped out to snuggle with Decker, embarrassing Joshua to no end. Personally, Joshua was still struggling with the idea that a kid as cool as Seth *wanted* to be his friend.)

Christmas is only a month away, he silently told his wolf. *We've got lots of work to do to be ready. It will go quickly.*

51: ELISE

Elise had missed five calls and three texts to call into Central while she was in the shower. Her stomach tightened at the number. Something big had happened. She stood naked in her bathroom, dripping water, as she called in.

Clarice answered the phone with, "Oh my God, where have you been? I guess you're on Decker time so it's still early for you and you were in the shower. I figured you weren't out shopping. I never understood why people shop Black Friday weekend. All the crowds and standing in long lines and everything. It makes me glad we don't do Christmas."

"Clarice, why are you calling?" Elise could hear her cousin typing quickly, a sure sign that she was frantically tracking information.

"The warlock in Belgrade is on the move. He landed in Heathrow an hour ago."

Heathrow. It would be hours, if not days, before the warlock was in her area. He might stay in London, abandoning whatever the Wakefields had planned. If he came to the United States, he might be rejoining what remained of his coven. Why had he stayed in Belgrade? Why was he moving now?

Elise pulled a towel from the shelf. She wrapped it around her and headed into her bedroom. "Any clue where he is headed?"

"No. I've been monitoring people traveling first class for the last three weeks. If a Wicker boards a full plane, a ticket holder gets bumped. Thank God, witches always bump people out of first class or they would be impossible to track. The ticket holder has to buy the ticket a second time and it stands out like a red flag. First class has priority in boarding and getting off, so I think this is the warlock. I'm not finding anyone matching him on the list of official passengers."

Elise's phone pinged with incoming mail. She flipped open her laptop to pull up the security photo. The warlock was a young man, tall, blond, elegantly dressed and bejeweled. Was this Heath Wakefield?

"Oh no," Clarice cried.

"What?"

"A first-class passenger on a flight to Logan International just bought a second ticket. I'm checking security cameras on the gate he should have departed from. Yeah, there's the warlock." Clarice groaned. "The real passenger just handed the warlock his ticket and walked away. The bastard probably just waltzed through security in Belgrade. The plane took off from London fifteen minutes ago. The warlock is on his way to Boston. He'll land in six hours."

"I'll be at the gate." Elise opened her closet. She tossed clothes onto her bed. Pants. T-shirt. Bulky sweater to hide her guns and daggers. She added two Tasers to deal with puppets and extra magazines. "Can you set up clearance for me to pass through security with weapons?"

"Working on it. Oh! Oh!"

"What?"

"The warlock might be running from the Wolf King. The king's jet just landed at Heathrow."

"The king is coming to Boston?"

"I'm seeing if he filed a flight plan out of Heathrow. No, no, don't do that," Clarice muttered darkly at something on her computer. "Stupid. Stupid. Oh, come on. Yes! No."

"No, he's not coming to Boston?" Elise guessed since it was the last thing that Clarice said.

"He's on his way to New York. They're refueling now. They'll be back at the Castle later tonight."

Elise hoped to have everything wrapped up long before the king returned. The werewolves had left a swash of blood and destruction behind them in Utica and Milton. Logan Airport would be packed with holiday travelers. She didn't want to offer up that many innocent bystanders to the wolves. She checked the time. "Is there anyone available to back me up?"

"Aurore is free," Clarice said hesitantly. "She could be there within four hours."

"Oh God, no!" A Power would be worse than the werewolves. Elise wished she could rely on Decker but the vampire would just be waking up as the airplane landed. Elise would rather ambush the Wicker in the tight quarters of the gangway when the warlock wasn't expecting an attack than chance losing him outside of the airport.

"What about tall, dark, and hairy?" Clarice asked.

"Cabot is on his way back to New York." Elise put the call on speaker so she could towel dry her hair.

"How did that go? Did you...?"

"No," Elise snapped.

"You forgot protection?" Clarice stated as if it was fact.

"No! Six people in one house, three of which have ultra-sensitive hearing, was far too public for me. Besides, it turns out I'm a little too trigger happy."

"Shoot first, ask questions later?"

"Yes. It's going to take a while for me to work past some kneejerk reactions."

"How did Cabot take that? Guys usually are kind of ticked off when you nail them hard."

"He's actually very sweet about it. It was kind of funny; he squeaked when he'd trigger a reaction, like one of those dog chew toys."

Elise checked the time again. The problem of calling Cabot was he was riding herd on the prince. She needed to keep Seth out of any danger. News of the incoming warlock would pull Seth back to Boston. Cabot might be ten years older than his cousin, but he couldn't say "no" to the boy. Dominance overruled age. The roads were still a mess from the blizzard. The holiday and the snow combined meant that the trains were running at maximum capacity. Even if Cabot could talk Seth into taking the train back to New York alone, there would be no room for the prince.

Clarice sighed loudly as she continued to type. "Oh, you're so lucky. I met this guy at the supermarket. It was in produce. I was buying eggplant and potatoes for moussaka. He picked up a cantaloupe and said that 'we have to get married because I can't elope.' He didn't stare or drool like most guys. He actually managed to say smart and intelligent things. There's this little coffee shop in the store where you can sit and eat. We got a table—it's one of those little round things on one post—and were talking. Out of the blue, he asked if the carpeting matched the drapes. I thought he was asking about my apartment. I was just about to tell him that I have wood floors when I realized he meant my red hair! I was so mad! Do you have any idea how much those stupid tables cost? Really! Five hundred dollars is way too much for a piece of wood on a metal pole."

He was lucky that Clarice used a table on him. Elise wasn't the only one that was trigger happy. It came with the training.

"I have a visual of the warlock making a call while he was in Heathrow," Clarice said. "I'm checking the cell tower nearest to Heathrow for calls to Boston area codes. There's a shitload of them. I'm going to compare the numbers to those called in Belgrade when he took off. I might find matches. It's going to take a while."

"I need security clearances," Elise reminded her.

"I'll have them by the time you get dried off and get dressed."

Elise had time to prepare and hopefully surprise on her side. She checked on Decker, or more specifically, Decker's phone. Joshua seemed to be safe within the wards. If Heath Wakefield had been in Belgrade all this time and chose to return to Boston, then he was sticking to whatever plan that his coven put into motion.

52: JOSHUA

Joshua woke to the sound of the wind through bare branches.

Everyone had gone home. Elise lived nearby. Bethy headed out Friday morning to their grandparents' house for a delayed Thanksgiving dinner. Seth and Cabot were driving back to New York City. With Decker asleep, the house was silent and still. It felt strange and wrong. Joshua had decided to take a nap to speed up the hours before Decker woke up. There had been yet another power outage; his digital clock flashed 12:00.

How long had he been asleep? He rolled onto his back to stare out the window. Rain turned the world outside a sullen gray. He couldn't tell if it was morning or afternoon. He felt like he'd only been asleep for a little while.

The whispering of the wind grew louder outside. It was only when the branches started to scratch on the glass of his window that he remembered that there wasn't a tree that close to the house.

There seemed to be nothing outside until something shifted, an absence of light with two small darker spots for eyes.

Joshua yelped in fear until he realized what he was looking at. "Fred! Geez, you scared me!"

He was going to have to fix his doorbell. Too many weird things were waking him up.

Winnie was probably downstairs, knocking softly on the door in fear of disturbing Decker.

Joshua dressed quickly and padded sleepily downstairs to see what Winnie wanted. She'd be happy to hear that Jack was indeed fine. Elise was probably the "prettier than you" that Marie Antoinette warned Winnie about. In Joshua's book, however, Winnie was the better choice for girlfriend. Elise was scary.

Winnie wasn't on the porch, nor was her Vespa parked at the curb.

"Hello? Winnie?"

Fred loomed over him.

He and Winnie had traded phone numbers and such on the subway ride to the Frog Pond. Her voice mail picked up after six rings. "If I was granny, I'd know why you were calling," Winnie's recorded message said. "But I don't work that way, so you're going to have to leave a message."

Joshua hung up without leaving a message. Fred scratched and whispered and moaned in what seemed to be distress. Joshua felt sudden empathy for people in television shows that were supposed to respond to barking dogs. "What's wrong, girl? Something happen to Timmy?"

Cold and dark and the smell of an open grave swept over Joshua. He had the distinct impression that Fred had just smacked him as hard as he could.

"I'm trying to understand!"

Luckily Winnie had also let him friend her on the Find My Friend app. According to Decker's phone, she was about a mile away. Why would Fred be here if Winnie was there? As he puzzled over the location, he realized it was the Royal Pastry Shop. Didn't Winnie say something about Marie Antoinette loving the bakery?

Did this mean the dead French queen had kidnapped Winnie again? What was Joshua supposed to do about it? Bring more money for pastries? He didn't have one of the magic clock-thingies that Winnie had used during the séance. He'd gotten the impression that Marie would leave when she felt like it, no harm done.

Maybe the queen had some information for Joshua about the Wickers.

Luckily, he'd bought an umbrella. Something that could have been rain or sleet or very wet snow was falling. It drummed noisily on the taut fabric as he followed the GPS on Decker's phone.

The Royal Pastry Shop was a tiny little storefront shop. A sign stated that it offered Italian and American pastries.

He'd forgotten to eat before leaving the house. As he walked through the door the smell of sugary pastries hit him. He lost control to the wolf. When he gained awareness again, he was sitting across from Winnie at little folding table, inhaling cannoli and cream puffs. Winnie wore an angora turtleneck sweater and a beautiful silk scarf with a sophisticated flair. She had four macaroons on a plate beside a coffee mug that was labeled "Queen of Effing Everything." Scanning the bakery, he realized there was no indication that patrons were supposed to eat in the store, nor did they seem to sell coffee.

"*Bonjour Monsieur le Loup,*" Winnie purred in French. She flicked a finger from Fred to herself. "*Sir Frederick vous a récupéré pour moi!*"

Marie Antoinette had kidnapped Winnie. It seemed as if she'd also sent Fred to fetch Joshua. Maybe.

"I don't understand French," Joshua said. "I took Spanish. *Hola? Hablas Español?*"

She gave him a dark look. "*Je refuse de parler en Espagnol.*" He'd take that as a "no."

"Oh, this is going to be fun." The wolf stole one of her macaroons. "Fred all but dragged me here. I don't know why and you can't tell me."

She pursed her purple lips at the cookie theft. "*Vous êtes ici à cause de cela.*" She rolled up the left sleeve of her sweater. "*Winnie a besoin de votre aide.*"

Coiled about her wrist was thick vine like a heavy bracelet. Little tentacles of green and tiny leaves showed that it was still very much alive. The vine wrapped up her arm and disappeared under her sweater.

"Oh geez, what the hell is that?"

"Wickers." She lifted the hem of her sweater to show woven cables thicker than his arms wrapped around her waist. "*Ils veulent lui pour le livre que les gardes Dorothy. Je suis empêchant la construction de prendre Winnie, mais je ne peux pas l'enlever par moi-même.*"

Dorothy guarded the book of runes in Sioux Zee's vault. The Wickers were trying to get it by going after Winnie? Why had Marie gotten Fred to grab him instead of taking Winnie to Sioux Zee?

"Shit." He hadn't been able to tear the huntsman's hounds completely apart. They'd reformed too quickly. This thing was denser and hidden by her clothes.

Marie pulled at the turtleneck to show that the vine continued up to wrap around Winnie's neck. The plant looked dangerously tight already.

The choker of wood and leaves stirred at the change of light. A snakelike head slithered into sight and hissed at Joshua. Its blue eyes were weirdly human.

Joshua leaped to his feet, snarling. He reached for the loop of woven wood around Winnie's neck.

"*Non! Non!*" Marie warded him off with upraised hands. She demonstrated a little tug on the vine around her wrist. It tightened even as she pulled on it.

What the hell did he do? Even Elise's daggers didn't damage the magical constructs enough to kill them. They had needed Decker to deal with the hounds. The vampire would be asleep for hours.

Marie pulled down her collar again. "*Mordre!*"

"What?" Joshua started to pace. "I don't understand!"

"Hey!" the baker called from behind the counter. He was a surprisingly tall and muscular for a pastry chef. "Are you bothering her?"

"No! We're friends!" Joshua cried. "She wants me to do something but I don't understand French...well."

He trailed off as he realized that it would be hard to explain being with friends with someone without speaking a common language.

The baker flipped a towel onto his shoulder. "*Ma petite reine est cet homme vous tracasse?*"

"*Non, Giuseppe!*" Marie blew the baker a kiss. "*C'est mon ami.*"

Joshua seized on the important part of this exchange. "You speak French?"

"Only a little. I got that Rosetta Stone app so I could talk to her."

"This is great! What does '*mordre*' mean?"

The clerk gave him an odd look and then turned to Marie. "*Votre Majesté, que voulez-vous?*"

Marie held her cupped hands beside her temples. "*Monsieur le Loup mordre.*"

"Eh?" The baker apparently didn't understand the phrase or hands on her head any better than Joshua.

"*Monsieur le Loup!*" Marie tilted back her head, hands still cupped beside her temple, and howled like a wolf. "*Mordre!*" She chomped her teeth together.

"Oh!" Joshua understood.

The baker didn't. "I don't get it."

Everyone had told Joshua that a werewolf's bite was magical. Seth had stressed several times that even the smallest nip could turn a human into a feral. If a werewolf's teeth broke the skin on anyone but Decker, they'd become a monster. Joshua's decision to flee home had been a wise one.

He wasn't sure if he could bite though the vine snake without also biting Winnie.

"*Se dépêcher!*" Marie cried as the snake tightened its hold around Winnie's neck.

Biting at the snake's tail around her wrist would be useless while it had a choke hold. He'd have to bite off its head—while he was a wolf. He needed to transform here at the bakery. He glanced at the tall baker. Did he know about werewolves and ghosts and other scary stuff?

The baker stared at Winnie, slack jawed. "What—what—what the hell is that?"

No, the baker didn't.

"Things are going to get—weird," Joshua said. "Scary weird. Just—don't panic."

Yup, that was clear.

He hadn't purposely transformed into the wolf before. All the other times, he'd changed completely by random accident. Seth had told him that he had to embrace the beast, accept it as part of himself.

If he was going to save Winnie, he needed to be the wolf.

"Seriously, what is that?" The baker had gotten on thick oven mitts and a box knife. "It's hurting her. We need to get it off her!"

"Yes, we're working on that." Joshua closed his eyes tightly. Wolf. Wolf. Come out and play.

The baker's startled yelp told Joshua that he'd succeeded. Why didn't he ever feel different? He didn't even know what size of wolf he'd become until he opened his eyes.

He'd gotten humongous.

"*Bonjour Monsieur le Loup.*" Marie's voice trembled even though she sat calm and poised at the card table.

The baker was wielding the box knife and a tin platter like a shield. "What-what-what-what?"

I am never going to be able to come here again.

Joshua sighed and focused on the snake. It hissed at him, eyeing him back.

It was going to be weird using his mouth to strike instead of his hands. He'd been trained to protect his head.

Deep breath. Focus on your enemy. Don't let fear in.

And strike.

He snapped down on the thick neck, just behind the triangular head. It corded and flexed like a living thing despite the taste of wood and bark and leaves. He heard Winnie give a strangled cry and he ground down with his teeth.

The snake thrashed in his jaws. Its body uncoiled from Winnie with stunning speed. It whipped around him. The thick woven vines sprouted hundreds of shoots. The thing no longer looked like a snake but more like a millipede.

This wasn't working. He didn't know how to fight as a wolf. Winnie was free—they should run. He was good at running.

The thousands of "legs" grew even as he tried to figure out how to safely disengage from the construct. The tentacles wrapped around his body. They anchored Joshua to the floor before he realized what was happening. He frantically tried to pull free. Something was wrong with the floor. The white vinyl had turned translucent like ice, thinly covering a wet blackness what couldn't possibly be the bakery's basement.

He couldn't break free. The hundreds of vines wrapped tight around him, mummifying him as they pulled him downward. His paws went through the thin surface of the floor. The black was blood warm.

He whimpered in fear as the vines yanked him down into the darkness.

53: JOSHUA

The world righted. Joshua was still encased in vines but he was no longer in the weird dark, warm nothingness. There was bare cement under him. The smell of blood leaked through the woody cords holding him firmly.

"Oh my God! Oh my God!" a girl shouted beyond Joshua's living cocoon. "Dad! Aunt Belladonna! Dad!"

"You don't need to scream, Tansy," a second woman with a deeper voice called from the distance.

"Black wolf!" Tansy shouted. "It's a black wolf! I got a black wolf!"

"What did you do?" Belladonna drew closer. "You know that we need to stay hidden until we have the lost heir on a leash."

"I got impatient," Tansy said. "I thought if I could send a fetch to nab the spook girl, we could use her to get the book of protective runes. Speed things up. I landed the hook, but every time I tried to pull her in, something blocked me."

"Of course something blocked you! A fetch needs to resonate with the soul of the target. Spooks can use a spirit as a mask. This could ruin everything; the prince is going to spot your fetch!"

"I got a black wolf! When I couldn't reel in the spook girl, I threw some eyes into the mix to see what the problem was. There was a black wolf trying to tear off the fetch! So I nabbed him!"

"Which black wolf?" Belladonna said.

"How the hell do I know?" Tansy cried. "I was fetching a spook!"

"Get him in a cage, Rowan," Belladonna said.

"I'm working on it." Rowan was a man with a deep menacing voice. "Hold still."

There was a whimper of pain from a new voice that was quickly silenced. The scent of blood grew heavy.

"Okay, let's see what we have," Belladonna stated like a command.

The vines unwrapped.

Joshua expected to be inside something made of metal: a dog kennel on steroids. What they'd put him into was another woven vine thing. Its bars were thicker than his wrist, interlaced to a rattanlike weave. It seemed to be sized to the wolf; he barely had an inch of space on all sides.

The whimper of pain had been from a college-aged boy lying on a plastic tarp. The student's chest had been sliced open and the tendrils of the cage's vine grew out of his heart. The tendrils of the retreating fetch were gathering around the body of a woman cut open in the same manner. The stench of blood and fresh butchered meat hung heavy on the air.

The cage stood in a massive underground parking garage. The concrete stretched out in all directions; the structure most likely took up an entire city block. A forest of square cement support columns held up the low-slung ceiling. Wide scattered lights barely touched the cold darkness. Somewhere in that darkness, Joshua thought he could hear pigs grunting. The noise echoed eerily in the huge space. Except for a scattering of furniture, five tall work lamps on stands, and the dead bodies, the garage stood empty. The place felt gravelike.

Joshua couldn't see any way out. There didn't seem to be any ramps leading to other levels. If there were doors to stairways, they were hidden behind the support columns. There were no helpful "exit" signs, nor any other normal signage. No painted parking stalls. No arrows indicating flow of traffic. No random oil stains on the pristine concrete. The space might have been built as a parking garage but the Wickers had taken it over before it had ever been used as one.

The three Wickers stood staring at Joshua from a safe distance.

"Tansy, you have a monster's luck." Belladonna looked nothing like how Joshua imaged witches. She was a stunning blonde woman in a deep jewel blue cocktail dress, studded with sapphires, and draped with a sable fur stole. She wore four-inch stiletto boots to make up for the fact she was short. If it wasn't for the assault rifle that she kept aimed at Joshua, she would seem like a movie star about to walk the red carpet.

"Oh my god!" Tansy was a junior-high-school-aged girl with

two blonde ponytails. "He's huge! You could put a saddle on him! Hey! Once we get the leash on him, can I ride him?"

The wolf flung himself against the cage bars, snarling. The cage seemed to shrink smaller.

"I'm not sure that would be wise, sweetie." Rowan looked harmless with a receding hairline, glasses perched on the end of his nose, and an apron that stated "Danger: Men Cooking." His hands, though, were soaked in blood up to his elbows.

"The leash will make him docile, Rowan" Belladonna stated firmly.

"As long as it's the right black wolf." Rowan turned to a basin on one of the work tables to wash the blood from his hands. "It could be that damn Thane again."

Belladonna shouldered the rifle. "Cabot is in New York City with the prince."

Tansy squealed, bouncing up and down with glee.

The wolf roared in fear. He was all alone. No one knew where he was. With Decker asleep for hours, no one would miss him. No one would think to look for him until it was too late. He bit at the cage bars, trying to break open a hole large enough to wiggle through. It repaired the damage he did to it faster than he could bite through it. The cage shrank little by little until the bars pressed tight against his sides and he couldn't move.

"Are we sure the cage will hold?" Rowan dried his hands on a clean white towel. He'd missed some blood and it stained the terry cloth.

"It will hold. The Monkhood coven spent decades refining the spell to hold even the strongest alphas."

"Yes, my dear sister, but the Monkhoods are all dead." Rowan picked up heavy rings from the sink's lip and slid them on. "They were either made feral or torn limb from limb; else we would have never inherited their spell books."

"The spell wasn't what failed." Belladonna checked the time on her diamond wristwatch. "This throws our time schedule off. We only have four hours until we're up to our neck in pissed-off werewolves. Heath hasn't arrived from London yet."

Belladonna and Rowan glanced hard at each other.

"Tansy, go fetch the other bag," Rowan said.

Belladonna nodded as if he'd agreed with something. Neither one looked entirely happy about the decision.

What did they have planned, Joshua wondered? What were they going to do? What was this end game of theirs? Why had they killed so many people to capture him?

"It can't be helped." Rowan pulled on a leather welding glove onto his right hand. "Heath will not make it back in time."

He pulled a silver chainmail glove on over the leather one.

"Don't rub it in." Belladonna shifted a wheeled tray closer to the cage. It looked like something out of a hospital operating room, stainless steel cleaned to gleaming perfection. "I know you want this as much as I do."

Rowan produced a narrow silver case and sat it on the nearest planting table. He fumbled left-handed with the catch. Inside was one of the angelic daggers. He cautiously took it out with his double-gloved right hand. The dagger flared bright as an arc-weld in his protected hold. He laid it quickly on the steel tray. "Perhaps, but I'm not happy with the cost."

Tansy left and returned wheeling a large suitcase. "This is so awesome. Do you know what I'm going to do with my wolves? I'm going to take over Disney."

"You don't need werewolves to do that." Belladonna motioned for her to put the suitcase on one of the planting tables.

"All of Disney!" Tansy swung the case up. "Disney World. Disney Paris."

"You still don't need wolves to do that," Rowan said sadly.

"No one wants to help me get my favorite television shows back on the air," Tansy started to unzip the suitcase.

"That's why they were cancelled in the first place," Belladonna said.

Rowan gave his sister a warning look. He brushed Tansy aside to take over the case.

Tansy crossed her arms over her chest in defiance of the older witches. "I'll take over Disney and have them made! *Firefly. Xena* with the original cast. *Farscape.*"

"It's a waste of power, dear." Rowan flipped the lid open to reveal a lush grey wolf pelt. The head lay on top, glass eyes inserted into the skull so it stared mournfully out at Joshua. "I will be recognized as a god."

Rowan swung the pelt around so it draped over his shoulders and lowered the skull so it sat like a hat on his head. "Let us take our last steps of hiding in shadows."

Joshua cringed. The skin was from a werewolf. A person like him. A man that walked and talked and watched television and had parents someplace. He'd died protecting Joshua. Daphne had used his friends to kill the man. The Wickers had treated the man as less than a dog, butchering his body down while knowing full well how human he really was.

And they had Joshua trapped and helpless. Were they going to kill him and skin him too? Seth warned him that the angelic blade was one of the few things that could kill Joshua instantly.

"Tansy." Rowan caught the girl by her shoulder. He moved her closer to the cage. "Hold still. I'm sorry. This was to be Daphne, but the stupid fool got herself killed. Heath won't be back in time. He was our second choice."

"What?" Tansy's voice went sharp with fear.

Rowan picked up the angelic blade. It flared brilliant in dim garage. "This takes a blood sacrifice of a witch full into their power, born to the wearer's immediate bloodline, killed by a Virtue's dagger. A child or a parent. Daphne and Heath would have been better since they were out of your aunt's womb and there's no fear of adultery there. I have to trust that your mother was faithful."

The wolf roared with anger and fear. It threw itself against the bars. Rowan was going to kill his own daughter! If the Wickers could murder their own children, what did they plan for Joshua?

"Be done with it!" Belladonna snapped.

Rowan caught his daughter's pigtails. He pulled her head back sharply.

"No! Daddy!" Tansy cried.

"Shhhh, be quiet baby." Rowan lifted the gleaming blade to her neck. "Daddy needs to do this right."

Her father's power held Tansy rigid and silent as he repositioned the dagger again and again, gleaming blade millimeters from her skin, painstakingly choosing his cut.

"Rowan!" Belladonna growled softly.

"It would be a shame to waste all that fuss and bother on a bad cut. The poopy diapers. The teething. The vomit. God, I hated the vomit. She's finally gotten old enough that you can have a reasonable conversation with her."

When Rowan found his mark, he cut without warning. Blood fountained from the wound. It pulsed in time with Tansy's racing heart. As the warm stickiness sprayed over Joshua, the air seemed to thickened, pressing down on him.

Tansy whined involuntarily of pain and fear.

"Thank you, baby." Rowan kissed her on the temple as he raised the blade high over his head. "Daddy loves you very much and you're making him very happy."

He drove the dagger into her heart to its hilt.

Tansy's mouth flew open in a wide circle of voiceless pain and horror.

The pressure increased on Joshua until it felt like something had wrapped tight around him.

What do I do? What do I do? He could barely think past the rage of his wolf.

"Be still," Rowan snapped.

Joshua's body obeyed against his will, just like when Seth made him sit after chasing him across Cambridge. The wolf continued to growl.

"Be quiet," Rowan ordered.

Joshua had no choice but be silent. He sat huddled in the cage, covered with Tansy's blood, panting.

"Good girl." Rowan kissed his daughter's temple again. "You were perfect, baby." He laid her dead body on the floor. Her eyes stared unblinking into Joshua's. "It's done. He's mine. Now what? Send him after the spook? He must know where she is."

"No, we don't need to find Decker's house any more. We got the ultimate prize, we just skipped all the steps leading up to it."

"But the spook must know where Decker's house is, else she wouldn't have been with the lost heir. The vampire will be awake soon. The spook will tell Decker that we've taken the wolf. We should at least send puppets to kill Decker before he wakes up."

The wolf roared with fear and anger.

Belladonna dismissed the suggestion with a flick of perfectly manicured fingers. "We're spread too thin. Decker is the Grigori's tool; he might not put himself at risk for a werewolf. The prince is a more immediate problem. He would have known the moment Tansy made the fetch where we are. We might have less than four hours before he gets here. We need to set up protective wards and open the breach quickly. The prince has to die before the king returns."

He couldn't let them kill Seth. What could he do to stop them? He couldn't even move.

Joshua had done some kind of spirit communication with Jack and the Wolf King, if one could call that "talking." If he could get to the right meditative state, he might be able to get hold of Seth. Warn him. Tell him that it was a trap and Joshua was the bait.

He struggled to calm himself. Breathe deeply. Focus inward. Fall into the darkness and find the green. Be one with the Source.

Quickly.

Not productive.

Breathe deep. Clear the mind. Let the fear go.

He stood in the dappled forest.

"Seth!" He ran through the bracken. "Seth!"

He saw something flicker through the forest. "Hey!"

The shimmer of white warned him that he hadn't found his brother. He'd found the Wolf King.

"Um, sir? Help!"

The great white wolf came out the shadows. Without the restriction of a ceiling, he seemed big as an elephant.

"Oh shit," Joshua whispered.

"What are you doing here?" The Wolf King asked in a voice like thunder.

"Wickers have set a trap for my brother. Seth. The Prince of Boston. I'm the bait. I need to warn him."

"Ilya," the Wolf King whispered. "I should have sent all the Thane in New York to fetch you instead of focusing on the Wickers themselves. I can no longer move effortlessly through the Source; I will not make it back in time. Listen carefully to me. Do not lose your temper. Anger will give control to the wolf. You need to *be* your wolf. Your wolf needs to be you. If you're at odds with yourself, you cannot break free."

"I can break free?"

"You must or all will be lost. Your brother. Boston. Everything. In that order."

"Must is not the same as can!"

"The Wickers don't understand our magic completely. It's why they failed before. The Source isn't what they think it is. You can use it to free yourself. You need to be one creature in heart and mind. Be careful, though, it can destroy you too."

54: SETH

"Seth! Seth!"

Seth jerked awake in the front seat of the Land Rover. They'd started home hours ago but the aftermath of the blizzard on the holiday weekend had made a mess of the roads. Traffic was at a standstill again as emergency crews cleared yet another accident. He blinked at the snowy surroundings. They were nearing the Sturbridge Exit on the Massachusetts Turnpike, less than a third of the way back to the Castle.

"Did you just call me?" Seth asked Jack.

"Hm? No."

Seth frowned, considering the dreamlike impression of someone calling him. It sounded like Joshua. That was impossible. Joshua wasn't in the Boston pack; they had no magical connection beyond the fact that Joshua was in Seth's territory. Joshua couldn't "call" to him.

Seth reached out to check on his brother. Decker's house was empty. They'd taken Joshua shopping the day before, restocking his refrigerator and freezer with food. Joshua told them that he planned to go back to sleep until Decker woke up. His brother should be home. His brother should be safe in his bed.

"Something is wrong." Seth turned in his seat to look back toward Boston now sixty miles behind them. "Joshua isn't in Cambridge."

"What? Where the hell did he go?" Jack muscled the Land Rover into the fast lane. "There's a turnaround ahead. We can head back to find him."

The bright star of a werewolf should be easy to spot anywhere in Boston. Seth scanned his territory quickly, afraid that Joshua had been somehow magically spirited out of his territory. There! Under Boston Commons. His brother's connection with the source glinted within the darkness, much weaker than it had been before. Snarled tight around Joshua were threads of power linking him to a person that wasn't a werewolf. Wooden constructs moved in the shadowed hallways connecting the garage to buildings around the park.

Seth felt sick as he realized what it meant. "Oh God, the Wickers have Joshua! I think they have a leash on him."

He was going to lose Joshua just like he'd lost his little brothers. He shouldn't have left Joshua alone at Decker's. Seth knew that the vampire would be asleep during the day. The boy might be able to fight but he had no idea what he was up against.

"Call Haji and Leung." Jack braked hard to pull into a maintenance vehicle turnaround. "Tell them to meet us in Boston. If they get on the next plane, they'll be there in an hour or two. Where are the Wickers holding Joshua?"

"Boston Commons." Seth shifted his focus off of Joshua to his location. What he found made him gasp in dismay. "Oh no, there's a tear right beside him."

"A breach?"

"The start of one. It can't be a coincidence. The Wickers must know a way to create one."

"Why would they do that?" Jack snapped. "They might be resistant to breach-borne but they're not immune."

"They're putting up wards. They'll be standing in the eye of a storm. We'd have to wade through breach-borne to get to them."

"We? No. No. No we!" Jack cried. "You can't go after him, Seth. You can't risk yourself to save him."

"We can't wait for the Thanes. It's the Sunday after Thanksgiving. They're not going to be able to get on a plane." Seth swept his hand to take in the bumper to bumper traffic. "They're not going to be able to get here quickly!"

"Call Elise and Decker. They can get there even before we can."

"Decker is asleep." Seth paused to verify that. Whoever took Joshua might have killed Decker. No, the vampire was still in his underground bunker. "We can't wait for Decker. The Wickers created the breach but they can't control it. It's going to tear open and dump breach-borne all over Boston. If enough people are caught up in it, we're not going to be able to save the city. There will be thousands of monsters within hours of the breach opening, if not hundreds of thousands."

"What the hell are they thinking?" Jack whispered.

It was a trap exclusively meant for him, Seth realized. Anything else, the Thanes would wade in alone. The nearby bloodshed would rip the breach open and the Thanes wouldn't be able to close it. Seth would have to be part of the battle. Obviously the Wickers thought Joshua was his heir. They couldn't control Seth or Jack because the wolves that created them had been cremated long ago. The Wickers must believe that if they killed Seth while Joshua was on a leash that they would have control of Boston. If Joshua became prince, then he could create a pack of wolves devoted to him. The problem was that Joshua was part of the New York pack. He wouldn't inherit Boston; Jack would.

It left Seth with a decision of charging in, risking death, and sealing the breach now before anyone died, or waiting until hundreds or thousands of innocent people were dead.

It didn't seem like much of choice.

What had happened three years ago? Did his family really die because of some natural event that no one could have controlled, not even his father? Or did the Wickers tear open a test breach in preparation for today? Or was that a first attempt that went horribly wrong? Had they planned to kidnap him and skin his father? Was that why the king wanted Seth and his little brothers in New York?

The idea of his father butchered like Samuels sickened Seth. He tried not to think about it but the thought loomed huge. He could have been in Joshua's place. Alone. Trapped. Scared.

The Wickers' secret lair had a several hidden passageways leading to it, all but one of them guarded by now active constructs. Why was one left clear? Were there more Wickers racing to join the two holding Joshua captive?

"Speed up." Seth explained the open passage to Jack. "If we get to the entrance before the remaining Wickers, we can just walk in without fighting our way through constructs."

Seth had never closed a breach before. The king had explained how to do it in great detail. He'd felt Alexander close up breaches within Boston, but that was while Seth was still in New York, watching from afar. Fear roiled in his stomach as they reached Boston Commons an hour later. Jack wedged the Land Rover into a tight parking space a block from the park. Elise waited on the sidewalk, her Jeep illegally double-parked with government tags displayed in the front window.

The breach was still small and new. Magic welled up like blood from a fresh, shallow wound. The power hadn't found a host yet, but that was only a matter of time. Seth could sense reality around the breach weakening. At any moment the small tear could rip open into a huge massive wound. Magic would flood out, infecting everything in its path not firmly rooted in another power source. The wolves and Elise, being a Virtue, would be safe. Everything from mice on up would be taken over. Changed. Twisted. Filled with the insatiable need to devour life.

Seth could feel all the people moving through the Commons on street level, in the underground garage and the nearby subway stations. Thousands of holiday shoppers surged through the area, unaware of the danger hidden under their feet. It would be a bloodbath.

"It's a virtual maze underground," Seth waved to indicate the Commons that stretched several blocks in all directions. "They've got Joshua in a cage in the bottom floor of the parking garage. The breach is within feet of him. The level isn't connected to the upper floors. There's several ways into the space from surrounding buildings and the subway. The only unguarded way in is through the basement of the Masonic Lodge. There's stairs heading down into an underground hallway."

"Wait." Elise put out a hand as if to catch Seth by the wrist. She remembered who he was and stopped herself before actually touching him. "Let me go first. The power of the Lord will protect me."

Seth locked down on a growl of impatience. It would be stupid for him to blindly charge into the fight. If he was killed, Jack would be deep in alpha amnesia for a week or more and unable to close the breach.

Elise paused to kneel in the grass, daggers down and touching the ground. She'd chosen an area already in shadows, screened from the sidewalks. "Blessed be the Lord, my rock, who trains my hands for war, and my fingers for battle; he is my steadfast love and my fortress, my stronghold and my deliverer, my shield and he in whom I take refuge. Amen."

Seth felt the power gather around her. The area brightened noticeably as ghost wings flared from her back. Oddly the people passing by had glanced her way as she knelt, but as she prayed, they paid less and less attention to her until she seemed invisible to them.

The Masonic Lodge was a huge stone building dating from the turn of the last century. It been built to impress, all stone and ornate details. It had multiple levels of basements, the first level of sub-basement were two large dining rooms.

The Wickers had puppets standing guard in the lowest level basement. It was a true basement filled with odd bric-a-brac. The men were armed with impromptu weapons of hockey sticks and butcher knives. Elise ghosted past them, unnoticed. Seth and Jack followed in her wake, protected by whatever magic surrounded her.

"That's a little creepy," Jack whispered. "I'm not used to being ignored so blatantly."

"I wish I could always be that invisible," the Grigori murmured.

Seth led to a doorway on the far wall. The large ornate door had once been an important entry. It had been updated recently with a keypad lock.

"This feels like a trap," Jack said.

"I need to get close enough to touch the breach." Seth ripped the door open, shattering the frame around the dead bolt. "Quickly. We're running out of time."

Stairs led down to a narrow stone lined hallway. At the end, a modern steel door opened into a massive low-slung space of the Boston Common Garage.

The scent of blood hung thick in the air, a powerful wave of coppery warmth. It washed over them as they came through the door. Under it was the taint of something bitter, dark and oily. The hair on the back of Seth's neck rose and he found himself growling.

The three Wickers stood within pentagrams with warding glyphs scribed at each point of the star. There was witch and two warlocks. The older male wore Samuels' skin, the skull perched upon his head with the body draped down his back. Flanking the Wickers were two large wooden cages. A black wolf crouched within one, silent and watching. Joshua gave no sign of how sane he remained. The second cage held four piglets. The animals ran in wild circles within the cage, squealing in fear.

It was the wet black breach, though, that caught and held Seth's attention. It smeared across the floor like an oil-slick between them and the Wickers. The air above visibly roiled, the magic spilling out distorting the light. At the moment the breach was only an inch wide and five feet long.

"Seth!" Both Jack and Elise cried as Seth raced to the black opening.

"I need to close this!" Seth knelt beside the breach. It looked like an optical illusion, the blackness hovering inches from the ground. It was growing larger even as he reached for it. Magic spilled out of it, shimmering like heat across the concrete. His body reacted as if he'd plunged his hand into boiling water. His hand jerked back without his conscious control. He steeled himself and reached again. The sensation of harm remained, but he knew it wasn't heat he was feeling. There were no words to describe it. His entire being, though, rebelled against it. He fought to keep his hand within the sheer nothingness, blindly searching.

"Let the pigs loose, Heath!" the witch cried. "Before he can close the breach."

The vines of the cage unraveled, spilling out the piglets. The animals fled blindly straight toward the breach. The air thickened and darkened and surged toward the pigs. Their squeals deepened as the magic took the pigs. They shimmered darkly as they changed form, growing massive. Their ridged backs became taller than a man, covered with a course gray hair. A dozen massive, razor-sharp tusks grew in haphazard patterns. Some were on their lower jawbone. Others on their snout. A scattering grew out of their cheeks and across their skulls and down their spines. Extra pairs of beady red eyes appeared, each monstrous boar growing a different number.

Seth ignored the boars, trusting Jack to protect him. He had to stay focused on the breach. His fingertips brushed over a strand as fine as spider silk. There! He caught hold of the thread and pulled to snap it. The line went taunt, digging deep into his fingers.

One of the boars charged toward Seth. Jack tackled it to the ground. They rolled away, growling and squealing. The vines from the boar's cage slithered toward Seth, trying to wrap around him.

Elise slashed at the tendrils. "Hurry! We're overmatched here!"

Seth yanked with all his strength. The thread snapped. He tapped the Source, pulling power to him, flooding the area with his magic to counter the breach.

A boar slammed into Elise, ramming her into a support column. The concrete shattered from the impact. Her ghostly wings vanished. She started to slump to the ground, unconscious.

Seth caught hold of the boar before it could gore her. It was like wrestling with a truck.

"Seth, watch out!" Jack shouted.

There was the thunder of an assault rifle on full auto fire. Jack fell as a storm of bullets plowed through him.

"Jack!" Seth flung the boar away.

The bullets punched through Jack, spraying Seth with blood as they exited Jack's body. They'd been silver, though, and left behind poisoned wounds that wouldn't heal until they were cleansed with Earthblood. Jack fell to the ground. His cousin flailed, trying to get up but too wounded to rise. A second boar charged toward him.

"No!" Seth intercepted the boar. As he attempted to kill the monster, the vines from the piglet's cage snaked around his ankles.

I've killed Jack, Seth thought. We're going to die here and with us, all of Boston.

55: DECKER

The house was too quiet. Decker woke full of misgivings. What had happened while he'd been dead to the world? In the short time that Joshua had been living with him, they'd established a pattern. Joshua was always in the kitchen, waiting for him, at sunset. The boy was always surprisingly loud. Why was the house so quiet? Had the prince decided to take his brother back to New York City?

Decker hurried up the basement steps, his worry growing as he discovered the kitchen dark and empty. The newly uncluttered rooms echoed loudly as he called "Joshua?" There was nothing left in the house to mute how empty his life was without the boy.

Even as the echo died away, someone knocked loudly on the front door.

It was the purple-haired girl with the spirit guide. She yelped in surprise when Decker flung open the door and hissed at her.

"Where is Joshua?" Decker growled.

"The Wickers took him!" She held out a piece of paper that shook violently as she trembled in fear. "I think. I'm not sure. Marie was at the helm at the time. The bakery guy was pretty rattled but he said something about there being a freaking big black wolf that was wrapped up by some kind of monster snake. I think it was Joshua. I think the Wickers took him. Marie left a note but I haven't had time to translate it."

He snatched the piece of paper. It was a pastry bag with French handwriting in smooth ballpoint ink on the back. *"My* dearest Silas. Those foul witches tried to take my little Winifred with a fetch. Of course I couldn't allow it. Unfortunately, I could not remove it myself so I asked my gallant Chevalier to bring your young wolf companion to my rescue. Alas, in freeing me, he was snared and the fetch carried him off. He is being held within the tunnels under the park with the darling Frog Pond. Godspeed. Marie."

That trollop, Joshua wasn't hers put at risk!

There was a postscript that he nearly missed. "They were after my Winnie in order to find your residence. I believe that is what those from the Far East would call karma." A second postscript added, "I just love these new pens. No more ink splatter, blotches or smears!"

He crumpled the note with a snarl.

The girl fled down the steps to her purple motorized bicycle, the oddly named Vespa.

"I didn't know what to do!" the girl called. "Marie left me at the bakery with the baker whimpering hysterically about giant wolves and wooden snakes and gateways to hell. I have no idea what really happened. I've been waiting for you to wake up so I could give you the note."

Where was the prince? He was to return to New York City that morning, nearly four hours away. Surely he knew that his brother was taken.

Decker struggled to clear his mind and focus on the prince. Where was Joshua's brother? Southwest and distant. Possibly still in New York City. It could take hours for the prince to drive to Boston.

If the Wickers had tried to kidnap Winnie to gain access to Decker's house, then they would be expecting an angry vampire. Most likely they would have something prepared to kill Decker if he came thundering down on them.

Decker had been faintly hoping for the release of death. If he found it saving Joshua, so be it.

Decker had been a hundred and fifty years old when he saw his first train. It had been a massive roaring thing, bellowing out black smoke and steam. It had seemed like a magical thing to him, chained to the ground, yet rushing along at impossible speeds. It had been the first hint of how lost he'd feel as mankind developed more and more advanced technology. Children now played with toys that went faster than that first locomotive.

He'd read about the proposed Tremont Street Subway in the Philadelphia newspapers as he approached his second century on Earth. It was the first of its kind in North America and thus big news. He could not wrap his head around the idea of a vehicle propelled simply by electricity until they started to appear in Philadelphia.

The two original stations of the Tremont Street Subway served Boston Commons. Park Street was a surprise rabbit hole, covered by a small brownstone head house with a dark tin roof. It looked like a public restroom from the distance. The Boylston head house was at the far other end of the Common, at the intersection of Boylston and Tremont Street. The squeal of train wheels on steel rails as the Green Line turned a tight corner underground betrayed the presence of the hidden trains.

In the nearly sixty years that he'd lived in Boston, the tunnels servicing the stations had constantly been altered, expanded and closed as the subway grew and merged with other rail lines. He did not have to imagine the maze of resulting underground passageways; he and the several generations of Grigori had climbed through them countlessly, hunting monsters. Saul. Lauretta. Elise.

The dark unused spaces at the heart of the city were frequent spawn points. The Grigori needed him to find the beasts within the maze. Needed him. Used him. Left him alone when they went back to their uncluttered houses. He had lived centuries repeating the cycle with each new generation. As toddlers they loved him utterly. As they grew older and more aware of the world and their place within, they came to distrust him. They despised him when they were idealistic teenagers. Hard reality sometimes changed them for the better; they grew to love him once again. Sometimes, though, it only made them hate him more, hence his exile from Philadelphia.

Of the New World Tribes, he'd only known the Virtues. They'd protected him from the Powers and guarded the Dominions, who could not defend themselves if he'd attacked them. They shared the hunt, sometimes their meals and occasionally their bed, but never the little mundane things of life. Saul had never taken him shopping. Lauretta had never done laundry with him. Elise never asked him to pick a paint color.

He was starting his fourth century on Earth and he'd just discovered the simple joys. Joshua had lived less than eighteen years. Decker wasn't going to let some power-hungry witch steal a full happy life from his puppy.

He boarded the Red Line at Harvard Square. The car emptied out within minutes of him stepping onto it. His cold anger made the rest flee the train completely at the next stop. No one dared to board the next three stops. He crossed the Charles River alone and dove under the city. Minutes later, the train rattled and squealed into the Park Street Station.

He paused on the brick platform to take his bearings. The high arched ceiling had not changed in all the years that he had lived in Boston. The lighting now was bright as daylight, stunning after the darkness of the night. Behind him the doors slid closed on the subway train and it rattled away, leaving him wholly alone.

Where was his Joshua?

His talent pointed high on the blank wall before him. He knew, though, that the Green Line crossed overhead, running from the Government Center to Boylston Station. He walked upstairs. The support columns were all clad in gleaming stainless steel that reflected distorted images of everything around but him. It was as if he didn't exist.

A train sat waiting, doors open, engines humming loudly, its running lights flashing brilliantly.

He stepped onto the last car. A dozen commuters bolted from it like rats fleeing a sinking ship. The doors accordioned shut. The train pulled out of the station, the electric engine humming loudly.

There had been few changes to Boylston Station since he had arrived in Boston half a century ago. The misaligned platforms still bookended a dark cave of tracks. The train wheels continued their high-pitched squeal as the subway cars turned the sharp corner.

The southern tunnel branch toward Pleasant Street, however, had been abandoned. The outer tracks were on the far side of the outbound platform. A work train sat in the shadows beyond the fencing that kept the curious at bay.

He paused to concentrate on Joshua's location. If Decker had his bearings right, the boy was due north and very close. It would put him close to the Frog Pond, if not directly under it. The question was, how did Decker reach him? What he needed wasn't Joshua, but the door that led to him.

Decker struggled to shift his focus off the boy. If the prince was correct, then the witches did not mean to kill Joshua but to make him into a tool. He should be safe as long as the Wickers had a use for him. Finding the path to him was key to Decker rescuing Joshua from them.

His fears abated slightly, his talent picked out something within the dark abandoned southern tunnel.

He caught hold of the fencing and tore it open wide enough to let himself pass.

The southern tunnel led down a gentle incline, allowing the side tracks to cross under the mainline even as it curved out of sight of the platform. A bare fifty feet there was a door in the tunnel wall. A small sign commanded "No Admittance." Someone had used bright yellow spray paint to fake graffiti to either side of the doorway and then on the wood itself painted a poorly done warding glyph. Just glancing at it filled him with tingling unease. A normal mortal would be compelled to avoid the door out of irrational fear.

"Protection is not our forte, is it?" Decker whispered. Such a thing could only keep him out as long as it wasn't damaged. The wards on his home were carefully hidden from view and easy access. If someone actually managed to force their way into his house, they wouldn't be able to destroy his protective wards. He glanced about for something to mar the glyph.

He spotted cans of spray paint further down the tunnels beside the rusted tracks. Sloppy. The witch wouldn't be able to see in the cavelike darkness. She must have assumed no one else would be able to either.

He fetched the cans. He knew what it was—vandals started to use them to spray graffiti in the poorer sections of the city shortly after he moved to Boston. He and Elise tripped over the young "artists" in some of the most unlikely places. He'd never actually tried to use spray paint. Somehow he missed that obsession during his period of experimentation in the late 1960s.

The brand name of the spray paint was Monstercolors.

"Truly? That's what you used?" He turned the can in his hand. He'd noticed that there was an assumption that goods were being sold to people like himself without a clue on how they should be used. It wasn't like the olden days where a gas lamp was the height of technology that a normal person used. Everything came with instructions, or at least, warnings on how not to use them. On the back of the can were directions. Shake. Point. Spray. Simple enough.

He painted his chest bright yellow on his first attempt. Apparently a common enough mistake, hence the reason for the eye protection warning.

His second attempt covered the warding. For good measure, he sprayed over the graffiti too, just in case they were some kind of magic that he didn't recognize. The one on the right stated "we aim to misbehave" inside a vaguely horse-shaped outline. The one on the left seemed to be the name Tansy written in leafy stylized letters combined with a stencil of the yellow flowers and green saw tooth leaves. Judging by the fact that the tingling unease disappeared only after he covered all three paintings, he'd missed the fact that the two "graffiti" had hidden some kind of backup wards.

The door was locked. He kicked it in. At one time, the space had been a small brick-lined equipment closet. The back wall had been chiseled away, exposing a long, narrow, dimly lit corridor. Had the Wickers created this secret passage? It was difficult to tell. The Monkhoods' gambit had been centuries ago. The Wakefields could have been quietly redirecting construction in Boston for decades without drawing notice of the prince. As long as they didn't spill blood, they were undetectable.

The light bulbs had been replaced with grow lights. Was this some attempt to thwart him? Yes, the lamps mimicked sunlight for plants but surely Wickers understood that daylight had a magical component beyond just being bright light.

Something rustled in the distance; the muted stir of leaves.

Oh! The grow lights were not for him.

He focused on his power and flicked out his hand, summoning his sword. It pulsed in his grip, blood warm and hungry. It spilled quiet need into him. If he turned around and went back to the crowded platform, he could feed upon the humans waiting there. They would be easy prey.

He stalked down the dim corridor, fighting the urges that his curse whispered to him.

The plants in the hall were general guard dogs, obviously meant to stop humans and slow down werewolves. They reached out green tendrils to bind him. They withered to dust when he slashed at them. Their magic flowed up his sword's blade to spill into him. It was warm and heady, like slowly sipping corn whiskey. He could feel his control slipping. With the death and destruction that lay ahead, was that a bad thing? Perhaps it was time to embrace his inner monster and let it wreak havoc.

If he guessed rightly, he was heading toward the Common's sprawling underground parking garage. Since there was an entrance kiosk with automated payment machines within steps of the Frog Pond, he could emerge directly below it.

The corridor ended with another locked door.

"Little pig, little pig, let me in." He kicked it hard. It flew from its hinges to skitter across an expanse of concrete.

The huge space had all the earmarks of an underground parking garage—poured concrete, thick support columns, exposed electrical conduits, a wide ramp heading up into darkness. The ceiling was much higher than normal. Some of the ones Elise had taken him to, he felt like he needed to duck. There weren't any signs to direct traffic or the lines painted on the floor to indicate legal parking areas. Obviously the Wickers had taken over the lowest level of the parking garage while it was under construction.

Grow lamps blazed against the cave-dark shallows that pooled in every corner. Plants crowded around the doorway, potted in huge galvanized steel watering troughs. Blood lay in large pools, scenting the air with the heavy coppery perfume. He breathed deep, drawing it in. The euphoria that proceeded complete loss of control flooded through him.

He stalked deeper into the garage. Elise was unconscious on the floor. The Thane lay bleeding, possibly dead. The young prince was being wrapped in vines. He struggled to free himself while he kept a herd of monstrous boars from feeding on the fallen. The Wickers stood within protective spells, apparently too startled by his entrance to act.

Decker ignored them all for his real target. Where was Joshua?

There. Huddled in a cage. Looking miserable. The black wolf got to his feet as Decker strode across the pavement.

One of the boars rushed into Decker's path. "Little pig, you've been busy."

He lashed out with his sword. The tip sank deep into the monster's chest. Power roared up the blade in hot wave. Decker drank deep of it. The boar fell, withering away to nothing. He stopped, wavering in place, trying to remember what he was doing as the power eroded away what was man.

"Oh God, it's Decker!" a man wearing a wolf skin shouted in fear. "Stop him! Do something!"

"Do *something*?" Decker laughed. "Oh yes, the Grigori have been around since the dawn of man. You've fought the wolves for thousands of years. But me? You have no idea how to fight me, and that terrifies you."

The witch open fired on Decker with a rifle.

The bullets plowed through him, barely registering on his awareness at first.

Decker laughed at the futility of it all. "No, no, silver bullets are for wolves, not vampires. I am corruption."

"If you bleed, you can die!" the warlock wearing the wolf skin shouted.

As Decker burned through the excess magic to heal, he grew aware that he'd taken massive damage. "True, but you've taken the only thing that matters from me. I'm here to take him back or die trying."

Which would be soon if he didn't replenish his depleted magic base. He slashed at another boar, devouring its power. "Luckily you've provided me a wonderful banquet of choices here."

He cut through the vines woven into bars. Joshua whined even as Decker freed him. The wolf stood motionless, held by something more than just the cage. To break the magical hold on Joshua, he would need to kill the warlock wearing the skin. The Wickers stood within protective wards against magical beings. He wouldn't be able to harm the man, not even with his sword. He needed something non-magical—like Elise's guns. He turned and stumbled to where she lay.

"Heath!" the witch cried even as she changed out the magazine in her rifle.

"I'm working on it," the younger warlock murmured.

Two massive constructs came spinning out of the darkness. Studded with blades, they careened into him. They sliced open a hundred sharp thin wounds. It took him to his knees.

Joshua whimpered loudly.

"Silence! Sit!" Rowan commanded as if the boy was nothing but a dog.

Decker snarled and lashed out at the nearest construct. The power flooded through him as the top clattered to the ground, its blades shattering under the impact. "Don't treat him like that! He's not a dog. Not a puppy. He's a man! My dear, dear friend, and I will not allow this to continue."

Good, brave speech but his legs were refusing to obey him.

56: JOSHUA

"Do not lose your temper," the king had said. *"You need to be your wolf. Your wolf needs to be you."*

What the hell did that mean?

Joshua struggled to stay calm. *Deep breaths.* He closed his eyes to the chaos in front of him. The sounds were too horrible. Cabot gave awful whimpers of distress between snarls of anger. Seth—his little brother—chanted "No, no, no" as the vines trapped him. The boars made terrible noises that sounded too much like them eating Elise. Decker was far too quiet, as if he'd already died.

Joshua opened up his eyes again.

Decker stabbed the spinning whirly death thing. It clattered to the ground, blades ringing as they struck the concrete. The vampire poured blood from dozens of wounds. He got to his feet with a shaky laugh. "You can't kill something that's already dead." He stumbled sidewise toward one of the boars. "Especially when you've scattered so many delicious treats about to feed on. Just stand there, trapped in place by your protective spells, while I heal."

"Stop him!" Rowan pointed at Decker.

Joshua's body sprang forward without his conscious thought. He slammed into Decker, knocking him from his feet.

"Kill him!" Rowan shouted.

Joshua froze, teeth inches from Decker's face. Kill Decker?

"No biting," Decker murmured.

436

Joshua whimpered. He didn't want to kill Decker. His wolf didn't want to either.

It wasn't until Decker pressed hands to Joshua's face that he realized he'd shifted to human.

"I don't want to hurt you," Joshua whispered.

"Then don't."

Decker was bleeding from a dozen places. He needed magic to heal. He needed to feed.

Think of it as CPR, Joshua told himself. He leaned down and pressed his mouth to Decker's.

No, his wolf stated, *it's love. We love him.*

It became a kiss, full of desperate fear and sorrow.

The Wolf King told him to embrace his wolf. To be one. Fine, it's love. If he had to be bisexual to save the world, so be it.

The Source blazed through Joshua as the vampire fed. Massive potential pulsed with his racing heart. How could he use it to break free? He could feel Cabot lying on the ground, bleeding, barely conscious. Seth struggled just beyond, cocooned in vines. His brother blazed with his own connection to the Source as he desperately tried to keep their cousin alive. Seth was pushing power into Cabot's healing ability, a fine web of magic woven from his outstretched hand to Cabot's body. Beyond was the Wicker with hold of the leash, its tendrils connected to Joshua.

Judo was the art of turning an enemy's attack against him.

The Wicker had a hold on him, but it also meant he had a hold on the Wicker.

Seth believed Joshua was his only possible heir because he had hundreds of years of breeding that might allow him to control the power of Boston. Joshua was praying that meant the Wicker couldn't withstand the same level of magic.

How did he channel the power onto the Wicker? He could see the tendrils. Could he grab hold of them?

The answer was yes. It felt like a garden hose, heated by the sun, with a strong current of water running through it.

"Are you *kissing* him?" Rowan cried. "Stop that! Kill him!"

The demands hit Joshua but the compulsion to obey was instantly washed away by the flood of magic.

He focused on twisting the flow, turning it back along the channel.

Rowan screamed. He dropped to all fours and transformed

into a small yellow mutt-looking wolf. Rowan charged toward his sister. He hit the edge of her protective spell and rebounded, snarling with anger.

Belladonna tossed away her empty assault rifle with a curse. "Well, this is a wipe." She pulled small-caliber pistol out of an ankle holster. She shot her brother twice in the head. Rowan collapsed into a bleeding heap beyond her protection circle.

"What the hell?" Heath cried.

"The leash disappeared when he transformed," Belladonna said. "It's in some other dimension or something. We can't control the lost heir. Everything is pointless now. We need to kill them all."

The female pointed her pistol at Seth.

"No!" Joshua leapt in front of Seth, transforming into a massive wolf to better shield his little brother.

Belladonna emptied the pistol into Joshua. The silver bullets struck white hot and continued to burn. He stumbled and fell. He couldn't get up.

Belladonna ejected the empty magazine and reloaded. "Where's your gun?"

"We never need them," Heath said.

"We never face off with Grigori and werewolves at the same time." Belladonna pointed the freshly loaded pistol at Joshua.

"Fight me, bitch!" Elise rose from the ground, gun in hand.

Belladonna swore, turning to face the Grigori. "For God's sake..."

Elise shot Belladonna in the forehead. "Yes, for God's sake."

"Mother!" Heath cried as the witch fell to the ground.

Elise turned and shot him twice in the chest. She shot the two remaining boars. She walked unsteadily across the concrete to shoot Heath in the head to be sure he was dead.

It was over. Joshua closed his eyes. Everyone was safe.

Distantly he felt Decker lift him from the ground, but that didn't matter. Everyone was safe.

"We need to get him to Doctor Huff's," Decker said from far, far away.

57: SETH

Seth was going to lose one of his family members, if not both. Jack was only alive because the power that Seth focused on him held the silver poisoning at bay. He could hear Joshua fighting for breath in the back seat, but Seth couldn't sense how badly his brother was hurt.

For some odd reason, Decker sang just above a whisper. "You've got to stay, just a little bit longer. Please, please..."

The words tore at Seth. They reminded him that he barely knew his brother and could lose him forever any second. "Oh, shut up!"

The silence was even worse.

Dr. Huff jerked open her door, already in full roar. "What part of 'closed' do you not understand? This better be an emergen..."

She trailed off as she took in who was on her doorstep. Her long black hair fell loose over her shoulders instead of braided into her normal pigtails. That and the lack of black lipstick and dark eye shadow, Seth barely recognized her. "Oh no! Oh God, what happened to them?"

"They've been shot multiple times with silver bullets." Seth carried his cousin into the house. Behind him, Decker proved that the vampire was inhumanely strong as he carried Joshua as if he wasn't the size of a pony. "Jack's wounds seemed to be all through and through. Nine entrances and nine exits. All of the bullets stayed in Joshua."

"Jack to the bathroom." Dr. Huff pointed down the hall. "There's bottles of Earthblood in the hall closet. I don't know if I have enough for both of them. Use it sparingly." She pointed toward the door to her clinic. "Joshua needs to be to be taken to the surgery. I need to get the bullets out of him before we can flush his wounds."

Dr. Huff's bathroom was filled with sorts of girly shampoos and soaps and candles. It was clearly a private sanctuary for her. Blood smeared the sides of her massive tub as Seth lowered Jack's body into it.

"Here." The Grigori carried in a five-gallon glass bottle filled with Earthblood. "The seal is broken on the other bottle. This is the only one that's viable."

"That's not enough!" Seth cried in panic. "We'll need at least twice that!"

"My family has some Earthblood stored in Watertown. I can get there and back in ten minutes."

"Go."

Earthblood needed to be stored in glass to keep its potency. Seth undid the stopper and wrestled the big jug into place so he could carefully pour the shimmering liquid out over Jack's wounds. All the while, his awareness was on the operating room on the other side of the building. Joshua lay unmoving on the steel table as Dr. Huff gathered her surgical instruments.

He should go make sure Joshua lay still as Dr. Huff removed the bullets. If his brother struggled, he could hurt the very human woman. If he left, Jack might die.

"Seth," Jack whispered. "I'm sorry."

Seth's heart seized in his chest. "No, you are not going to die on me, Jack."

"I've screwed up so many times. I should have gone to the barn with Samuels. I should have sent Ilya to New York. I should have made you..."

"You did what you could! I'm the prince! I should have known..."

"You're sixteen, Seth. Everyone keeps forgetting that because you've stepped up and *been* the prince. You shouldn't have to be making these kinds of decisions."

"I don't care."

"Then go take care of Ilya. Your brother needs you."

Dr. Huff was shaving Joshua's fur away from the bullet holes so she could see the wounds clearly. At any moment, she would start digging out the slugs. Seth couldn't imagine staying still as someone did that to him, not even someone he trusted as much as Dr. Huff.

But if he left Jack, he'd die.

"Jack..."

"Go!"

Seth staggered to his feet. He picked up the bottle of Earthblood. He knew Jack was right. He had a duty to keep Dr. Huff safe. If Joshua bit her, she'd go feral. But even as he started down the hall, he could feel Jack get weaker.

Seth stopped in the living room, stranded between his remaining family members. Jack or Joshua? Which one did he save? Both had just put their lives on the line for him. Joshua was his duty to protect, a puppy in his territory, and his brother who already once been lost to the family. Jack would rather die than fail Joshua again. But to lose Jack? Seth couldn't bear that.

The door suddenly open and Alexander stalked into the vet's surgery.

"Sire!" Seth was never so glad to see his foster father. Relief swept through him so strongly that his knees gave out.

Alexander paused to put his hand on Seth's head. "Get to your cousin." The king took the bottle of Earthblood. "I'll see to your brother."

"Yes, sire."

58: DECKER

Decker had spent over three hundred years living in the shadow of the Wolf King but he'd never met the creature. He recognized Alexander instantly. It felt like someone had opened the door to summer; magic radiated off the king in a wave of sun-warmed green.

The Wolf King was surprisingly average height, although at one time he would have been considered tall. His hair was snowy white and gathered back into a braid. It was difficult to tell if the color of his hair was because he was a white wolf or merely ancient. He wore a charcoal gray suit and tie tailored of the most recent fashion.

Decker stood holding Joshua's head as Dr. Huff shaved away the fur around the bullet wounds. All his instincts were screaming to run. He tightened his hold.

"Your majesty," Decker managed to whisper. It pleased him that anything came out. Now if he could keep from letting anything improper leak out. This time his humor would get him killed instantly. He didn't want to upset Joshua.

Dr. Huff's eyes went wide over her surgical mask. She glanced behind her. "Oh! Oh God!"

Joshua growled weakly.

"Sh," Decker whispered. "We're safe. There's nothing to harm us."

The king gave Decker a long hard stare. "You're the Grigori's pet monster."

That was his heart leaping up his throat. It been a long time since he'd felt fear this sharply. He'd almost forgotten how horrible it was. "Yes."

Joshua growled and tried to get up.

"Hush." Decker leaned down to press his forehead to Joshua's. "He's here to help you."

Joshua whined but laid still.

"Why are you even here?" The king moved no closer. "Do you not know that a werewolf's bite is a wound that will never fully heal? He could cripple you for the rest of your very long life."

"He needs me," Decker said. "I cannot abandon him in his time of need. If he hurts me, so be it. It will be without malice." *Good, now stop talking. Don't make any jokes.*

"We will keep him still," the king said to Dr. Huff. "Get the bullets out of him."

We? Decker had expected to be chased away. He pressed his lips tight on the questions. If he started talking, something stupid could slip in. Best to be quiet while things were going the way he wanted them.

"This is a topical. It will numb the pain." Dr. Huff flushed the wound. "Not for long, but it's better than nothing. Sweetie, I'm going to have to ask you to be brave."

Joshua whimpered.

"Just do it," the king ordered. "He's growing weaker as you baby him."

Dr. Huff frowned over her mask at the king but picked up a scalpel and pair of clamps and started.

She dropped the bloody, misshapen bullets into a pan one at a time. They made dull chimes of metal on metal. They were joined by countless wads of gauze soaked in blood. Joshua had gone still, barely breathing. Decker didn't want to believe he was dying, but the evidence was too clear.

Dr. Huff rinsed the wounds out with Earthblood. "There. It's done."

"Ilya." The king brushed her aside. He gathered Joshua's limp body. "I have looked for you too long for you to die on me."

The heat from the king became white hot and Joshua flared into brilliance, as if his entire body became light itself. When the light faded, the black wolf had become a confused-looking boy.

"Who are you?" Joshua whispered.

"I am your king."

"King?" Joshua frowned at him a moment and then his eyes went wide. "Oh shit! You're the Wolf King!"

The boy flailed in the king's hold. He transformed into a black wolf pup and leapt at Decker.

"He's shy," Decker lied as the puppy burrowed under his arm.

"I see." Alexander stared at Decker for a minute before nodding. Decker wasn't sure what the nod meant.

"I need to go see to my Thane." The Wolf King turned and walked out of the operating room. Surely it was a day that miracles could happen.

59: ELISE

"We have to stop meeting like this," Cabot whispered weakly as Elise poured Earthblood over his wounds. The gleaming liquid splashed over the bullet holes and drained out of the bathtub bloody red.

"Yes, we do," she said.

She'd been afraid that both Cabot and Joshua would be dead when she returned. She never thought she'd be so happy to see the Wolf King. Judging by Seth's face, Cabot's baby cousin felt much the same. Seth sat in the massive bathtub with Cabot. She could feel his power radiating off him like the morning sun. It filled the bathroom with the scent of deep forest.

"We should try just dating like normal people," Cabot said. Was his voice already stronger? "Dinner. Something fun. Regular stuff instead of this witches with silver weapons."

"I'm open to that." She emptied the bottle over the bullet wounds. Yes, they were healing shut.

"How about Friday?" Cabot said.

She took comfort in the fact that he'd probably be fully recovered. The Wolf King's return to United States, though, changed their relationship. "Friday works. Probably. We should check our social calendars. Make sure we're not conflicting with something."

He nodded, understanding the unspoken part of her reservation. "Like saving the world?"

"Yes, something like that." She was thinking God and Wolf Kings deciding that they were otherwise unavailable, but saving the world was what Thanes and Virtues did.

✧   ✧   ✧

The Wolf King was born before even Icarus strapped on wings and took his mythical ill-fated flight. The first verified human flight had been 1903. It meant for two thousand years of his life, flying was something only birds and a handful of Grigori did. It was only natural, then, that the Wolf King didn't think werewolves should fly. It was something to be done only in emergencies. Having landed safely at Logan International, the Wolf King declared that he would not reboard his private jet. He ordered the Thane at the Castle to drive the king's fleet of Bentleys nearly four hours to Boston. The main roads were crowded with holiday travelers and the side roads were still being cleared from the blizzard. Driving to New York City was extremely impractical but no one even tried to sway the king from this course.

The decision delayed the process of the werewolves decamping. The night was ticking closer and closer toward dawn.

Elise found Decker in Dr. Huff's deep walk-in closet. The Royal Vet had an impressive array of patent-leather boots and goth black clothes. Ghost traces of amber, musk, and leather scented the narrow, deep windowless space.

The vampire had tucked himself under a rack of leather corsets and lace boleros. A black wolf puppy slept in his arms. The puppy stirred to growl sleepily when Elise opened the door.

"Hush, it's just Elise. Go back to sleep," Decker petted the puppy until it tucked its head back under his arm. The look on Decker's face was heartbreaking. He knew time was running out.

"The Thane called," Elise said. "They're stuck on the highway behind a big pileup. They'll be here after dawn. You should go home before Isaiah arrives."

"I'm not leaving," Decker said. "Joshua needs me."

The man had already faced down the king; he would not flee before the king's son.

"You're going to be asleep and helpless."

"I don't care."

It was what Elise was afraid of. Once the Wolf King took Joshua away, Decker would stop caring about anything. "The Wolf King is not going to be able to keep him in New York City long."

Decker gave her a confused look. "What?"

"Joshua's heart is going to be here in Boston. He likes living with you. You're important to him. Seth is going to be here. Sooner or later, Joshua will be back."

Decker's eyes widen with the realization. "Yes, he will be." He sighed and dimmed. "The house will seem so empty until then."

"You are my oldest friend. You have been nothing but patient and loyal to me." Elise reached out to take his hand. She couldn't remember the last time she touched him with gentleness. She'd forgotten how cool his skin felt. The vivid memory arose of him holding her in his lap when she was four or five and sick with a fever. His hand felt so good against her forehead. She'd repaid his kindness by throwing up on him. Since she'd returned from Greece, she'd repaid him by treating him like a tool. Something taken out and used when needed but otherwise kept in a box and ignored. Friends were not things to be used.

"I'm just starting to realize how much I've misunderstood everything. My mother tried to warn me that I was giving my vows too much of myself. She kept saying 'God loves individuality, otherwise he wouldn't make snowflakes.' I thought that was just trite nonsense that she said to pacify me." Usually the phrase was in response to Elise's criticism of her mother's relationship with Decker. "I tried to make myself the perfect weapon and in doing so, I abandoned everything that made me Elise. I've lost track of everything important to me. I don't even know what I like to do for fun."

Decker gave her a sly smile. "You liked making dioramas."

He meant the plastic cowboys and Indians tying a vampire to a stake to be burned.

She smacked him out of sheer habit. "I'm sorry. It was cruel. I hope Joshua threw it away."

"You were a child and bored. I should have made my house a welcoming place for the living instead of one massive trash bin. I could have had an entire room full of toys."

"It would have made me more suspicious of you as I got older."

"Perhaps, but it would have made your childhood more bearable."

It might have, but she doubted it. She'd been happy when she was very young. Much of her unhappiness had come from her own growing surety that she knew how the world worked. It was time to question everything instead of accepting things at face value.

"We can't change the past but we can make any future that we want." I can be someone I like instead of this hard, angry woman. "I want to find out what I like to do for fun. We can even start with dioramas."

60: SETH

Seth braced himself for a fight. The immediate danger to his family was over but his brother wasn't safe. Seth needed to somehow face down the king to make sure Joshua stayed in Boston. The idea of fighting the king was frightening, not for his own well-being, but for the fact that he didn't think he'd win. Still, he'd trained for this fight his entire life.

Step one was to get the king alone where none of the Thane could hear the argument. The king would never allow himself to seem weak in front of them. Luckily the rooms in Dr. Huff's offices were small and the Thanes were exhausted from their long flight from Belgrade.

Seth chased the king's lawyer, Bishop, from the room with a hard look and then shut the door. "You need to make a choice. Isaiah and Joshua can't exist in the same house. You've been too lenient on Isaiah; he will not leave Joshua alone. Either you must move Isaiah elsewhere—his grandfather's in Russia—or leave Joshua in Boston."

"I must?" Alexander gave no hint to his mindset in the dry quiet words.

The king was never swayed by emotional outburst. During the last three years as he trailed behind the king, Seth had watched passionate pleas fail every time. Only cold logic would move him.

"I do not dictate this; the facts stand by themselves." Seth forced himself to speak calmly. "My only part in this is that I will not stand by and allow Isaiah harm my brother. I will assume that the first offense is a pattern of intent and I will kill Isaiah."

"That sounds like you are dictating."

"Isaiah has made it clear over the last three years that he will not respect me or leave what is mine in peace. If you had supported me, then perhaps I would have options, but as it stands, I have only one means to control Isaiah."

There were times that Alexander was more like a granite statue than a man. He looked at Seth with his long unending, unblinking stare. It always made Seth's eyes hurt trying to match the king's gaze. In the end, Seth always had to look down, blinking furiously.

It didn't occur to him to glance up. He wondered how many times that Isaiah had made that mistake.

"Sire, the leash is destroyed." That was Seth's strongest point. "There is no reason anymore for anyone to try and harm my brother with the exception of Isaiah. Joshua has a safe place with Decker, who has proven for half a century that he can be trusted. My brother can remain with Decker until I return to Boston."

Seth wanted to push—include himself in the deal—but he knew that now wasn't the time. Alexander would only give him one thing and it had to be that Joshua stayed out of Isaiah's reach.

"You believe the only solution is to leave Joshua here or to move Isaiah elsewhere?"

Seth couldn't think of any other solution. "Joshua is too dominant to send to another territory for the interim. If the alpha died while he was part of the pack, he would inherit the alpha over any blood relative. He doesn't know the first thing about being a werewolf. He'd be completely lost as the pack tore itself apart."

"He can be taught." The king's tone gave no clue to his intent.

"He's happy here. If he's unhappy, he'll run. He's very good at running. I had trouble catching him in my own territory. He might go back home to his parents and the newborn marquis won't know how to deal with that."

"If he runs, I can find him."

Alexander could find Joshua anywhere. Historically, Alexander had a short fuse for wolves that caused him grief.

The last thing Seth wanted was Alexander's anger coming down on Joshua. "He wasn't given a choice about being a werewolf. He's been resisting integrating the wolf. He managed during the fight to work with the wolf. If he is unhappy..."

"You should know by now that I do not care about anyone's happiness."

He plowed on with his reasoning. "If Joshua is unhappy he'll start fighting his wolf again. He still can go feral."

"He is stronger than you give him credit for."

Yes, he knew that, but he was hoping to rattle Alexander's determination. One thing he'd learned in the last three years, Alexander ultimately cared only about their people as a whole. He did not allow fondness of any one individual to sway him.

Perhaps that was the key.

"I need an heir. We need to rebuild the Boston pack. You lost all the bloodstock with the exception of me and Jack."

Alexander was silent for a moment. "I have lost entire packs before," he stated quietly. "Before the treaty with the Grigori, it was common. With you and Jack, I have more than I have had in the past to rebuild. When the time is right, we'll start to rebuild your pack."

When the time was right. In other words, not now.

Seth locked down on a wave of sorrow that went through him. The king wasn't going to listen to reason. Joshua had lost everything. Friends. Home. Foster parents. It seemed as if the king was willing to drop him into the hell of being Isaiah's whipping boy. "Give him to me, then. Make him part of Boston's pack so I can protect him fully. Please."

"If I give him to you, do you pledge to keep him safe? To put him before even Jack?"

Was Alexander balking because Seth had left Joshua with Decker? Or because Seth allowed Joshua be taken and nearly killed in the first place? A few days ago he would have blithely promised anything, but the last few hours had been grim reminder that all his power could be rendered moot. What had the old Marquis of Albany said? Good intentions meant nothing in the face of reality?

Seth knelt in full subservience to his king. "I don't want Joshua hurt. He's a good person. He's nearly died to protect me. He's my brother. The only one I have left. Please. Let me do all that I can to protect him."

Alexander put a hand on Seth's bowed head. "I put him in your care."

Without any more of a warning, Seth felt Joshua's presence within the Boston Pack. Decker had tucked himself into a deep windowless closet rather than go home for the oncoming day.

Joshua slept as a small black puppy across Decker's chest. For the first time Seth could sense that Joshua was still weak from his near-death experience. Despite that, his brother was calm and content. He obviously felt safe with Decker.

Seth pressed hands to his face as relief made tears burn in his eyes. "Thank you, Sire."

"Protect him from all things, even himself. If you truly think its best that he stay with the Grigori's pet monster, then take whatever steps are needed to make it a proper place for him."

"What?" Seth was sure he misheard the king.

"Your brother may stay in Boston. He should have a proper wardrobe, cash in hand, whatever they use as bank notes now, and a vehicle. See that he's educated in a manner befitting a prince."

"I—I—I will. Thank you, Sire." Surprise and dismay kept Seth rooted in place as the Wolf King walked out of the small examination room.

He'd won? Joshua could stay in Boston? Seth cocked his head, replaying the conversation. Yes, somehow he'd managed to convince the king to do what he asked. Three years and he'd never been able to sway the man. It made Seth uneasy to have finally succeeded. What was he missing?

Albany had warned him that the king acted on what he saw written on the wall too big for any normal person to see. Had the king kept Boston off-limits because he knew that the Wickers that had killed Anastasia would strike again? Did the Wakefields create the breach that killed Seth's family three years ago? Now that the coven was dead, did Alexander believe that Boston was safe enough for wolves?

Or was it something else? The king operated solely for the whole, not the individual. His brother had an unprecedented alliance with Decker and a Virtue. Was the king setting Joshua up?

Albany had said that time gave a person the ability to see such things. Time was something that Seth had very little of, both in the way of experience, and wiggle room. He had to act now. He had to trust his instincts that Joshua needed to be kept as far as possible from Isaiah for all the reasons he gave the king. Until he could see the writing on the wall, he'll take his cues from the one person that could.

The king.

"See that he's educated in a manner befitting a prince."

Seth knew that being a prince meant more than just getting a high school diploma. It was being taught how to see the world as a political arena. It was not something learned out of a book but from someone who been trained to think and act like a prince. If the king wanted his brother to learn, then there was only one person able to teach him. Seth.

He stood up. He'd been equating being the prince simply to being in Boston. It was so much more than just that. He hadn't been staying in contact with his neighbors. He hadn't been making decisions on rebuilding his family's home. He hadn't been seeking out alliances with people like Elise and Wise Woman Sioux Zee and her granddaughter Winnie. He hadn't even contacted his wife in California to make plans about their future together.

He had much to do. It was time for him to do it.

61: DECKER

"The Four in Hand is the simplest tie knot." Decker paused to remember the process. The fact that Joshua was wearing the tie changed the motions his hands needed to make. He hadn't worn a necktie for decades. They had, however, been a standard for men's fashion for over a century. His ability to tie one had become ingrained. "Wider end over the narrower one, under, around, under again, down through."

Joshua blushed while the wolf wagged his currently nonexistent tail. It was the cutest little hip wiggle that betrayed the wolf's delight in the process.

Decker understood for the first time the phrase "beam with happiness." He felt as if the joy had to be turning into pure light and pouring out of him. His puppy was going to the werewolves' private school in Cambridge. His puppy was staying in Boston. Most importantly, his puppy was happy.

And confused.

"Under, around, what?" Joshua peered down at the knot that Decker just tied. "Do I really need to wear one of these?"

"Yes, the school has a strict uniform policy set by your father, Gerald Tatterskein." Decker had used it as an excuse to drag Joshua to upscale clothing stores. (The month of cleaning and painting had left the boy looking like a ragamuffin.) Elise had attended Blackridge as a child. She knew what they needed to buy and where to find it. She volunteered to help and seemed to enjoy the trip nearly as much as Decker. Joshua liked the amazing collection of stores called "Cambridge Side Galleria" but hated the clothes. He seemed to think shirts should come without buttons and regarded neckties as some kind of cruel trick on men. Decker had to agree that most of the ties were truly ugly. What had happened to humans' color sense?

"Gerald was very old-fashioned for his time," Decker said. "Tradition was important to him. I believe it was because he lost his father so young. Your grandfather wouldn't have been heir if not for the fact that all the other possible heirs had been killed by a feral. It burned him out. He died before he was fifty."

"Oh, that's sad. Wait? What about Seth?" The tail wag stopped cold. "Is he going to be okay? He's not in trouble because I was kidnapped as a baby? That was the whole point of the Wickers' plan. I would have been heir instead of him."

"Seth is fine." Decker patted his puppy on the head. "I've lived long enough to be able to tell. Your brother is a much stronger wolf than your grandfather was. Being prince is not burning Seth out, which means he'll probably live to a very old age."

"Oh good." The tail wag started again. Joshua undid the knot. "So, wide end twelve inches lower than the narrow end. Cross over. Under?" His hands faltered and stopped.

"Around." Decker took hold of the tie just below Joshua's hands to illustrate. His grin widened as Joshua's blush deepened in shade. The activity was requiring them to be oddly intimate. Decker was having a devil of a time controlling his tongue. He mustn't tease his puppy. The fight with the Wickers had been a horrific experience for Joshua. The boy had been captured, witnessed multiple blood sacrifices, watched helplessly as his family was nearly killed, forced to attack his friend, and had been shot six times. The feeding had been least disturbing thing to happen to Joshua but Decker had promised Joshua that he'd never feed on him again. Technically, Joshua had force fed him, but who initiated it didn't count, not with the wolf added into the equation. Joshua needed time and distance from the fight. Decker wanted to make sure that he got it.

Joshua worried at the tight knot around his neck. The wolf growled softly in annoyance. "I wish I didn't have to wear this. It makes me self-conscious. Maybe it will be better when I see everyone else wearing the uniform but right now I feel like I'm doing cosplay. Badly."

"You look fine," Decker said. *Cosplay? What was cosplay?*

"These things always look so cool in anime," Joshua said mysteriously. "Am I too short for this outfit? I can't tell. The only mirror is in the bathroom and I'd have to stand on the toilet to actually see what I'm wearing."

They'd shortened and hemmed the pants but altering the jacket was beyond them. There hadn't been time to have the store tailor fit it. Joshua had the shoulders and chest of a man who did heavy work, but the waist and arms of a boy still growing. While the jacket fit his shoulders, its sleeves were too long and the waist hit too low.

"It's fine," Decker lied. "It's only for a few days. The other jacket will be ready for pickup next week. I'm sorry about the lack of mirrors. Since I don't have a reflection, I never thought to buy one."

Joshua continued to look stressed. Decker debated for a minute before cautiously wrapping arms about the boy. Yes, it embarrassed Joshua to be close, but it soothed the wolf. Joshua was stiff and still for a moment before relaxing against him. Good, it had been the right thing to do.

"It sucks that I'm not going to be able to stay up all night with you after I start classes," Joshua said into Decker's chest.

"We'll have five or six hours a day." In the winter. Once spring started in earnest, they'd have far less, but no need to mention that now. Decker suspected that wasn't the real problem since Joshua rarely lasted beyond three in the morning.

"Do you think it's really safe for me to go to school?" Joshua whispered.

Ah, the true source of Joshua's unease.

"What the Thanes found at the Frog Pond after our fight suggests we did manage to eliminate the Wakefield Coven completely."

"I mean—am I safe for other people to be around? I'm a bully magnet but now I have this whole other self with a short temper and sharp teeth."

"Which you can take out and show any bully."

"What?" Joshua cried in surprise.

"I'm sure that if anyone tries to bully you, all you need to do is to show them that you're a giant-sized wolf and they won't ever bother you again."

"I think you're missing the point."

"Hiding what you are is a slow painful death. It locks you in darkness with the one bully you can't silence—your own self-hate." Decker knew from experience. He didn't want Joshua to drink that poison. "There will always be people that hate. They will latch onto any flimsy excuse they can to justify their rage. If you let them cut yourself off by hiding away, they've won. The trick is to surround yourself with people who will love you for yourself."

"How do you find them?"

"By looking for them." Decker had gone out looking in the night for something to save his life. If it wasn't for his magical talent, he would have overlooked the scruffy puppy he'd found lost in the park. "You won't be able to know them on sight. Learn the temper of their heart. You'll find the ones that beat in time with yours."

Joshua leaned back to give him a suspicious look. "You're not just saying that—are you?"

Must not tease the puppy even though he makes it all so easy. "No. Leave yourself open to friendship and you'll find one."

62: JOSHUA

Nowhere in the official documents for Blackridge High School was the name Tatterskein mentioned. Its mascot, however, was a black wolf wearing a gold crown. The building reflected that it been founded in the early 1800s with massive amounts of money poured into it; everything was made out of polished stone, carved wood and leaded glass. The students wore a school uniform that was white dress shirt, slacks, jacket and sweater vest. The latter obviously because the heating system was still based in an earlier century.

It'd taken Cabot and Seth three days to assemble the paperwork and enroll Joshua under the name of Tatterskein. He had no idea how they'd gotten his transcript from his old school without his parents' knowledge, but there it was, sealed and stamped. The principal was a stuttering mess at their sudden arrival. Cabot and Seth wore expensive tailored suits. Joshua felt underdressed despite his new school uniform.

Seth did silent commanding presence while Cabot laid down the law. Joshua pulled at the tie that Decker had patiently taught him how to tie.

"He'll be living in Cambridge with a friend of the family," Cabot stated in a low, firm voice. "We are not providing their name or address; you have no need to know. If there is an emergency, you will contact me or anyone on the list I provided."

"W-w-who is he? He didn't attend Blackridge with the other Tatterskein child. Wait. He was born in March? He's Anastasia's baby boy? Ilya? You found him? Where? How?"

"That is not your concern," Cabot said. "Let me remind you that my uncle's estate is still the sole owner of the school. If you don't cooperate fully, as trustee I'll have you removed and find someone else that understands who is in charge here."

"No!" the principal cried. "It's wonderful news; we were all heartbroken over Anastasia's death. It's—it's—it's just we're twelve weeks into the term."

"That was unavoidable," Cabot said. "We have selected classes for him; we expect him to start on Monday. That will give you a work day to educate our teachers as to what their employment contract clearly spells out in terms of handling students who are Tatterskeins."

The man looked like a fish yanked out of the water, mouth opening and closing. He turned an alarming color just as if he wasn't getting oxygen. Joshua was fighting his own internal battle to stay human; otherwise he'd feel guilty for the trouble he was putting the man through.

"Do you understand?" Cabot asked calmly but forcefully. Getting no response, he sighed slightly. "Nodding will be sufficient."

The principal nodded vigorously.

"I can show Joshua around while you finish here." Seth stood up.

Cabot nodded without moving his focus off of the principal.

Out in the hall, Seth loosened his own tie.

"I spent too much time in that office, being raked over the coals by my father. Our father. He was very hands-on about running the school."

"You went to school here?" Joshua blushed because he sounded like an idiot. Obviously Seth attended Blackridge. His—Their family owned it. It put new meaning to "private" school.

"Kindergarten through eighth grade." Seth stopped and pointed at a locker. "This one was mine." He started to twist the dial. "I'm going to a private school in Manhattan but I really need to watch my step to keep from being kicked out. They're really annoyed with me right now for taking nearly a month off." He clicked open the lock and started to rifle through the belongings inside.

"I don't think you're allowed to do that." Joshua glanced around. Everyone was in classes; the hallways were empty.

"We own the school; we can do anything we want. It's part of the rules. Besides..." Seth pulled out a plastic baggie with some weed inside. "Drugs aren't allowed on school property."

Seth led the way into the bathroom where he flushed the contents of the baggie. "Jack gave you a phone and a wallet."

"I already have a wallet." Joshua had just pocketed the wallet when Cabot had given it to him. "My folks gave me a leather-working kit for Christmas last year."

He wasn't sure why his parents had given him the kit. Making his own wallet was fun but he'd asked for an iPad. Seth and Cabot had also given him a laptop.

"You can toss the wallet if you want." Seth threw away the empty baggie. "Just switch the stuff that's in it over to your old one."

Joshua hadn't looked inside when Cabot handed it to him. He took out his new wallet. A Massachusetts learner's permit was tucked into the ID window. It identified him as Joshua Ilya Tatterskein living at an address that wasn't Decker's house. It even had a photo of him. How did they manage that?

"The address is where we've lived since 1660," Seth said. "There's nothing there now but we will be rebuilding the estate once Jack and I move back to Boston. Half the teachers here know that the lot is empty, so we couldn't use that address for the school. Don't tell anyone where you really live."

Joshua Tatterskein. That was going to take some getting used to. His old name had been smeared all over the news, first as the sole survivor of the massacre at the barn, then for disappearing from his parents' house. His adoptive parents. He never loved his last name; he'd spent most of his life wanting to change it. He hated, though, having to cut the last connection he had with his family.

Joshua distracted himself with the rest of the wallet. There were three credit cards and a debit card all with his new name on them. The debit card came with a pin number written out on a sticky note. Cabot must have started the paperwork for them shortly after Halloween. The bill compartment contained a fistful of hundred dollar bills.

"Holy shit," Joshua breathed. "There's four thousand dollars here!"

"We take care of our own," Seth said.

"Four thousand dollars? Why?"

"Because you might have an emergency where you need lots of money fast. Buy whatever you need. Anything. We'll give you more if you run out. Seriously. Just call me or Cabot if you need anything."

"Oh, I'll need to add you to this phone." Joshua took it out. The contact list had a dozen names, mostly unfamiliar. "What the hell? Who are all these people?"

"Those are Thanes that we trust. Bishop is the king's lawyer. If you're arrested, you call him first and then us. And the one that says Albany? That's the landline for the Court of Albany. If you have a problem and for some reason, any reason, you can't get ahold of anyone else, call them. Tell them you're my brother and you need help."

Joshua scrolled up and down the list. The overkill made him uneasy. "Is this school really safe? I mean—there's like twenty numbers here. Back home I only needed three people's numbers: my mom and dad's and the next-door neighbor's. You really expect me to get into that much trouble?"

"This is our school but we do share it with other—special— families."

"What do you mean? Not short bus special, right?"

"No. Like witches."

"Wickers?" Joshua shouted.

Seth hushed him. "No, not Wickers. Witches. And don't go calling them Wickers, or they'll have the right to be pissed off. There may be Grigori here."

"Like Elise?"

"Sort of. She's a Virtue, which puts her in a different power level. They might not be related to her so don't consider them allies. There will also be kids like Winnie. Their families are under our protection; they attend Blackridge via scholarships."

"Is this place like Hogwarts? Is there going to be some weird dark arts teacher I need to avoid?"

"No and no. This is completely normal high school with an extremely high acceptance rate to Ivy League colleges."

"Are there *normal* kids that go to this school?"

"That depends on your definition of normal. Either they're going to be filthy rich—which isn't normal—or they're special."

"How am I going to tell the difference?" Because he wanted to know which ones were witches.

"Well, Grigori are easy. They're all drop-dead beautiful and use Grigori as their last names and look like they want to kick everyone's ass. Witches and the other special kids? They'll be the ones running from you."

"Because I'm a werewolf?" He whispered despite the fact they were alone in the hallway.

"Yes."

"How will they know?"

"You're a Tatterskein." Seth walked to a display case full of trophies and photographs. "Here." He tapped a picture of a boy that looked a lot like Seth. "That's our father. He was the school's chess champion. He took second at the Nationals and went on to be a grandmaster. This is your mother. She went to school here too. She won the Nationals for chess. They were extremely competitive, even after they fell in love."

"Oh." He hadn't considered what his biological parents looked like. She had been a tiny, fierce thing. "Obviously I take after my mother."

Seth pointed at more photos. "Here's Jack. He was state's champion in archery. This is his mom. This is our grandfather. In the library, there's the rest of the family. You can go through the yearbooks and find pictures of all the Tatterskeins back to the late 1900s. Jack might threaten to fire the staff but he won't. These people know how to deal with us. They'll take care of you, just like they've taken care of all the rest of us."

"Do the teachers know that we're werewolves?" Joshua whispered again.

"No. They just think we're very eccentric rich snobs. A lot of money and two hundred years of tradition buys a willing blindness to the facts." Seth patted him on the shoulder. "You'll be fine, but if you have any problems, call me. Don't think you're bothering me either. I've spent most my life wishing that you hadn't been kidnapped. I *really* wanted my older brother back."

Joshua had thought it odd that Seth and Cabot had made such a big deal about him being Ilya. To him, they were strangers suddenly claiming him as their own. It was weird to suddenly realize that they'd known about him all his life. Most likely they had thought often about him; he would have wondered about Seth if he'd known he had a little brother. Cabot and Seth both had known what his real birthday was. Had they solemnly celebrated it every year? Had they marked his absence at the holidays?

Considering how they acted toward him, they had.

"Okay, I'll call," Joshua promised.

"That includes help with classes."

The offer surprised Joshua since Seth was a year younger than him. "Really? I'm taking AP Physics C and AP Chemistry."

Seth took a sheet of paper out of his breast pocket and held it out. "Plus AP European History, and AP Comparative Government."

"What?" Joshua snatched the paper from Seth's hand. He hadn't paid attention to the classes that the werewolves wanted him to take. He whimpered at the course schedule shown on the paper. "Are you insane? We're three months into the term! What the hell? Do you want me to fail?"

"You're not going to be graded on those two classes, so don't worry. We didn't want to screw up your grade point average so you can start college classes next fall."

"Who says I'm going to college?" Joshua had grown used to the idea of his dreams being blown out of the water.

"The king. He picked those classes. He wanted you to have a better foundation in history, politics and law. It's part of being heir to Boston. When you go to college, you will have to take more of the same."

"Oh." Joshua frowned at the paper, trying to imagine his future. It was like dealing with a jigsaw puzzle that had been scattered to four corners of one of Decker's messy rooms. When he ran away from home, he'd thought he was giving up college. He'd told himself that it didn't matter because the main thing he wanted was simply to get away from his hometown. Away from the bullies that he'd grown up with. Away from people who thought reading was a waste of time, that fantasy books were "for dorks," and that a "good time" was getting as drunk as possible. He'd escaped, in a very weird definition of the term.

"When I go to college," Joshua repeated. He was picking up puzzle pieces and turning them in his mind, trying to see how it fit together. "I can stay here in Boston? I can stay with Decker? I never wanted to live in a dorm. I figured it be like living in the locker room at high school, only worse."

"You can walk to Harvard from Decker's," Seth said.

"Harvard?"

"Every Tatterskein born for the last two hundred years has attended Harvard. I'll be the first not to go. You'll be accepted—that is, if you want to apply. You could go to MIT or Boston University."

Seth clearly thought of the other colleges as poor second-rate choices.

"I wanted to go to Harvard." Joshua admitted. "It's just—I thought—we're werewolves."

"And monsters don't go to college?"

"Well it seems a little redundant. We're stronger and faster than normal people. Nearly impossible to kill. And extremely rich!" Joshua waved his wallet stuffed full of hundred dollar bills as proof.

"Brains will always beat brawn," Seth said. "We're rich because we're well-educated, not because we're werewolves."

"Harvard," Joshua whispered, gripping the idea tightly. He was going to go to Harvard.

"You can pick any major. The king will want you to audit classes in history and political science but you won't actually be graded for them unless it's a required course for your major. What do you want to be?"

He had thought that "werewolf" had become the answer to that question. He had believed the word would define him so completely that there would be no room left for anything else. If felt as if an invisible straitjacket had been torn off, leaving him free to be anything he wanted. It was an exhilarating thought. What did he want to be? An architect? A historian? Surrounded by books? A librarian? A bookstore owner? A pie shop owner?

A pie shop owner?

"No! No pies!" he cried as he recognized the source of that idea.

Seth raised his eyebrows in confusion.

"We're not sure yet. We'll figure it out."